PUFFIN BOOKS

D1079001

Books by David Gilman

Danger Zone: The Devil's Breath
Danger Zone: Ice Claw

MAX GORDON HITS THE ▶ DANGER ZONE

ICE CLAW

DAVID GILMAN

PUFFIN

PUFFIN BOOKS

Published by the Penguin Group
Penguin Books Ltd, 80 Strand, London WC2R ORL, England
Penguin Group (USA) Inc., 375 Hudson Street, New York, New York 10014, USA
Penguin Group (Canada), 90 Eglinton Avenue East, Suite 700, Toronto, Ontario, Canada M4P 2Y3
(a division of Pearson Penguin Canada Inc.)
Penguin Ireland, 25 St Stephen's Green, Dublin 2, Ireland (a division of Penguin Books Ltd)
Penguin Group (Australia), 250 Camberwell Road, Camberwell, Victoria 3124, Australia
(a division of Pearson Australia Group Pty Ltd)
Penguin Books India Pvt Ltd, 11 Community Centre, Panchsheel Park, New Delhi – 110 017, India
Penguin Group (NZ), 67 Apollo Drive, Rosedale, North Shore 0632, New Zealand
(a division of Pearson New Zealand Ltd)
Penguin Books (South Africa) (Pty) Ltd, 24 Sturdee Avenue, Rosebank, Johannesburg 2196,
South Africa

Penguin Books Ltd, Registered Offices: 80 Strand, London WC2R ORL, England

puffinbooks.com

First published 2008
1

Text copyright © David Gilman, 2008
All rights reserved

The moral right of the author has been asserted

Set in Monotype Sabon
Typeset by Palimpsest Book Production Limited, Grangemouth, Stirlingshire
Made and printed in England by Clays Ltd, St Ives plc

British Library Cataloguing in Publication Data
A CIP catalogue record for this book is available from the British Library

ISBN: 978-0-141-32303-9

www.greenpenguin.co.uk

Penguin Books is committed to a sustainable future
for our business, our readers and our planet.
The book in your hands is made from paper
certified by the Forest Stewardship Council.

For Suzy
May the adventure never end

DANGER ZONE:EUROPE

Select a location **PYRENEES**

Bearly there!

European brown bears, cousins of the
North American grizzly, used to live in
their thousands in the forests and valleys
of the Pyrenees but hunting and
destruction of their habitat meant that
by the 1980s there were only a handful
left. In 1996 brown bears from Slovenia
were introduced to the area to try and
encourage a population increase but,
even now, the species remains
endangered and in 2004 a bear, believed
by environmentalists to be the very last
native female Pyrenees bear, was
shot by a hunter.

KEY FACTS

HIGHEST SUMMIT:
– Pico d'Aneto (3404 m)
(42° 37' 56" N, 0° 39' 28" E)
COUNTRIES: France, Spain and Andorra
MAJOR LANGUAGES: French, Spanish,
Catalan. Also Basque, Occitan,
Aragonese and Portugese.

SNOWBOARD SPEAK

Alley-oop – a half-pipe move where you flip at least 180 degrees in an uphill direction.
Bulletproof – frozen or super-hard snow.
Fakie – riding backwards.
Mogul – a snow bump formed by skiers.
Rolling down the windows – madly waving arms while trying to recover balance.
Vultures – crowds who gather at the dangerous sections of a course.
Wipeout – a crash.

HOW TO SURVIVE AN AVALANCHE

- Shout so others in the group are aware of danger – this isn't loud enough to trigger an avalanche.
- Hold on to something – grab a sturdy tree or boulder.
- Start swimming to stay above the surface – head for one side.
- Get rid of your snowboard/skis – they'll get in your way as you try to stay above the snow.
- Create an air pocket near your nose and mouth.

1

It was too beautiful a day to die.

Max Gordon gazed up at the mountain peaks that scarred the crystal-clear sky. A whisper of mist soared up the valley beyond them, twisted briefly and escaped across the peaks. Flurries of snow scattered from the rocks like a flock of white butterflies disturbed from a meadow. But this was no gentle English summer landscape. Max was two thousand freezing metres high in unpredictable weather and no one knew that he and his best friend, Sayid Khalif, were there.

A blanket of snow the size of a football pitch clung precariously to the rock face a hundred metres above him. One shudder from the breeze, a single tremor from the overladen trees, and a thousand tonnes of snow would avalanche down and crush him and his injured friend to death.

Fifty metres away Sayid lay twisted in pain and fear. Max had to reach him and get him off the mountainside. There wasn't much time. A sliver of the loosely packed snow crunched down, tumbling beyond Sayid.

'Don't move!' Max shouted, an arm extended towards the boy in warning as he trod carefully, using his upended snowboard to probe the snow.

Max's breath steamed from his exertion as he slumped on to his knees next to Sayid. Using his teeth, he pulled off his ski glove and tenderly cradled his friend's leg.

Sayid cried out. His eyes scrunched up, then widened at the pain.

'Sorry, mate,' Max said, keeping one eye on the threatening field of loose snow above them.

'It's broken,' Sayid mumbled.

'Your leg's all right. Probably just a twisted ankle.'

'You think so?'

'Yeah,' Max lied. 'Serves you right, going off-piste. The whole idea was to stay on safe slopes.' He eased Sayid into a sitting position, straightened the crooked leg and wiped snow from the boy's face.

A stupid bet: Sayid on skis against Max on his snowboard – who'd get to the bottom first? But Sayid had veered off several hundred metres back and dipped into this dangerous cleft. It was a deceptive snowfield promising fast skiing and Max's warnings had been ignored. When Sayid hit the fallen tree trunk lying just below the surface he'd tumbled forwards for another ten metres. He was lucky he hadn't snapped his neck.

Max busied himself with the broken ski. Pulling the tie cord from Sayid's ski jacket, he strapped the good ski across the snapped piece – forming a cross.

'You making a splint?' Sayid said.

Max shook his head. 'You don't deserve one, you idiot. This is your way out of here.'

'Are you kidding? I'm in agony. I need a helicopter.'

Max finished the binding. 'You won't need anything if that

lot slips off the mountain,' he said, nodding towards the snowfield.

An ominous crunch reinforced his warning as a huge chunk of snow gave way. It growled down the far side of the slope, a frightening display of weight and power.

'Max! What do we do?'

'If we don't get out of here in a hurry, panic would be a good idea. We've gotta move, Sayid. Grab the cross-piece.' Max clamped Sayid's hands on to the broken ski, which now served as a handlebar. 'Sit on the good ski, hold on tight, and aim for down there.'

Sayid scrambled for something in his pocket. 'Wait. Hang on!' He pulled out a string of small black beads, spun them round his fist, kissed them and nodded nervously at Max. 'OK. Go!' he said.

Sayid's fear for his life overcame the stabbing pain in his foot as Max shoved him away. Looking like a child on a tricycle whose feet had come off the pedals, Sayid sliced through the snow, the rush of wind carrying his yelps of fear back towards Max.

Max had just clamped his boots on to the snowboard when the mountainside fell. The scale of the huge block of snow mesmerized him. It dropped in slow motion, a fragment of time during which he knew he could not outrun anything that powerful or fast. A shudder came up through the ground. Max bent his knees, lunging away as the blurred power smashed the trees two hundred metres to his right. Swirling powder smothered him and the gust of wind from the avalanche pummelled his back. He threw his weight forward and curved away as fast as he could. The avalanche ran parallel to him for more than a hundred metres, growling destruction, like a frustrated carnivore hunting its prey.

A surge of adrenalin pumped through Max's veins. The lethal risk of riding the edge of this terrifying wave was forgotten as a wild excitement overtook him. He laughed out loud. *Come on! Come on! I can beat you. I can win!*

A boulder-sized chunk of snow broke loose from the main fall and careered towards him. A sudden reality check. Max arched his back, veered inside the block of snow and felt the swirling edge of the avalanche smother his knees. *Don't fall! Not now!*

And then it was suddenly over. The monster snowfall smashed only metres away from him on to compacted snow, rocks and the treeline.

Spraying crisp, white powder, Max turned the board side-on and stopped. Looking back. he saw that where he and Sayid had been only moments earlier was now unrecognizable.

The silence was almost as frightening as the short-lived roar of the avalanche. Sayid had skimmed beneath snow-laden branches and gone through the other side. He was well out of harm's way. Max gulped the cold air. The voice inside his head was still laughing with victory but Max was under no illusion. If that avalanche had veered his way, he'd have been buried alive and crushed to death.

In the ski village of Mont la Croix the small emergency clinic was used for immobilizing broken limbs and stabilizing patients before they were sent to a city hospital. It was usually adults, crying in agony, who were admitted, people who thought skiing could be tackled without getting fit, practising, or that any idiot could do it. Any idiot could – they were often the ones with the broken legs.

Max watched as Sayid was wheeled out of the emergency room, an inflatable splint covering his leg from his foot to his knee – a specialist dressing that kept the limb immobile and cushioned against any ill-effects from being moved.

'I told you it was broken,' Sayid moaned.

'How bad is it?' Max asked the young French nurse.

She smiled, then spoke; her accent had a melodic attraction. 'It's not serious. A bone in his foot is cracked. We offer only emergency aid here. We will send him down to the hospital at Pau. It's a couple of hours away, and there they will put a plaster on his leg.'

'By helicopter?' Sayid asked hopefully.

'No, no. You are not sufficiently injured for that,' she said, and smiled again.

'I could always make it worse,' Max suggested.

'Do not joke,' she said, gently chastising him. 'You were lucky today. It was a miracle you were not swept away by the avalanche. They have banned off-piste skiing now.'

Max was already feeling a twinge of guilt for letting Sayid get into trouble. He had promised Sayid's mother, who was a teacher at their school, that he would keep an eye on her only son. 'Can I go to the hospital with him?'

Before she could answer, Sayid said, 'You can't. You've got the finals tomorrow. If the roads ice up you'll never get back in time. Max, it's all right. I'll be OK. You're almost there. You can win this championship.'

Sayid was right. Getting this far in the Junior X-treme

competition was a small miracle in itself. Even though his dad had helped, Max had limited funds. He had done every odd job he could to earn money. It didn't buy him the best equipment, but it was enough to help cover the costs needed to get to the French Pyrenees and compete.

Max had trained for two years to enter this contest and his teachers had encouraged him every step of the way. Dartmoor High wasn't a normal secondary school. Built into the rock face like a small medieval fortress on the northern edge of the Dartmoor National Park, it offered a sound education with an emphasis that engendered self-reliance. The often treacherous moorland tested not only the boys at Dartmoor High; it was tough enough to be used as a combat training ground for British soldiers and marines.

What Dartmoor didn't have was snow slopes, so Max had relied on skateboarding to work up his skills. A slither of downhill tarmac road with a wicked lump forced up by the roots of a hawthorn tree gave him a perfect take-off ramp. The deep heather cushioned his falls, and there'd been plenty of them, but between that and the dry ski run at Plymouth he had learned some of the skills needed to compete. There were two remaining events and tomorrow's was crucial.

The nurse saw Max's concern. 'Perhaps I can help,' she said. 'The roads, they are icy, so the ambulance will probably not return from Pau in time to take him before tomorrow. It is possible we could give him a bed here for the night.'

'That's a great idea, Max,' Sayid said. 'I don't fancy you trying to carry me up the three flights of stairs at the hostel.'

'Your room is upstairs?' she said. 'No, then you stay here for the night. Wait a moment. I will go and arrange it now.'

She left the two boys alone and went to an administration desk, where she flipped over pages, checking a chart.

Sayid smiled at Max. Hostel beds had wooden slats with hard mattresses, and the showers had a tendency to gasp and splutter just as you were covered in soap. A comfy hospital bed with personal attention was like a mini-holiday. Almost worth the pain.

Max looked through the window. He'd lost track of time. It was late. Cones of light from the streetlamps cast deep shadows across the village's jumbled buildings. A perfect winter picture, but treacherous underfoot. He would have struggled to get Sayid down those streets, make sure he got hot food and then nursemaid him into bed.

'All right, Sayid, you jammy devil. I'll come and see you in Pau after the competition. OK?' Max told him.

Sayid nodded. But as Max turned to go he took his arm. A distraught look crumpled his face.

'What?' Max said quietly.

Sayid hesitated, then shook his head sadly. 'Max, I lost Dad's beads.'

'Where?'

'When I went through those lower branches.'

Max remembered Sayid's downward path as they raced the avalanche. The beads were important to Sayid. Max unconsciously touched the old stainless-steel chronograph on his wrist. His dad had worn it when he had climbed Everest twenty years ago and given it to Max on his twelfth birthday. The inscription on the back plate said: *To Max. Nothing is impossible. Love, Dad.*

A few years ago Max's dad had rescued Sayid and his

...ner from assassins in the Middle East, but Sayid's father nad been gunned down. The string of beads – his father's *misbaha* – was, like Max's watch, one of the few things he had from his father. A *misbaha*, a string of either thirty-three or ninety-nine beads, was used to help its owner do anything from meditating to alleviating stress. They were, in their own way, very personal and, even though these prayer beads, or worry beads as they were more commonly known, were only of ebony, they were priceless as a tangible link to Sayid's dead father.

Max's dad had risked his life to save Sayid's family but what had Max done? Put Sayid's life in danger by taking on a stupid bet. Sayid may have gone off into dangerous snow territory but Max felt responsible. Just like his dad had done.

'I'll take a look after the competition,' Max told him.

'Don't. It's too dangerous up there,' Sayid said. 'They're not worth getting killed for.'

Snow and ice crunched underfoot as Max made his way down the half-lit streets towards the hostel on the edge of the ancient town. The gloomy light created sinister shadows, embellishing the old stonework with rippling darkness. The high Pyrenean town had given very little away to the modern world and the fifty-year-old streetlamps were now more quaint than effective.

He carried his snowboard and Sayid's broken skis across his shoulder. A pizza and a mug of hot chocolate would be a treat right now. The efforts on the mountain had drained his energy and niggling anxieties about tomorrow's competition gnawed

8

away at his mind. Occupied by these thoughts, Max missed the shadow that flitted between buildings across the street. But then he heard a grunt of effort and looked up to see a figure leap from a low wall, hit the street running, kick against a car for balance, roll and lope effortlessly away. All in one easy fluid movement. *Parkour*, thought Max immediately. Freestyle urban running, which had been developed by a group of French enthusiasts and now had a dedicated following in cities around the world. They used buildings, cars, bridges – in fact, anything in their way – as an obstacle course. This runner was fast and perfectly balanced. The black-clad figure disappeared from view, but only for a few seconds. Scratchy exhausts from off-road motorbikes suddenly tore the silence from the streets. Their headlights picked out the runner from the darkness as they roared into the street from different alleyways. Within moments the riders swung their machines into a tight circle. Cutting and weaving, their studded tyres gave them perfect grip on the icy surface as they taunted the runner, now barely able to take a step without being hit. The bikes competed to make the most noise, and exhaust fumes cast an eerie veil over what was fast becoming a vicious attack.

Four of the six bikers wrenched their machines to a standstill, a four-pointed star blocking any escape, as the other two revved and slid their bikes, sideswiping the runner. The noise suffocated any cries from the desperate victim, who fell and rolled, narrowly avoiding the wheels of one of the bikes. But then, as he got to his feet, he was shouldered by one of the riders who roared past.

Max suddenly realized that the bikers were going to maim or kill their defenceless victim. He reacted instinctively. His snowboard scratched across the ice, moving fast – he had already covered twenty-odd metres. He needed to find a gap between the bikes and put as many of them on the ground as he could.

Bending his knees, throwing his balance forward, he picked up more speed. The runner was down, winded, maybe even injured, and the bikers were going to ride over him.

Max lifted Sayid's unbroken ski, held it across his body and swept between two of the stationary bikers. It shattered as it hit the unsuspecting riders, knocking them aside and throwing them into the others. It was sudden chaos. Bikes and riders fell, engines stalled, another machine slid away out of control. Max's sudden blitz had taken them all by surprise.

The sliding bike's headlamps spun crazily across the faces of the downed bikers and Max saw they were about his age. One of the attackers rolled to his feet quickly; though still dazed, he glared into Max's eyes. This was an older boy by a couple of years. Max stared. The boy's head was an unusual shape. His cheekbones and nose protruded forward and his chin receded. Snarling and gasping for breath, he revealed ragged, broken teeth. Max couldn't remember where he had seen a face like that before. Then, with a shock, he knew.

His father had taken him on a diving holiday off Aliwal Shoal in KwaZulu-Natal, South Africa. The muddy rivers that run into the sea there are a haven for Zambezi sharks. The reef was five kilometres offshore and the water had good visibility, but as they surfaced the local diver signalled, shouting a shark warning, 'Johnny One-Eye!' – the local nickname for those ragged-toothed killers.

This boy reminded him of one of those cold-staring,

emotionless creatures. A thin white line – an old knife wound – ran from his ear down across his neck. It was a warning signal that he fought close-in and dirty. Max was bigger than any of them except Sharkface, but he was outnumbered. They would quickly overpower him, put him on the ground and kick him into submission. Or worse.

Max released the board's bindings and pulled the slightly built runner to his feet. Time to go. The black ski cap had been torn free in the struggle; a tumble of auburn hair fell across the runner's face.

It was a girl.

The café's steamed windows blurred the empty streets. Max and the girl ate pizza and drank hot chocolate. Occasionally a car would crunch by and once they heard the high-revving engine of a motorbike. Max tensed, but it passed without stopping. The girl reached out – a small gesture of assurance. Max liked the warmth of her touch, but squirmed his hand away to fiddle with his food. French girls were more demonstrative than any of the girls he knew at home, and they seemed unafraid to express their feelings. Max concentrated on his pizza.

Her name was Sophie Fauvre. Her slight, elfin build put her age anywhere between fourteen and eighteen. She had lived in Paris until two years ago, and Max was right, she was a *parkour*, and the discipline of urban free-running was something her elder brother Adrien had taught her. But those boys who had boxed her in tonight – they had been sent deliberately to hurt or kill her.

'Someone sent those blokes? I mean, how do you know it wasn't just a bunch of yobs having a go?'

She frowned. 'Yobs?'

'Er . . .' He scrambled for a French equivalent. '*Loubards.*'

'No, no. They are paid to stop me. They are kids, sure, but they're like feral animals. The men with the money buy them anything they want, and they do as they are told. If they had hurt me tonight the police would have put it down to a malicious accident.'

'Then why would these people who are buying off street kids with fancy motorbikes want to hurt you?'

She hesitated. Hadn't she told him enough? He was an innocent who had jumped into danger to help her.

'Have I got food on my face?' Max asked.

'What?'

'You were staring at me.'

'Sorry. I was thinking. Look, you don't understand. My brother has gone missing. He called us from a town called Oloron-Sainte-Marie; it's a few kilometres down the valley. And then he disappeared. I thought I could find him. People I have spoken to remember him but nothing else. So, now I have to go home. Perhaps there is news there.'

'To Paris?'

'No. To Morocco.'

'Ah. Did I miss the Moroccan connection somewhere?'

She laughed. She liked him. Which was not a good idea. It wasn't going to help her complete her task. He had a habit of rubbing a hand across his tufted hair, and then, as he smiled, his eyes would flick self-consciously away. Nice eyes, though, she thought. Blue or blue-grey, she couldn't be certain in the soft light of the café.

'Now *you're* staring,' she said.

Embarrassed, Max quickly recovered and put a finger to his mouth. 'You've got cheese in your teeth.'

And as soon as he said it he wished the earth would open and swallow him.

He walked her back to her small hotel through the winding streets, keeping in the middle of the narrow road, the brightest place, away from light-swallowing alleyways. The cold night air began to bite, even through his padded jacket.

He ignored the creeping ache in his body, alert for any movements in the shadows. Fear kept the circulation going better than any warm coat.

Sophie told him that her father used to run the Cirque de Paris, but over the years had turned more and more towards animal conservation. Her Moroccan mother had been taken ill several years ago and the family had returned to her homeland, where, after her death, Sophie's father founded an endangered-species conservation group. Like other conservationists who tried to stop the illegal trade in animals, threats and violence were not uncommon. The traders made big money. People like her father were bad for business.

'My brother Adrien discovered one of the routes was through Spain and across the Pyrenees. There are no customs posts any more, so every day thousands of lorries cross from the ports in the south of Spain.'

'And your brother found one of the animals?'

She nodded. Cupping her hands to her mouth, blowing moist air to warm her gloves. Her shoulders hunched against the icicle-snapping cold. Max wondered, for all of a nanosecond, whether he should put his arm around her.

'An endangered South American bear was shipped out of Venezuela, through Spain and into France,' she said. 'Buyers pay a huge premium for anything endangered.'

'Why? Do they have private zoos?'

She shook her head. Maybe Max Gordon really did not understand the cruelty of the world beyond his snowboarding dreams.

'Trophy hunters. They kill the animals. Shoot them. And one day one of the killers will be the luckiest hunter of them all. He'll be able to say he shot the very last animal of its species.'

They reached the corner of the *pension*, the small hotel where she had a room. A car eased along the street behind them; its exhaust growled as the studded tyres purred into the layered snow and ice. Max eased Sophie behind him into a shadow. It was a black Audi A6 Quattro – high-powered, four-wheel drive, fast, sure-footed and expensive. As it came to the intersection it stopped. A tinted window purred down. Two men: the driver and his companion. They wore black leather jackets over black roll-neck sweaters. They were big men. Dark cropped hair, their faces unshaven for a couple of days – designer stubble or tough blokes? Max settled for tough. Their cold, hard stares went right through him.

The window glided upwards, then the car eased away. Maybe they were just tourists looking for their hotel late at night, but there were no ski racks on the car and they didn't look as though they were into snowball fights for fun.

'Do you know those men?' he asked.

'No. I have never seen them before.'

'Probably nothing,' he said, smiling to reassure her, despite his own sixth sense warning him otherwise.

The night porter shuffled towards the *pension*'s door on the third ring of the bell.

'I can order you a hot drink, if you would like. Before you go?' she said.

'No. Thanks. I've gotta get back. Big day tomorrow.'

'Of course. Good luck for that.'

The sallow-faced porter stood waiting silently.

She lowered her voice. 'Thank you, Max. If there is anything my family can ever do for you, my father would be honoured.' She went up on tiptoe, placed a hand on his shoulder and kissed his cheek. Max's head bobbed to meet her lips and, uncertain where to put his hands, he fumbled and dropped his snowboard. He felt the heat rising into his neck and face.

The night porter gazed at him in bored pity.

She stepped through the door. Smiled again. 'Sure you don't want a drink?'

'No. Honest. Thanks. I've ... I've got ironing to do,' he muttered uselessly.

She said nothing, then nodded and turned, walking further into the half-lit reception area, as the porter, now with unconcealed disdain, latched and bolted the door in Max's face.

Cheese teeth and ironing. What a disaster.

The truth was he *did* have ironing, but it had nothing to do with making himself look any less untidy.

Max's snowboard rested across the two single bed bases

15

in the room he shared with Sayid at the hostel. The mattresses had been shoved to one side on the floor. A towel and a newspaper were spread out beneath the board and, holding the pointed end of the iron downwards, he pressed a stick of wax against the hot surface and dribbled the melting liquid across the board's surface, which was badly scratched from sliding across the road.

The heat opened the board's pores and allowed the wax to penetrate. Twenty minutes later, when it cooled, he scraped off the excess wax and rubbed hard with the back of a pan cleaner, buffing the surface.

His kit was as ready as it could be. All he had to do now was secure a place in the top three of the wildwater kayak race next morning and he'd be ready for the final in the freestyle snowboarding event.

He checked the alarm clock.

The wake-up call was only three hours away.

Max slumped on to one of the mattresses on the floor fully dressed. He pulled the duvet over himself and fell sound asleep.

And then – what felt like two minutes later – the alarm clock's bell clattered him awake.

2

The X-treme sports competition's heats had been held over the previous week. Three events: cross-country mountain bike on the lower slopes of the mountains, wildwater kayaking and freestyle snowboarding. The points system for each event quickly decided who went through to the next stage. Max was one of the youngest competitors, each of whom had to be between fifteen and eighteen and attend school in Europe. Bobby Morrell, ex-US junior champion, was leading the points board so far. He attended the International School near Toulouse in southern France. Max knew he was the boy to beat. Thankfully, because of the costs involved, the mountain bikes and kayaks were provided by the organizers and were all standard. There was no unfair equipment advantage; success was down to a competitor's skills. But the snowboarding was another matter. The really good riders had specialist boards for different events. Max would have to make do with his own, modest, middle-of-the-road board – if he got through the kayak race in good enough time.

The water roared.

'Max Gordon?' the steward shouted.

'Here!'

The previous heats had determined who was who time-wise, and at this stage of the competition the fastest kayakers went last. And that was Max and Bobby.

The American shook his hand and they touched knuckles. 'Good luck, Max. Remember, watch that drop at the halfway mark. You get it wrong and it'll force you to the left where the river splits. Don't get pushed down there. That's damned nearly a grade-four river in these conditions. That's real dangerous. It'll put you under. That can kill you, Max. Yeah?'

Max nodded. He liked the American. The eighteen-year-old champion always passed on his experience to the younger competitors. They both wanted to win but for Bobby it was nowhere near as big a deal as it was for Max. The 5,000-euro prize money would go a long way to helping Max buy equipment and pay for travel expenses if he wanted to continue competing in these events in the future. His dad didn't have much money to speak of and although the school had managed to secure a grant for him to stay on and study, any extras were up to Max to find.

He fitted the splash apron around the kayak. He nodded to the stewards that he was ready. The roaring water almost deafened him to the beeps of the electronic starter. The steward helped with the countdown, spreading his fingers wide, the palm of his hand towards Max's face. Five fingers, four, three, two . . .

Max's shoulders bunched; his grip tightened on the double-bladed paddle. *A deep breath. Charge the energy. Win this thing. Go fast . . . go fast . . . go . . .*

One!

The start klaxon shrieked and Max plunged the kayak into the first swirling wave.

He immediately realized the water was trickier than the previous time trials. It twisted and pounded him. The snow melt further up the peaks meant the heavy run-off was being funnelled like water down a narrow drain.

He thrust the paddle's blades left and right; threw his body from side to side for balance. It was all about countering the strength of the river with skill and judgement. Wildwater kayaks are long and narrow, and their rounded hulls make them fast, but unstable and hard to turn.

Water thundered over him. He'd misjudged one of the eddies and nearly rolled, his helmet deflecting him from the boulder that was the cause of the spurting power. He had to use the curved boat to his advantage. The river was widening. Slower water nearer the bank gently swelled into calmer pools. Max stayed in the rough and tumble, curving turns – using the boat to pick up the energy of the water and hurtle him along. The dangerous bend wasn't far now. No one would be on that side of the river anyway – not by choice. The rapids were treacherous there.

Max saw the foaming water snarl angrily past hidden boulders; these were the fastest jets, the edge of the wave train. He took the curve, and felt the lift and surge as the tongue of water powered him along, its roar muffling his shout of joy.

The cold, stinging water lashed his face and as he turned to shake his head free of it, he saw another kayak, protected by a promontory, clear the calmer-flowing water near the river bank.

It couldn't be Bobby, he'd never have passed him this far

downriver. Besides, he wouldn't start his run until Max was across the finishing line. Maybe there'd been a problem with the previous competitor, a German girl who was doing well in all the events. Had she got caught up? Had a problem? Hadn't they relayed the information back to the start line? His mind raced as he battled the crashing water. No, this was a more rugged kayak than the X-treme competitors were using, carbon-fibre-made, and it certainly took the rapids in its stride, and whoever was in the kayak was pounding across the current. Which meant he had a lot of strength and skill. And he was coming straight at Max.

Collision course.

He was going to sink him!

It was Sharkface.

Max dug in the paddle, forced the water around it, threw his body weight to one side and sideslipped the kayak so that the attacking boat glanced off.

It shuddered into him, nearly rolling him over.

The two boys fought the confused water almost side by side. Sharkface swung his paddle in a backward slash, catching Max off balance. Max's boat spun, nearly capsized, and was saved only by Max counter-balancing in the opposite direction, but in doing so he was vulnerable. The scarred boy held his paddle above his head and, like a mighty sword blow, hammered it down on to Max.

Max braced for the impact, held his paddle across him and took the blow square on. Now it was the other kid who had lost his balance and was vulnerable. Max powered the paddle into the water and in a couple of strokes took the fight to him.

Side by side they thundered down the white water, and for every stroke in the water that kept them upright, another was hammered into their opponent. Like two swordsmen on horseback, they cut, slashed and battered. A glancing blow sliced beneath Max's helmet, the edge of Sharkface's paddle cutting into his forehead. Blood mixed with the cold water, closing his eye.

A surge of anger almost lifted Max out of the kayak as he yelled and slammed his body weight and paddle down on to the boy.

Sharkface slumped. The water sucked his uncontrolled boat away. Max balanced his own kayak and wiped the blood from his eye. He was still going fast, but now he was looking at the back of his attacker. The unconscious boy had still not lifted his head. His paddle was churned away in the water and both kayaks were at the dangerous bend. Sharkface was on the wrong side of the river. If he got sucked down there, even if he was conscious, odds were he would drown. As unprovoked and vicious as the attack had been, Max wasn't a killer.

He saw a curving channel of water, paddled furiously and felt the nose of his kayak lift, then settle, as the faster, stronger and more dangerous current took control.

Within seconds he reached the other boy, the kayaks now side by side as Max shielded the uncontrolled boat from the rapids. If he could dig in his paddle and slow the pace he could force both of them away from the side tributary that now exerted a huge pressure on the river's flow.

Max's shoulder tendons felt as though they were tearing, but he kept the paddle in the water, throwing his weight against Sharkface's kayak, taking the strain for them both.

And then the river eased, the noise lessened, and slower water gave Max the chance to control his own kayak's progress by letting the other boat slip away. It nudged the bank, the water acting as a buffer, making it roll over gently on its side.

Max steered past, aiming for the centre of the main river again. With a final backward glance he saw Sharkface clamber groggily from the kayak and slump down on the bank. Someone hadn't liked the fact that Max had helped Sophie last night. And she was right – they were paying a lot of money to give these violent kids whatever they wanted, and to buy their obedience.

The adrenalin kept Max going, but in his heart he knew the attack had cost him valuable time.

As he rounded the final bend, the finish line was two hundred metres away, crowded with spectators and officials. He caught a glint of sunlight on the road that snaked up the mountain pass.

A stationary black car and two men, both in black leather coats, stood watching. One held a pair of binoculars to his eyes.

Max heard the spectators shouting.

He focused on the finish line and flexed his arm muscles in an almighty surge of power. Seconds later he heard the electronic buzz as he passed through the time gate.

He eased towards the bank and eager hands helped steady the kayak. Using the paddle for support, he pulled himself out. Exhausted, his lungs gasped for oxygen. One of the stewards shouted for a paramedic.

Max ignored the stewards' fuss and pushed his way through the crowd to get a clear view of the time board.

It wasn't his best, but he had still beaten two of the others. He'd get through to the snowboarding final on those points. Had he made better time and accumulated more points he would have been in with a stronger chance for the last phase of the competition. Now it was going to take something extraordinary in his freestyle event to snatch back those points.

He looked up towards the mountain pass.

The men and the car had gone.

The organizers bussed the competitors back up the valley and gave them two hours to eat and prepare themselves for the final event of the day. This last week had been pretty relentless because it was about stamina as well as skill. Bobby Morrell was the clear favourite now, as he'd achieved a scorching time on the river. There were three other contenders besides Bobby and Max: the German girl, who had trained on the purpose-built snowboard course in Munich, a French seventeen-year-old who was clearly the favourite of the home crowd and a Dutch boy who had surprised Max by managing to reach this stage. A Hungarian girl, lithe and beautiful like a gymnast, and who looked Californian with her modern, short hairstyle, had originally been a favourite. Buzzy and always smiling, she was also well liked by everyone. The boys were drawn to her like petrol-heads gravitating to a Ferrari. But they kept a respectful distance when they learned that she'd hooked up with Bobby. They were an 'item'. Her name was Potÿncza Józsa, and she seemed more competitive than most. Even Bobby would stand back and shake his head at her focused determination. Pronouncing her name was a tongue-twister so she always introduced herself, and then added, 'But call me Peaches; everyone does.' And that's how everyone knew her.

Initially she seemed to have had the Dutch kid beaten hands down, but she'd blown it at the kayak event with a stupid mistake. Bobby had tried to console her, but she was too angry with herself. With a kiss for luck she left Bobby to concentrate on the competition and went back to the hotel for a hot bath and probably, Max reckoned, a good cry out of everyone's sight. In a way he was relieved she'd lost her placing. Peaches would have been a lot tougher to beat than the Dutch boy. He wasn't too much of a threat, because he had even less experience than Max at freestyle snowboarding. So: five contenders remaining; two runs each to battle it out for the championship.

Max needed four stitches to the cut over his eye. The medic decided that a steri-strip would not staunch the bleeding and did the needlework in the field tent as Bobby Morrell stood watching.

'You could ask for a late start for the final, Max,' Bobby said.

'No. I want to get on with it. Did you see a loose kayak on the big bend?'

'Yeah, black with a white scattered kinda design.'

Max nodded. 'Anyone in it?'

'No. I thought it must have broken loose earlier in the day. The marshals should have checked the river. A loose boat like that could've caused big problems. They were tough conditions out there today.'

Max winced as the antiseptic and sutures stung; the medic apologized.

Morrell studied him a moment. 'Was that kayak out there a problem for you? Is that how you got cut? Listen, you can ask for a re-run. I won't object, and I bet the others won't either.'

The French medic dabbed the wound. 'It's done. Don't worry, the girls, they like a scar,' he said.

Max pulled on his ski jacket. Bobby was right. He could ask for another go at the river if he wanted. He shook his head.

The mountain was waiting.

The specially constructed snowboard run was a long, sloping drop from the start gate until the end, where the sculpted curve flared upwards for take-off. The accumulated points from the previous X-treme events meant Max was in third place. There was no time for regrets about the wildwater – he was still in with a chance. The Dutch boy had done a fairly mediocre jump, leaving a deficit of points that could not be made up on his next attempt. He was out.

Max readied himself. Tingling nerves, deep breaths, good old-fashioned stage-fright which he settled into a concentrated visualization. He was cool. This was it. Go!

Jump one – pile on the speed, focus on the middle of the ramp, hit air. He needed a big ollie – a high jump – so he hit the ramp hard, kicked the tail of his snowboard down and lifted the front with his leading boot. He pulled his knees up high, carrying the momentum, and grabbed the toe-edge of the board with his trailing hand. It was silent. No scrape of snow on board. No wind. Nothing. He threw his arm high, needing a backside 360 – a big one: a huge, stylish spin of three hundred and sixty degrees. He felt the swish of air on his face; saw the blurred crowd, then the mountain, then the slope as he spun. He'd done it! His legs dropped and the board hit the slope.

The energy rush was great. When he slid into the finish area, Bobby Morrell gave him a high five. It had been a well-executed jump with something he had had little practice at. In its simplest form it was not considered too difficult a feat, but Max had taken a slow, high twist, and that was all about style.

The German girl was next, and then Bobby.

Max watched as the girl gave a stunning performance. The crowd roared, whooping and cheering. His heart sank at her skill and the points that illuminated the board. Max was now pushed into fourth place, but when Bobby Morrell dazzled everyone his score pushed Max into fifth place. After all that effort he was one ride away from being out of the competition.

Max needed something so spectacular that it would wow the judges. He had seen a blistering jump made the previous year by a top-class American snowboarder – a high-speed exit from the start gate, hitting the ramp fast, and a double flip. A single inversion was relatively easy using the body's natural tilt as the board hit the ramp's wall, but to somersault twice in the air? To succeed Max needed a lot of height and a perfectly balanced landing – and a lot of experience. By the time he stood at the jump-off gate again he had made up his mind.

He was going for the big one.

The crowd's faces blurred, the curving downhill run seemed narrower and snow began to fall, thick leaf-like flakes spiralling downwards. The mountains would have fresh powder – nice, deep, unspoilt conditions. It'd be quiet up there, not like here; no cheering and screaming going on from all those faces, knowing that this was his make-or-break jump.

Max had a knack of being able to replicate what others could do. It was as if he had a camera in his brain that clicked a million frames a second and fed the information to his body. A muscle memory. *Don't take your body where your mind hasn't already been*, his dad once told him. *See the problems, see the route, work it out – then go. It may take only the blink of an eye, but let the mind go there first.*

Max knew he could do this jump.

His run-in was fast; he soared up the snow wall and, easing the pressure on the toe-edge of his board, he kept his head high and squared his body. He was airborne. Throwing his rear shoulder at an angle, he reached down for the edge of his board, grabbing it between the foot bindings. He had to hold on, against the pull of the somersault. Bringing his legs up into his body, he felt the tug of air on his jacket's fabric as he completed another backward curl. He gripped his fist even more tightly on the board's edge, heard a muted, almost hypnotic roar from the crowd as they realized what he was doing. Another rotation! His fingers were slipping from the board's edge; if he lost his grip now he'd fall badly on to his back and neck. Clamping his hand tighter, knuckles aching and with leg muscles coiled, he felt the final somersault complete. Earth and snow-speckled sky blurred his vision. The big hit was in the landing. He had to take the shock through his legs, but it was his stomach muscles that needed to be tight to keep his body balanced. His snowboard thumped on to the ground, his arms went out for balance, but his centre of gravity had shifted and he tumbled backwards.

In that instant he knew it was over. Max grunted in pain as his back hit the ground and his body slid, uncontrolled, towards the crowd.

He had dared to win – and lost.

Bobby Morrell was the first to help him up and release the bindings. His look said everything. It had been an awesome jump and if the landing had worked out as planned Max would have gone to the top of the leader board. Bobby put his hand behind Max's neck and touched his forehead with his own. A small, intimate gesture of friendship and respect.

'Another year of this and no one will touch you, man. I swear,' Bobby said quietly. 'Not even me.' He gave Max an encouraging smile and went to take his place for his next run.

As Max sat and eased the stiffness out of his leg, a few people leaned forwards and patted his shoulder. Some murmured encouragement, others commiserations. They were a good crowd. And most of them knew that even though Max had thrown away the championship none of them could have achieved what he had done.

Max had wanted so badly to win. He held on to his disappointment. He couldn't show it in front of everyone. The other board riders were better than him; more experienced, older, had better equipment. That was all true, but his mind was starting to make excuses and he swore at himself to shut up. He'd done his best. Leave it at that, he told himself, and watch the others as they fight for the final three places.

He stayed for the awards ceremony. Bobby Morrell won,

the German girl came second and the French boy third. Max told Bobby he was cutting out for a few hours, while there was still light, but that he'd join the party later.

He slipped quietly away, took the ski lift up to the top of a run and carved his way through the deep, freshly fallen snow. The mountains soared thousands of metres above him, and now that the snowstorm had swept through the valleys Max found himself in a pristine wilderness.

He went fast, making long, sweeping turns – happiness surging back. He stopped and let his gaze take in the quiet, majestic beauty. No matter what happened in any future competition, it was free-riding up here in these massive snowfields that made him feel this good.

With a gentle rush of the board through knee-deep perfect snow, Max curved a line down the valley. He suddenly realized he was close to the avalanche area where he and Sayid had been the day before.

The snowfall had sculpted the landscape into windswept angles so finely shaped it made everything look sleek and fast, like the leading edge on the bodywork of a fast car. As beautiful as it was, Max knew that avalanches were still a danger, especially if anyone else was on the slopes. He had some mountain knowledge and knew more than most other free-riders just what to look for in these high, dangerous conditions. That's what Sayid had failed to realize yesterday. He saw the off-piste run and wanted to cut up the snow and enjoy the thrill of the deep powder.

Max scanned the rock faces and mountain peaks. In the distance Le Pic du Midi d'Ossau soared like a gargantuan reptile's head, the slashed summit like a jaw gasping for air at nearly three thousand metres. The malevolent eye of the mountain stared heavenward, ignoring the puny human being on the valley floor.

Max checked the deep gullies above him. There was one *couloir*, a narrow chute formed by rocks at the top of a cliff, that whispered puffs of snowflakes. Max reasoned that they were due to an updraught of air twisting through the narrow crevices.

Everything seemed fine, but his instincts were prickling, warning him of something being not quite right. He had learned to follow those primal feelings when he was in Africa, where he had grappled with death and survived its swirling darkness. But now . . . What was it? What was wrong here? Still no sign of movement. The snow embedded the silence. Perhaps he was being overcautious; maybe he was still emotionally uneasy because of losing the competition. No, it was more than that – but he didn't know what. He glanced down at his father's watch and realized there was something he could salvage out of the failure.

It was a calculated risk – but he'd try and find Sayid's beads.

Max took a final glance across the shimmering valley. Satisfied that all appeared to be safe, he eased his board down into the deep snow. Like crushed diamonds, it flurried away as he rode towards the treeline that Sayid had ploughed through. Bending down and searching the lower branches, Max spotted the dark shapes against the white backdrop. Draped like a forgotten Christmas-tree decoration dangled Sayid's *misbaha*. Max picked it carefully from the branch and tucked the ninety-nine strung beads into his ski jacket's pocket.

It was time to leave; to get Sayid out of the city hospital; to pack their bags and go home.

A sudden blur of movement startled him so that he crouched quickly in anticipation of a perceived danger. Three hundred metres away a skier plunged from a high crevice; a black, billowing figure, he dropped ten metres or more, hit the snow with enormous skill and turned his skis in a furious dash across the face of the mountain.

It was one of the weirdest things Max had ever seen.

A bare-headed man, a monk, with a bushy, grey beard. His shoulder-length hair streamed behind him, thick and wild as a horse's mane. He wore only a cassock, which flapped wildly as the air buffeted him, the hood acting almost like a drogue parachute behind his head. His concentration was so intense he glanced neither left nor right and didn't see Max.

Moments later, dropping from the same *couloir*, tumbling snow veiled another figure. As bizarre as the monk had been, so this skier was menacing – like the Grim Reaper stalking his victim. Sleek, carbon-smooth through the snow, the second man was a phantom, a silent Fury. The only sound he made was that of his skis slashing the surface. Max could barely see him, for as the skier tore through the white shower he seemed to disappear from view, before suddenly appearing another ten metres down the hill. The ski ghost wore a body-hugging, one-piece ski suit, black helmet and visor; even the skis were black. The reason Max could not see him clearly was that his outfit was fragmented by a disruptive pattern, white shreds of crinkled lines, like the veins of a leaf. It was perfect snow camouflage.

Max hadn't moved. The monk and his pursuer were level with his line of sight when the phantom, without losing a moment's pace, lifted one arm quickly behind his neck, grabbed something and brought it forward. It was a rifle, camouflaged with black and white stripes, like those used by soldiers and marines for winter warfare. With a practised, rapid movement he brought the rifle to his shoulder while still skiing at speed.

'No!' Max screamed, his yell echoing across the valley.

In an instant both skiers turned their faces in his direction, but the gunman was the first to react. He stopped in a shower of snow. The rifle never left his shoulder and Max heard the frightening crack of the gunshot.

The monk floundered and, like a beginner on skis, seemed suddenly disjointed. He stayed upright, fighting the sudden loss of coordination. Max knew he had been hit. And he needed help. Max took off towards the wounded monk, crouching low on his board, his hand skimming the snow to balance his speed. He zigzagged in anticipation of a shot from the gunman, but it never came. Instead, a more frightening roar, like a massive wave breaking on the shore, swept over him.

The blast of ice-cold air hit his face. It seemed that the whole mountainside roared. The gunman executed a fast, sharp turn away from Max, the monk and the wall of snow thundering down towards him.

The wounded man looked right at Max. And pointed with a ski pole – the trees! They had to get below the trees if they were to have any chance of survival. Max could see the escape route and the monk was already pushing downhill as hard as he could to outrun the mountain god's wrath.

Max's dad had always told him it was natural to be scared, that fear had a purpose and could be overcome, but what he hadn't told him was that anything could be this terrifying.

His gasping, rapid breath was drowned by the increasing roar behind him. His muscles ached with the effort of speed and manoeuvre, but he stayed focused on the spot he had to reach. The mighty fist of wind behind him was pushing him off balance. Max wasn't laughing now. There was no thrill in this chase. The avalanche wasn't any distance away this time. It was raging all around him. Out of the corner of his eye he saw the trees being flattened, snapping and cracking like kindling wood – the snow wave was overtaking him.

And then the monster hit him.

Swept into a maelstrom of confusion, he felt his snowboard's bindings being ripped from his boots. Ice-cold fingers snatched at his face, tearing away his ski mask and, like grains of wet sand, snow was forced into his ears and mouth.

Memory kicked in. Some long-forgotten lesson from his father. Snatches of words. Survival. All about survival. Remember! *Don't ever go skiing alone in the mountains.* Rule one – broken. *Never go skiing where there have been avalanches.* Rule two – broken. Avalanches happen where there's new snow clinging to the mountain on the side facing away from the wind. He knew that! He knew it! And he had ignored it all in his stupid reaction to losing the competition.

As fast as the snow hurled him along, this secret voice in his mind taunted him. *Survive! How?*

Swim! Stay on top of the snow as if you were doing a front crawl.

Max churned his arms, trying to keep his face upwards towards the fleeting glimpses of sky visible through the snowstorm. He spat snow from his mouth, shook his head.

Keep looking at the sky! The avalanche's energy vibrated through him. Like a dog with a rat, it savaged him, shook him and then spat him free. For a moment the silence engulfed him. It wasn't that the avalanche had stopped but that the wet snow had compacted in his ears.

A glimmer of hope. Blue sky. A deep breath. His arm lunged for the golden line of light. A sunbeam. A narrow band between the blue sky and the whiteout. *Breathe! Suck in the air! Reach for it! Break free from this crushing monster and live!* Darkness engulfed him.

Savage teeth bit into him again as he went head over heels, tumbled left to right. He was totally disoriented.

Finally the mayhem ended. Max was trapped, spreadeagled. A huge weight crushed his chest. Blue-tinged snow told him he must be lying on his back, facing the sky. How deep was he buried? If only he could scoop away the snow from his face and create space to breathe, but his arms were trapped. He must be a metre or more below the surface. He began to panic. He knew that if he fought the weight of the snow the energy would be sucked out of him. He had to take control of his mind. He had to calm down. Max tried to move his head, but managed only a few centimetres. Avalanche snow wasn't fine and powdery; it was wet, heavy and compacted. How much longer would the small area above his face allow him to breathe? The weight of the snow was crushing his chest, settling heavier by the second.

There was, he realized, no way of escape. What would kill him first? The cold or having the life squeezed out of him? He would lie frozen in this tomb, and when the snow melted his body would be washed down into the river where, only hours earlier, he had fought Sharkface. Like flash photography, his mind showed him pictures of the kayak attack. The same white, scattered design on the kayak that the killer had on his ski outfit. The gunman – slightly built – fast and light on the snow – quick to manoeuvre. Young? Couldn't tell. Sharkface? No. Sharkface was more thick-set – had broader shoulders – didn't have that fast, fluid movement of the skier.

Max's mind was wandering. The exhaustion and lack of oxygen dragged his consciousness down an underground passageway. Colours swirled: purple, brown, blue, a kaleidoscope blurring his senses.

When Max was in Africa, a lethal poison had taken him through death's door. A shaman had saved him. The medicine man was a *BaKoko*, a shapeshifter, and had given Max a power that both confused and frightened him. When his concentration was centred, and his breathing slow and deep, he was sometimes able to project himself as an animal.

Max's dad had taught him never to reject primitive beliefs and Max vividly recalled flying as a falcon and running as a jackal. But he did not know how to trigger the transformation at will. And what animal could escape from where he was now? Buried alive.

A gentle warmth washed over him. He was falling asleep. His core body heat, essential if he was to live, was seeping away. Sleep was bad. Sleep was death. Now there were memory snatches of Sophie. Warm café. Smeared window. Hard, tough men gazing at him. Angels of death maybe. Was that what they were? Angels of death come to find him? The bear, Sophie had said. She was looking for a bear, stolen and shipped and probably destined to be shot.

A bear would hibernate. Sleep deep in a snow hole. It would roll and claw its way out into the spring sunshine and sniff the sweet, clean air. Max's hand felt as though it clutched an ice-pick. Impossible. He didn't have one. The swirling colours merged, sucking him into a vortex. Max fought the sensation but his thoughts were being broken up into tiny pieces. And then he felt a surge of strength.

He struck out, felt, rather than heard, something rasp against the packed snow. His senses sharpened. A musty tang of sweat, like a wet dog smell, fur and stale air, filled his nostrils and caught at the back of his throat. An instinct made him grunt with effort as snow fell from the space he'd scooped out in front of his face. Through the indefinite light the ice-pick looked like a claw – a bear's paw that raked the snow – *his paw*!

The sky seeped its blue more deeply into the crystal particles. It seemed he was going to burst through, but his chest and legs were still crushed by the pressure of the compacted snow, an invisible hand squeezing the life out of him. He was losing consciousness.

Someone smashed through the packed crust. A face. Wild. Spittle and snot clinging to a snow-caked beard. A madman dressed in black. His arm reached in, like a poacher snatching a rabbit from a snare, and he slapped Max's face. Max gasped, spat out snow and focused. The man's mouth with its old broken teeth made shapes but no noise came from it. Max's ears were still packed with snow. It was the monk, now digging furiously with his bare hands. There are only two ways to survive being buried by an avalanche: have a transceiver and hope rescuers reach you in time, or be lucky enough for another skier to see where you're buried.

The monk grabbed Max by the front of his jacket and heaved. Max kicked and wriggled in an attempt to reach the daylight. Cold air stung his face. The monk's calloused hand wiped away the snow caked around Max's eyes. Max clambered out of the hole. The landscape had changed, but he knew he must have tumbled hundreds of metres down the mountainside, swept perilously close to the sheer drop that existed about halfway up the mountain. The monk's cassock, matted with snow, looked cumbersome. The old man sat back, exhausted. A pink stain snaked across the snowfield behind him for twenty or thirty metres, showing where he had crawled, which told Max that the man was bleeding badly. Thankfully the monk had seen where Max went under the avalanche.

Max took a few moments to settle his breathing. Slumped on his knees, he carefully checked his arms and legs. Nothing broken. The old man was muttering something. Max pulled off a glove and tried to dig the freezing wet muck out of his ears.

'I'll help you,' Max shouted. But he couldn't hear his own words. The cold must have done something to his eardrums.

Clumsily, he staggered the few steps through the loose snow to the old monk. Now that he was closer, Max could see he was a big man. And he was barefoot. The avalanche must have ripped away his boots and skis. His tangled hair fell across his face; his beard – snarled strands of white and grey, like lichen – was congealed and matted. Through the blanket-like thickness of the monk's cassock Max saw a spreading bloodstain.

Marbles of snow scattered around Max's feet. There was

another tremor. The mountain was still unsafe. The monk was shaking his head, still muttering, pulling the hair from his mouth and eyes, fixing Max with a frightening, almost demented stare. He tried to get to his feet but fell, unable to wade through the deep snow. Max staggered closer, but fear suddenly gripped him. The monk had slid a metre away. The snow was shifting like sand on a steep dune. The monk's eyes widened: he knew what was happening and fell forward, trying to lie horizontally, hoping his legs wouldn't be pulled from under him.

The movement settled. Max lay as flat as he could, as if lying on ice, trying to rescue someone from going under.

'Don't move! I'll grab you. I'll get you down.' He could just about hear his own voice now as it boomed inside his head. But as he yelled he had no idea how he would get himself down from the mountain, never mind the wounded man.

The monk snarled in his effort to reach Max; blood-flecked spittle caught his whiskers. His eyes locked on to the boy's as he reached out. Max grabbed his wrist and realized for the first time that the man's other arm was injured, from either the avalanche or the gunshot, and he must have overcome tremendous pain to dig Max out.

And then the slope moved again. A huge sheet of snow, like an ice-floe, shifted away. Max held tight. The old monk growled. Max was holding him against the pull of the snow. He jammed his legs into it for grip and realized his chest and stomach were pressing against a boulder just beneath the surface. That's why the spot where he lay was not moving.

'*Ez ihure ere fida – eheke hari ere*,' the monk shouted in a language Max had never heard before.

'I don't understand! *Je ne comprend pas!*' Max yelled, hoping the man understood French.

The monk's grip loosened, so Max tried to take a firmer hold. The bare arms below the cassock were muscled and sinewy, but they were slippery with blood and sweat and gave him nothing to grab effectively.

Max stared in horror.

Two hundred metres away, silently and without warning, a massive chunk of snow disappeared. It had dropped into a void. And then other huge slabs followed and vanished. The slope they clung to was false. The snow had dammed itself up over the top of a massive chasm and this last tremor had released the pressure. Gravity sucked the crust of snow down and the snowfield the size of a football pitch had disappeared into nowhere.

The monk saw the terror in Max's eyes. He twisted his head, saw the horror and squeezed Max's arm tighter. If another slab fell away they would both be dead – a drop of at least five hundred metres had opened up, like the mouth of a volcano, and it belched powdered clouds from the weight of the snow as it impacted far below.

The monk shook his head. It was useless. He knew he was going to die. His wounds were draining his strength and life force.

'Don't let go!' Max screamed.

But the monk's hand, slippery with blood, was losing its grip.

Max's arm felt as though it was being torn out of its socket, and his ribs hurt from the pounding he'd taken, but despite the pain he pressed himself against the hidden boulder and pulled on the man's weight as hard as he could.

The monk shouted again, the desperation as strident as before, this time in French, but a sucking, collapsing roar overtook the first words, and all Max heard was a broken cry. '... *allez* ... *Abb* ... *aye!* ... *le crocodile et le serpent!*'

Max stared in disbelief. There were only twenty metres of snow left behind the monk, the rest had gone. When this slab dropped, they would both die, plunging into a grey, mist-shrouded nothingness.

The monk's other arm snatched something from around his neck, broke the cord that held it and threw it at Max. It was a crucifix and what looked like a medallion, but Max's eyes were on the wounded man's as they pleaded, and his faint, desperate words reached out again. '*Ez ihure ere fida – eheke hari ere.*'

Max shook his head. Why didn't the man realize he could not understand him? And then the remaining block of snow fell, and the monk with it, sucked from Max's grip. His eyes stayed on the boy's, as his clawing fingers ripped away Max's glove, his father's watch; nails raked his skin.

In the fraction of a second it took before the monk was swallowed by the churning mist, he shouted one word that Max had no problem understanding.

'Lucifer!'

3

The ski patrol found Max less than an hour later, straddled across a jagged rock which, in turn, stuck out in space across a massive precipice. He was hypothermic and unconscious. The four-man team, wary of the gaping void, roped themselves together and brought Max up on a rescue stretcher. Within ten minutes they had eased him a safe distance down the slopes and called in the Mountain Air Rescue helicopter, which flew him straight to the main hospital at Pau, less than half an hour by air to the south.

Max stayed in the darkness of his mind, at times plummeting through the blackness as if that terrible vortex that had sucked out the bottom of the world was still trying to claim him. The helicopter's mechanical shuddering snatched at his consciousness. Once, through half-open eyes, he saw the blurred whirring of blades against a grey sky, and felt the exhaust vapour sting his nostrils. He tried to get up but he was strapped down and the winch man placed a gloved, comforting hand against his chest. The man smiled. Everything was OK. He was safe.

Max was still unconscious when the helicopter landed. His neck was braced in a medical collar, his arms and legs secured.

The French medical team was excellent. Being this close to the mountains and the main highway, they all had extensive experience in shattered bones and hypothermic victims.

Inside the building the team listened to the airborne medics' concise assessment of their patient. The doctor quickly realized that the young man the trauma team was helping on to the gurney was fit and strong. His muscle tone was good, his heartbeat steady and there was no sign of internal bleeding.

The doctor ordered an MRI scan. The nurse had already cut away his damaged jacket and was about to cut off Max's cargo pants and fleece, when he opened his eyes.

'Don't cut my clothes,' he said. 'They're all I've got.' He slipped back into unconsciousness.

The doctor hesitated. There was something in the boy's desperate plea that he recognized. Max could not know that Dr Marcel Riveux was a volunteer in the mountains during his off-duty hours; that he was someone who understood the lure of the high valleys and felt an affinity with others who knew the thrill of the slopes.

He shook his head at the nurse. And instead of cutting Max's clothes away, he helped ease them from his body.

The hospital was well equipped with the latest technology. The highly specialized teams of doctors meant that each patient received the most up-to-date treatment.

Max lay in the doughnut-shaped Magnetic Resonance Imaging scanner, eased slowly beneath the machine's all-seeing eye. This tomb swathed him in technology. Illuminated only by the equipment's beam, the darkened cocoon scanned his brain and spine. The machine made deep, resonant sounds. One like a car alarm running out of power, another a badly tuned guitar amplifier, both giving way to a hissing like a steam train. This sighing breath mimicked a breeze catching tree branches. Max saw dabs of light, speckled like snow on high boughs, as the sound soothed him into darkness and sleep.

The consultant was fascinated by his young patient. Everything seemed normal; there was no brain damage, no skull fracture. But the deep-brain activity indicated that Max had gone into an unusual neurological condition. Images scanned of Max's brain were like satellite shots of Earth taken from space, coloured details of shape and form, but different areas of his brain were hot spots of activity. A twisted knot of colour, the neocortex, responsible for thought processes; the limbic system, which took care of emotions and dreams – both showed heightened activity. But it was the area called the reptilian brain – responsible for instinct, survival, breathing and heartbeat – that made the consultant conduct another test.

The PET scan had nothing to do with taking a sick animal to a vet – it stood for Positron Emission Tomography and used a highly specialized piece of equipment which would investigate the biochemical composition of the brain. This boy had almost animal instincts. The scan showed virtually no sign of trauma for someone who had experienced extreme danger. For one moment during the scan the consultant thought Max had died. His brain had gone into an almost death-like state, but he realized that this animal instinct, or whatever it was, had sent Max into a kind of deep sleep – like hibernation. No different from a bear in winter. The consultant's logic grappled with the rare glimpses of the extraordinary activity within Max's brain. There were secrets within the boy. Whatever they were, he needed more time to analyse them, but one thing was certain – he knew the boy was special.

Max finally awoke, stiff and sore, in a hospital room with the muted sounds of two nurses talking. The younger of the two had her dark hair tied back, and her slender fingers traced information on a chart at the foot of his bed. The other woman was older, more like the age his mum would be if she were still alive.

He lay still, his instincts keeping him from moving – like a wounded animal. His mind absorbed the information and tried to fill in the blanks. He had no idea how he had got here, or which hospital he was in. And then he remembered. Jumbled words from a dying man hammered inside his skull. The memory triggered a gasp of breath and the two women looked at him.

'Ez . . . fida – eheke . . .'

The older woman moved closer and touched his brow. 'What did you say?' she asked in her accented English.

'I don't know . . .' Max muttered. The foreign words wouldn't form on his tongue. He saw the monk's wild face again. Watched as his mouth made the sounds. Listened again.

'Ez ihure . . . ere fida – eheke . . . hari . . . ere.' Max stumbled over the words.

The nurses looked at each other, and then the younger one spoke gently. 'Do you know what you have just said, young man?'

Max shook his head. The women looked concerned. The same nurse said, 'I am French Basque. That's my language. Do you speak it?'

'No,' Max said. 'What does it mean?'

The two women spoke to each other in rapid French. Max couldn't catch it. The young one eventually shrugged.

'It means: Trust no one – they will kill you.'

The hospital team was thorough. Max had been X-rayed, scanned, checked, cleaned up and pronounced uninjured except for bruised ribs and the after-effects of the cold. He was lucky to be alive, but they insisted he be kept in overnight. It had been Bobby Morrell who raised the alarm. When Max had told him he was going back into the mountains, Bobby immediately warned the ski patrols when they heard the avalanche.

The doctors' usual questions had to be answered. Where were his parents? Was he on school holidays? How long was he staying in the Pyrenees? Where was he staying? How much money did he have?

Max explained everything, and someone said something about contacting his father, then they left him in peace. Max lay quietly for an hour or more, watching the image in his mind play over and over again.

He had been sucked into two startling events: Sophie and the monk. In both cases he had been involved in different, violent attacks by men using the same black and white camouflage. He really should tell the police. What would his dad do? He'd think it through and make his own decision about what course of action to take – and then do it. *There*

45

are times you're put in a situation that only you are meant to sort out, Max.

'Where are my things?' Max asked the young nurse when she returned to check his temperature.

She opened the small wardrobe in which Max's clothes were hung. From a drawer she pulled out a sealed brown envelope. Inside were his blue nylon Velcro wallet and his green silica Maldovite wristband. His father's watch was missing, the scratches on Max's wrist confirming that the terrifying events hadn't been a dream. A dull ache, a sense of loss about the watch, momentarily distracted his feelings from the nightmare scenario he had recently escaped. He said a silent *Sorry, Dad.*

In addition to Sayid's *misbaha*, there were the two items the monk had ripped from his neck and thrown at Max seconds before he died. The first was a rosary and crucifix, its necklace broken, most of the beads now missing, and the second was a leather cord looped and tied through a brass disc, slightly bigger than a ten-pence piece. Inside the circumference of this ring four equidistant spokes secured what looked like a small rounded crystal floating in the centre of the circle.

Max fingered the disc and curled it into his palm. He suddenly felt very possessive about the dying man's urgency in giving it to him. Max might have lost his own treasured possession, his father's watch, but this pendant was so vital to the dying monk, so important, that he had entrusted it to the boy who tried to save his life. Trust, that was a huge responsibility, his father had always told him.

If only his dad were here now. Making the right decision about what to do would be so much easier. Maybe he should phone him and tell him about the last desperate moments of the monk's life. But his father was in London, recovering from the torture he had suffered in Africa, and still struggling to remember things. The doctors believed he was making slow but definite progress, and because his dad worked for an international agency that sometimes helped the government uncover massive environmental threats, he was being well cared for in a private nursing home. Max couldn't burden him with any of this. He knew that when the authorities finally got through to the nursing home in England to explain Max's accident, someone else would take the call. Which bought him time.

'What is that pendant?' the nurse asked, interrupting his thoughts.

'It's nothing,' Max told her.

But he knew the burning secret he clenched in his fist was probably the answer to the events on the mountain. And the words spoken forged a powerful warning.

'. . . *allez . . . Abbaye! . . . le crocodile et le serpent!*' Go to the abbey. The crocodile and the snake.

Trust no one – they will kill you.

Lucifer.

They will kill you.

Lucifer.

A monk pursued by a man in black. Shot and wounded. An avalanche. A desperate fight for life. And a message.

A secret message.

*

Max stood at his room's window, looking out across the low rooftops. Pau is a small city that sits on a bluff above the Gave de Pau, the river that flows beneath the cliffs at the city's southern edge. The panoramic view of the Pyrenees meant that on clear days the saw-toothed mountains seemed endless. Less than twenty kilometres away, their snow-capped peaks in the background of the Château de Pau made the view every tourist's perfect holiday snap. But tonight was something different. Tonight the mountains held a tight grip on a mighty power that threatened and taunted him. Max slid the window open and felt the rush of wind.

A storm, like a massive battle, had struck the mountains. Thunder and lightning clashed, their percussion slamming across the city. The fire-lit sky smashed open the darkness and created a whirling exhibition of unparalleled energy. The world shook and trembled. Red- and blue-light lightning unleashed from the cloud-to-ground strikes crinkled the darkness. The light illuminated clouds and mountains, ricocheting around the peaks like a circle of fire. It was more stunning than anything Max had ever seen in any firework display.

An almighty crash and flash of light cut across Max's face. He recoiled, but quickly turned back to face the storm's anger. He gripped the sill, squinting against the biting wind. The mountains had failed to kill Max, but this enormous power seemed to be telling him that it could still reach out and destroy him.

The Pyrenees flared in a final, pounding thunder, as nature's design created a lace-wing of shredded light that descended from the clouds. Exactly the same as the camouflage used by Sharkface and the monk's killer.

Max had been given the responsibility of guarding the pendant, of finding answers in an abbey. He decided not to tell the police. Not yet anyway. But there were two people in his life he could trust. One was his dad; the second person was Sayid.

'I can't believe you were rescued by a helicopter,' Sayid moaned. 'It took me two and a half hours in the back of an ambulance to get here.' He was in another room, the lower part of his leg in plaster. 'I mean, how cool is that? A rescue chopper!'

Max smiled at him. 'Stop moaning or I'll hide your crutches. Listen, they're gonna chuck us out of here in the morning and we have to make a plan.'

'Plan is we go home, isn't it?'

Max nodded. 'The flight's booked for the end of the week, but I reckon they'll try and pull strings to get us back earlier. But I want to stay.'

'The competition's over, you can't do anything about that,' Sayid said. He didn't need to add how sorry he was that Max had lost the final.

Sayid fingered the *misbaha*. Max had risked his life to get it and nearly died in the process.

Max second-guessed his thoughts. 'Sayid, it wasn't just those that took me back to the slopes. I was meant to be there. Some things you can't explain, but if I hadn't lost the final I would never have been up in the mountains.' He held up the broken crucifix and the brass ring pendant with its opaque stone.

Sayid squinted at the stone. 'Where did you get these?'

Max told him everything.

A shudder went through Sayid as he listened. He liked his adventure in small doses: like the time he and Max outran the farmer's dog in a local orchard as they pinched apples; that had been exciting enough, thanks very much. His friend was proving to be a magnet for bigger trouble.

Max's story rattled him. He and Max had decided to make the winter holidays a fun thing, so while Max worked to save money for the trip and competition by doing odd jobs, Sayid sorted out local people's computer problems. What Sayid secretly longed for was the chance to be like Max, even to try and match his attitude. His best friend seemed able to determine a plan of action and act on it. Sayid would do anything to help him, that was chiselled in stone, but he knew in his heart he did not possess the instinct – yes, that's what it was – an animal instinct for survival. Only Max had that.

The avalanche his friend had saved him from clearly wasn't as huge as the one that had swept Max away. The thought of a massive snowfield and mountainside crashing down filled Sayid with horror. To be buried alive; crushed. What a way to die. Max was right: he owed his life to the single-minded determination of the monk.

'I want to find out more about this monk,' Max said.

'You don't think we should just hand this problem over to the cops? Blimey, Max, someone tried to murder him.'

'He saved me.'

'That doesn't mean you're responsible for him dying,' Sayid said.

'He could have left me buried, Sayid, he could have got

50

himself down the mountain and reached a doctor. I owe him. He was desperate. He was begging me.'

'He was warning you!'

'And that was important as well.'

Sayid knew it was useless trying to dissuade Max once he'd made up his mind. 'I'm not going back to England on my own, Max. You've got to promise not to let that happen, yeah?'

'I'll come back and get you. I promise.'

'So you need to buy some time. How long?'

'Another day at least. How are your acting skills?'

'You mean this terrible pain that has suddenly shot up my leg into my back and the terrible headaches I'm getting?'

Max smiled. 'Don't overdo the headaches bit. They might do a brain scan and discover there's nothing there.'

Bobby Morrell had left messages with the hospital staff when he'd phoned to see how Max was getting along. Max dialled the number of the hostel where he and the other competitors were staying in Mont la Croix. Bobby was on the slopes – where else? Max knew he'd be back once the light faded. He was going to need the American's help. Making sure the hostel manager repeated everything carefully, he left instructions for Bobby.

Max shed the hospital pyjamas and dressing gown, and immediately felt better the moment he pulled on his cargo pants, fleece and boots. It just made him feel 'together'. He ran his fingers under the tap and mussed his hair. He slipped the brass pendant over his head, tucking it out of sight beneath his sweat rag, but he wasn't sure what to do with the broken rosary.

The young Basque nurse walked in with a tray of food, fully expecting to see Max in bed. 'What are you doing?'

Max thought quickly. 'I have to go and sort out my friend's equipment. Clothes and stuff. We'll be going back to England. The doctor said it was OK.'

'But only tomorrow, I think. No?'

She placed the tray of food down, shook her head impatiently and placed her hand on his forehead, then held two fingers to his wrist. With her free hand she absent-mindedly tugged at his shoulder, straightening his fleece, as she counted his pulse rate. Max did not object. Big sisters can fuss, he knew that. Not that he had one, but he had seen Baskins, one of the most troublesome boys at school, who liked nothing better than a scrap with his mate Hoggart, reduced to impotent rage and frustration whenever his family visited. His older sister would fuss his hair, straighten his clothes and generally make life a misery. Kerfuffle. Max understood some girls just couldn't stop themselves from doing it.

The nurse seemed satisfied with his pulse, but she was hesitant about something.

'Is everything OK?' Max asked her. 'No snow or ice inside me that needs defrosting?' he quipped, but she didn't understand.

'It is OK,' she nodded. Her fingers touched the crucifix in his hand. 'I have seen this before.' She hesitated. 'Did you steal it?' she asked very carefully.

'No! Course I didn't.' He was more shocked that the crucifix had been recognized than at being thought a thief.

'Will you tell me where you got it?' she asked him, gazing directly into his eyes. Max knew that if you lied the dead

52

giveaway was in your eyes. So, do what? Turn away, think of an answer, cover your hesitation by doing something else? No. Look her straight in the eye, don't blink – and don't tell her the truth.

'I found it on the ski slopes.'

He held her gaze. After a moment's consideration, she nodded. 'It is possible. I have heard he skis on the high mountains.'

She knew the monk? Max's heart beat faster. Just as well she wasn't taking his pulse now. He stayed as nonchalant as he could. 'Who?'

She slipped the rosary from his hands, traced a finger down to the bottom of its crucifix. There was a piece broken from the bottom corner. 'Once in a while he would come down from the mountains to celebrate mass in our own language. I have kissed this cross and I have always seen this small piece missing. He is a Basque monk.'

'So, Basque is something different from being French?'

'Of course. We have our own language, our own culture. The Spanish Basques are more aggressive for their independence, some are terrorists, but on this side of the Pyrenees we love French culture as much as our own. There is no conflict for us.'

'Are you certain it belongs to him?' Max said.

'What is it you are doing? You know something, but you are frightened to say.' She spoke softly, and then, carefully, repeated the warning he had muttered when he recovered consciousness. '*Ez ihure ere fida – eheke hari ere*. Why would you say that?'

Was she suspicious or did her uneven English accent suggest

someone who was worried for his safety? Concern or suspicion was all in a person's voice inflection, and Max wasn't sure how to read her intentions. He decided to ignore the question. She may well be a big-sister-type caring nurse, but Max had been there when Baskins's sister told all his mates that her brother used to wet the bed when he was a little boy. Trust no one.

Max eased the rosary from her fingers. 'I'll take it back to him,' he said.

'But he is a recluse. He lives somewhere in the mountains. There is a word, *Cîteaux* . . . You understand?'

Max shook his head.

'It means a place where no one lives except wild animals. He has a sanctuary, a hut, in the Montagne Noire,' she said.

'The Black Mountain? Are you sure?' Max hid his shock. He had been there barely a couple of weeks ago. As part of his altitude and fitness training, Max had hiked for three days, on and off trails of the Montagne Noire, before the competitions started. It was a wild place, subject to sudden snowstorms, but because of its orientation the effect of Atlantic mists and rain caused snow to settle for no more than a week or two. That meant there was vegetation which supported wild mountain goats, which in turn fed birds of prey. Max had been warned that if he went too high wolves and bears could still be found. Climate change meant bears were not hibernating as they used to. It was not the place to get injured, for then the chances of survival would be almost non-existent. Max wasn't that keen to go back up there.

'Do you know his name?' he asked.

'Brother Zabala. He is a big man with a beard and long hair.'

There was no doubt in Max's mind that it was the same monk who had saved his life in the avalanche and then fallen so horribly to his death.

Max clutched the rosary even tighter. A warning voice deep inside told him that he was about to plunge into the darkness of a dead man's secret.

4

Max was relieved to see the battered blue van at the far end of the hospital car park. Snowboards and windsurfers in their covers were strapped on the roof rack. The sliding door was open and Bobby Morrell was sitting in a folding chair, as were a couple of other teenagers Max recognized from the competition. The gendarmes were strict about drinking in public and no one wanted a spot fine or trouble with the less-than-amenable police, so Bobby and his friends sipped hot coffee and ate home-made hot dogs.

'Hey,' the American said with a big grin when he saw Max. 'Got your message. Thought you'd be in hospital a while – but look at you. Got your backpack in the van.'

Max nodded at them and gratefully accepted a mug of coffee. 'I'm OK. Hospital food's grim and, can you believe it, they hacked off my jacket.' A hot dog was already filling his mouth – squelching, soggy sausage doused in ketchup. Sweet mush slithering down, satisfying his hunger.

'Yeah? Not a problem,' Bobby said, and gestured to one of the others, who ducked inside the van and came out a moment later with a really cool snowboarder's jacket. 'Try that. One of the guys left his gear in my van. He's about your size. Take whatever you need; he won't be back for a couple of weeks.'

The jacket was a good fit. Max nodded his thanks. 'Where's Peaches?'

Bobby shrugged, made a grunting, squashy sound and shoved more food in his mouth. 'Cut out. Just a poor loser. We'll connect in Biarritz at my gran's place. Girls, eh?'

'Yeah,' Max said, 'girls.' Wishing he had Bobby's experience.

With a gulp, like a cormorant with a fish, that made the hot dog sit somewhere in his windpipe for a second, he finally managed a breath.

'I never had a chance to thank you, Bobby. If you hadn't alerted the mountain ski patrol I'd have still been out there like an ice cube.'

They were both talking with their mouths full, unable to eat fast enough.

Bobby spluttered flecks of food. 'Nah, that was nothing. Anyway, didn't think you'd make it with an avalanche like that. But you did. That's cool. Sometimes you get lucky. I didn't come down and see you cos we had an ace party and did some riding on the new snow. I figured it was no good being here holding your hand. Y'know.'

'Can't miss a good ride,' Max agreed. He washed down what was left in his mouth with a swig of coffee. 'You said you could put us up for a couple of days.'

'Sure. My crazy grandmother has a place in Biarritz. I figured we'd get a couple of weeks' surfing, then we'll split and head for the Alps. They're expecting good snow and we can get work in the chalets. Bed and food and free ski passes.'

Max was silent. He cleaned his teeth with his tongue. The coast was less than two hours away if they went down the motorway, probably double that if they took the country road. He had everything he needed in his backpack for a couple of days in the mountains, but he wanted to make sure Sayid was looked after until he got back.

By tomorrow the doctors would probably want him and Max on a plane back to England. Trouble was, Max didn't want to go back. Not yet. The kayak attack was clearly meant to cause him serious injury for saving Sophie in the village that night. If the organized crime gangs dealing in endangered species were using these mountain passes to ship animals through Spanish ports and into France and the rest of Europe, Max was at the sharp end right now.

In his heart he knew that even though animal smugglers might have associated him with Sophie, the real mystery was something entirely different. Pursued across the snow and shot, Zabala had made an enormous effort to pull the rosary and the pendant from his neck before he died. Max still heard the man's desperate and insistent shouts just before he fell to his death, telling him to find an abbey and whatever connection it held to a crocodile and a snake. Why? It was something so important the man gave his dying breath trying to pass it on to him with a final warning about Lucifer. The Fallen Angel – was that part of the mysterious monk's message? Max knew what his dad would do. He'd honour the dying man's pleas and try to discover his secret. If the police became involved any impetus would be lost as they set up a lumbering investigation, so they shouldn't be told – not yet anyway. Max had to make a decision. Stay and find out more about the monk, or go home and forget the whole thing? *There is no choice, is there, Dad?*

Fragmented pieces of clues, shards of information like a broken mirror. *How do you put all that back together?* he wondered.

'Keep Sayid with you. I need to go and look for something. It's important, Bobby. But you have to trust me, I can't talk about it yet.'

'What I don't know, I can't tell.' Bobby smiled. 'What do you need?'

Max quickly explained his plan. He had no sooner finished than he saw the distant blue-tinged headlights of a car as it turned off the road towards the hospital. He had run out of time.

It was a black Audi.

Bobby's van lurched up to the hospital entrance, then stalled. Raucous music blasted the night air as the snowboarders piled out and tried to push-start it.

The two night-duty staff were quickly out of the hospital's doors, demanding they turn off the music. There were patients sleeping! After some furious gestures from the staff, Bobby finally realized they did not like his taste or the volume of his music. He did as he was told and turned it off, mumbling apologies about being lost, saying that he was an American, that this was a really pretty town but how did anyone find their way around this one-way system? He managed all of this in really bad French, despite the fact he could speak the language fluently.

Finally everything and everyone quietened. Bobby

conveniently got the van started just about the same time he saw Max move through the entrance, past the now-unmanned security desk, and into an elevator.

The corridors and wards were quiet and mostly in semi-darkness. Two or three voices murmured somewhere in the distance. There was a clink of metal from a trolley, a sigh from a closing door and the hum of an elevator as it sank down to the basement. Max walked quickly; he did not want to be seen or heard up here on the wards, so he stayed close to the wall, where the downlighters created the most shadow. His father had taught him to stalk animals in the jungle so they could get close enough to capture them in the camera lens. Walking on the edge of the foot lessened any sound of impact and that's what Max did now, but he moved quickly.

The corridor's windows looked on to the car park and six floors down he could see the dull sheen reflected from the men's leather jackets as they got out of their car. Max recognized them instantly as the men from the mountainside road at the kayak rapids. They glanced around the near-empty parking area. One nodded to the other and they split up. The bigger of the two men walked towards the reception area, the other skirted around the back of the building.

Who were these guys?

A chair scraped. Someone moved. Max pressed against the wall and peered round the corner into a nurse's duty room. A night nurse had pushed her chair back from her desk. If she came out into the corridor she'd walk right into him. Max looked at the room's reflection in the corridor windows opposite. The nurse tapped a handful of patients' files into a neat block, tucked them under her arm and moved towards the door. No matter what explanation Max could come up with, she would be suspicious and phone security. Skulking in a corridor was going to be a difficult one to explain.

Max reached into his pocket and found a coin. He lobbed it gently across the doorway, saw it land edge-on and roll against a filing cabinet. The nurse heard the tinkering coin, turned to follow its path, searched for it, and finally bent down to retrieve it. By which time Max was gone.

He passed a few private rooms and felt uncertainty tug in his stomach. Was this the correct floor? He couldn't remember the room; it all looked different at night. Then, like a homing beacon, he heard the sound he needed.

Within moments he opened the door to Sayid's room. His best friend lay in bed, mouth wide open, snoring as contentedly as a pig in straw. Max shook him gently. Sayid gasped, turned over and began to snore even more loudly. Max shook him again, harder this time, but he didn't budge. He put his hand over Sayid's mouth to try and make him gasp for air. His friend suddenly became quiet, then started to spasm. Max released his hand and Sayid sucked in a lungful of air; as he did, Max tipped the glass of bedside water over his face.

Sayid choked. Max held his spluttering face in his hands and whispered urgently, 'Sayid! Quiet! It's me!'

Sayid's eyes blinked open. He stopped coughing and gazed blearily at Max. He mumbled, 'Max . . . hey . . . what are you . . . they . . . gave me . . . drugs . . .'

'What?'

'Yeah . . . tol' them . . . I . . . er . . . I was in a . . . lot . . . of pain . . .' Sayid laughed stupidly. 'It worked . . . see? Ha ha . . . worked a treat . . .'

Sayid started to fall asleep again. Max shook him. Sayid opened his eyes again. 'Max. Hi. Just had a dream about you . . . you poured water . . . hey, whaddya doing here . . .?'

He was clearly out of it. Max couldn't spend any more time trying to explain, or, come to that, get his friend out of bed and dressed. Max shook him again. 'Sayid, listen. We have to get out. Stay with me a bit longer, mate!' he said, gently slapping his face.

Sayid rallied. 'Yeah, yeah. Right there, Max. Go where . . .?'

'I'll explain later.' Max hauled him out of bed, with Sayid trying to help. He got him into the wheelchair, raised the leg support and stuffed a blanket around him. Sayid's head nodded on to his chest. Max tugged Sayid's hair. His head snatched up again.

''S OK! I'm awake!' Sayid slurred.

Max opened the cupboard and dumped Sayid's clothes and boots on to the bed. He bundled them into the cotton blanket and shoved it on to Sayid's lap. He realized that if Sayid fell asleep again he'd slide out of the wheelchair. Tearing a length of sheet, he wrapped it beneath Sayid's armpits, tying him securely.

Max heard the hum of the elevator. Someone was coming.

Grabbing the two crutches, he jammed one down the side of the torn sheet binding and locked the support grip of the other on to Sayid's arm.

'Sayid, listen. You've got to stay awake long enough to shove open all the doors with that crutch, otherwise your foot's gonna get clobbered when we go through them. Ready?'

Sayid nodded, licked his dry mouth. 'Water,' he croaked.

Max held the water carafe to Sayid's lips and let him guzzle a few mouthfuls.

'That's enough, mate. You're not a camel and there're no toilet stops,' Max said.

A quick glance out of the door told him the coast was clear. He pushed the wheelchair into the corridor, turned away from the main lift and aimed straight for the left-hand side of two big swing doors. He heard the lift stop and the floor signal 'ping'.

'Here we go! Hold on!'

Sayid gripped the battering-ram crutch. They hit the door. The long corridor on the other side was a cluttered service area. There were a few wheelchairs, a couple of trolleys and a left-hand bend to negotiate. But Max could not get around the corner. Someone had jammed a cleaning wagon full of disinfectant and mops across the corridor, using it as a last place to park its awkward bulk. Max had seen the sign for the service lift but this way of escape was blocked.

Max looked over his shoulder. Whoever had been on their way up must, by now, be close to Sayid's room.

'Hang on a minute, Sayid.'

Max ran back to the double doors, peered through the laser-thin crack and saw the approaching figure of the stubble-faced man. His bulk and size looked out of place in the clinical sterility of the hospital. Max reasoned he had convinced the nursing staff to let him in. Maybe he'd told them he was a relative. Whatever ruse he'd used it didn't matter – he was here. The night nurse accompanied him, and Max heard her say, *The boy has already discharged himself . . . but his friend is still here.* The man stayed in the corridor as the nurse stepped into Sayid's room.

The man waited. Max held his breath. He could hear the soft creak of the man's leather jacket as it strained to hold his muscles. The dark face turned and looked directly at the double doors. Where Max crouched was a darker area than the corridor, but he knew that if he yielded to his instinctive fear of being seen, then that is precisely what would happen. *If you're being hunted, don't move. It's movement that gives you away.* His dad's words echoed in his mind. Max dismissed his fear. Stand still, he told himself. Tough it out. Give in to the temptation and it would cause a change of shadow and light. Anyone with a hunter's eye would spot it immediately. And Max knew that the man in the corridor was more than a hunter. He had the look of a seasoned killer.

Max did not move.

The man turned and stepped towards him. Max readied himself. The best he could hope for was that he could ram his shoulder against the double doors and knock the man off his feet. Reality check. Body weight like that won't go down easily, even if taken by surprise. But he had no choice. There was nothing else he could do. The man was less than half a dozen paces away. Max held his breath and readied himself. The torsion in his body bracing him for a bigger shove than any rugby scrum demanded.

'Monsieur!' the nurse whispered urgently.

The big man stopped and turned to face her.

'He is not here. Perhaps the bathroom? It's this way. I had better check,' she said quietly.

The cones of light above the man's head darkened his face, but his eyes penetrated the shadow. Max held his breath, heart banging away in his chest. It was a split-second moment – was the man going to take those extra few paces and push open the door? In less time than it took to think about, the heavy-set man turned and followed the nurse.

Max sighed as quietly as he could.

There was nothing else for it but to jolt Sayid down the flight of steps to the floor below. It was a slow, muscle-straining process, and by the time they got there Max felt his T-shirt clinging to his back with sweat. He prayed he wouldn't have to do this down every floor. He turned the corner, avoided another cleaning trolley, and, like a welcome sign on a lonely night, the service lift doors were already open. Max said a silent *thank you* to whatever night cleaning staff had last got out on that floor.

Max wheeled Sayid inside the broad-sided lift. His finger hovered over the floor buttons. Where had the second man gone? The back of the hospital was most likely. Safest bet for Max and Sayid was the basement. That might offer another hiding place for a while and then a way out. Max pressed the button.

The lift doors shuddered closed and the creaky lift graunched its way down. When it finally groaned to a halt, a maze of service corridors faced Max and Sayid. Air-duct pipes ran along the ceiling and liquorice-twisted cables, colour-coded red, green and blue, clung to the rough cement roof. A choice had to be made.

'What do you reckon, Sayid? There should be an underground car park for the ambulances somewhere . . . left, right or centre?'

Sayid's head nodded on to his chest again.

'I'll take that as a "yes" then to all of the above – and take pot luck,' Max said.

He pushed the wheelchair straight ahead, towards the darkened end of a corridor – more of a tunnel than anything else – but Max had smelt a slight whiff of car exhaust from somewhere, and he thought it came from that direction.

No sooner had he made the decision than he heard someone push the bar on a fire door a couple of floors above. He waited a second. He listened. Nothing. But then there was an almost inaudible footfall of a rubber sole catching the lip of a step. Someone was moving slowly down the emergency staircase. There were only a dozen steps between Max and the first turn of the stairwell. If whoever was coming down decided to move more quickly they would see Max and Sayid in no time at all.

Max put his hand over Sayid's mouth. His friend's eyes widened.

'We have to hide. Someone's coming,' Max whispered.

That got Sayid's attention. A rush of fear pumped adrenalin. He steadied the crutch as Max pushed him towards the nearest door. Gently, they eased through to an older-looking corridor. A fluorescent ceiling light crackled and flickered over a linoleum floor. A different smell here. Not disinfectant. Something else. Max couldn't put his finger on it. He stopped the door swinging closed behind them from disturbing the air – a sound that would be heard to anyone half listening. And Max's guess was that whoever was creeping down those stairs would be listening for any sound at all.

There was no time to go further. A double-tiered trolley stood in the corridor. Neatly folded on top were a rubber under-blanket and a cotton sheet. Opposite, a door with a slide bolt and with a fanlight window above was the only other exit to be seen. A small sign read: *Morgue*.

'Hang on a sec,' Max whispered.

He eased the bolt. Inside the room was a wall of stainless-steel refrigerators, each with a door big enough to slide a body in, and there was another trolley, like the one outside. It was obviously used for bringing bodies from the wards or, as Max hoped, from down that other corridor, where he reckoned the underground car park was located and where ambulances might arrive to deliver their fatalities.

Max knelt next to Sayid and whispered in his ear, 'We'll go in there. It's pretty gloomy and there's a trolley we can hide in like this one. You go underneath; I'll go on top with a sheet over me. Chances are whoever it is won't want to go poking around a mortuary. I should be able to hold my breath long enough to fool them.'

Sayid shook his head. 'Not a chance.'

'This is no time to be squeamish, mate. Someone's coming down those stairs and I bet it's not nursey to tuck you up for the night.'

'No. Can't go in there, Max. Can't,' Sayid whispered back.

'They won't hurt you. They're dead,' Max assured him. 'They're in the fridge, like last week's leftovers.'

Sayid's eyes scrunched tight and he shook his head adamantly. There was no time to argue. Someone had pushed a swing door on the floor above them. Whoever was up there, they were checking the corridors.

'All right! Blimey, Sayid, you don't half make life difficult at times.'

'Me!' Sayid hissed.

A door clanged shut above their heads. They looked up, trying to imagine the intruder walking back towards the stairs. Max grabbed Sayid's arm.

'Wheelchair stays here, you climb underneath this trolley. I'll go in there,' he said, with a nod towards the mortuary door.

Sayid eased himself on to the bottom tier of the trolley as Max threw the sheet across the top so that it draped over the whole thing.

He poked his head under the corner of the sheet. 'Stay dead quiet until I come and get you.'

'This is no time for making jokes, Max!'

'I'm not. He's going to come through those doors, so whatever you do – don't move!' Max told him.

Sayid lay rigid, clutching the clothes bundle to his chest as Max dropped the sheet corner back.

Inside the mortuary he eased the door closed so the lock didn't catch, its edge resting against the frame, then he climbed under the trolley as he had shown Sayid. This sheet was shorter than the last. It wouldn't cover the length of his body or the whole trolley. Max pulled off his boots and socks and rolled his cargo pants to his knees. Tucking a boot under each armpit, he lay down on the top of the trolley, pulled the sheet over his head and straightened himself out, as if at attention, determined not to move. The cold air on his bare feet made him want to rub them together. They would be drained of warmth and blood any minute now. Placing his heels together, he let each foot drop away naturally from the other. No sooner had he settled his breathing than he heard the swing doors whisper open.

Max prayed Sayid didn't lose his nerve.

5

The man who moved almost silently down the last couple of floors had spent more than half his lifetime in the French Foreign Legion. His young life of violent crime had been officially forgotten with no questions asked when the Legion accepted him that day in Marseilles twenty years ago. They gave him a new identity and, more importantly for him and others like him, a new family – the Legion. When he left that legendary fighting force he found better-paid work that utilized his specialist skills.

The Legion had given him the name Corentin, a Celtic Breton name meaning hurricane, and he had the strength and energy of a storm. But he had stealth as well as power and now he moved lightly along the half-lit corridors. Despite there being no obvious signs of either boy, Corentin's instincts told him someone had been behind those swing doors. Having easily convinced the nurse he'd left the building, he had worked his way methodically downwards. Now he'd heard something move. He carried a concealed 9-mm semi-automatic pistol – a Glock 18 – and a short-bladed fighting knife. Close-quarters unarmed combat was part of his armoury, but he wouldn't need any of these weapons or skills. He was hunting kids, not killers.

Sayid smothered his face into the bundle on his chest, desperately hoping that his shallow breathing would not be heard. Under the edge of the sheet he could see soft-soled black boots. Whether it was the stress and fear of the situation or still the effects of the drugs, Sayid began to feel faint.

Corentin walked past the hospital trolley for another ten paces until he reached the end of the corridor. Turning back, he hesitated at the mortuary door. He was a man who had seen a lot of violent death, and been responsible for some of it, something which demanded energy and aggression, but a mortuary was a silent place where the spirits of the dead lingered. Old superstitions. Perhaps an unconscious fear of knowing that one day he would lie on a cold slab while a pathologist began the ritual cutting to determine how Corentin had died. Knife, gun, explosion. What would it be? He didn't think about it. It didn't matter. But a mortuary . . .

Corentin eased open the door and smelt the sickly sweet aroma of embalming fluid and whatever else these doctors-of-death used. He looked quickly. Stainless-steel cabinets, a trolley and a body.

OK. Clear. He backed out. His instincts screamed a warning. He'd let a stupid childish fear absorb his concentration and now someone was behind him. He whirled around, the automatic in his hand even before he'd completed his turn, already levelled to shoot the silent intruder.

'It's me!' his partner hissed, arms half raised.

Corentin dropped his aim. 'Thierry. For God's sake!'

The two men had worked together for a dozen years, each as well trained as the other. 'You're getting twitchy in your old age,' his friend said. 'Anything?'

'No. You?'

'There's underground parking back there. This place has lousy security. You'd think in this day and age –'

Corentin interrupted him. 'Did you see either of those kids?'

'Not a sign. It's a fool's errand. What could they know?'

'Enough to give us what we want. Let's get out of here. We'll call it in. The trail's gone cold.'

Corentin followed his partner through the swing doors, but not before sliding the bolt home on the mortuary door.

Let the spirits of the dead stay where they belong, he thought.

Max waited. The low, muted voices he had heard speaking in French were indistinct. He heard the bolt slam home, then the swing doors swish open and closed. He lay still for another couple of minutes, just in case it was a clever trap to lure them out, before tossing the sheet aside.

His heart had thudded as solidly as the bolt when Corentin had rammed it across the door, but he still tugged at the handle in hope. It didn't move.

Max tapped, still wary of being heard. 'Sayid. I'm locked in. Sayid?' he called softly. He listened. Nothing. They couldn't have snaffled Sayid, could they? Suddenly gagged him and bundled him out?

Max pulled the trolley to the door, toed down the wheel locks and clambered on top. He could see the other trolley through the half-open fanlight. There was no sign of the two men. 'Sayid!' he hissed, louder this time. Once again he listened and, frightening as the man pursuing them had been,

71

his friend's snoring now scared him even more. He couldn't escape without Sayid's help.

The fanlight, hinged at its base, pivoted outwards and offered far too narrow a gap for Max to squeeze through. He extended an arm as far as he could and tossed one of his boots at Sayid.

Bull's-eye! It hit the side of the sheet exactly where Sayid's head should be. A sudden gasp of breath was the response. Good! That should do the trick. No sooner had Max felt the gratifying sense of success than the gasp settled once again into a rhythmic, nasal snore.

Sayid was out for the count.

Max was trapped.

Bobby Morrell sat in the van about three hundred metres from the hospital. The road was on a slight incline, so he had a good view of the hospital, both front and back. The two other snowboarders were already tucked up in sleeping bags on the mattress in the back. This was taking longer than Bobby had anticipated. He was about to jump out of the van to try and find Max and Sayid when two men came out of the shadows from the back of the building and walked to an unlit corner of the hospital's car park. They climbed into a black Audi that Bobby hadn't even noticed was parked there. He ducked as the blue-tinged lights swept across the van when they drove off.

Dude. Those are mean-looking guys. They don't eat Sugar Puffs for breakfast.

Maybe it was better to wait in the van after all. Just in case they had friends.

*

There was no way Max could ram open the door with the trolley and there was no other door out of the freezer room. If he could get his weight on to the fanlight and force it down, smash it from its hinges, he could probably crawl through. But even if he succeeded shards of glass might rip his legs when he wriggled through, and if he cut the femoral artery in his groin he would be dead within minutes – even though he was in a hospital. Medical help just wouldn't reach him in time.

Sayid's unabated snoring irritated Max like a persistent, troublesome wasp as he fingered the window, hoping to find a weakness, maybe a loose hinge that could be wrenched away. It was solid. Layers of gloss paint over the years had sealed them into the woodwork. Only the hinges' barrels remained oiled, allowing the window to be opened and closed. Then Max noticed the small corkscrew-like ratchet threaded with cord, used for opening and closing the fanlight.

He tugged gently but it was obvious the window was at its maximum opening. If he could cut the cord and make a small loop he could lean out of the window and snag the bolt head.

Max wrapped the cord through his hands and tried to snap it, but it was too tough. He saw, though, that where the cord had gone through the ratchet it had frayed with constant use. He eased the cord down until he could get a firm grip with both hands – and yanked. The cord snapped. With the single length he formed a quick slip-knot so that when he snagged the bolt it would tighten. He tried to reach out through the fanlight, but because he'd narrowed the gap he couldn't get his shoulders and arm out at the same time.

He peered down. The head of the bolt was about a metre below. Dangling the cord through the gap, he worked blindly, fishing with his mind's eye, trying to get the loop to catch hold. After half a dozen attempts he felt it snag. Keeping the cord in his fingers, he pulled his arm out of the gap, peered down again and saw the noose was tight around the bolt. Easing his arm back through the gap again and pressing his face against the edge of the fanlight, he yanked sideways as hard as he could. It didn't budge. The bolt was pressing firmly against the door and its frame. Somehow he had to loosen the bolt enough to let it slide free. It would take an earthquake to rattle that thing free. OK. Earthquake time.

Still balanced precariously on top of the trolley, he pulled his socks on to his freezing feet and laced up the remaining boot. Knowing the bolt was just below the door handle, he steadied himself with one hand, gripped the cord tightly with the other and repeatedly kicked the door, while at the same time yanking the cord. Frustration mixed with fear – he didn't know if those men were still in the building – and he hammered the door loudly enough to wake the dead. Thankfully, no one in the room complained.

Come on! Come ON!

Another kick, a sudden lurch, and the bolt came free. The door swung open as the force of his kicking dislodged the trolley. Max fell back; the trolley lurched forward and rocketed into Sayid.

Max rolled on to the floor as Sayid blearily opened his eyes and yawned.

'Max?' He cleared his head, remembering why he was hiding. 'Where's that bloke?'

'Gone,' Max said as he retrieved his boot. 'Which is what we'll be in a couple of seconds.'

'Good stuff. Why've you only got one boot on?'

Bobby flashed the van's lights when he saw them emerge from the same dark area as the two men.

'I was getting worried,' Bobby said as Max pushed Sayid to the sliding door.

One of Bobby's friends helped Sayid into the back of the van and made sure he was wedged on the mattress by sleeping bags.

'Not half as worried as me,' Max said, folding the wheelchair.

'Did you see those two bone crunchers?'

'Yeah. They were after us. I wish I knew who they were. I reckon they think I'm part of Sophie's anti-animal-smuggling group.'

They were in the cab by now and Sayid had covered himself with a sleeping bag.

'What? Who's Sophie?'

'It's a long story,' Max said to him, unfolding the grubby map from the dashboard. 'Anyway, I need to get to . . .' His finger traced the mountain route through to the coast. 'About here. La Vallée de la Montagne Noire.'

'What about Biarritz? You need some rest, man,' Bobby said, easing the van into the empty streets.

'You drop me off, tell me where you'll be and I'll get to you by tomorrow night.' Max rubbed the weariness out of his face. 'Right now I have to think things through, and I need to stay awake. Got any music?'

'Sure. What about him?' Bobby said, looking at Sayid, who was asleep again, mouth open, moments away from snoring.

'He's had enough sleep for a lifetime. Go for it.'

Bobby hit the play button. A raucous tune spilled out of the van as they turned towards the mountain road. Bobby and the others would be at the wild Atlantic in a few hours.

But Max had a rendezvous with a dead man.

6

Sentinel mountains blocked the night sky with even blacker silhouettes.

The snow sat above the eight-hundred-metre line on this side of the Montagne Noire. But the close-cropped pasture and stony ground made the going hard, so Max used goat and cattle tracks that were scuffed into the slopes to wind his way higher until he found shelter from the increasingly cold wind.

Shepherds used these stone-built mountain huts when bringing in the goats and sheep for market: gathering in the scattered animals was a task that could take days. Max had walked for over three hours since Bobby had driven over the mountain's lower pass and left him to head for higher ground. Max had barely slept in the past twenty-four hours. Fatigue had set in. He had already pushed himself this far, so it made no sense to risk a fatal mistake. Lose your footing on these steep slopes, tumble down through those rocks and serious injury was a given.

Max ate dry food from his backpack, and although there was kindling and wood in the small stone hearth he wasn't going to advertise his presence by lighting a fire. Neither did he climb into his lightweight bivvy bag. He wanted to be able to move quickly if trouble came out of the night.

He pulled back his sleeve to check the time, forgetting momentarily his watch had been ripped away by the dying monk. *Dad, I'm sorry. I couldn't do anything. I tried. I just couldn't save him.* A brief shiver of loneliness ran through him as thoughts of his dad flooded his mind. His father in the nursing home, his mind a netherworld – consciousness flitting between understanding and forgetfulness. He would recover, the doctors were certain, but Max feared that one day he might sit with his dad, look into his eyes and see no recognition there.

Max hid those fears, but they were a constant companion, partly responsible for his determination to carry on when others would have turned back. Zabala may have passed on a secret legacy but Max's dad had given him a much greater gift – his love – that, and the ability to meet a challenge and see it through.

Max fingered the pendant. It yielded no clue, but its secret had caused murder.

Nestling into the deep, warm hay, he set his mental alarm clock and listened as big, white cows snuffled the grass on the mountainside. Broad leather belts supported dull-thudding bells around their necks and the steady clonking lulled him into a deep sleep.

Max could see mountain peaks, one after the other, stretching to the distant horizon. The night wind had blown away cloud and pollution, leaving a diamond-bright sky. His polarized sunglasses helped keep the glare at bay but he still had to shield his eyes as he peered across the white-blanketed mountains. He had walked for four hours after waking, climbing higher into the mountain, remembering where he had been previously when training.

Stepping carefully through the snow-dusted scree, he saw the stone hut he was searching for. The last time he had been here a storm had swept in and deposited thirty centimetres of snow across his path. That was less than three weeks ago and he'd been forced to stay sheltered for a whole day while the sun melted it enough for him to make his way down again. He had huddled in the building's animal shelter, wishing he could have found his way inside the big hut. But a solid door had barred his way.

Now as he got closer he could see that the heavy-planked door yawned open, the push and pull of the wind creaking the old hinges. Scattered paper had been sucked out of the room by the airstream; a couple of sheets lay sodden in the entrance and others were scattered across the face of the animal shelter. A sheepskin was stretched out being cured on the sunny side of the hut and a couple of hessian sacks were hooked on nails. What looked like a home-made crutch, a sturdy pole with a flat, well-worn piece of wood fastened to the top of it, stood propped against the wall. Had the monk been injured once?

Max stepped closer. His eyes scanned the surrounding valleys and mountains. On the weather side of the slope snow clung tenuously, deep in places, drifted into half-pipe channels elsewhere. A snowboarder's dream – a desperate man's nightmare. Anyone less skilled than a brilliant skier or board rider would hit those sculpted walls at speed and come to grief.

But on the slope where Max now climbed there were barely

a few centimetres of snow, while over the crest of this ridge the cold air current turned the Atlantic moisture into deeper falls on that flank of the mountain. It had taken hours to get here by road and foot, but he realized that a fast skier could probably reach the mountains above Mont la Croix in half an hour – forty minutes if he wasn't racing. But the monk was an expert, and he'd been trying to escape a killer. A helter-skelter ride for his life.

He'd have plummeted down the far side of the mountain and in less than an hour appeared where Max had stopped to pick up Sayid's *misbaha*. A shot, an avalanche and a desperate cry in an ancient language had brought Max to where he now stood.

Max's skin crawled.

He turned slowly – three hundred and sixty degrees – letting his eyes look at the near and far distance. Someone was watching him. He could feel it. Nothing moved. A speck of black in the sky high above circled. An eagle. Was it that? Was that what made the hairs on his neck bristle? The lone raptor shrieked. Its cry carried easily by the wind. The eagle's eyes had two hundred times' magnification when it looked down. It would see Max's eyes staring right back. With a final twisting turn, the eagle spun away on another thermal.

Max went back to the hut, an unconfirmed warning banging through his body like a fire alarm.

And his instincts were right.

The monk's killer was watching Max's every move through a high-powered spotter scope from a vantage point more than a kilometre away.

*

Max had imagined something quite different from what he found inside the hut. For a start it was bigger than it appeared. The thick walls offered resistance to the cold and wind, and although Zabala had been a recluse he had obviously led as comfortable a life as he could, given the confines of the building.

An overstuffed chair, bookshelves, a portable radio, oil lamps and a log-burning stove were as much as anyone living alone needed. A sturdy bed with a deep mattress and an old duvet covered by a red knitted throw took up one corner of the room and Max felt a pang of envy. It would have been a cosy and warm safe haven. Would have been before someone had trashed the place. Only the bed had not been upended; everything else was turned upside down. Bookshelves were trashed, books were torn and even the old woollen carpet had been turned back on itself, exposing a solid stone floor. Max automatically pressed the back of his hand against the stove. It was, of course, ice cold. *A cold grate is as welcoming as a grave.* He couldn't remember where he had heard that but he wasn't going to argue with the sentiment. He dropped his backpack and began to sift through the damage. He picked up a few books; there was no sense in trying to tidy the room.

It looked as though a storm had wrecked the place. A mini-tornado that ripped and scoured the walls. The chair was slashed, its stuffing pulled free. The mattress had a surgical slit down its side and book bindings had been skinned from their pages. Curved daggers of glass remained embedded in the smashed photo frames.

Violent upheaval. Was the monk's killer responsible or

could it have been a wild bear that had tortured the room? They were up here. The damaged climate meant they weren't hibernating as they should. A hungry bear could have done this.

Max saw dark flecks splashed across the whitewashed wall, more on the edge of the mattress and bigger globules settled on the floor like dribbled paint. He brushed his fingers against them, and, like breaking the skin on cold porridge, the smudge told him it was blood.

The signs of struggle were everywhere. Zabala, who was a big man, must have connected a blow. That gave him time to escape and ski across and down the mountain. After the avalanche the killer must have come back here and made a frenzied search – for what? Max fingered the pendant. It was obvious.

He bent down, sifting through the debris. There was precious little to salvage, and nothing seemed of any intrinsic value. And nothing that gave Max any clue as to Zabala's secret. The books were varied and Max realized that they covered a whole range of subjects. He began sorting through them. Quantum physics, astronomy, astrology, religion, myths and legends, conservation and animal behaviour. The monk had been an extremely well-read man.

A scrapbook's pages lay scattered. Max sifted through them. There were faded newspaper cuttings about Zabala. He gathered those that weren't torn and folded them into his pocket to be read later – something more interesting had caught his eye.

Max picked up one of the broken photo frames. He eased out the shattered glass and swore as he felt the edge cut into his finger. Damn! Small cuts seemed to bleed worse than bigger ones. He pulled at the sweat rag from around his neck, but couldn't undo the knot one-handed. His finger oozed blood; he wiped his hand on the side of the old chair. A piece of cloth lay among the papers and he quickly wrapped that around the dripping finger. There was a small first-aid kit in his backpack – but the wound could wait. The picture held his attention.

He carefully pushed out the remaining glass and took the photo closer to the light at the window. The old black and white print looked as though it had been taken at least twenty years ago. The two men in the picture stood smiling, side by side. They wore trousers and short-sleeved shirts. The sun was shining; their eyes squinted against the glare. Each had an arm around the other's shoulders and each held a clipboard, so it probably wasn't a posed picture, more of a casual, off-the-cuff photo that someone had snapped. One for the album. The bigger of the two men already had those bushy eyebrows, wild twisting bristles that Max had seen close up a couple of days ago. It was Zabala. He was clean-shaven and his hair was trimmed short.

The man who stood with him was more gaunt, his sallow complexion almost noticeable in the monochrome photograph. His eyes had a sunken look. He had his head tilted back slightly – he was laughing. It was a moment of shared joy about something. Friendship. The photograph was a medium close-up. The two men filled much of the frame, but Max could see that the picture had been taken in front of an archway; a narrow one, like an entrance to an old building. The Gothic arch's apex was cut off above the men's heads and the background was out of focus, but just to the left of the picture a shape curved down from what looked like steps. It was low to the ground, its outline irregular. Jagged. Two sections gaped open, half hidden by the gaunt man. It was a statue of a crocodile.

It had to be the abbey! This was where Zabala and the other man had worked.

A scream severed his concentration.

Max turned and ran for the door. A shadow filtered the sunlight. Another shriek. It wasn't human. Max barrelled out of the doorway into the glare. With barely seconds to react, he saw the eagle swoop out of the sun a few metres away. Its glaring eyes fixed on his. The talons aimed at his face and neck. Acting on pure instinct, Max yanked the sheepskin from the wall, pulled it across his arm and presented it to the raptor.

The eagle came in at speed. Max wouldn't be able to stand the impact. But then it heaved those mighty wings into a braking stall and the curved weapons dug satisfyingly into the sheepskin.

It flapped once again, settling, finding its balance. Max couldn't bear the weight on his arm. The crutch. Of course. That's what Zabala used it for. Max grabbed it and rested the back of his arm on the support.

The bird seemed content. Suddenly the thumping in Max's chest and his racing pulse were due to excitement rather than fear. To have a king of the skies resting on his arm, its head turning, its eyes, ever alert, meeting his own, this must have been how rulers of long-lost empires felt. Standing above the rest of the world, a breeze teasing eagle feathers, a sense of power surged through Max. He laughed. The bird stared in a seemingly disapproving way. It opened its beak, its head swivelled, it shrieked again.

If the bird had come on to his arm so easily it meant it had done the same with the monk. Max looked around. On the weather side of the animal shelter was what appeared to be a stone-built storage area for bins, bunker-like with heavily planked lids, as sturdy as the hut's front door and covered in frozen snow.

You weren't likely to get a bin collection up here. So what was being kept there? Max staggered under the eagle's weight, propped his arm up again and, with his free hand, heaved off one of the lids.

It was a perfect outside larder. Cuts of sheep were laid out on racks; dead mountain hares, some gutted, others not, none of them skinned, hung from nails. Jars of fruit and tins of food were stored lower down and to one side were haunches of what looked like goat and deer. This area was less ordered. Almost as if whatever had died or been killed was hacked into pieces and dumped here – probably carrion gathered from the rocky gullies – as Max had seen no sign of any weapon in the hut.

Cîteaux, the nurse had told him. The place of wild animals. That's why the eagle came. Zabala must have fed him when food was scarce on the ground. Max took one of the hares and presented it to the eagle. The curved beak snatched it. Max ducked as the wings unfolded and beat the air. Transferring the hare from beak to talon, the eagle flapped lazily away, glided another thirty metres, then settled on a rocky outcrop to enjoy its meal.

Max rubbed the strain out of his arm and looked around. He wasn't sure about raptors, but animals were creatures of habit. They would hunt and sleep when their body clock told them to. The eagle wouldn't be the only creature that was in close proximity. He scanned the snowfields and broken ground that staggered the mountainside. *Just wait. See if anything moves. Be patient. Stay still. There.* A smudge of movement. Max cupped his hands each side of his eyes, creating tunnel vision, blocking out extraneous light and focusing his attention.

A couple of hundred metres away a huge brown bear, its dark coat smudged with pale, almost blond fur, stood to its full height, which Max reckoned must have been almost three metres. It dropped down on to all fours, scraped away at the snow and nuzzled the ground. The bear had used the boulders as cover, moving closer, making sure that the place it visited was safe. This human scent was different from the more usual, staler smell. Now it searched for food.

Max watched the bulk rise up again. That bear could move at a hell of a rate. Odds are it'd be on Max like a swarm of wild bees on honey if it decided to charge. Just how hungry was it? The bears usually stored up on fruit and berries for their winter hibernation, but with climate change nature's cycle was all over the place. Spring flowers were out on the lower slopes already, so maybe he'd have eaten further down. The brown bear was a protected species, but that didn't stop farmers from shooting them if they thought their sheep were threatened. Max watched as the bear sashayed towards him. Its shoulders rolled in a swaggering display of muscle. It stopped every few metres to sniff the air.

Perhaps it *was* the bear who had smashed up the hut. If Brother Zabala had been feeding animals, then they still expected him to be here. It was more like a wild zoo than a monk's retreat.

Fifty metres away the bear stopped, stood on its hind legs and roared. Max froze. It didn't seem like a friendly greeting. *OK. Don't run or do anything stupid. And don't look it in the eye.* Humans often got in the way of wild creatures and failed to understand animals' aggressive behaviour towards them. It was simple. You're in their way and on their patch. The bear moved closer still, its head swaying like a radar scan picking up Max's movements and smell.

Time to go. But something held him. A moment of instant recognition that stopped him from backing slowly away. The breeze had shifted. The bear's warm, musty smell wafted downwind to Max. Damp fur like a wet dog and a rich earthy tang like fallen leaves in a forest. The smell immediately conjured the image he'd experienced in the avalanche. The sense of *being*. And of feeling a powerful strength he knew he did not have as a boy. As if he had been a bear.

Now mesmerized by the towering bulk, and trapped by his memory, Max broke the golden rule. He locked eyes with one of the most dangerous creatures in the world. He saw the incisors as its snout pulled back, saliva dripping, eyes glaring. If it was a challenge this puny creature wanted, then the bear would oblige with all its fury. Max heard the thud of its weight as it dropped on to all fours – and charged.

Bears can run as fast as a horse, their awesome strength can rip a car apart if they're searching for food – and they are not inclined to listen to reason.

Max made an instant decision. He knew he couldn't outrun or fight the bear, but he could offer it an alternative to ripping him apart. Max's vision blurred as he dived to the ground. The bear grunted and roared as it sped towards him. Five metres, three . . . another stride and it would have him. Max would be under its paws in seconds. Twisting on to his back, he kicked both legs against the bunker's wooden doors that held the food store.

Wood splintered. One gate came free of its hinges. Max spun away. The bear's power was on him. *Think hedgehog!* a voice in his brain shouted at him. *Roll tight, don't resist.*

It took enormous willpower but Max did as the voice instructed. The bear's paws rolled him, its slobbering jaws and rancid breath snuffled into his chest, but Max kept his arms tightly locked across his face and body and his knees tucked up. Someone kicked him hard, at least that's how it felt – the bear had cuffed him, like a plaything – and he was lifted off the ground by the force of the blow.

Max was not going to survive this assault.

Risking a peek through his arms, he saw the bear had knocked him a couple of metres away, and for some unknown reason hesitated in following through on the attack. Its head lifted, it sniffed the air and then gazed back to Max. The next few seconds were vital for Max's survival. He couldn't make the safety of the hut, and the bear hadn't gone for the alternative offering of food from behind the storage bins' shattered door, which were now five long strides away.

There was one chance.

Max stood up, faced the monster and yelled as loudly as he could. The yell became a roar, thunder coming from his belly, booming in his chest, which bellowed like a fog-horn out of his mouth.

The startled bear stopped dead in its tracks.

Max lunged for the storage bunker. One, two, three paces . . . four . . .

The bear hurled itself forward, maddened by its escaping prey.

Five!

Max barrelled into the dead carcasses. Sheep, goat and deer torsos, haunches and heads. Some were frozen more than others and the offal stank. No sooner had he squirmed into the charnel house than the bear plunged after him. The low stone structure restricted its power, allowing only a front paw and its head to get into the shattered doorway. Max kicked back, pushing himself further out of reach. But then his back thumped into the wall. The bunker was only a metre and a half deep; another big push and the bear could winkle him out, hooking a claw into his head as if it were a ripe plum.

The bear's head burrowed into the carcasses and yielded to the instinctive temptation. Dragging out a haunch of deer, it gripped the meat in its jaws and sauntered away – its anger expended, the urgent need for food satisfied.

Max waited a few moments, making sure the bear had retreated back to the distant rocks. He crawled out of the storage bunker, stretched the tension from his muscles and checked himself over. The bear had done little more than play with him. A slash of claw marks had caught across the back of his jacket, releasing feathers which caught the breeze like dandelion seeds. Max felt the back of his head; his hand came away dabbed with blood. His clothes smelt and the stench seemed to have penetrated his skin and hair.

The bear attack could have left Max totally helpless up here. A shattered leg, a broken back and he'd have lain out on this mountain top only hours away from death. Eagle, wolf, vulture and storm would have stripped him to the bone. He'd been lucky.

Brother Zabala had been a wild man of the mountains all right; his survival skills kept him alive all the way up here, but he'd also forged a bond with these wild animals. You had to be tough and intelligent to live here and achieve that.

His mountain wilderness must have presented dangers every day, but it had been a more lethal intruder who caused his death. The violence of a human killer was more frightening than the basic instincts of a wild animal.

Now that Max had found the monk's sanctuary and seen the photograph, the man was even more of a mystery. Perhaps becoming a recluse was not a simple, straightforward choice. A well-educated man, Zabala had chosen to hide away and keep his secret with him.

And he had passed that secret on to Max – Lucifer and the pendant.

Well, Max had come this far. He had discovered who the monk was, where and how he lived, all of which had given him more information about the man. He looked across the peaks. The snow would come in by morning. The long, soft line of precipitation-filled cloud on the horizon would push in from the sea, be squeezed by the cold mountain air and dump snow from here down to the lower slopes. Max could survive on what food was stored here, but he might be snow-bound for days. Survival-induced adrenalin seeped away, leaving a deep-seated tiredness. He needed to push himself now, because otherwise it would be easy to light a fire, find a corner of the hut and sleep for a very long time. Max had to get himself together, clean up and make his way to the coast.

Sometimes you do things because you choose to and at other times because, no matter how unpleasant it is, you know it's got to be done. If Max made his way down through the villages looking and smelling as he did, he would draw attention to himself and suspicious villagers might warn the local gendarmerie.

No good thinking about it then, that would just make matters worse. It was time.

Max stripped off his clothes, leaving on his boots, socks and boxers – the ones with the man's face in the moon. The cold air bit like a thousand ants but soon turned into a punishing contradiction of cold heat when he scooped handfuls of snow and scrubbed it over his body. He yelped, then laughed. This was crazy, but it would scrub off the dried blood and invigorate his aching limbs.

'Yeaeeeow!' he yelled across the empty mountains. He 'shampooed' his hair with snow, feeling the back of his head carefully. There was no wound. The sticky blood had been from one of the dead animals. He gasped as his flushed skin puckered into goose bumps; the wind had veered and swept up from the snowfields, adding an extra chill factor.

Max was pretty pleased with himself. He'd found Zabala's mountain retreat and learned more about who Zabala was, discovered a photographic clue to what might be the mysterious abbey – and he'd brought a wild eagle off the wing and survived a bear attack.

He threw his head back and howled like a wolf, then did a jig in the snow, arms flailing, feet stamping. Max Gordon! The only boy on top of the world!

He bared his teeth and made strange, imbecilic sounds, just to make himself happy. And it was then, as he bent down to pick up his clothes, that he saw the shadow.

He jack-knifed upright.

Standing watching him was Sophie Fauvre.

7

Max got dressed in minus zero seconds – at least that's what he wished. A stumbling, one-leg-hopping charade of a silent movie as he tried to pull on his clothes.

Sophie turned her back, covering her look of amusement, and waited, listening to the grunts and groans from Max's efforts to dress himself. What a strange boy. She felt conflicting emotions. On the one hand, she was wary of his presence here at Zabala's hut, but on the other, charmed by his unaffected manner. She'd come across plenty of boys his age who tried to show off, or pretend to be something more than they were. That was natural, she supposed; boys had a much harder time of it, emotionally that is, than girls. Not that she would ever admit that to any of them. Anyway, in truth, boys never grew up. Perhaps that was why they became soldiers and firefighters, or trekked around from Pole to Pole. Women just got on with life and didn't make a fuss. Having said that, this Max Gordon seemed to be – what was the English expression? – 'pretty much together'. Except, it seemed, for dressing himself.

Max kept a fumbling, running commentary going as he pulled on his clothes. How surprised he was to see her. How there was this monstrous bear with an appetite to match, and that if she'd appeared minutes earlier she'd have been in danger. And an eagle who could take you home and pick your bones, that's how big he was. In fact, this was no place to be up here alone, even though he was, up here alone that is, unless you were used to the mountains. Which he was. Sometimes.

He was rambling.

He fell over once, got a boot stuck in his trouser leg, but eventually managed to complete the manoeuvre.

Finally, he called to her. 'Er . . . right. Done.' A sheepish grin covered the last flush of embarrassment. And he realized he hadn't asked the most obvious question: 'What are you doing here?'

A chunk of snow slithered down his back and settled in his boxer shorts. He squirmed. It looked as though he was trying to do some kind of exotic dance. She gave him one of those cool, disdainful looks: a raised eyebrow, then a shake of the head, as if answering a boy moving shoulders and hips in opposite directions was beneath her dignity.

She picked up her small backpack. 'I came to see Brother Zabala. Where is he?'

'You know him?'

She walked towards the hut's entrance, Max at her side. 'My father knows him. He helps wild animals in this region. The bear and the eagle you saw –'

'I didn't just see them. I was nearly their breakfast,' he interrupted.

'Well, those *wild* animals you so foolishly tried to play the tourist with were some of the creatures we helped save. Brother Zabala has lived here for years. He is like a guardian to them.'

Max's irritation got the better of him. He was suddenly suspicious of the petite, attractive girl. 'You haven't really answered my question. What are you doing here?'

Without thinking, he had grabbed her arm. She pulled away from him. 'What's wrong with you! I thought he might know where my brother is! My father and my brother worked with Zabala!'

The missing brother. Max had completely forgotten about him.

'I'm sorry, Sophie. Things have been a bit crazy these last few days.' He stepped back and gestured for her to go into the hut.

As she walked inside she gasped – a hand to her lips. Max remained silent, watching her reaction. It seemed genuine enough. Was it simply a coincidence that she was here at the same time as him?

Trust no one – they will kill you.

Come on, you idiot. Look at her! She's a girl who's looking for her missing brother. You *helped* her! She's the reason those thugs are after you. Remember?

She stepped through the trashed room, looking at the devastation. In a futile gesture of doing something to take her mind off the terrible sight, she picked up a couple of books and put them back on the shelves. Max couldn't read her mood. Was it sadness or fear that made her speak softly?

'Where is he?' she asked.

'I don't know,' Max lied. 'I was training up here a few weeks ago. I came back just to get away from everything, after the competition, I mean. I haven't been here long.

I found the door smashed open. So I checked to see there was no one hurt in here.' It sounded horribly lame as soon as he uttered the words.

She said nothing. But Max could see uncertainty nagging at her. Did she believe him?

'Do you know Brother Zabala?' she asked him.

'Only what you've just told me.'

'But when I got here you seemed surprised that I knew him. You already knew his name. How did you know that? What aren't you telling me?'

Max kept his cool. Her sudden incisive questions demanded a logical explanation. He moved towards her, and she retreated a step backwards.

'It's OK, Sophie,' he said, a hand extended to calm her as if she were a frightened animal. 'Look . . .' Max picked up a dog-eared book on astrophysics. Opening the cover, he showed it to her. 'His name's inside. In all of them, probably.'

An old-fashioned rubber stamp had been used to imprint the framed words *Ex Libris* on the inside page. Beneath the Latin inscription the name Zabala had been written in ink, a bold flourish to the letter Z.

She seemed alarmed that the answer was so simple. Picking up the books she'd placed on the shelf, she leafed them open. In each one the same inscription told the reader it belonged to the owner's library. She nodded. 'I'm sorry, Max. I shouldn't have doubted you. Now what do we do?'

The most obvious thing would be to tell the police, Max thought. He'd already decided it wasn't what he wanted – but why hadn't she suggested it? Maybe she was just thinking out loud. But before he could make any suggestions of his own she spoke quickly and certainly. Almost too quickly, it seemed, but maybe that was just his imagination getting the better of him.

'I don't think we should say anything to anyone.'

The answer surprised him. 'Why not?' Max said.

'Brother Zabala has wrecked places before.'

'You think he did this himself?'

'It's possible. He has a temper and he drinks a lot. The locals think he is a madman. No one comes up here, Max, unless it's by mistake. We tell the police, it could turn bad for him. I don't want that.'

An instant way out for Max. Keep quiet and no one would be any the wiser about the missing monk. That would give him the time he needed to find the mysterious abbey. The less he told Sophie the better. Let her think this was a drunken trashing by Zabala. There was no way he was going to point out that the dark splashes on the wall were blood.

'You don't think it has anything to do with those thugs who chased you that night? You're the one who told me they were being paid to stop you. Maybe they tried to stop Zabala as well,' Max said, testing her.

She thought about it, then shook her head. 'Attacking him would make no sense. We are the ones who save the animals and relocate them. Zabala is a recluse; he serves no purpose for them. No. I think sometimes the poor man is overwhelmed by the loneliness. Let's leave things as they are. He will come home.'

Brother Zabala was never coming home, Max wanted to tell her.

*

They ran downhill fast. Sophie led the way, adjusting her stride for the terrain, using the ground well. Her poise was perfect, never faltering when she altered course to find another route. Max winched his backpack tighter. He didn't want any untoward movement throwing him off balance. The athletic girl was a natural *parkour* – she jigged across the uneven ground and kicked against embedded rocks to propel her forward. Max was determined to keep up but, looking across the treacherous slopes, he knew he'd have found an easier way down, one less likely to cause injury as the result of a fall. But there was no sense in challenging her, he'd run down mountainsides before. *Take your mind there first.* He concentrated, but was pleased to hear she was gasping for breath just as much as he was.

Sophie was unsure about Max. Her instincts warned her he was a boy who could bury secrets deep inside and he definitely knew something about Zabala. When she had picked up the books she had seen the picture frame, the edge of dried blood on the glass shard, and the picture was missing. Max had taken it, she was sure of that. And what else had he taken? When she reached Zabala's hut, she had seen the sun catch something underneath the knotted sweat rag around his neck. It looked like a pendant, but she couldn't be sure. One thing she did feel certain about was that he wasn't wearing it that night in the café.

A dog barked; cows scattered a few metres, then settled. An old Basque farmer looked up from where he dozed in the last rays of the day's sun. By the time he focused his ageing eyes he saw only a few fleeting seconds of a boy running fast, faster than any sane person would on those slopes; as if

Inguma, the malevolent Lord of Nightmares, was chasing him. Kids today, they scoff if you tell them the legends, the old man thought, but if that Lord of Darkness came after you there was no place to hide. That boy ran as if Inguma was biting his backside.

These valleys and mountains were closer to the Atlantic weather patterns and the snow Max had seen approaching now shrouded the mountain peaks, but it fell as light rain as Sophie finally led Max to the narrow, twisting road in the valley. Tucked under a tree, behind a hedgerow, was a small car, barely visible on the deserted road. Neither had spoken since they started their helter-skelter run down the mountainside. Both still needed to get their breath back, but Max's thoughts whirled. Did she live in Morocco, as she said? This looked like a local car. Had she lied? Had their meeting on the mountain really been by chance? Max was uncertain. Sophie had seemed to test him coming down the mountain – or had she just assumed he was fit enough to keep up? Max had to decide how to play it. He either went his own way or kept her in sight, and that meant keeping her with him, telling her just enough of a lie to avert any further suspicions she might have about him being in Zabala's hut.

Was Zabala's death associated with the animal smugglers? Max didn't think so. Zabala died for another reason, something to do with the abbey. There seemed to be a connection between Sophie's family and Zabala – did she know more about the reclusive monk than she had said?

She caught Max's glance of uncertainty when he first saw the car. 'It's hired,' she said. She opened the car's boot and threw her backpack in. Max did the same. She slammed closed the lid. For a moment they stood looking at each other, drizzle washing sweat from their faces. She gazed at the boy, who, impervious to the rain, stared at her.

'Where to?' she asked Max.

He hesitated for only a heartbeat. 'Biarritz,' he answered.

They drove south of Biarritz's airport, near the sweeping curve of road that skirted the runways, and which would lead a motorist down the coastal road and, within an hour's drive, across the border into Spain.

Max remembered Bobby Morrell's instructions and headed for the sound of the crashing waves. A major surfing destination, Biarritz had been 'discovered' in the 1960s by a Californian film-maker – surf this good had to be experienced – and since then it had become the surfing capital of Europe.

They drove up a twisting road, past a modern and, by the look of it, very expensive low-rise block of flats. The road curved away into darkness. A high, grass-covered bank, topped with razor wire, hid the dark shape of an old building behind rusting iron gates. It was the end of the road.

'Kill your lights,' Max told her. They sat in darkness for a few moments. Max, uncertain if he'd found the right place, didn't want to raise anyone's suspicions if he was wrong. 'Stay here,' he said as he got out of the car.

It's a château, Bobby Morrell had told him. Well, it wasn't as fancy a building as Max had imagined. It was unfussy, stark and surrounded by this fortification. It was more like a state-built monolith. The moon cast a sallow glow across the landscape and then disappeared as clouds tumbled across it.

There were no grounds to speak of, as beyond the wild bushes and defensive wire the scenery was scooped out and shaped into a golf course. Distant low-level security lights from the clubhouse helped illuminate some of the undulating land. It seemed as though the château's owners had sold off whatever they had owned and retreated behind the grassy embankments that surrounded the house, and which now supported the razor wire. Max stood in the eerie shadows. An iron gate barred the way. The only sound was the surf crashing a few hundred metres away.

Max's fingers traced the gate's framework, hoping to find a bell or a security button. It was dark here. His hand brushed a thick chain and then found the padlock binding the gate closed. As he reached through, someone grabbed his arm and yanked him forward, banging his head against the bars. No time even to cry out! Something sharp pressed under his chin. A cloud shifted away from the moon; light glinted on a broad-bladed kitchen knife that now stung his skin. Blood trickled down his neck. He gagged. He was held fast, unable to move. A leathery face pressed against the bars, eyes narrowed in suspicion. An old woman, her twisted hair covering her features. Moonlight. Clouds. The image of a witch.

Her rasping voice hissed in his ear. 'I told you, there's nothing more! Nothing!'

Then, as if from heaven, lights flared. A figure ran, blurred by the powerful beams. Max could only see out of the corner of his eye; the woman still had him jammed into the railings. Then a familiar voice. Bobby Morrell.

'It's OK! He's my friend I told you about! Comtesse! Let him go!'

The grip loosened; the blade pulled back. Max pushed away from the gate and held a hand up to his eyes to ease the glare. Bobby reached the other side of the gate and stood next to a strong-looking woman. She was short and bony; thick, unkempt grey hair fell down to her shoulders. She wore what looked to be a kaftan, or a nightdress. Max couldn't tell. In truth, he didn't care. He looked at the dribble of blood on his fingers from the nick. The old woman turned on her heel and merged into the light.

Max felt Sophie at his shoulder. She glanced at the bloodied fingers. He shook his head. It was nothing.

Bobby opened the gate. 'Sorry, pal. It's Gran, she gets a bit confused at times.'

Max and Sophie stepped into the château's courtyard, the chain rattled through the iron bars and the padlock snapped closed.

'Truth is,' Bobby said as he tested the chain, 'she's as crazy as a loon. Definitely one sandwich short of a picnic.'

'And you let her out?' Max said.

'Only when it's full moon.'

Max noticed that Bobby didn't smile when he said that.

Max shuddered. It felt as though he was being ushered into a prison.

Or a lunatic asylum.

8

The kill, when it came, would be swift, silent and merciful. The victim would feel a searing, numbing pain from his neck, down through his chest, into his heart and lungs; splintering ribs, puncturing vital organs. The cold shaft piercing his body from the sky would stifle any cry of pain.

The hunter's name was Fedir Tishenko – Fedir meaning 'a gift from God'. His Slavic mother, Olha, had cherished him; she had desired a child for many years and God had finally blessed her. She worshipped her son as much as she feared his father, Evgan. Fedir would soon learn to share her fear. His father was a warlord. Barbaric, cruel and powerful, he ruled clans across three Slavic countries. Despite national boundaries, there existed stronger tribal loyalties, forged in blood. This was a society closed to anyone who had not taken the same oath.

Fedir was raised to be his father's son, a life of violence unfolding rapidly. Evgan groomed him for succession by teaching him endurance, the fighting skills of a warrior, the cunning of a predator and the ability to withstand pain. Fear, he had told him, must always lie in the other man's heart. A man born to rule must scythe dissent as the wind gods destroy the wheatfields. Appease the gods, worship the ruler – or die.

Evgan and his men revelled in their reputation for causing havoc.

Ancient folklore told of men from the northern Neuri tribe who could transform themselves into wolves. These dread legends were kept alive by peasants and villagers during their festivals, when men known as *vucari*, or wolf men, hid their faces behind wolf masks.

And the threat of the real *vucari* was the power behind Evgan and his clansmen.

The gods and spirits of the mountains were one thing Fedir's parents agreed on. His mother nurtured Fedir's respect for ancient ways. Steeped in mythology, the Slavs worshipped pagan gods, and one day a terrifying event confirmed all her beliefs. It was the day men came to fear the son more than the father.

When Fedir was twelve years old he returned home from the village school to find his mother lying beaten on the floor. A storm raged outside, one of the worst in living memory. Fedir confined the chaos within himself until his mother was comforted. Then, stepping back into the malevolent tempest, he set out to kill his father. Evgan had always expected that one day his son would challenge his authority and leadership – but not this soon. He watched the boy climb the steep hill towards him, saw the strength in his legs and the power of his shoulders. He could almost smell the stench of hatred from his son. It made no difference though, he was just a boy. Time for another beating.

Fedir charged his father. The man cuffed him aside; Fedir went down, blood trickling from his nose. But the power to avenge his mother for the constant fear and pain his father had inflicted upon them surged him back into the fight. He landed a blow, catching the old man off guard, and then another. His father laughed and struck him again.

The clansmen jeered. This pup of a boy tackling an old fighter like his father! Why, they'd seen their leader kill men with his bare hands, three times, no, four times the boy's strength. Alcohol fuelled their chanting. The boy just wouldn't stay down. He was battered, the rain-lashed wind washing his wounds. Fedir spat blood-clotted phlegm. But still his hatred drove him on.

With sudden sleight of hand he pulled a knife from a man's belt.

The men hushed. A knife fight. The boy's father knew this was a skill the boy had learned well, taught by the master. Himself.

If he did not end it now the boy would come at him every day of his life. Even he had to sleep. It had to be finished. He unsheathed his own knife.

'I shall take you from this life, boy! I gave it! I shall take it! Last chance!' his father shouted above the howling wind.

A thunderclap smashed down the hillside. The shock wave pulled at his father's clothing; the men ducked as if a mighty hand had knocked them down. But Fedir did not flinch. He lunged. His father twisted, blocked the attack, smashed the blade from the boy's hand with a savage, bone-breaking strike.

The men heard it. The snap. But the boy did not cry out as he sank to his knees. Pain sucked the strength out of him, rushing like water from a burst dam. He looked up into the swirling sky. Dust, leaves and debris danced in a whirling mockery of his failure. He felt his father grab a handful of his hair. The knife ready to strike, as if for a sacrifice. It didn't matter. Better to die than endure the brutality any longer.

Time froze. The men were transfixed. The knife swooped down. The boy screamed.

'PERUN! Save me!'

The clansmen swore for the rest of their lives that the moment the boy cried out to the god of lightning, thunder tore through the blackened clouds, wrenched them apart and threw a spear of lightning down into their leader.

The explosion flattened them all. The sky fire scorched the earth and the thunderclap deafened them. The charred remains of Evgan lay twisted in the blackened hole where the bolt had struck. The corpse smouldered, unrecognizable. A few metres away Fedir's blast-thrown body was scorched from head to toe.

But he was alive.

It took two years for the herbs and medicines to restore his strength. His mother took control of the clans, honoured by the men for bearing an indestructible son. And the boy's legend, like his strength, grew stronger every day. What did not change was his scarred body. The lightning had burned off his scalp and withered his skin like a reptile's body, crinkled with a scale-like covering. His mother had ordered a wolf be slain and skinned. Its skull cap, still moist with blood, was pulled on to her son's face to try to heal the raw skin.

When it came time to remove the wolf's pelt, part of the membrane had grafted on to one side of Fedir's face, giving it a partial covering of fur.

Fedir wore his disfigurement like a badge of honour. If

anyone averted their eyes in repulsion they learned the harsh reality of his cold, unyielding will.

Death was a given if Fedir Tishenko was displeased.

From the age of sixteen he began a reign that changed the face of Eastern Europe. No one stood in his way. His single-minded determination destroyed enemies and rewarded friends. An empire was built – 'Perun Industries'. The company logo, a white on black, disruptive, scattered pattern, did not symbolize anything obvious to a casual onlooker, but to those who knew, it was chain lightning – in honour of his saviour, the lightning god.

The land Fedir ruled harboured deep treasures of energy beneath the surface – oil and natural gas deposits which gave him wealth and even greater power. By the time he was twenty-five years old he was one of the richest men in the world. He influenced stock markets and had politicians and governments at his beck and call. He sought no publicity, he bought no football clubs, he became as mysterious as the legend surrounding him. And when he was thirty-one years and one day old, he sold everything to the powers-that-be.

And disappeared.

That was five years ago.

Now he hunted in the silence of the night. It was his creed to calmly punish disloyalty and incompetence. Lessons had to be taught so that others would learn. This boy he hunted had made a grave error. In a town near where Zabala had lived the boy had got drunk and spoken about the smuggled animals. Tishenko's new private world, this mountain kingdom, could have been compromised. There was only one punishment.

The sounds of Tishenko's hunting wolves were far behind

the boy. His strength gave him confidence as he ran across the hard-packed snowfield. He would outrun them, he was certain of it. He knew the landscape and where the glacier crept down the mountain pass there was a way up the side of the ice. The wolves could never follow him.

Tishenko could see his victim's plumed breath, watched as the boy kept looking over his shoulder, perhaps unable to believe his good luck that he was not being pursued, that the deadline for escape had been achieved, that he might live. Freedom beckoned. That was the most wonderful gift for a frightened mind – hope. But he had failed to look into the night sky behind him.

Tishenko eased the black-winged paraglider into position.

Moon glow sprinkled the snow. Tishenko's muscles tightened, his breathing steady as he watched his fractured shadow steal up behind the boy, who had only seconds to live.

The specially made titanium hunting bow needed strength and skill to draw, hold the target and release the arrow to kill effectively. Tishenko did not wish to cause undue suffering. Fear was torment enough.

With barely a whisper through the air, his darkened wings made him a creature of the night, gliding between moon and victim. A hurried sigh and the broadhead-tipped arrow flew in the night air and plunged into the running target.

The boy dropped instantly, prone, arms outstretched, without any conscious thought of what had struck him. A puddle of blood darkened in the cream-tinted snow. Death took only seconds. His last sensation was feeling the rough, wet crystals against his face and being drawn down into the cold, embracing ground.

The wolves would pick up the blood scent. The body would be devoured. Tishenko knew others would need watching before his plan to harness the most powerful force in nature could be completed. When that was done a new order would be created out of the destruction.

As Tishenko turned the paraglider across the desolate but hauntingly beautiful snowfields for the place that was now his home, deep inside the Swiss Alps, a raven flew across the face of the moon. Ravens do not fly at night, nor should they cross such desolate areas.

It was an omen. Of something unexpected.

The boy, Max Gordon?

Time would tell.

Like a dark angel, Fedir Tishenko drifted beyond the killing ground.

Max's room in the château was basic. An old iron bedstead, a worn mattress, a duvet, bare floors and hand-painted wooden shutters across draughty windows. A spindle-backed chair served as a clothes-horse. Almost like home, he thought. He had wrapped the duvet around him: this was his first opportunity to have a proper look at the newspaper cuttings he had taken from Zabala's scrapbook. With little help from the bare, forty-watt light bulb, he scrutinized the French reports, getting his brain to think in the other language.

Twenty-three years ago Zabala had caused a furore by claiming that a catastrophic event was going to take place in south-eastern Europe. He had, it seemed, little evidence that pointed to a disaster. Everyone scoffed. Zabala was ridiculed; accused of dabbling in astrology, the predictive, unproven art, instead of keeping within the discipline of astronomy.

So that's what he was – an astronomer.

Zabala's riposte to his critics was that in ancient times Egyptian, Greek and Persian cultures had embraced celestial attributes and associated them with major events in history. Zabala refused to disclose his research and insisted that Lucifer . . .

Max gasped. Zabala was talking about Lucifer all those years ago! The last word he said before he died. Someone walked over Max's grave. He shuddered. That moment of terror on the mountain persisted with startling clarity in his mind.

Lucifer would return, bringing cataclysmic destruction, Zabala had insisted in the newspaper. The journalists' articles derided Zabala rather than offering any facts. Perhaps there were none to report. They didn't even mention where he worked, so Max decided that the man had become something of a figure to poke fun at. However, Zabala insisted throughout that he would provide definite proof, that his research was not yet finalized, but that all the signs were there.

Signs? The newspapers scorned him.

It was getting late. Max clambered on to the bed and switched off the light. The old house creaked from the wind sneaking under its floorboards and rafters. Despair whispered through the run-down building. The shutters, edged in fuzzy half-light, pushed and pulled, moaning from the breeze.

Maybe this was all a wild-goose chase. An obsessed man, demented by a half-baked prediction, forcing himself from society into the mountains because of something that didn't happen. He had turned his back on the world and become a reclusive monk. If Zabala had raised the alarm all those years ago, had been proved wrong because nothing happened, then from a rational point of view Max was getting caught up in an old man's fantasy.

Max checked his thoughts. Someone had attacked, pursued and killed the elderly monk. That wasn't a fantasy. Stark terror had strangled them both in the moment before Zabala's death. But Max had hung on. Had done everything to save him, just as Zabala had done for him. Just as his dad would have done.

One of the articles made a final, sober statement. Zabala was nothing more than an unknown, publicity-seeking, third-rate scientist, possessed by the demon of failure. He had become a religious zealot who should carry a placard telling the world, The End is Nigh.

Max lay in the gloom. Someone padded barefoot along the corridor – candlelight seeped around the doorframe, paused, then moved on.

He slipped out of bed and put the chair under the door handle. A crazy woman with a knife had nearly cut his throat. He didn't want her, or anyone else he was unaware of in this crazy place, coming back to make sure he was all tucked up for the night.

Sleep tugged at Max's mind. He fingered the stone pendant and dismissed the whispers of doubt that plagued him about Zabala's sanity. The only way to find the killer was to have something he wanted badly enough. Zabala had found Lucifer's secret and Lucifer had taken his revenge.

Max would find the secret.

And Lucifer would come for him.

9

The château was no less stark in daylight. Two huge balconies hung precariously from the art deco building. A turret that looked like a small bell tower peeked above the castellated roof terrace. The roof's eaves were rotten and most of the big windows were boarded over. At the turn of the nineteenth century it had taken four hundred men twelve years to build an aristocrat's dream. Its grim history of bad debt, misery and sadness had by now soaked into the neglected structure.

Max had slept badly: the mattress was lumpy, the room draughty and the ancient water pipes kept up a constant groaning. As he wandered through the corridors towards the voices and the smell of coffee and bacon, he noticed that there was barely any furniture anywhere. And when he finally reached the main living room, it looked more like a city squat than a French château. Bobby Morrell, his two surfing friends and Peaches sat with Sayid and Sophie. They lounged with plates of food on their laps on big, overstuffed chairs which looked as though they came from the Second World War. A big dining table, once beautifully polished but now scratched and burned by innumerable pots of hot tea being placed on its surface over the years, teetered on thin legs, supporting fresh bread, jars of honey, jam and marmalade. There were bacon, eggs, coffee, fruit – just about anything anyone could want to eat.

Peaches' laughter, as always, threw light into the room, and Bobby nearly choked as he laughed with her.

'Hey, Max,' Bobby called. 'Good sleep? Help yourself, pal. Look who's here!'

'Hiya, Max!' Peaches said, giving a girly wave. She sat knee-hugging on the old sofa next to Bobby and Sophie.

Max nodded and smiled. Everyone seemed more interested in Sophie and Peaches than in his arrival in the room, as their chatter, fractured with gestures and shrieks, amused Bobby and his friends.

He looked at his friend now, smiling through a messy fried-egg sandwich. Sayid hobbled forward and hugged Max.

'You should've given me a shout when you got in last night,' he said, being careful not to drip the egg yolk that ran through his fingers on to Max.

'I tried, but you were snoring like a train. What's going on?'

Sayid limped to the table. 'Isn't this great? Loads of nosh, Max, and the sea –' he pointed across the vast balcony, whose doors, leading from the lounge, were closed – 'is right there, only don't try and go on the balcony, it's condemned. Drop a bread roll on there and it'll collapse. The whole place is falling apart,' he said quietly, then more cheerfully, 'Sea's only a couple of hundred metres down that path. Great surfing. Peaches rocked up yesterday and she, Bobby and his mates were down there all day. They wheel me down as well. I sit under a big brolly. The Comtesse makes sure there's plenty of grub whenever we want it. I read comics all day. Bobby's got every superhero comic in his room, says he's been coming here since he was a kid. I can't believe his gran's a French countess. She's all right. Bit weird. But, well, y'know, they're not like the rest of us, these aristocrats, are they? And you've gotta try these croissants and jam. It's all home-made, almost as good as my mother's *ataif*,' Sayid said, remembering the joy of the small pancakes stuffed with nuts or cheese and doused in syrup.

'Thanks for the potted history, Sayid. As long as you're not going hungry or anything. Nice to know you weren't too worried about me, yeah?'

'Listen, Max, if I spent half my time worrying about you, I'd be a nervous wreck. Sophie said she found you on top of a mountain.'

'Did she? I don't know much about her,' Max said as he helped himself to the fresh fruit.

'She told us about Paris, and a circus and her dad. Then they did the girl-talk thing. Chatter mostly. Why they think anyone is actually interested in any of this stuff scrambles the brain. I mean, look at those two.'

They glanced at Sophie and Peaches.

'Boys and shopping. How boring can you get? So, what mountain were you on top of?' Sayid said as he reached for more food.

'How's the foot?' Max asked, warily looking to see if anyone was paying attention and might hear what he wanted to tell Sayid.

'S'all right. What mountain? Don't hold out. Come on.'

'The old monk's place.' Max spoke quietly. 'Someone had trashed it. Looks as though there was a hell of a fight there, and I reckon it happened before the avalanche. I think they were searching for the you-know-what.'

Sayid looked blank.

Max stared at him.

'Oh yeah. Right. Of course. The . . . yeah. The thingy,' Sayid said, remembering the pendant. 'Bloody hell, Max. This is getting dodgier, isn't it?'

'By the minute. Maybe it's time you went back to England.'

Max didn't sound that convincing. He wanted Sayid to stay a while longer. His friend was good at figuring out complex problems and if Max found more clues, he would be grateful for Sayid's help.

Sayid hesitated. He also wanted to know more about the mystery that was unfolding, despite the nervous tingle of trepidation that fluttered in his breakfast-filled stomach.

'Well, let's talk about that later, yeah?' Sayid said, delaying his own uncertainty.

'OK,' Max said, pleased Sayid was prepared to stick around for a while longer. 'There's a library down the corridor. When you get a chance, nose around, see if there's anything about old abbeys in this area. I don't want anyone seeing me do it and asking any awkward questions.'

Sayid nodded and smiled. Looking through books wasn't dangerous at all. He could manage that.

Max nodded in Sophie's direction. 'What do you think of her?' he asked, before gulping down a glass of fresh orange juice.

'Sophie? Dunno. What was she doing all the way up there anyway?'

'I'm not sure. We'll have to wait and see.'

Max's doubts about Sophie persisted. He hoped he might be wrong in thinking she was more deeply involved in Zabala's death than he suspected. He just hated coincidences – Max, the mountain and Sophie.

One thing he was wrong about was the witch who seemed intent on cutting his throat last night. Comtesse Isadora Villeneuve was a petite woman. The moonlight had been unkind to her, Max realized. Her finely etched features, distinctive cheekbones and emerald-green eyes showed she must have been a beautiful woman when she was younger. Her sun-damaged, wrinkled skin now gave her a look of weather-beaten leather, as coarse as the thong holding the thatch of hair in place at the nape of her neck. She wore a different dress; still a cotton kaftan but shot through with iridescent colour. Her bony fingers were, in fact, arthritic, swollen with painful inflammation. She smoked – that wouldn't help her skin either, Max thought, as she approached the others. She took a plate from her grandson, Bobby, asked if Sophie had had sufficient to eat and then turned her gaze on Max.

Max faltered under her stare.

'I apologize, young man, for last night,' she said as she moved towards the table. 'I have nothing left to pay the debtors. They have stripped my home, taken my land. I thought you were one of them trying to sneak inside and threaten an old lady.'

'I'm the one who should apologize,' Max finally managed

to say, searching for an appropriate level of politeness. 'I didn't mean to frighten you.'

She smiled. A glimpse of what her beauty must have once been. 'I think I was not the one who was frightened. *Oui?*'

It was said in such a gentle way, by no means a taunt, that Max smiled back. 'I was scared stiff,' he admitted.

She cocked her head, looking for the mark under his chin where she had put the working end of the kitchen knife. 'Did I hurt you?'

'No. It stung a bit. Like a wasp sting. It's OK now. It was nothing.'

She studied him a moment. 'From what my grandson tells me, you don't scare easily. I like that in a boy. Robert,' she said, glancing at Bobby, his legs slung over the edge of the sofa, flopped like a girl's rag doll, 'is brave when he faces the sea and the mountain, but you have a different courage, I think.' She stopped smiling. Max felt embarrassed. 'And a dark side. Am I right? I see it, you know. It's in the eyes. It's always in the eyes. Robert does not have it. But you . . .'

Her smile returned, brushing aside the moment of perception. 'Eat. We always have enough money to feed my grandson and his friends.' She laughed. 'Why do you think I am so poor!'

She floated away, that's how it seemed to Max, her feet gliding across floorboards and rugs. Bobby, unshaven and looking as though he hadn't yet woken up properly, stretched over to the table for another roll. 'The old girl's all right this morning. She, er, sees things. Y'know, spooks and stuff.'

'Ghosts?' Sayid said quietly.

'Yeah. She wanders round at night making sure they're all settled. Says they're her dead friends, and granddad.'

'So you think she's psychic?' Max asked.

'I think she drinks the wrong stuff,' Bobby said, filling his mouth with the roll. 'Anyway – surf's up.'

The wave curled; the offshore breeze brushed a fine spray from its crest, as Max gybed the windsurfer, caught the wind and ricocheted across the snapping white peaks. Borrowed from one of Bobby's surfing buddies, the wetsuit, a rich blue, with a curving yellow line across shoulders and hips, looked cool, but fitted badly. Max's shoulder joints strained, his knees took the impact of a big lift, but he misjudged the gusting wind and crashed into the cold Atlantic.

'He learned that in north Devon,' Sayid told Bobby, as they sat on the edge of the half-moon beach.

'Swimming underwater, y'mean? Idea is to stay on top.' Bobby laughed as he watched Max drag the windsurfer ashore.

'That was rubbish,' Max gasped as he sank on to the beach's grass verge.

'This isn't a great place for boardsailing. I'm gonna do a bit of surfing. See you guys later,' Bobby said as he ran to the breaking waves, surfboard under his arm. Peaches and his friends were already cutting across the face of a curling wave.

'We can't hang about here all day,' Max said. 'I didn't want to just disappear again. Bobby's cool about us hanging out, but I've got to find the abbey, Sayid, and I want to do it before Sophie gets back.'

The girl had gone to Biarritz to return the hire car that morning. She'd been fairly noncommittal about everything, but had said that she'd come back to the château if he wanted her to. She and Max were dancing around the same unspoken mistrust – both wanting to know more about each other's involvement with Zabala. Mutual suspicion bound them together.

'I looked in all the old guide books at the château, and the only abbey I could find is hundreds of Ks from here, way up north,' Sayid offered.

Max towelled himself dry. The wind was dropping; the weather would worsen soon and then Bobby and his friends would be off to Switzerland for more snowboarding. He had to use Bobby's local knowledge while he could. Trouble was, Bobby Morrell's local knowledge extended mostly to surfing conditions and girls, which at any other time would be an asset, but not now. Max looked across the sand dunes to the château. The Comtesse stood at a window. As Max gazed in her direction, she moved away. Max felt something more than the trickle of cold Atlantic water that slithered down his spine.

Time to take another risk.

The black Audi slipped through the early-morning streets like a feral cat searching for prey. Biarritz's roads were deserted; cars were clumped on pavements – parking, as in all cities, was a nightmare. Within a couple of hours traffic would choke the narrow streets and then Corentin and Thierry would never find the small side street they were searching for.

They had lost the girl, and the boy had slipped through their fingers back in Pau, since when both had vanished, but the girl had rented a car and with any luck she'd be returning it today. The two killers had entered the northern side of the city, turned down Avenue de l'Impératrice, past the Hôtel de Palais, where the rich came for self-indulgent pleasures of five-star luxury. There must have been every top marque parked in the hotel's car park, Corentin thought, as they glided past. Thierry was checking a street map, cursing under his breath as he tried to figure out the bottle-necking one-way street system. Corentin had no envy for the rich or their lifestyle; his path had been chosen for him when he was a boy. And as a man he had made good, casting aside the mindless violence of his childhood. The Legion had channelled his aggression, taught him to think and behave. He adhered to a set of values that seemed right, and it was known that, if a contract touched some deep instinct within Corentin, he would do a job without payment. There were times when he saw killing someone really evil as an act of charity; a contribution towards society.

After a few minutes of avoiding the wrong-way street signs, the car eased into a narrow road. Shops were still shuttered and closed. Thierry pointed to a lane behind the marketplace. A small sign: *Simone's Autos*. An archway led to an inner courtyard, where older cars were parked.

Corentin and Thierry watched, and waited, for Sophie.

Comtesse Villeneuve sat at a small baize-covered card table at the window, her back to the door. She slowly turned larger than usual cards, while a cigarette smouldered. After a moment of watching her, Max raised his hand to tap on the door, but before his knuckles found the wood she lifted the cigarette to her lips and, without turning, said in a low voice, 'Don't stand there all day, young man. I've been waiting for you.'

Max, unnerved by her knowing he was there, walked closer. Through the window he could see Sayid still under the umbrella, more for protection from the sea mist than the weak sunlight. He was stretched out on the ground, using his wheelchair as a footrest. Bobby had caught a good wave: his angular body scuttled towards the front of the board, his sea-soaked hair twisted like seaweed – his speed and elegance on the surfboard demanded attention.

'What do you mean, Comtesse?' Max said, turning to face her.

'You're not the same as these other boys. You're not as carefree. You think. Your brain – it works. I don't know what it thinks about, but you look at everything, you see things other boys do not. You are careful before you speak. You hold secrets. You are unsure of the girl. Well, maybe that is correct. Some girls, like Mademoiselle Fauvre, are . . . complicated. You watch her, you watch me. You have many questions that need answering. *N'est-ce pas?*'

'I didn't think it was that obvious.'

'My dear Max, I am an old lady. Age is like standing on top of a mountain – you get wonderful views of everything – before you fall, of course.' She laughed at her own mortality and his serious expression. 'Come along, Max. What is it?'

Trust no one! But there was no choice. Max felt time was running out. 'I'm looking for a Basque abbey and I've no idea where it is. At least I think it's Basque.' The helplessness of not knowing depressed him. He was stumbling along, caught up in a complex mess not of his own choosing.

'The Basques? Ah, there's a strange and unique people. These are their mountains that go down to the sea and they are also shrouded in mystery. Their people are blessed with ancient blood. Did you know that thousands of years ago they migrated from Finland? That they travelled down across Europe, bringing with them their own beliefs and a determination to find a new land? There is very little written about them. It's as if they are their own secret. And there are few remaining who can speak their language. No. Of course you did not know. Why should you?'

She paused, gazing out across the sea, past the crumbling stonework. When she turned to look at him again, Max felt as though she knew his deepest secrets. Maybe she was some kind of witch after all.

'My late husband was a soldier of France. Wherever we went he studied the people and the place, as if he was looking for an ambush. Just like you.' She laughed. 'You are safe here, but you are correct to exercise caution.'

'Even with you?' Max dared to ask.

She thought for a moment. 'Yes. You have given me information, now I share what it is you are seeking. Yes, caution. Always.' She went back to shuffling the cards, as if their conversation had ended.

'It's really important I find this place. It's an abbey with something to do with a snake and a crocodile.'

Her hands immediately stopped fingering the cards. Max's heart thumped. She knew. She looked at him. He didn't flinch. Challenging her to tell him. Her eyes never wavered from his face. Less intense than moments ago – more dreamy-looking. Why should this boy seek a place filled with exotic knowledge, created by a most extraordinary man? An Irishman, a Basque father and an Irish mother. Basques and Celts, rich in esoteric myth and legend. What was this boy doing? Why did she feel a sense of discomfort? A separate energy possessed this Max Gordon. A primeval element that could be evoked.

'Sit down,' she told him.

Max dragged a rattan chair over and sat. She beckoned him closer. He scuffed forward a few more centimetres.

'Give me your hand.'

He did as she asked and she held it tenderly in both hands. Max felt her calloused fingertips trace the whorls and lines on his skin. She half closed his fingers, studied the deepening creases in his palm, then turned his hand again, stroking the back of his fingers. She hesitated. There were sadness and loss in his hand.

'Your mother.' She shook her head gently. 'You were so young when she died.'

Max said nothing, remembering his dad holding him, and his tear-filled eyes. He'd never seen his father cry before – or since.

The Comtesse waited, sensing the boy's subtle energy of strength and determination. No evil. But a darker power lurking, accessible.

'Your father's energy flows in you. You grieve for him – but he's not dead.'

'No,' Max replied, his dad clearly in his mind. She whispered a truth Max had not dared tell anyone.

'You blame yourself. Something happened in the past. And you feel guilty.'

Max swallowed, his throat dry. Memories of the race to save his father when he was captured in Africa still tore him with regret. If his rescue mission had reached his dad sooner, then perhaps Max could have saved him from being tortured. And his dad's mind wouldn't now be fractured like a cracked mirror.

The Comtesse decided. The boy's search was for genuine reasons.

'It is not an abbey you seek, Max. It was built by a scientist-explorer in the nineteenth century. It is named after him. The Château d'Antoine d'Abbadie.' She smiled. 'Actually, it's a tourist attraction.'

'What?'

'Not very well promoted, and I doubt many know of it.'

'Where?'

'Hendaye, on the Spanish border. An hour or so from here.'

He had misunderstood Zabala's frantic, desperate cries in his dying moments. What he had heard as 'abbaye' was the name Abbadie.

'Can you keep this to yourself?' Max asked her.

'A tourist attraction? No,' she teased.

'That you've told me. Please. Don't mention it to Sophie. I need to see something for myself first.'

'All right. I have been a confidante of kings and queens.'

Max's eyebrows raised. Royalty?

'Not in this life,' she said quietly and without any trace of a smile to show that she might be kidding him. 'You have my word.'

Max turned away. He needed Bobby's van and Sayid's brain.

When he left the room, the Comtesse relaid the cards. They were Tarot, believed by some to show the journey from birth and the confrontation with universal forces. Fire, Air, Water and Earth were concealed in the pack. She turned over four cards – and felt a sudden pang of fear.

A high priestess – the power of the unconscious. Mystery.

The Skeleton – destruction and renewal. Mortality.

A tower struck by lightning – a stroke of fate. Catastrophe.

The final card showed a young man, a staff on his shoulder, a boy on a journey – a quest. A leap into the unknown.

Max Gordon was in mortal danger.

10

Bobby Morrell's two friends straddled their boards, a hundred metres from the shore, waiting for a swell that promised a curling wave. Peaches, further out, saw the dark rising wave and beat them to it, riding it as far as she could before cutting the board back over its crest.

Bobby shook his wet hair, reached behind him and unzipped his wetsuit. It was a way of buying time. Max had just asked him for the loan of his van. Sayid had just told him that Max could drive anything, but his head was telling him that he couldn't let an underage kid without a licence loose on a French autoroute. He towelled his hair, then looked at them.

'Guys, I'm sorry. No can do.'

'Bobby, if Max says it's urgent, I mean, I can vouch for that. He doesn't just say things for the sake of it,' Sayid urged.

Max held up a hand to stop his friend going on. 'He's right, Sayid. It'd only take one cop pulling me over and they'd have us home on a plane and Bobby here would be dragged into it. Sorry I asked,' he said to Bobby.

'No hard feelings, Max.'

'Course not.'

Bobby looked down the coastline, glanced out at his friends.

'Weather's gonna change. Those dudes are cutting out tomorrow. Hendaye's not great for surf, but there's a good break out near the rocks. I wouldn't mind going down to see how it's doing. Me and Peaches could catch a few waves. I could drop you guys off.'

He was trying to help, and still wasn't asking questions. Max nodded. 'That's perfect, Bobby, thanks.'

'This place mightn't be open, y'know. It's seasonal round here. You want me to phone and check?'

'Thanks,' Max said again as Bobby reached for his mobile.

Bobby gathered up his gear and dialled the French directory enquiries. Max watched him. Sayid caught the look in Max's eyes. Calculating, looking through the other person, figuring out if there was another motive for helping.

'What?' he said quietly.

Max shook his head. 'Nothing.'

Bobby had stepped away, one hand covering his ear against the noise of the crashing surf.

Sayid couldn't believe it. 'You don't trust Bobby?' he said quietly.

'I don't trust anybody, Sayid. I'm sorry. I can't.'

'And what about me?'

'You have to ask?'

'Maybe I should. You get some pretty dark thoughts, y'know. This sort of stuff can do your head in. You're not alone, Max. You've got friends.'

Sayid was right. But Max knew at the end of the day his instinct was always to go his own way. He didn't like depending on too many people. Why? he often wondered. The answer was always simple. Because not everyone realized the importance of being reliable.

Bobby walked back to them. 'I only got the caretaker, but they're open.'

Max smiled his thanks.

Sayid hauled himself out of the wheelchair. 'I'd better get rid of this thing if we're going museum bashing.'

'No. We're going to need it,' Max told him.

Sophie Fauvre eased the hire car into the bustling Biarritz street. Small farmer's trucks, laden with produce, jostled to reach the unloading bays of the indoor market. Outside, other stallholders set up their tables. The cobbled street was blocked. A van pulled out and Sophie pushed the car's nose into the space, edging backwards and forwards until it was parked. She was within sight of Simone's Autos.

The crowd jostled her along until the archway let her sideslip the stream of people. Simone's front office was little more than a hole in the wall. As Sophie moved round someone blocking her way, a vegetable cart jockeyed for position near the market's main doors and a shiver of light from a car's windscreen caught her eye – a black Audi. The big man leaned against the bonnet, casual, hands in pockets, just watching the market crowds.

Turning her face quickly, she stepped into the shaded archway. They'd found her. How? Only Max and the people at the Comtesse's château knew where she was. But she'd phoned her father. Maybe someone was monitoring her calls. She stripped her mobile of its SIM card and threw them separately into rubbish bins. She'd have to live without one for a while.

In a few strides she was in the office of Simone's Autos.

'Ah, mam'selle. *Ça va?*' Simone Lavassor beamed at her, tugging bangles over her wrist. 'A good holiday?'

Sophie nodded, but glanced quickly over her shoulder, making sure that the men hadn't spotted her and were at this minute making their way towards her.

'Something wrong?' the woman gently pressed her.

Sophie shook her head. 'The road's jammed. I've left the car opposite the market stalls.'

'But the car is fine? It is not damaged?'

'No, no. Course not. Just didn't want to hang around, sitting in traffic.'

Something wasn't right. Simone stared at her. 'You are in trouble?'

Surprised, Sophie laughed. 'No! Of course I'm not.'

Simone studied her, fussing with the collar of her flowered shirt. The office was always draughty at this time of year – and it gave her time to think. This young girl was lying. Good lie or bad lie?

'A man came here asking for you. Said he was a relative, heard you were visiting. Wanted to surprise you before you left for the airport.'

Fear tingled Sophie's neck. She had not been mistaken. It was one of the men from Mont la Croix.

'A man dressed in black, with a couple of days' stubble. Dark hair. Good-looking.'

'That's him.'

Sophie dropped her shoulders, sighed, shook her head, play-acting despair.

'You know him, mam'selle?'

'A man I met when I was skiing. He's been pestering me. Following me everywhere. I think he's one of those obsessive types. You smile at them once and they think you're offering to marry them.'

'Ha! Older men! They are all the same. You should stick to people your own age. I showed a kindness to old Monsieur Labrecht when his wife died. Some soup, some cleaning. The next thing . . .! I can't bring myself to tell you.'

'The man's out there. I saw him down the street. I don't know what to do,' Sophie said.

'He's stalking you!' Simone reached out a comforting hand to the troubled girl. 'Don't worry, *ma chérie*, you can go through the courtyard.'

She shuffled from behind the counter, took Sophie's arm and guided her through the door to the archway, pointing to where the hire cars were untidily crammed. 'On the other side of the yard, there's a back door. Monsieur Fouché's shop, a *chocolaterie*. Divine. Look at the size of me. I resist him but not his chocolates. One day I shall yield to his desire. Go. Tell him Simone has sent you. He'll let you through the shop.'

Sophie kissed her cheek in thanks and manoeuvred through the cars. Simone watched her go. There was a time when she too was slender and agile, and handsome men pursued her with a passion. Now? Ah, now she was a woman of years.

But life was not all bad. There was always Fouché and his dark chocolate crushed raspberry delights.

Corentin and Thierry were old hands at what they did. They had reconnoitred the streets around the market before Sophie arrived. They knew where she would go if she got spooked.

Corentin wanted her to see him.

When Sophie ran through Simone's yard she failed to see Thierry waiting across the street. And despite her fast-paced escape, Thierry kept far enough behind her not to be noticed. Corentin cut and thrust the car through the congested side streets and by the time Sophie had hitched a lift in a young man's car, Thierry had climbed into the Audi, and the two killers followed her with ease.

Max stood behind the two front seats and stared through the windscreen as Bobby drove the van at the speed limit towards the Spanish border. Peaches sat in the passenger seat, knees tucked up as usual, iPod playing, eyes closed, lips muttering, and – as usual – was out of the real world. They turned off the A63 motorway on the St Jean de Luz south slip road on to the D912, a smaller, twisty road that would take them, hopefully, to the château. Max was worried. Not only was he dependent on Bobby for shelter and transport – which, as grateful as he was, was irritating because he'd rather look after himself – but the young American had never asked a question about what was going on. Never since Pau, when Max had phoned him asking for help at the hospital, never once on the drive into the mountains and Zabala's sanctuary, nor when Max and Sophie turned up late at the château. And this morning Bobby volunteered to drive them without question. Wouldn't it be natural to at least ask what you might be getting into?

As they approached the outskirts of Hendaye, Bobby slowed down.

'Any idea where this place is? The caretaker guy didn't have a clue about directions. Probably hasn't been any further than his local town his whole life,' he said to Max.

'The Countess said there were no signs but we should look out for a hairpin bend. It's on the right somewhere.'

Bobby winced. 'I've got a confession to make, Max.'

Was this going to confirm Max's doubts? He waited.

Bobby grinned sheepishly. 'My gran isn't a countess. She was the housekeeper until the old countess died twenty years ago. She left the château and all its debts to my gran. She's been selling off furniture and fighting debtors ever since. She's a bit loopy. She thinks she is the countess now, but she has a heart of gold and I'd hate to do anything that'd cause her problems. So, this thing you're involved in seems to be getting complicated. If there's anything you think you should tell me, I'd like to know.'

Max's mind raced, plucking out events from the past couple of weeks. Was this it? Had Bobby finally broken cover? Could he be involved in any of the trouble? *Ez ihure ere fida – eheke hari ere.* Trust no one – they will kill you. Max just didn't believe it. Of all the danger he'd been in, he couldn't pinpoint any in which Bobby might have been implicated. But the black Audi had arrived at the Pau hospital soon after the young American. Coincidence? And Zabala's mountain hut? Bobby had dropped him off in the valley that night and then . . .?

A gut-wrenching moment. Sophie appeared the next day – was there a chance these two could be working together? It fitted neatly enough. Max's mind shouted back at him. No! This is stupid. It's paranoia. Not trusting anyone was like mental quicksand. Doubt and fear smothered and drowned any rational thought. No!

He shook his head involuntarily at his own thoughts.

'That's OK, then,' Bobby said, misunderstanding.

'That's not what I meant. You're right, Bobby, I shouldn't drag anyone into this. It is serious and the reason I don't want to tell you is because it would make you vulnerable. Once we've been here to this Antoine d'Abbadie's place, I'll leave. Me and Sayid. All I can say is, I need to find something. Although truth is I don't know what I'm looking for. I would never cause any harm to you or your gran, no matter who she thinks she is. I promise.'

'That's cool,' Bobby said. He leaned across to the dashboard, took his mobile phone and handed it to Max. 'You might need this. I've got another. I'm on speed-dial one.'

'Thanks,' Max said, momentarily surprised by the generosity of the gift.

The surfer nodded. It was cool. It always was.

'There,' Max said, pointing at the bend in the road. 'It's there.'

The young driver's dream of asking the beautiful girl for a date lasted all of five minutes when Sophie jumped out of the car, apologized and told him she was late to meet her boyfriend. The lie slipped easily from between her lips. The driver shrugged. It was life. But it could have been a more beautiful one had she stayed.

Sophie found the safest route across the barbed-wire-topped gate: she clawed her fingers around a gate post, balanced, flicked her hips across the wire, then twisted her body mid-air, landing with both feet together, neither on her toes – that would have pitched her forward – nor on her heels

– that would have jarred her spine. It was effortless. She ran almost silently into the château. Where was Max?

'I cannot tell you,' Comtesse Villeneuve said as she studied the girl, who now seemed mildly agitated.

'Countess, listen to me. This is not a straightforward matter of a wayward fifteen-year-old kid on the run from going back home. He's involved in a really dangerous situation.'

'He behaves more like an older boy. He has seen death and known loss. That can mature a boy beyond his years.' She gazed at the girl, whose light olive complexion now seemed a little flushed.

Sophie had pulled off her cap, ruffled her hair and sat down facing the elderly lady. 'It's dangerous,' she repeated helplessly.

'For whom?' No expression. No hint of suspicion or guile. A straightforward question. Would the girl answer truthfully?

'For everyone who knows him,' Sophie said.

The Comtesse did not know whether she trusted Sophie or not. Those almond eyes were impenetrable and she liked to read people through their eyes. A grey slab of cloud pushed between sea and sky, dimming the room. A contour of diffused light surrounded Sophie's body. Invisible to the naked eye, seen only by those with the gift to see. The old lady watched the agitated flow of colour-drenched energy swirl around the girl. She was distressed, but hiding it extremely well. There was pain there, grief too, and fear. The fear was not of physical harm but of a young woman's emotional uncertainty.

Where Max's aura had been broad, unbroken, symbolizing his strength and health, this girl's was fractured – enormous energy, screwed down tightly like a lid on a jar. Daggers of red light shot out from this quivering shadow-body, like sun spots bursting from the fiery surface. The girl's conflicting emotions made the Comtesse gasp. She could not help herself.

Sophie Fauvre either was in love with Max Gordon or wanted to kill him.

The nondescript entrance to the Château d'Antoine d'Abbadie could easily be missed by passing motorists. There were no big signs demanding attention and the château wasn't visible from the road. Bobby drove the van slowly under the canopy of trees that lined the narrow tarmac drive. A parking area, denoted by coconut-mat fencing, was on the right-hand side after about a hundred metres. There was one other car parked, with German number plates, and Max could see a middle-aged couple, obviously tourists, waiting further ahead, where he could just make out the edge of the grey stone building. That must be the entrance.

'Wait here. I'm going to check it out and make sure this is the right place,' Max said.

The bare branches of the tree canopy still obscured the building, but now Max could see its shape. A black slate roof capped the stone walls. The château wasn't that big but it had the look of a small medieval castle, some ramparts on the one side, about three storeys high, while the nearer side looked like a more typical French château. This d'Abbadie bloke must have had a lot of fun, Max thought, because it was all a bit nineteenth-century Disney. But there was also a creepy feeling. Chimeric gargoyles, imaginary creatures from mythology, snarling or laughing, Max couldn't tell, glared down at him from the corners of the building. Mythical equivalents of scrapyard dogs. No entry! they snarled silently.

He stopped in his tracks. Facing him on the building's huge stone wall was a massive snake, a giant anaconda, sculpted into the stonework. Its body squirmed, twisting, head facing upwards; in a big S, its tail curled in a figure eight. Heart thumping, knowing this château was the key to Zabala's death, Max walked another few metres to the front of the building. The site of the incomplete photograph he had found in Zabala's hut was revealed. Eight front steps, broad at the base, narrowed as they ascended to the double-studded red front door. The Gothic arch, cut off in that photograph, was joined together beneath a statue of a shield and a sword. Another snake twined itself along the blade to the handle. Two palm trees shielded the entrance.

Crocodiles gazed blindly at him, one each side, straddling a low balustrade that ran down the steps. Their chiselled tails curled upwards towards the door, mouths gaped, front legs gripping the stone, as if ready to strike.

Max's jaw clenched so tightly it ached. He'd had experience of crocodile attacks before and these lifelike creatures made him shudder. Max's dad had taken him to ancient tombs in Egypt. Crocodiles were revered as part of the pantheon of gods. Max remembered the crocodile deity was called Sobek and was believed to have emerged from the 'Dark Water' to create the world. He also guarded the dead. These two crocodiles guarded the portal to a hidden world.

Max stepped between them towards the entrance, half expecting them to come to life, to whip their heads around and strike. But the creatures held within the stone sculpture lay silent as he approached the château and its secret.

11

'You pay extra for a guided tour, which we don't need, and it's about half price if you're under thirteen,' Max told Sayid as he pushed the wheelchair towards the entrance. The van had merged into the coast-road traffic, with a promise from Bobby to return in a few hours when they called him. 'So you're under thirteen if they ask. I can't get away with it but you can.'

'I thought I looked older than that,' Sayid moaned.

'No. In fact you look about ten.'

'Ten!'

Max laughed. 'Well, you behave like a ten-year-old. Now shut up and look stupid if they talk to you. That shouldn't be too difficult.'

The small window at the side of the front door showed an office, where a middle-aged man, who minutes earlier had been thinking only of going home to the fish lunch his wife had prepared, now looked with anguish at the fair-haired boy trying to pull another youngster in a wheelchair up the steps. It was not worth offering to help and risking an injury to his back, the man reasoned; besides, the boy looked strong. But how would the youngster view the château in a wheelchair?

'Not exactly geared for disabled access,' Sayid winced, as Max jammed the wheels up another step.

'Yeah, well, I'm hoping it'll help us fool him later. We're going to be here some time. I have a plan.'

Sayid looked at his friend, who gave him an encouraging smile in return. Max's plans usually meant trouble. Sayid had told Max he didn't want to be left out – but he knew he needed a degree of bravado he would find difficult to muster.

Max turned and looked at the German couple, who were already halfway up the steps.

'*Bitte?*' he called gently towards the stout man, whose face lit up with relief at hearing his own language – someone asking for help. He immediately walked back to Max and took control of pulling Sayid up the steps.

Max's German was fairly basic – he was better at understanding than speaking the language – but he could pull off a good accent and his limited vocabulary would be enough to achieve what he needed. The German tourist spoke rapidly. Max only grasped about one word in three but he quickly assured the tourist that everything was OK. *Alles ist in ordnung.*

By the time they reached the studded door it seemed as though they had known each other for years. Just what Max had hoped for. The Frenchman selling tickets couldn't see Max and Sayid to one side, nor the crumpled notes in Max's hands.

Max groaned.

The German turned. '*Was? Was ist los?*' he asked.

The tourist's concern for the boy seemed genuine as Max

shook his head sadly. The look on his face said everything. He didn't have enough money. The stout man waved his hand in a dismissive gesture, turned back to the ticket seller and, using sign language, indicated he was paying for everyone.

Sayid looked over his shoulder at Max. What a clever ruse. How did Max get away with things like that? The Frenchman smiled, ushering 'the German family' inside. Max thanked the German for his generosity and explained the couple could go around the château on their own. *Unbegleitet.* And that he'd be happy to help wherever he could.

The ticket seller, by way of appeasing his guilt, as well as protecting the floors and the banisters, not to mention the risk of walls being scraped, agreed to Max leaving the wheelchair in the entrance hall. Sayid got himself on to his crutches, as Max tucked it into a darkened corner. The wheelchair would play its part later.

Black walls decorated with an ornate design of bright blue and gold enamel panels made the place seem like a miniature royal palace. Max tried to look appreciative when the tourist, referring to a German-language tour pamphlet, explained that the chapel they now gazed at was a private place of contemplation for Antoine d'Abbadie and his wife, Virginie, and that the scientist-astronomer, who died in Paris in 1897, lay buried with his wife in a crypt under the altar.

Max saw the ticket seller go back into the office, thanked the German for his explanation and pointed the couple towards another room, as he eased Sayid away.

'Come on, Sayid. We need to get around faster than a tourist.'

Sayid was well practised on the crutches and quickly

developed a swinging momentum as they moved towards the next room along.

'Blimey, hang on. I can't keep up!' Max laughed.

It wasn't true of course, but it made Sayid feel less of a hindrance than he thought he was. 'Where do we start?' he said.

'Dunno yet. We'll check down here first. There's a load of stuff about Ethiopia,' Max said, as they walked beneath richly painted scenes of ancient Abyssinia, as it was then known. 'If Zabala spent who knows how many years working here, then maybe it means something.'

They stepped into a bedroom. The decor was overpowering. The four-poster bed seemed small compared to the lavish surroundings. Arabic letters flitted across large canvas panels.

'What does that say, Sayid?'

Sayid looked at the delicate calligraphy. 'Er, not sure. Something about . . . Oh, hang on, it's an old Arab proverb. My granddad was always saying things like that: "Never throw stones in your own drinking well's water."'

Max looked blank.

Sayid shrugged. 'I think that's what it says. Whatever that might mean?'

'Well, "Don't do anything stupid close to home, as it'll come back on you!" Or "Make sure you're connected to mains water." How would I know?' Max said.

'You're the one looking for clues!'

'That's not one of them, I'm sure. Come on.' Max moved quickly to another room, keeping an eye out for the ticket seller, but there was no sign of him, and he couldn't hear the Germans anywhere either. He could see the edge of the car park through a window. Their car was still there. Good, that meant he didn't have to do what he'd planned just yet. He entered the château's dining room. Wood-panelled to shoulder height, buffalo skins on the wall and Antoine d'Abbadie's family motto boxed next to his coat of arms. It was a Latin inscription.

'What's that say?'

'Erm . . . it's Latin . . .'

Sayid groaned. He knew Max's ability on the subject.

Max hesitated. 'I think it says, "Life is but smoke."' The phrase immediately reminding him of his African Bushman friend, whose people believed that life was a dream and one day we would all wake up in the real world.

'Do you think it might be a clue? Life is smoke. I mean, we've got Latin sayings, Arab verses, it could be any of these things,' Sayid said.

'Like that, you mean?' Max pointed at the backs of the dining-room chairs surrounding the marquetry inlaid table. They were covered in green velvet but on each one was an Arabic letter. Max stood back, walked around the table. 'What do they mean?' he asked Sayid.

'I'm not sure, Max.'

'What? Suddenly you can't spell?'

'It's Amharic. Ethiopian.'

The German spoke in English. He was in the doorway, smiling as Max spun round, instincts suddenly wary. When he had left the tourist couple at the chapel it would have been natural for them to carry on their tour on that side of the château. And Max believed he would have heard even the softest of footfalls across the hall and down the passageway.

Why so silent? Perhaps Max had been distracted by Sayid and all the different languages on display.

'I thought you were English, though your German accent is good,' the rotund man said, smiling at Max. He gestured with the tour pamphlet for the château. 'If you get the letters on the chairs in order they spell out a warning: "May traitors never be seated at this table."' He gave Max and Sayid another smile, and handed Max the pamphlet. 'We have another one. Enjoy the tour, boys,' he said, ushering his wife into the corridor.

Sayid slumped on to one of the dining-room chairs and rubbed his aching leg. 'Well, traitors not being welcomed to nosh might be something.'

Max shook his head. 'This is all window dressing. None of it concerns us. If Zabala worked here for all those years he would have been involved in the science bit. There's a library and observatory upstairs.'

He checked the corridor. The Germans were just going into one of the other rooms, so he and Sayid turned into the main hallway, where the carved, wooden-banistered stairs began.

'Come on,' Max said. 'Piggyback time.'

As he pumped his legs up the stairs, the extra weight stretched his tendons and muscles, but it was effortless; the knowledge that he was getting closer to where Zabala had spent his working life boosted his strength.

On the upper landing there were huge paintings of tribal chiefs from Ethiopia dressed in white robes, with spear-carrying warriors protecting them, the whole tableau set against a deep blue sky. The vibrancy of the château's decoration seemed so out of place when compared to the rough simplicity of how

Zabala had lived on the mountain. Max reminded himself that Zabala became a monk after he stopped working here, because of his failure to convince everyone that something terrible was going to happen. The Academy of Sciences ran the château after Antoine d'Abbadie's death, so Zabala would have had the full weight of the French scientific community against him when he failed to prove that Lucifer – whoever that was – would cause some kind of mass destruction. A Basque outsider, a man consumed by his failure, but eventually murdered because his prediction must finally have some validity. Who would benefit from stopping Zabala's theory becoming known?

Distorted shadows lengthened across the walls. The dark wood sucked in what natural light was left to the day. Arabian shields and swords, once held by warriors, adorned the walls. Antelope trophy heads stared in dumb fear, gazing sightless over the flamboyant neo-Gothic castle they would never have seen in their natural lives.

Max suddenly felt all the paintings and decorations overpowering. The weight of colour on the walls and ceilings, oppressive, like a clown's face overladen with make-up, concealing misery beneath a false smile. They turned a corner into another room.

'Wow!' Sayid said in amazement.

Bare floorboards, a long, solid-looking table sat square in the middle of the room bearing a few relics of scientific machinery, and an old manual typewriter. Charts, files and folders were neatly stacked in purpose-built bookshelves from floor to ceiling. An explorer-scientist's lifetime's work. The darkness, from the almost black timber of the ceiling, swallowed the very top shelves of books. This was getting close to where a scientist or researcher could stay in splendid isolation and concentrate on the complexities of their project. No overkill on decoration here. It was as if Max and Sayid had stepped behind a façade and found the true heart of the château. Was this where Zabala's secret lay?

Curved, cast-iron supports bore the weight of the gallery that went round the whole room halfway up the wall. The ceiling must have been about six metres high and not a space was to be seen between the soldier-rigid volumes. Dulled gold on black lettering spread across the top of the far wall. It was in Basque and Max had no idea what it meant.

But he loved books. And maps. In fact anything that told a story about somewhere different. And sea charts showing reefs and sandbanks, tides and warnings of danger. He could almost smell the adventure in them. But here was something unique – being allowed to peep through the curtains on an extraordinary man's life.

Max knew his dad could spend years in this room, examining every paper written by d'Abbadie. He ran his fingers along book spines. A gentle hum drew his eyes to a humidifier in the corner. Yes, that made sense. They were barely a kilometre from the page-rotting dampness of the Basque coast. These books could be either packed away and held in some philistine of a building in a city, or allowed to remain here where they belonged. A tribute to the achievements of one man and his desire to explore the world and its people, the stars and planets, and his dream of living in a pretend castle.

From what Max could see, the lower shelves were mostly astronomical publications. The folders were protected by strong, thick, brown paper. He touched his finger along their edges, pulled one from the shelf and placed it on the table.

'Sayid, grab another one of these. From about twenty years ago, just before Zabala left here.'

The folder was heavy, the big pages cumbersome. Max's hand hovered over the intricate data. A star chart. Lines bisected each other, stars had numbers, some had letters. Magnifications, magnitudes, it was a meaningless panorama of the galaxy as far as Max could tell. He flipped the pages quickly. There was nothing that could even resemble the name Zabala.

'They're missing,' Sayid said.

'What?' Max moved to where his friend shuffled along the wide shelves, the only places big enough to hold the star charts.

'The folders go way back. Look –' he pointed one out – '1904, all the way up, 1927, and so on. How long would Zabala have worked here?'

'I don't know,' Max said.

'Well, if he was here for, say, ten or fifteen years, up to twenty years ago there's a whole batch missing.'

It made sense. If Zabala had tried to prove something and failed, gone public and brought embarrassment and derision on his scientific colleagues, they would have taken anything he had researched and archived it somewhere, or at worst destroyed it.

'See if there's a book or something that would list any of the scientists that worked here,' Max told Sayid. 'I've got to check on something.'

Max automatically looked at his wrist, but of course his father's watch was missing. A twinge of regret, which he pushed aside. 'Time, Sayid?'

'Nearly half-four. They close at five.'

Max nodded and walked quickly to the stair landing. Looking out of the window, he saw that the Germans' car had gone. He ran to another window that looked out on to the fields towards the coast. The Frenchman was locking a small garden-type gate that closed off a footpath towards the cliffs.

Max pounded downstairs to the entrance hall and glanced at the office. The man's scruffy black anorak was on a hook, so that meant he was probably doing his rounds. He'd be back.

Max trundled Sayid's wheelchair down the corridor into the chapel, then folded the chair and hid it behind the door. Odds were the ticket seller would check inside the château before locking up for the night. Even if he went into the chapel he wouldn't spot the wheelchair.

And if Max was lucky the man would see that the Germans' car and Sayid's chair were no longer there and believe that the whole 'German family' had left.

Max sprinted upstairs, two at a time, got back to Sayid and moved closer to him so his voice wouldn't echo.

'Tell me when it's quarter to five. Anything?'

Sayid had an embossed leather book on the table next to a rolled-up plan. 'I found Zabala.' He grinned. 'I couldn't find any kind of register, but I reckoned those scientists wouldn't want to miss out on their bit of glory, so they wouldn't chuck anything away with their own pictures in.' Sayid opened the ledger-sized book. 'Different photos of the scientists who worked here until the 1970s, then it looks as though the place was closed down.'

Sayid was pointing at a group photograph. The caption was

in a small typeface but Max could read Zabala's name. Two rows of men: the front row seated, the others standing. Looking, with his shorter beard, very much as he did in the one from the broken frame, Zabala stood with his arms folded and a briar pipe clamped between his teeth as he smiled for the camera.

'But I saw newspaper cuttings from the 1980s,' Max said.

'Then my guess is he carried on doing his own research here afterwards.'

'There must have been a reason. What's here in the château? Stuff from Africa, different languages, astronomy –' Max remembered the newspaper piece on Zabala – 'and astrology. He mixed the two. So there's a link somewhere, Sayid. The Arabs were major players in astronomy . . .'

Sayid closed the book.

'Astronomy was OK because that could be used to tell farmers when to rotate crops and what have you, but astrology was unlawful.'

'OK, so perhaps it's just an astronomy clue. Europeans mixed the two. There's a load of stuff here about old d'Abbadie's journey across Africa. Keep looking. And do it quietly. What's this?'

He unfurled the rolled plans.

'Architect's drawings of the château,' Sayid said.

They held the uncooperative edges of the plan flat. Max scooted his finger around the drawing, tracing the internal layout of the château in case there was a hidden room they had missed, or, more likely, that was kept purposefully from the public.

'Here's where we are now, here's the observatory . . .'

'We should look in there,' Sayid said.

'Yeah, I know. I just hoped there would be something in this room that would help us. This is where all the records are kept. The observatory hasn't been in use for a quarter of a century.'

A footfall scuffed the floor below. The Frenchman was on his rounds. He wheezed and coughed. Lights were going off all the way through the château, but were replaced by the softer glow of all-night security lights, small spotlights strategically positioned to throw a cone of illumination across a corner or edge of stairway.

Shadows changed the shapes of the walls, defacing the huge paintings, making an eerie no man's land of the pockets of darkness.

Max needed to get into the office. He'd spotted the control box for the château's alarm system when they had first entered the building and it needed to be switched off if he and Sayid were going to spend the next few hours hunting for clues.

Max paused and crouched, watching through the banisters. The old man was pulling on his jacket. He moved towards the front door – going through his nightly routine.

A warning creak, like a snapping stick, seemed to thunder down the stairs. Sayid!

Had the old man heard? He turned but didn't look up, then stepped back into the office, took his cigarettes from the desk, closed the office door and moved towards the main entrance.

Max turned, stepping lightly but rapidly upstairs.

Sayid had frozen, as if his foot had trodden on an anti-personnel mine that would spring up and explode if he moved. He winced when he saw his friend emerge from the staircase void.

The door downstairs clunked closed.

Max gave a thumbs-up to Sayid, who nodded, eased his foot forward and swung himself towards the library. Max peeped out of the window and saw the man hobbling towards the gate pillars at the end of the drive. The office door was unlocked. Max could smell the lingering residue of tobacco in the air as he slipped inside.

He opened the alarm box's cover. A simple series of switches with the master switch clearly marked.

It was off. The Frenchman must have forgotten to switch the circuit on. Maybe the château was so secure no one could get in anyway. Security systems were a nuisance and a curse when one was forever being dragged out of a warm bed for a false alarm. Whatever the reason, the main switch was off and that was all Max was interested in. Now they could get to work.

Once again he ran quickly back up the stairs, stepping across a darkened corner. Yellow, crinkle-cut moonlight filtered through the stained-glass window. At the top of the staircase the life-sized statue of a young Ethiopian warrior stood silently, a glass lamp held high, guarding the darkness of the stairwell, showing the way. Max murmured, 'Thanks, mate.'

The château, full of half-light, relics and mysteries, whispered silence. Max could hear the gentle turn of paper rustling in the library. As he left the upper landing, turning into the passageway for the library and Sayid, he had no idea they were not alone.

Something moved in the shadows below.

12

Bobby Morrell didn't have a chance when they came for him.

As darkness fell and the swollen moon escaped the confines of the horizon, he sat with a mug of coffee, a small fire burning on the beach. The salt-encrusted wood sparked fairy-light blue flame, embers heated the stones surrounding the fire and a wave, almost reluctantly, curled and hissed across the sand. It was a cold night. He and Peaches had caught a few waves on the break near the rocks, but the wind had freshened, pushing clouds silently through the valleys and peaks of the mountains behind him. Ripples scattered across the surface, nudging the anchored speedboat a kilometre or so offshore. Locals fishing. A picturesque scene. Bobby was content. A surfer's chosen loneliness – down a mountain on a snowboard or riding an undulating wave, its curling power ready to fling you forward – just him and his board. Another few weeks and he'd be back in school. Then college. Then what? He didn't know. What he really wanted was to be on his own with the elements. He'd get a degree – business studies – and set up a sporting empire on the web. Five years from now someone else could run it. He'd go and find the perfect wave and the highest mountain.

Countless waves around the world waited for him and his board, and there were high valleys choked with snow just begging for him to slice them open with a sweeping curve. Life should be that simple. Bobby was part of the great outdoors. Connected is how he felt. Part of. Integral. Symbiosis. That was cool. Symbiosis – interdependent. Mountains and sea needed him and he needed them.

School was not symbiotic.

That's why he liked Max Gordon. That kid was 'connected' as well. Max was cool. He'd take on a challenge. He'd give it a go, as the Brits say. Yeah. He'd take Max to Hawaii one day and let him see real waves on Oahu. That'd chill his blood. Winter storms in Alaska created huge rollers that travelled thousands of kilometres until they hit Oahu's north shore. Monsters. Wow. Yeah. Body-manglers. That'd test the kid's nerve. Those waves come at you like an express train, twenty metres high. Higher.

Max'd like that.

He looked out across the bay. Peaches must have caught a wave further down and decided to call it a night. She was probably trudging through the sand right now. He'd keep the fire going. She'd be cold.

As the moonlight shimmered across the flat-water bay, he heard distant growls – off-roaders. Three or four of them were scratching around the night. He checked his mobile phone, nervous he'd missed Max's call. Nothing. Then something pushed through the bushes.

Bobby got to his feet, grabbed a piece of driftwood to protect himself and faced the figure who'd stepped into the firelight. The malformed head raised its face to the moonlight, as if sniffing the wind. The gashed mouth revealed pointed teeth. Its tongue licked saliva before it dribbled down its almost non-existent chin.

'You must be Bobby,' Sharkface said.

Max pulled books and files from the library shelves, searching for any clues. Sayid did the same. But all they found for their efforts were a few charts, a plan of the château and what amounted to a series of yearbooks of scientists. Max was on the upper level, moving along the gantry below the emblazoned Basque letters on the roof beams. He looked at them and dismissed them. The words were a legacy of the generous spirit of Antoine d'Abbadie, encouraging the readers in his library to work and seek wisdom. It didn't matter. Max didn't understand a word.

His eyes were glazing over. He'd been in the half-light too long and trying to read the foreign words on the spines of the folders and books was giving him a crick in his neck. He was looking without seeing, concentration flagging.

And then something caught his eye. He took two steps back. Words had been scratched along the edge of a shelf. Faint, barely visible, and they were small. It was doubtful if anyone would notice them unless by chance. Or unless they were looking.

What he needed was a piece of chalk to highlight the letters. But there was no chalk. What else? Max looked down to where Sayid sat at the trestle table, poring over a volume. He saw what he needed. He ran to the end of the gantry and down to Sayid, praying what he wanted would still be in place.

The old typewriter.

'What? You've found something?' Sayid said as Max stuck his nose close to the old metal keys.

'Something,' he said, his fingers already lifting the faded ribbon spindles from the machine. Within seconds he was back at the bookshelf. He rubbed what little pigmentation there was with spit on his finger, then ran the ribbon across the bookshelf's edge. It worked. The faded scratches lifted slightly, but he could only see a few of the words. *Luciferi primo cum sidere frigida rurar carpamus . . .* There were more words too worn to be seen. Max muttered the inscription to himself. Lucifer! There it was.

If only Mr Chaplin were at his shoulder. The softly spoken teacher at Dartmoor High had found the route to Max's fleeting attention span in class by teaching them ancient Greek and Roman history. And as Dartmoor High was built on a one-time outpost of Rome's XX Legion, that meant soldiers and battles – and Latin.

'What is it?' Sayid said quietly, looking up to the gallery.

Max studied the words again. '*More* Latin. I dunno. Something to do with . . . er . . . to do with hastening . . . the first morning light.' He shook his head and shrugged apologetically at Sayid.

'Thicko,' Sayid said.

'I can tell you all the battles the Twentieth Legion fought. I can't help it if they spoke in ancient Italian.'

'Lucifer, though, eh?' Sayid said.

'*Luciferi*. Yeah.'

Max scanned the books wedged immediately above the scratched words. A folder was hidden behind them, its corner alerting an enquiring eye to find it. Max reached in and pulled it free.

The worn brown paper had sloughed, like dead skin. He opened it and a few pages fell out. Max shuffled them. The first sheet was a hand-drawn circle with symbols and numbers around the edge, and inside the circle what looked to be three or four triangles of different sizes.

Scrawled across the top of the page, in a barely legible script, were three more Latin words: *Lux et veritas*.

'There's more!' Max blurted out as he made his way down to Sayid. '*Lux et veritas*. That means "Light and truth", I know that much.'

He laid the sheets of paper on the table, but Sayid's attention was elsewhere. He had found a volume of documents.

'Blimey,' Sayid said. 'Look at this.'

Sayid placed the big book next to Max's folder on the table. A diagram filled the page. It was an intricate symbol, a zigzag pattern, all angles and lines. Where the lines did not touch, the spaces formed shapes which made the pattern look like a field of diamonds, while the spaces between the lines made star patterns. This was something.

'You know what this is?'

'Yeah,' Sayid said, still gazing at the drawing.

'It's all right, Sayid. No hurry. Take your time. You don't have to share the secret if you don't want to.'

'Well, it's just a bit of a surprise, that's all. My family had books on Islamic art and I've seen this before. Wow. Amazing.'

Max stared at Sayid, who was transfixed by the drawing.

He turned it this way and that, and no matter which way up it was held the pattern stayed the same.

'I'll tell you what this is . . .' Sayid said, the intricate drawing still holding his attention.

Max sighed, and waited.

'This is the Divine Order,' Sayid told him.

'The what?'

'It's pure geometry. I think the Arabs got it from the Greeks, but they perfected it. Anyway, that's what it represents – that the chaos of the universe is part of a plan. At least, I think that's what it means. And this shape, this diagram, shows the chaos of the universe in a defined order. All very precise.'

'You've lost me, Sayid.'

Max's mind raced. His dad had taught him so many things when they travelled together, but this didn't trigger any memories. He knew the ancient Greeks had learned from Egypt and Babylonia, and that the Indians and Arabs had mastered astronomy and mathematics, but where did this fit in? Was there anything his dad had told him that would help solve this puzzle?

The thought of his father, alone and struggling with his own illness, stabbed at him. His dad was bigger than life. His strong, adventurous, clever dad. Max let the feeling slip away. No good dwelling on it. But he remembered his dad telling him about the Greek masters. The bloody conflicts of ancient times fascinated Max, and he'd visited battlefields with his father. It was about the time he just couldn't settle down at Dartmoor High. So his dad told him stories. They walked in the heat of Greece, where warriors had fallen in great battles, his father explaining how the use of geometry had enabled men to build siege machines for thousands of years. It was his father's way of helping him concentrate in class, giving him something vibrant to grasp when the subject demanded concentration rather than imagination.

Max had struggled at school. When his mum died, the shock and grief resonated through him, a silent weeping he could barely hold in. And to try and understand even the most basic elements of geometry – the square of the length of the hypotenuse is equal to the sum of the squares of the lengths of the other two sides – would make his brain seize up at times. So his dad told him about Pythagoras. A Greek master mathematician, a vegetarian mystic who believed he could prove the secrets of the universe through geometry. Secrets of the universe. Now Sayid had told him that the drawing meant exactly that.

'If it's in this book, then I reckon it's not part of any clue,' Max said. 'But maybe it tells us that Zabala was searching for something to do with astrology or astronomy and was using geometry to help him solve the puzzle.'

Max took the second piece of paper from the folder. It had a row of five numbers across and five down. And only one word, a symbol and a number were written across the top: *Mars* = 65.

'Mars equals sixty-five,' Max said. 'What's that supposed to mean?'

'Mars is the god of war.'

'I know that, Sayid. But he's not sixty-five years old, is he? And he doesn't live at number sixty-five Acacia Avenue.'

'I'm only trying to help. Keep your shirt on. I'm the bloke who helped you get through your maths exam last year, remember? Your mad monk must have put it here for a reason.'

'He wasn't mad, I'm sure of it. He was a scientist and he's giving us another clue along with everything else.'

Max studied the piece of paper a moment longer, gazing at the numbers, willing his mind to make some sense of them.

11	24	7	20	3
4	12	25	8	16
17	5	13	21	9
10	18	1	14	22
23	6	19	2	15

'I read a book once about spies in the Second World War and they used a code system like this, but that was something to do with letters in a box, not numbers,' Max said.

'I remember that, you were going on about it for ages. And?'

'And ... I dunno. I can't remember how the system works.'

Sayid looked dismayed.

'No good pulling a face, Sayid. I told you about it as well. How come you don't remember?'

'Because I was probably doing your maths homework at the time.'

Max touched his finger on to each square.

'There's always a pattern with numbers. They always mean something,' Sayid said.

'Obviously,' said Max, 'otherwise they wouldn't be here,

would they? Anyway, I can tell you one thing – all these numbers, up, down and across, add up to sixty-five. They have to be these particular numbers in this particular order to do that.'

Sayid checked. Max was right. Each column and row totalled sixty-five.

'There's hope for you, yet.'

'Well, I'm not thick, y'know. I just struggle with maths a bit,' Max huffed.

Sayid fingered the scrap of paper. 'I've seen something like this before. It's called a magic square,' he said.

'Magic like in abracadabra?'

'Nah, the Arabs got it from the Indians when they invaded. Yonks ago, seventh century or something. Then a mathematician . . .' Sayid lifted his head for a moment, scratching around in his memory. 'Al-Buni. That was him. He got into astrological stuff in about twelve hundred and used it for –'

Max interrupted him. 'Sayid, we don't have time for a history lesson. Just tell me what a magic square is, will you? Or at least this one. Mars equals sixty-five means something. Zabala wouldn't have gone to all this trouble to hide something if it weren't vital.'

'I don't know what these numbers mean. Honest, I haven't a clue. But the sixty-five bit, at least that's a start,' Sayid said, frowning with uncertainty.

'I suppose so,' Max said, 'but a start in what direction we don't know. Not yet anyway. I reckon we'd better get back and study this at the Comtesse's.'

Sayid nodded, his mind also trying to make sense of the jumbled ideas entangled in his head. 'Let me think about it some more,' he said, folding the paper neatly.

'OK. Numbers are what you're good at. But we've got to check the observatory before we go. We won't have another chance to come back,' Max said, tucking the drawing of the circle into his pocket and pushing the worn folder back into the shelves.

Sayid tidied the trestle table as Max carefully rethreaded the typewriter ribbon.

The observatory was on the same floor and by the time they reached it there was no sign of any disturbance in the library, nothing to draw suspicion of a search.

The observatory was an uncomplicated room. There was no decoration. Dark wooden floors gleamed with reflected light from two mullioned windows, one left, one right, which allowed an almost perfect rectangle of moonlight to stream in. The room was mostly bare, clearly used as a place for work, research and compilation of any findings done in the library. A Gothic arch was set in the middle of the room, flanked by old wooden bookcases displaying research-drab folders. In the arch's alcove an old-fashioned telescope about two metres long was cantilevered on what looked like spoke wheels. It sat solidly, its barrel pointing up at about forty-five degrees. A small wooden seat on a slider was fixed to the floor beneath the whole apparatus.

'Stay away from the windows, Sayid. Just in case anyone is out there.'

Max stroked the telescope's barrel. In the archway's ceiling, louvred windows could be opened to access the sky.

'You lie down there,' Sayid said, pointing to the wooden seat, 'then you slide under the telescope and watch the stars cross the meridian line.'

'How do you know that?'

Sayid smiled and pointed to a sign barely visible in the archway. 'It says so. I'm going to have a go.' Sayid was already manoeuvring himself on to the floor.

'Sayid, we don't have time.'

'Course we do. C'mon, Max, you know all about the stars. Let's have a look. It's a clear night. Open those shutters up there.'

Sayid was already settling himself beneath the telescope's eyepiece. Max jiggled with the rods that opened the arched ceiling. 'The moon's too bright, Sayid. You won't see much.'

'Stop moaning, Max. Just do it.'

Max finally got the old louvres opened. He was afraid the whole system might collapse on them, but he stopped when he felt the opening rods getting stiff.

'That's fine,' Sayid said, grinning. But then he grimaced as he struggled to focus the eyepiece.

Max gazed around the room. What else is here? Have we found everything now? The folded paper was burning a hole in his pocket. He just wanted to get to a safe place and pore over it.

Irritation began to bite. 'Sayid, give it up. C'mon, we've got to get out of here.'

Sayid's eye was glued to the telescope, shuffling himself a little forward, a little back, until he was as comfortable as he could be, waving an arm for Max to quieten. A tinge of light moved to one side of the room. Max's heart jumped. Something dark had shimmered. Imaginary monsters lived in these old walls. Gargoyles climbed down from their lofty perches, their claws scratching walls, their hunter's eyes seeking prey. But it was a trick of the light, aided by Max's imagination. Or was it? The wind, turning from the sea, snared itself across the battlements. The gargoyles' open jaws cried out, desperate for life.

Sayid looked up. The haunted wailing seeking out the boys' fear.

'It's just the wind,' Max said.

Sayid smiled half-heartedly and put his eye back to the telescope. Max decided to let him stay where he was for a few moments. The light that had shimmered came from the far side of the room.

An old burnished mirror, its copper surround a patina of dulled green, barely reflected any light at all. It must have been one of the original mirrors in the house and the glass was now a murky brown colour. Max looked at his reflection. The boy who stared back at him had no eyes; the light from above cast deep shadow across his face, obliterating any reflection from his pupils, blackening the sockets. The thin red line of a scar still puckered the skin across his eyebrow, and his bunched jacket gave him the appearance of a hunched creature. He smiled, half expecting to see fangs instead of teeth. But then he gazed beyond his own image. Pulling his cuff down, he wiped away the dust on the mirror's surface. It was clearer now.

Something in its reflection caught his eye.

Max turned and moved towards the opposite wall where an old wooden panel hung, its dingy paint seeming testimony of its age. It was about fifty centimetres long and half as wide. Small, tarnished brass eyelets, hooked on barely visible nails, held it to the wall. The painted image, faded and dull, hung in the darkest corner of the room and was out of place; the only picture in the whole room.

It had that kind of medieval look about it, where the figures didn't seem quite real – flat and two-dimensional. There was a mountain range in the back of the picture; dirty, dust-covered peaks, any resemblance to snow long gone. But the image was easy to understand. A faded star, the yellow and white paint still recognizable, hovered above the peak. To the right of that another star, equidistant. And to the front of the mountains, lying in the foreground, was a monk. His head rested on a log or a boulder – Max couldn't decide which – one hand held a telescope, crude, like the first ever made. The monk looked old, almost biblical; his ragged beard covered his chest, but his free hand's index finger pointed towards himself.

Max scanned the tiny writing on the engraved metal square screwed to the frame's base. It was in French and said that the château was dedicated to St Anthony the Hermit. Max concentrated, looking at every brushstroke on the wooden panel. There was a scratch or mark in the bottom left-hand corner. He tilted the panel and let the light pick up the picture's texture. The mark was barely visible unless you were looking for it. It was a Z.

This was no medieval painting, it wasn't even done at the turn of the last century. Max lifted the panel down on to the floor, surprised at its weight. Why the hermit was looking through a telescope made no sense, but the two words in old-fashioned letters did. One lay to the left and below the old man, and the other was opposite: *Lux Ferre*. Max jerked his head up, almost fearful that anyone else might have seen the clue. Sayid was engrossed and only dust particles hovered in the moon-glow. The château was silent. Max was on his hands and knees, staring down at the picture on the floor, gazing at the eyes of the old man. The way the figure was painted allowed the viewer to look directly into his eyes – even with the telescope balanced in front of the man's face. It was as if he were looking directly at Max. Appealing.

The hermit pointed to a tiny dab of light beneath his beard. Another star. Next to his neck.

Max touched the pendant at his throat.

Bobby Morrell had run for his life. The sand slowed him but he was strong and athletic enough to ignore it. Besides, high-octane fear drove his muscles towards the sea. The one place of safety. The dark waters would swallow him, his wetsuit the perfect camouflage. And Bobby could swim a long way underwater.

Up and over a sand dune, across the last stretch to where the moonlight corrugated the beach. The tide was high, he'd make it, no problem, then he'd warn Max. He didn't know how, but he'd stay out in the sea until these thugs beat it. Then swim for the rocky headland. He'd find a way.

In those first few strides he had screamed Peaches' name. Yelled at the top of his lungs into the night. Telling her to run. Telling her to hide. But the attack came fast and took him by surprise. They'd been hiding in the trees and bushes near the dunes. The motocross bikes coughed once, throttles turned, wheels churned sand. They leapt from the darkness, wolves hunting a vulnerable animal.

He was in the shallows, but they were already on him.

Wheels sprayed wet sand and spray. Well rehearsed, they criss-crossed him, one from the left, another from the right. There was a faltering moment when he couldn't move, and a third biker knocked the wind out of him.

Bobby sprawled, face slamming into wet sand. The sea was tantalizingly close. The pain shot through his back. They'd winded him badly, but it wasn't the first time the American boy had been slam-dunked. How many tonnes of water had tried that before? He breathed through the pain, pushed his feet into the sucking sand and lunged for the water.

They let him make three, four strides and then powered their bikes into the shallows. One of them held a club, or a stick, he couldn't see; his eyes focused on the beckoning refuge. He needed deep water.

The blow spun him around. The back of his head hit the water. He went under, gagged. Salt water flooded his nose and mouth; gritty sand choked him. Gasping for air, he was struck by the irony taunting him. *You're gonna die in six inches of water!*

Someone grabbed his wetsuit, hauled his face out the water and shook him. He spluttered, regained his breath. The faceless figure, silhouetted by the moon, hissed with pleasure.

'We're not finished with you yet,' the twisted mouth said.

Unless anyone had ever felt the grip of a crashing six-metre wave, its hungry power pummelling you below the surface, they couldn't know the strength of someone who spent every spare moment in the water. Bobby twisted hard and fast. His fist, clutching wet sand, weighted like a cosh, slammed into the boy's head, whose cry of surprise and pain made him release the hand that gripped him.

Like a seal escaping a killer whale, Bobby slithered free and struck out for the deeper water. Within seconds he was swimming. The bikes couldn't follow him now. He kept going. Head down, a crawl stroke, breathe, pound the water, breathe. *Keep going! Gotta warn Max. Gotta warn him!*

He twisted, pushed his back against the swell and faced the shore. He'd put a couple of hundred metres between him and the bikers. They weren't going anywhere; they just stared at the sea, watching him.

He laughed. If they were waiting for him to tire they had a long night ahead of them. Bobby Morrell could swim like a dolphin. He'd cut across the headland, get ashore by the rocks and into the grassland behind the château. The distant crashing waves muted the sound of an engine. At first he didn't understand. It couldn't be a motorbike.

He turned.

Slicing through the water, the speedboat was coming straight for him. They'd had a back-up and with this moon they didn't need a searchlight. He was an easy target. The boat roared around him, the waves bobbing him even more clearly for them to see. They turned again and thundered in for the kill.

He ducked his head, pulled himself underwater and kicked, praying the propellers wouldn't mangle him. The muted roar of the powerful outboard reverberated through the water and the shock wave plucked at him. He broke the surface, sucked air and swam. The boat was turning, lining up another attack; he had to keep going for the headland. But he'd miscalculated.

The boat had spun so quickly it was already bearing down on him. The engines slowed. Too much speed had made them overshoot their target on the last run. But the thumping power was still enough to finish him.

If he was to survive he had to know when the hit was coming. He turned, faced the boat, waited, took a deep breath and, when it was three metres away, kicked hard to one side. But it was not enough. The boat cuffed him. His ribs cracked. Pain. He gasped, swallowed water and rolled, clearing his lungs of water.

Cold reality bit like a blade.

He wasn't going to make it. He was going to die.

They circled him slowly, engines barely ticking over, gazing disinterestedly as the dark sea began to claim him.

He saw the boat ease alongside, a metre away. *Help me.* They watched. Unmoving. *Help me. Please.* Had they heard him? Were the words only in his head? One of the men in the boat handled a spear-ended boat hook, raising it like a lance. The men were grinning. They were going to spear him like an injured fish.

The man lunged.

Bobby felt the tip pierce his wetsuit and the hook catch his skin. Water slipped across his face, which dipped below the surface, then bobbed free again. He gazed at the shining orb that blessed the darkness with its light.

The man in the moon was smiling.

Mocking him.

13

Max pulled the pendant over his head and gazed at the blind stone. Twirling the brass ring between his fingers, he turned it against the moonlight and then the dim ceiling light, but nothing revealed itself to him. So if the pendant sat as a star on the hermit's neck what did the other two stars in the painting signify? Max knew he was pushing his luck. It was getting late. He didn't know if the Frenchman returned to patrol the grounds or whether the dim lights would stay on all night.

'Sayid, I need to have a look through there.'

Sayid slid the wooden chair backwards and rolled himself free of the contraption.

'Be my guest. I can't see much. That's the trouble with stars – they're too far away. And the moon's so bright. I've angled it away a bit, but it's still too bright to see much.'

Max slid into the seat, pulled himself under the telescope's angled eyepiece and began to focus. He squinted his eye across the eyepiece and tilted the barrel of the telescope down to where he hoped the Pyrenees would come into view. It was too sharp a movement; the magnification blurred everything. He tried again and the glaring moon, escaping the cloud cover, made his eye water. This was going to take more time than he had available. He tried again, promising himself no more than a few minutes to sweep the skies.

He focused and refocused, changed angle and direction, but nothing obvious presented itself. As he lifted his head away in frustration, ready to quit, the pendant swung loose on its cord, tapped the eyepiece, almost snagging it.

He tucked it back into the sweat rag, but with his face further away from the eyepiece he saw there were grooves etched inside it. Something like a camera lens that you screwed filters on to. But this diameter was small.

Pulling the pendant free again, he slipped it over his head and fingered the brass ring. It fitted perfectly. Careful not to cross-thread it, he turned it until it sat snugly in the eyepiece.

He looked through at what now revealed itself to be a polished, opaque crystal. Back-lit by the moon's glow, numbers and a diagram, both blurred, were visible, etched into its surface.

The blind stone had revealed its treasure.

'Sayid!' he whispered, without taking his eye from the viewfinder. 'Write these numbers down. Quick.'

Sayid pulled out the piece of paper with the magic square on it.

'OK,' Sayid said.

'There's a space between each of these . . . 7, then 24 and 8. Then a dash. Then 10, 4, 9, 12, 25. Another dash. Yeah?'

'Got it.'

'Then 7, 11, 9 and 17. That's the lot.'

Sayid repeated the numbers, with all their space and the dashes.

Max could see something else but it was blurred. Whoever had etched these tiny inscriptions on to this stone must have spent hour after patient hour doing it – it was the work of a craftsman. Or a determined scientist.

Max eased the eyepiece slightly, refocusing it. Now the numbers became blurred but the rest of the drawing revealed itself.

He looked up at Sayid. 'There's a drawing etched on this thing. Get me something to write on, will you?'

Max put his face back down to the eyepiece as Sayid grabbed one of the old brown files from the shelf, tore it down its middle and gave it, and his pen, to him.

Sayid stopped. 'I think I heard something,' he said quietly.

Max dismissed the frustration from his mind; it would get in the way if he had to make a snap decision. 'Like what?'

Sayid shook his head. They listened. It was silent, except for the eerie moaning of the wind torturing the gargoyles.

'Stay at the door. You hear anything definite, tell me. I need more time.'

Sayid moved to the doorway as Max put his eye back to the telescope.

Max put the folder on his lap and drew what he saw using his other eye. It was a long-sided triangle in a circle. Very similar in shape to, if not the same as, the drawing he had found earlier. But there was a single letter at each point of this triangle – E, S and Q.

Max had the next part of the secret. The vital element of the dying monk's legacy. In less than a minute he had drawn a rough copy. He unscrewed the pendant from the eyepiece and folded the file's cover in half, tucking it into his jacket pocket.

Time to go!

He pulled himself free of the sliding chair, closed the louvred window and walked quickly to Sayid.

'Sayid, I've got it. We're getting out of here.'

Too late!

Max saw the ghostly image of a man walking up the stairs towards them. It was the German. And he was smiling. Max realized he had been the one who switched off the alarm system.

'That's good, Max. We could not find it.'

Max realized with a sickening lurch that he and the woman must have known he would be at the château today. How? Who had told them? It didn't matter right now. Max had played into their hands and they had waited in the darkness, giving him all the time he needed to try and work out Zabala's secret.

The shock lasted no longer than the words spoken. Max got between the approaching German and Sayid, shoved Bobby's mobile phone into his hand and pushed him towards the château's main bedroom. 'Go, Sayid! Phone Bobby!'

Sayid didn't argue and, like a stick insect in fear of its life, loped away on his crutches.

The man stopped, shook his head and lit a cigarette.

'Max, there's nowhere to go.' He stopped mid-stairs, gazed upwards and shrugged, watching the smoke drift lazily into the moonlit stairwell. 'I am not alone.'

Out of the darkness two figures bounded up the stairs past the nonchalant man. Bikers. One armed with a motorcycle chain, the other some kind of short iron bar – a wheel brace. They were going to hurt Max and Sayid badly. There was no sign of Sharkface, but Max recognized the tough-looking teenagers as being part of his gang.

'Don't kill him. Not yet. Go for the injured boy first,' the German called.

If they got to Sayid, Max knew they would inflict so much pain on his friend that he, Max, would sell his soul to have them stop.

But he wasn't ready to turn and run. *In trouble? Always do the unexpected, Max.* Dad's voice. Max smiled. It checked them. 'A length of chain and a wheel brace? Think again, porridge brains.'

Grabbing an Ethiopian shield and a set of lethal-looking antelope horns off the wall, he attacked, jumping down the top three stairs and smashing into the dumbstruck bikers. The German turned and ran, one of the bikers tumbling head over heels after him, catching the back of the man's legs, crashing the bodies down together. The German yelled in pain and anger.

The second biker regained his balance and swung the chain hard towards Max's head. Max ducked, turned his shoulder, raised his arm, felt and heard the power of the blow clattering across the shield, and lunged. The boy's eyes widened as Max went for his throat. The fear served Max well; it was exactly what he wanted. The boy faltered, took a step backwards, found himself trapped against the banister – as Max drove the attack home. The horns went each side of the boy's neck, pinning him next to one of the monster creatures carved into the main staircase. A flicker of shadow and light, its eyes gleamed, as if relishing the helplessness of the boy held so close to its jaws.

No sooner had the biker been pinned than a whisper of

air came out of the darkness. Max spun, raised the leather shield – a knife thudded into it.

The German's voice cried out a command from the pit of darkness below: 'We need him alive!'

But the pounding of more feet told Max that kids don't always do what they're told by adults, no matter how much they're being paid. The first figures moved into the light. He could see the knives in their hands now, the moonlight glinting on dull metal. Max was defenceless except for the shield. They would soon get through that. He turned to run, but a twang and a shuddering impact into the wall stopped him dead in his tracks. An arrow had pierced the half-light just in front of the attackers. Max looked up. Sayid stood awkwardly against the balustrade, a short African hunting bow in his hands – and let another arrow fly down the stairwell. It thudded into one of the silently screaming gargoyle's heads. The bikers faltered, holding back, keeping themselves out of sight. Max seized his chance.

In a few strides he was at Sayid's side. 'That's all the arrows there were,' Sayid said, trembling with the effort, fear and excitement.

Max was already bundling him back towards the château's main bedroom. He had done enough to stop the savages for a few moments.

'You saved my neck there, Sayid.'

Sayid smiled. 'I did?'

'Yeah. Though another couple of centimetres closer and it would have gone *through* my neck.'

'I've never fired a bow before,' Sayid said, as Max shoved the door closed behind them.

'I'd never have guessed,' Max said through gritted teeth as he pushed a big piece of antique blackwood furniture across the door. It took all his strength to shift it, but the fear of who was coming up the stairs helped his efforts.

'There's no reply from Bobby's phone,' Sayid said.

'Then we'll make it up as we go along,' Max said – but he wasn't smiling. They were in real trouble now without any back-up.

Satisfied the piece would keep anyone from forcing the door for a while, he took his bearings. Could they hide here? Heavy furniture, cabinets and tables supported by legs of twisted wood; a leopard skin on the polished floor. Latticed windows, a chaise longue, a boxed bed, the wooden sides almost touching the ground. There was nowhere they could conceal themselves and not be found in seconds. Heavy blue curtains draped the bed and windows; a door led to a dressing room. It was almost pitch black in there.

Grunts and shouts came from the other side of the bedroom door. They were pushing hard. The furniture shifted a few centimetres.

Max gripped the lip of a big table and heaved it in place. That would buy precious minutes. All those curtains! They had to be of some help. Max snatched at the corded tie-backs, his eye catching the benevolent stare of Antoine d'Abbadie and his wife, Virginie, their gold-framed portraits gazing down above the black marble fireplace. Max felt a twinge of guilt for the ugly stench of brutality he had brought into the eccentric man's home. The concerted effort of that brutality, banging and shouting behind the door, that was trying to reach Max and Sayid.

'Sayid!'

Max nodded towards the small dressing room. Sayid hesitated – they'd be found if they hid in there! But Max was already tying all the cords together, making a rope. Sayid knew Max would have a reason for his command and he did not want to face the violence that threatened them outside the door. He did as he was told.

Once in the small room Sayid saw there were doors leading to a balcony behind the room's heavy curtains. Max was ahead of the game – he'd already seen the terrace on the château's plans. Sayid opened the doors, while Max feverishly pressed his palms across the small room's panelled walls. He found the latch he was searching for. A click. A narrow door creaked open, revealing a passage: a slender tunnel of blackness leading into the body of the building.

'Servants' corridor,' Max said quickly. 'Right. Get ready.'

Max joined Sayid outside, drawing the curtains and shutting the doors behind him – the German and the bikers might waste valuable seconds before they realized there was a balcony.

Sayid's mouth was dry. His voice croaked in a worried whisper, 'Ready for what?'

Max dropped a metre of the home-made rope over the edge and coaxed Sayid forward. 'Dead easy,' he said. 'All you have to do is clamber over the balcony, put your good foot into this loop and I lower you down. Smell that sea air? That's freedom.'

Some of the curtain tie-backs were broad swathes of strong material and Max had fashioned a loop with one of them at the end of the cord. He smiled. 'No rush. Take your time,' he said with a comforting, though false, calmness.

A huge thump against the door convinced Sayid to clamber over the balcony. Knuckles white with tension, he nodded. Crutches gripped in one hand, the other holding the rope, he eased his good foot into the sling.

Max took the cord across his back and braced his legs for Sayid's weight. 'Step off gently. There – got you,' he whispered.

The cord bit into Max's back, but he lengthened the rope half a metre at a time, then allowed his legs to walk forward slowly towards the balustrade, taking the strain in his thigh muscles. Sayid was still a couple of metres off the ground. The cord was too short! Max leaned his body across the balcony's rail to try and give Sayid the extra length that his own body provided. The rope burned into his back and it felt as though the skin on his hands would tear from his bones. Sweat ran off him and the railing pressed against his bruised rib. He had to let go, he couldn't hold on any longer. Sayid would smash his leg. He'd failed.

But then the weight disappeared. Max opened his eyes. Sayid was on the ground, looking up, waving. Max hauled the rope back up, looped it through the balcony's uprights and lowered himself down. Once on the ground, he yanked the rope free and tossed it into the shadows. Even if their pursuers saw the balcony, they wouldn't see Max and Sayid's means of escape. That should convince them to waste time exploring the servants' corridor.

Max immediately urged Sayid into the shadows of the treeline. 'Look out for anyone coming, especially the German's wife. I bet she's out here with their car.'

All they had to do now was escape. How long did they

have before their attackers heaved the door upstairs open and realized the boys had escaped? Max took Sayid's weight, helping the boy to move quickly towards the trees. They reached the front of the château. Half a dozen motorbikes stood tilted on their stands. Was Sharkface here? He couldn't be. If he were he'd have led the battle on the staircase.

Max looked out into the moving shadows. Spider's webs of light teased the bare branches. One patch of darkness was blacker than the rest. On the left of the drive the Germans' car sat unmoving – and facing the gates. Tucked well in, so the driver could see if the old Frenchman returned.

Max put his mouth next to Sayid's ear. 'There's no sign of Bobby. He can't have seen our call. We're on our own. Get into those trees over there on the right. See the car? Stay on its blind side and keep out of sight. Meet me at the entrance gates.'

Sayid hesitated. Where was Max going to be?

'I'll be right behind you,' Max assured him, then turned and ran for the château's front doors. He had to buy them time.

Max barely made it to the Frenchman's office before he heard angry shouts from the top of the stairwell – the German's gasping voice shouting to unseen bikers. 'Find them! Find them! Search every room!'

He scanned the small, tidy office. Turn things around; make a disadvantage work for you. You're in trouble – think. C'mon! Put them on the spot. He grabbed a pair of desk scissors, he'd need those. Then, opening the alarm box's front panel, he saw the row of unlit lights and the master switch. How long did he have once he activated the alarm? He tried to remember what the Frenchman had done. He'd walked out of his office, closed the door behind him and then gone out of the front door. How long? The Frenchman was slow. Max saw him in his mind's eye. And counted. Close the office door, one . . . two seconds. Turn, three . . . four. Three, maybe four steps to the front door, five . . . six. Open the door, seven . . . Pull on his hat and coat, eight . . . nine . . . ten . . . eleven . . .

The Frenchman had patted his pockets, twelve . . . thirteen. Stepped back to his office, fourteen . . . fifteen. Open the door, sixteen. Done what? Reached for something on his desk. What? Cigarettes. He had picked up the forgotten cigarettes, seventeen . . . eighteen. Repeated his movements again, out of the office, into the hall, nineteen . . . twenty . . . twenty-one. The old man had quickened his pace, twenty-two . . . twenty-three . . . twenty-four. By now, Max remembered, he would have been back at the door, which was already open. Stepped out – and closed it.

Twenty-five seconds tops. The old Frenchman might have been slow but it was a practised pace, he did it every night of his life. To the second.

Max's finger hovered over the master control. Was he about to throw the wrong switch? Holding his breath, he flipped the switch and began a mental count – following the same procedure as the Frenchman. Door . . . one second. Turn, three . . . four . . .

Footfalls pounded on the stairs. Max sneaked a peek around the office door and saw the German, grunting with exertion, reach the hallway. He ducked behind the open front door and watched through the narrow gap between wall and door as the German stopped in the archway.

Five . . . six . . . seven . . .

Max could have reached out from the darkness and touched him.

Eight . . . nine . . . ten . . .

The man gestured and yelled, 'Bring the car! Bring the car! We need a torch! They've escaped! Rhona, *schnell*! Come ON!'

Eleven . . . twelve . . . thirteen . . . fourteen . . . Max hardly dared breathe. The clock was ticking; the alarm would go off unless he could get out the door and close it. That was his only chance. COME ON! Shut up and leave!

Fifteen . . . sixteen. The German turned back to the stairs. Max heard a car engine start, scrunching tyres, a car door open and slam. No headlights.

Seventeen . . . eighteen . . . nineteen. And then the German's wife ran into the entrance hall. She hesitated. 'Ernst!'

Twenty . . .

The voice carried. 'Up here!'

Twenty-one . . . twenty-two . . .

She ran towards her husband's voice.

Twenty-three . . .

Max stepped out, grabbed the door . . .

Twenty-four . . . twenty-five!

The door clicked shut behind him.

Silence.

Max blew the air out of his lungs with a massive sigh of relief. He leapt down the steps, past the guardian crocodiles to the motorbikes, then slowly and methodically pushed the scissors' blades into the rear tyre of each motorbike. There was an even more satisfying hiss of released air.

Max's plan had worked better than he had hoped. The

Germans' car had stopped right outside the entrance and the keys were in the ignition. Max didn't care about noise now.

He kicked the row of bikes. Nice to see the domino effect in action. The bikes clattered down. Handlebars snared wheels, brake and clutch levers dug into engine blocks and headlights cracked and smashed.

Max adjusted the driver's seat in the small Mercedes, turned the key, pulled the gear shift from Park to Drive and let the smooth engine glide him towards the entrance gates. He stopped the car, slid down the window and called, 'Sayid, your taxi's here.'

The boy stepped out of the shadows. 'Max!' He climbed inside. 'What was all that racket?'

'Fun,' Max said, smiling. 'Not half the racket there's going to be in a –'

The piercing screech of the château's alarm siren sliced through his words. Max and Sayid turned. Figures ran down the steps. Some tried to lift their motorbikes; two bigger silhouettes pointed and shouted something.

Max laughed, pushed his arm out the window and waved. '*Auf wiedersehen*, losers.'

Sayid beat his hands on the dashboard and shouted, 'We did it. We did it.'

Max turned the car towards Biarritz.

'Put your seat belt on, Sayid. What's wrong with you? You like living dangerously?'

14

Fedir Tishenko was superstitious. Portents and signs had guided many great men in history and Fedir modestly counted himself among them. Had he not been marked by the lightning god's hand? He doubted if any other human could have survived such a ferocious baptism.

The unseen powers of the universe guided his destiny unequivocally towards that chosen moment when he would shock the world by harnessing and unleashing the greatest force nature possessed.

But he was also practical. Superstition was the foundation of his belief, but cold logic had given him immense financial power. Desire for anonymity from the world's media was driven not only by his disfigurement but also by stealth and cunning. Behind the scenes he could influence governments, buy politicians and inflict whatever judgement he deemed appropriate on those who failed to live up to his expectations.

One hundred billion dollars buy a lot of influence and privacy. But he knew that no matter how exact he had been over the years a tiny speck of the unforeseen could create havoc. Like a Formula One racing driver getting a wasp under his helmet at three hundred kilometres per hour, or a precision piece of high technology getting a microscopic mote of dust in a vacuum-sealed area.

Deep underground he was driven past massive pieces of equipment resembling something a hundred times bigger than a jetliner's engine, an enormous disc, higher than a six-storey building, gripped and secured by steel frames attached to the rock face. Except this disc did not house fan turbines but energy conductors, overlapping, highly polished titanium tiles, solenoids that would snare and capture, then transmit the raw energy he would soon harness.

Energy crisis? A gash appeared in his crinkled face – a smile.

The world did not understand the meaning of the word energy, or crisis. What he planned would make any such concerns seem as insignificant as blowing out a candle.

Now, as he sat on the electric golf cart being driven through the cathedral-like halls beneath the mountains, a chill prickled his skin. It was not the cold, because massive heat conductors maintained a regular temperature down here at a hundred metres below the surface. No, it was this unexpected complication.

The monk, Zabala, had spent over twenty years searching for proof of some future profound, earth-shattering event. More importantly, it seemed, this evidence was the precise time, the exact hour when the cataclysm would occur. This is the information for which Tishenko had paid Zabala's closest friend a small fortune. The man had failed to obtain the secret from Zabala and Tishenko had taken his revenge – the body would never be found. But the man had learned enough to give Tishenko the exact day on which to inflict the terror of his awesome, earth-shattering revelation. He liked that word. Revelation. Yes, it would be *that* wondrous a moment.

Tishenko's scientists, tracking powerful weather fronts across the Atlantic, confirmed that the day the storm was expected to strike matched Zabala's prediction. But for Tishenko there was still a niggling concern. He wanted to unleash his cataclysm at the optimum moment in time for it to succeed. Absolute power demanded absolute knowledge.

Superstition picked at his logic like a child teasing a scab. Perhaps the monk had had something Tishenko did not possess, something almost akin to a sixth sense. Zabala had turned to prayer and meditation as well as science and mathematics. He had become like one of those ancient masters who felt an affinity with the universe, who understood things at a superconscious level. Zabala knew things.

And had proved his mystical prediction with facts. Perhaps the scientific community would have still scoffed at Zabala had he lived – but what if they had not? Today's climate change had scientists so worried that they swapped information like kids exchanging football cards. They might just identify where and what Tishenko planned.

Fedir, remember who you are, remember why you are so named – a gift from God. His mother's words caressed his moment of doubt.

Why was this Max Gordon boy involved? Tishenko's people had scoured the airwaves for months, ensuring that anyone who might even remotely offer any threat could be monitored. This illegal spying on known environmental groups, investigators, scientists and government departments had revealed no cause for alarm. Nothing would threaten Tishenko's plans, because no one knew of them – except Zabala.

But a meddlesome environmental troubleshooter, Tom Gordon, had been contacted. He was confined to a nursing home in England but his son was in precisely the same area as Zabala.

Tishenko hated coincidence. There was no such thing. It was destiny throwing forces together like a particle accelerator slamming together beams of protons at the speed of light – well, 99.999999 per cent of the speed of light to be precise, his mind chastised him – and not even the scientists knew what the resulting explosion would create.

Superstition gripped him.

They had checked back. Every Friday afternoon over the preceding weeks someone from the Pyrenees had used a landline phone and contacted Tom Gordon's nursing home. The location told them it had to be his son, Max.

The boy had phoned again when he was in hospital in Pau, after the assassination of Zabala, and then he had gone to the monk's mountain home.

Coincidence?

Fate?

Since discovering this information, Tishenko had tried to stop him. Just in case he knew something. But the boy had defied the threat of violence and death from Tishenko's people at every step. Now he represented that speck of the unforeseen that could destroy everything.

The American boy who helped Max Gordon had been dealt with. The Germans who were in charge of capturing the troublesome English boy at the château near Biarritz had failed and had already paid the price – their bodies would never be found. Now the biker gang of hunters would scour the area around Biarritz until Max Gordon surfaced. He had been to the château in Hendaye, so the possibility of his finding Zabala's secret was all the greater.

Max Gordon had succeeded, without even knowing it, in rattling him. Tishenko had to snare this boy and find out once and for all if he had discovered that vital piece of information of Zabala's that he so craved. Now there was an urgent need to double-check that the father had not instructed the son. How? There was one person who might be able to reach him. A man who was once Tom Gordon's friend but who had betrayed him.

Would sending this man be a risk too far?

Superstition demanded Tishenko send him to Max Gordon's father.

He gave the order – contact Angelo Farentino.

Max didn't know how to read Sophie Fauvre. She had smiled with relief when he and Sayid had walked through the door, but she kept her distance, almost as if she might be intruding on their friendship. Max nodded a kind of gruff 'hi', then, thinking he'd been a bit rude, smiled back, told her that Bobby and Peaches were still surfing down the coast.

The small sequence of events was just like being in a home of his own. She offered them coffee that was already made. Max thanked her and took the biscuit plate she put in front of him. Then, in a spurt of words, she told him about the man in the black Audi. Max looked worried, nodded, but didn't say anything. She reached out a hand and touched his face and smiled in a funny kind of sad way.

It was a toe-curling, stomach-churning moment as far as Sayid was concerned. He watched them both, ignored and probably not even noticed by either of them, for a few minutes.

'I'm going to change my clothes,' she said, leaving the two boys.

Max's ginger biscuit, dunked in coffee, wobbled and splashed back into the mug. 'Oh, right. Sure. OK,' he managed to say.

As Sophie turned out of sight Sayid pulled a face. 'What was all that about?'

'What?'

'All that. She was all over you. I thought she was going to wipe the biscuit crumbs from your mouth for a minute.'

'Don't be stupid.'

'If I'd had anything to eat in the last few hours I'd have puked. That's how bad it was. She's trouble, I'm telling you.'

Max pushed the chair away from the table. 'What do you know?'

'I know I'm hurting worse than being clobbered by Baskins and Hoggart cos I've been jumping around like a grasshopper with a broken leg.'

'Sayid, one of those blokes from the hospital was waiting for her, didn't you hear what she said?'

'And those others were at the château! Whoever "they" are, they know everything. Max, you're being set up. And guess who's the only person who's been around long enough to know where we are.'

'She didn't know about the château,' Max whispered furiously.

'You can't be sure! Just like you can't be sure that bloke was watching her! She said he was but that doesn't mean anything. He and his mate could be knocking on the Comtesse's door any minute now.'

Max felt the turmoil of uncertainty. This wasn't one of those moments when you had to decide on a course of action, like when the German and those bikers attacked them. His body and mind responded immediately then. This was worse, because it made heart and mind fight each other. They were surrounded by people who liked and cared about them. Who knew where they'd been? Who had betrayed them? It couldn't have been Bobby. He would not have brought violence to his grandmother's house. But where was he? Max couldn't get hold of him on the phone he had given them. Was that because mobile reception was poor down there or was Bobby deliberately not answering? And Sophie? Max shook his head. He didn't want to be thinking such distrustful thoughts about anyone here.

'I'm sorry, mate. But this is really serious stuff now and I don't mind telling you, I'm scared,' Sayid said by way of apology.

Max had to acknowledge that. 'Have another piece of cake. It'll take your mind off things.'

'I'm not kidding, Max!'

'I know,' he said gently.

Max understood that Sayid had been incredibly brave so far. His friend had put aside his own fear to help. He guessed there was an element of adventure that excited Sayid, but the reality of the danger was getting to him. Max had faced violence before – but it didn't stop him being scared either. The difference between them was that Max had to see this thing through. It's what his dad would have done.

Max walked through to the kitchen and the sound of the small portable television set which the Comtesse seemed to have on permanently, a slush of words and laughter. The old lady sat at a large wooden farmhouse-style table. A cigarette smouldered between her lips, one of her eyes half closed against the smoke, and a large glass of cheap red wine nestled in partnership with the half-empty bottle.

Piles of diced vegetables sat before her like a gambler's winnings. Max told her briefly about the unknown enemy waiting at the château for him. She wielded the long-bladed knife with a rhythmic certainty as she listened. Max wondered how she didn't lose the ends of her fingers. She looked up.

'I'm making soup and, before you ask, I didn't tell Sophie where you were,' she said without looking up.

'How did you know that's what I was going to ask?'

'It's obvious, *mon cher*. Who knew? There was me, and Robert, and Sayid of course. Who among us would betray you?'

'Where do you think Bobby is, Comtesse?'

She nodded. 'Your question makes sense. He's your first suspect.'

'No, I'm worried about him. He didn't answer his phone and the mobile he gave us is flat. So, if he is trying to contact us, why hasn't he phoned here? He was supposed to come back to d'Abbadie's château for us.'

Ash dropped from the cigarette. She blew it away from the

vegetables, then ground out the smelly stub in a curve of potato skin. 'Robert is a child of the sea and the mountain. He goes with the wind.'

'He wouldn't abandon or betray us, Comtesse, I'm certain of it.'

She stopped dicing and indicated with the knife the chair next to her. Max sat down obediently. She swallowed a mouthful of wine and pointed the remote control at the talking head on the television set, muting the sound.

'Let me tell you about my grandson. He is frightened of failure. His father expects great things from him. He is frightened of his father. He hides in his sport. Perhaps he thought you were involved in something that was too big for him.' She gazed at Max, who had listened carefully. He felt sympathy for the older boy, who was essentially alone in the world. He understood that. She covered his hand with her own. 'It is not the first time he has run away. And now he has this Peaches with him. He's a boy with his girl. Life is easier that way.'

Max nodded. He couldn't blame Bobby for leaving them in the lurch.

'Sophie asked me where you were. I did not tell her. She was emotional. Though she did not show it. But I saw it. You young people. My God, it's wonderful to have youth, but the emotions! You can keep them!' She smiled at his blank expression. 'You don't know what I mean?'

'No,' he said.

'You will. But Max, let me tell you, this matter is not finished. Be careful of everyone around you. Especially the girl.'

Was the Comtesse confirming Max's own doubts about Sophie?

'Remember my warning,' the Comtesse said. 'I saw it in the cards.'

Yeah. It was a great pity the cards hadn't told her where Bobby was, or who it was attacking them, and where they might be now. Second-guessing pretty pictures wasn't exactly an exact science.

Max took the piece of paper with the triangles enclosed by a circle from his pocket. This jigsaw puzzle of a mystery that he had stumbled upon needed all the pieces to make sense, fit neatly and give him the complete picture. The Comtesse seemed the only one around who had any inkling about all this weird stuff. Weird but important. But then she would be involved – and at risk. Enormous risk, given what had happened to Max so far.

She seemed to read his thoughts. 'I'm an old lady. I get very forgetful. I don't even know what day of the week it is sometimes. In a way it's quite nice. Time stops. What is it Bobby says about me? "One sandwich short of a picnic"?' She smiled. 'I have forgotten more than I ever knew.' She looked at the piece of paper he held. She raised her eyebrows. 'More secrets?'

Max unfolded it to reveal the triangles, circle and signs. 'Do you know what this is?' He turned it towards her and waited as she gave it barely a glance.

'It's a birth chart,' she said almost dismissively.

'Which means what?' Max asked.

'Somebody is born at a particular time. Someone who knows how to interpret these things looks to the heavens and the stars and planets, and draws a birth chart.'

Max thought for a moment. 'Like a compass? They point to the stars and planets.'

'That is one way of thinking of it, yes. It used to require great skill to do such things. It shows someone's life, their destiny. It shows events. It shows me nothing. I don't understand them. I don't do them. What do I know? I will tell you a secret, Max. It's too difficult. Like mathematics. I hated it at school. I am intuitive, not scientific. Besides, these days, things like this can be done on computers. Not for me, I think.'

She drained the bottle into the glass and dropped it into a bin full of other empty bottles.

'But this was done years ago. Maybe twenty or thirty years ago. And you can see it's hand-drawn,' Max said.

'Then the man who did it had the old skills,' she said.

Max gave that a moment's thought. 'Old? You mean, special?'

'I mean whoever did it was skilled in ancient wisdom,' she said as she adjusted the gas flame beneath a pan of simmering water.

'I found something else,' he said hesitantly.

She waited.

'It was a painting and it had two Latin words on it,' he said.

'No one speaks Latin any more. Not even lawyers, damn them,' she muttered.

'But you've got books on Latin on your shelves. I saw them.'

'You were nosing around?'

'I was looking for an atlas.'

'You found one?'

'No.'

'So? You're going somewhere?'

He'd probably said too much already. Better not to ask anything more. He nodded, put the paper back in his pocket and got up from the table. 'I'm going back to England. I think I need my dad's help with this.'

She lit another cigarette, found another half-bottle of red wine and topped up her glass. She swallowed a mouthful and turned the television's sound up. 'That is the most sensible thing you have said since you have been here. You need an atlas to find your way home?'

'No, course not.'

'Then you're looking for something else. Eh?'

She stopped her chopping again. 'What Latin words don't you understand?'

'*Lux Ferre*. I mean, I think I know what they mean but I don't understand why I saw them.'

'At the château?'

He nodded. The strong smell of the rough wine and her smouldering cigarette was mingling unpleasantly with the smell of the boiling vegetables. He wanted to get some air but he had to find the answer to this last question.

'So? They mean what?'

'Something to do with light.'

She nodded. But spent another moment dabbing ash from her cigarette. Then, as if making a decision, she nodded to herself. '*Lux Ferre* was used by ancient Roman astrologers. It means "Light Bringer". But the words were corrupted, they were joined together – Luxferre. You understand now? It became the word that now represents ominous darkness and evil. It means Lucifer.'

Max was silent. His mind whirled. Lucifer. The last word Zabala had screamed at him. Traces of the name in the château teased him, those words etched on the bookshelf and their meaning something about morning light, and now *Lux Ferre* – Lucifer.

He wasn't sure whether it was the steam in the kitchen making him sweat.

'I think you should go home, Max. I do,' she said carefully.

He nodded. He had already decided not to show her the numbers they had found or the other diagram he had drawn quickly from the pendant seen through the telescope. She had identified the man, or the entity, Max didn't know which, that Zabala feared.

How come Lucifer brought light? He was a force of evil. Or both.

'There is an old atlas in the library,' the Countess said nonchalantly as she peeled another potato.

If a birth chart was like a compass to the stars, then it might also hold a clue to where Max should go next. The Comtesse's library, stuffed with generations of old books, yielded an atlas, its musty pages still etched sharply with continents and names of countries that no longer existed. *Everything changes, Max. Empires are gained and lost, the climate falters, our fate is uncertain. So make plans but don't expect them always to work out. That way you'll get through.*

His dad's words comforted him as Max fingered the piece

of paper in his hands. The drawing he had made from the crystal pendant was a long-sided triangle which reminded him of when he did orienteering. To find where he was on the ground he would take a compass reading of two other visible objects and join the lines up, then this triangulation would give him his location. This drawing looked just like a triangulation. Max knew it could never be to scale, but he had a good eye and he had drawn the lines accurately. He laid it on the page showing France and some of its old colonies in North Africa. He turned the drawing around, like orienting a compass, but it made no sense, especially not the letters E, S and Q. Then he placed one corner of the triangle on the foothills of the Pyrenees, just about where he was now. The shorter base line seemed to point in the direction of the French Alps and Switzerland, but it was the longer line of the triangle that held his attention. It pointed towards North Africa. He grabbed a ruler from the table, laid it on the line. *Come on! Think!* Could this line be a direction? The scale of the atlas wasn't big enough for him to be that accurate, but there seemed no doubt in his mind that the line went straight into the Atlas Mountains in Morocco. And that was too much of a coincidence to ignore. Sophie lived there. The area on the map looked barren; a world away from the comfort of Europe. How to get there, and what would be waiting for him when he did?

Max, Sayid and Sophie sat around the big table in the main room eating bread and cheese. Max reached out and tore a chunk from a baguette, shoving a wedge of cheese into it.

    'We have to leave here, Max. Those men found me in

Biarritz and I do not know *how* they found me. And now Sayid has told me what happened at the château.'

Max felt a twinge of panic. What else had he told her?

'Was there nothing at all there? No clues?' she said.

Sayid looked innocent, filled his mouth with food and looked at Max. A sense of relief. Sayid hadn't said anything important other than they had been attacked.

'No, there was nothing. I think this whole thing is a wild-goose chase. Sayid and I are going back to England.'

'Great!' Sayid said, a little too enthusiastically. The buzz of the earlier encounter at the château had already left him. England was a refuge from all the crazy people in the world.

Sophie did not react. Max had secretly hoped she would. He told himself that her reaction might have given him a chance to see if she was involved more deeply in all this mess than she had told him.

'I'll phone the airport for you,' she volunteered.

'No. The Comtesse can do that,' he said a little too quickly. Realizing that he was still uncertain of her motives. That instinctive sense of survival overrode all other emotions.

Before Sophie could say anything the Comtesse scuttled into the room, waving the kitchen knife. 'Turn it on! Turn it on!' she cried, gesturing towards the television set.

Sayid was the nearest.

A moment later Max's face filled the screen.

No one spoke. The French news station showed an old picture of Zabala and Max's passport photograph. Then scenes intercut between the avalanche area behind Mont la Croix, a body being stretchered away and Zabala's mountain hut. The newscaster's voice was hurried but clear enough to understand.

The body of Brother Zabala, a Basque monk, had been found buried beneath a recent avalanche. The post-mortem showed he had been shot before the avalanche claimed him, but that he had also suffered a knife wound. An English boy – Max's passport photograph zoomed up on the screen – Max Gordon, was believed to be involved in the monk's death. As with all foreign visitors staying in French guest houses, his passport had been photocopied. The boy had been identified hiking in the mountain passes, approximately three weeks before the man's death, in the area where the recluse lived. In Pau hospital the boy had learned the whereabouts of Zabala and was seen by a local farmer running from the monk's reclusive home on Montagne Noire and – a close-up of Max's watch filled the screen – this watch was found clasped in the dead man's hand. The inscription on the back of the watch identified its owner: Max Gordon. Upon further investigation at the mountain hut – more images of police taking out boxes of material from Zabala's home, police crime scene officers, taped areas, sniffer dogs – evidence that blood found in the hut belonged to the dead man, and by DNA analysis samples of skin taken from beneath the dead man's fingernails indicated a struggle and matched the blood in Zabala's hut belonging to the English boy.

The motive for the monk's murder was unclear at this stage, the voice went on, but police were now hunting for this boy to help with their enquiries. Gordon, described as 1.75 metres tall, athletic build, untidily cut fair hair, blue-grey eyes, weighing approximately sixty kilograms, is considered dangerous. The public are warned not to approach him.'

Suddenly a reporter, someone called Laurent Messier, appeared on screen with a microphone. Max immediately recognized the building as the hospital in Pau.

'I am here at the hospital in Pau, where the boy, Max Gordon, was brought following the avalanche at Mont la Croix and where he was examined by neurologist Dr Fabian Vagnier.'

The microphone moved a few centimetres towards the consultant's mouth. He appeared appropriately sombre, his own desire for recognition bending the truth as he rattled off words too fast and technical for Max to catch, but when the reporter spoke to the camera again, he emphasized words Max did understand: *assassin et un sociopath.*

Everyone stood in shock. The Comtesse killed the sound, then stared at Max. It was Sayid who broke the silence.

'I didn't get all that. What was that bit at the end?'

Still no one moved.

'A French doctor said he did a brain scan on Max after the avalanche and that he found brain activity which was usually associated with violent behaviour,' Sophie said quietly. 'A killer's behaviour.'

'Bloody hell,' Sayid said under his breath.

Everyone was looking at Max. He rolled up his sleeve, showing the Comtesse and Sophie the faded scratch marks. 'I tried to save Zabala. He fell, he scratched my arm and grabbed my father's watch. I didn't kill him. But I did see the killer.'

'You recognized him?' Sophie said quickly, barely able to keep the alarm out of her voice.

196

Max hesitated but kept his eyes locked on hers. 'No, they were too far away.'

She nodded and looked down.

Max turned to the Comtesse. 'I promise you, Comtesse, I did not kill him.'

She had not moved, but the knife in her hand was slightly higher than before, held in a defensive gesture. Then, after a moment, she lowered it and nodded.

'Of course you did not. I believe you. But now you are in very serious trouble.' She looked at the silent screen and they followed her gaze.

A picture of Max filled the frame and emblazoned below it were the words: *Recherché pour meurtre.*

Max Gordon: Wanted for Murder.

15

Max had, as always, very little to pack – travel light, travel fast. He weighed up his options as he rolled his trousers and T-shirts and stuffed them into the backpack. How best to escape the police hunt and the attacks of whoever wanted him dead? He was beginning to feel like a fish caught in a net. Squirming to breathe, he knew panic was just waiting to smother him, and that's when big mistakes were made. Well, he wouldn't panic. He'd make a plan.

'You have to tell the police everything, Max,' Sayid said, interrupting his thoughts.

'No. I turn myself in now and we'll *never* find the secret. Listen, Sayid, Zabala was murdered for something so important that I can't let it die with him. The police have got enough evidence to put me away until there's a trial. This is a set-up.'

'What do you mean?' Sophie asked.

Still unable to read her intention, Max held her gaze.

'How did they find Zabala's body?' Max said.

'There must have been a melt,' she said.

'But there hasn't been. You saw the news; they went straight to the spot where he fell.'

'Someone told them!' Sayid said.

'That's right. And who knew?'

'The killer,' Sophie said calmly.

It wasn't a guess, it was stating the obvious, but why did such a bare fact feel like a challenge? Max wondered. Was it the way she said it – so coolly?

He nodded. 'Whoever's been chasing me needs me in a place where they can get whatever information I have. Setting the French police force on to me is a hell of a way of getting me pinned down, wouldn't you say?'

'You lied to me. You went to Zabala's hut to look for something. What?'

'I wanted to find out more about him,' Max told her, still unwilling to let her know too much until he determined how involved she was.

'And that's why you went to the château?'

'Because I discovered that's where he once worked.'

'And isn't it all obvious to you now?' Sophie could barely keep the irritation out of her voice. 'It's the animal smugglers. They're the ones responsible. You should have told me. You should have trusted me.'

Max knew it was far more than animal smugglers. The German had waited at d'Abbadie's château until Max had discovered the drawing on the pendant. It was only then that they attacked.

'I'm sorry, Sophie. The less you knew the better. I didn't know how dangerous it was going to be.' He still didn't want to tell her anything more.

'Is there any other reason you think Zabala died? Other than being murdered by animal smugglers?' Sophie asked, staring straight into Max's eyes.

Sayid looked worried. Was Max going to tell her everything? He didn't trust Sophie. A) She was a girl who was good at just about all the things Sayid couldn't do. B) She had crept between his friendship with Max – so he was a bit jealous. C) She was making a play for Max, and that was so obvious that even the old clock on the wall could have noticed. D) She seemed to be in the exact place where Max was, when it mattered, like at Zabala's hut, and just before the avalanche, when he saved her from the bikers. E) . . . Well, Sayid could probably come up with a whole alphabet of reasons why he didn't trust Sophie Fauvre.

'I don't know why he was killed,' Max told her. 'But there might be another reason other than animal smugglers. Though I'm not sure what it is yet.' Max chucked one of Sayid's T-shirts at him. 'C'mon, Sayid. There isn't much time.'

'Wait a minute,' Sophie said. 'Where are you going?'

'Where I think Zabala's clues want me to go.'

She waited, but Max said nothing more. He was waiting for her response. She looked concerned. All Max was certain about was that in a short while he had to get clear across France without being spotted. And that was going to be pretty near impossible. He had deliberately said very little to Sophie. The triangle etched on the pendant pinpointed Sophie's country of birth. With her involvement in the endangered-species trade and her mysterious appearance on the mountain, he was convinced she was caught up in this whole thing far more than she had told him. What Max had told no one was that he had to get to the Atlas Mountains in Morocco. He needed her to open the way for him.

'You should come home with me,' she said.

'Why would I do that?' Max said, barely able to conceal his relief – this was exactly what he had wanted her to say.

'Because you would be safe. For a while at least. And then you can decide what you want to do. My family owes you. My father would be honoured to help you.'

'Thanks. Give me a minute to think about it. I need a word with Sayid.'

She left the room and Max closed the door. Sayid shook his head.

'You're crazy, Max. Y'know, things about her don't feel right.'

'It's what I have to do, Sayid.'

'What? Walk deliberately into a trap?'

'Keep your voice down. We don't know exactly how she's involved. Not yet.'

'I think a boulder must have hit you on the head in that avalanche. You're getting deeper and deeper into trouble. Real big-time-very-messy-desperate-to-get-out-of trouble.'

'I know it's dodgy, but we'll sort it out when we get there. It's vital, Sayid. It's exactly where Zabala wanted his clues to lead us.'

'I can't go,' Sayid said.

'Course you can. I need your help. You know some of the info we found at the château was all about sacred geometry and you're good at working out stuff like that. You'll be fine. And I need someone to speak Arabic for me.'

'Max, my leg is hurting like hell. And I would slow you down. Besides, they speak Darija in Morocco . . . it's a dialect,' he quickly explained. 'I wouldn't understand a word.'

Max felt there was more to it than not speaking the

language. 'I promised your mum I'd look after you on this trip and I haven't done very well so far,' he said.

'Max, it's been a scary time for me, and in a twisted kind of way it's been fun, but I can't keep up with you. Not with this leg. I'd better go home.'

Max hid his genuine disappointment. Sayid had been there when he needed him. Was his injured leg an excuse because he was too scared to go on? Max mentally chastised himself. It didn't matter if Sayid needed a way out. He had already endured more than most boys his age. Max had already put him too much in harm's way.

'Yeah, I suppose. OK. Look, I'll get you to the airport.'

Sayid interrupted him. 'Max, you've got to get away. You can't come to the airport. The authorities will be watching. Keep it simple. The Comtesse can get me a taxi. We go our separate ways. We have to.'

Max pulled the drawstring tight on his backpack and stuck out his hand for Sayid. His friend took it. The boys embraced each other. Both felt the emotional tug of impending separation.

'Try and see my dad. Tell him I'll be OK. When you get back leave a message on your voicemail. Something about – I dunno – flying lessons, then I'll know you made it. If they pick you up in England because of me, just tell them everything except the bit about Morocco. I reckon that's going to be my route into France when I have to come back.'

'You're coming back to France? Why? Are you crazy?'

Max smiled and put his arm around his mate. Once he'd established if Morocco really was where Zabala had intended the clue to take him, then he would explore the third side of the triangle, which pointed across the French Alps to Switzerland. 'That's one bit of info I don't want to tell you. You already know more than anyone else. Let's get out of here.'

The Comtesse had filled baguettes with cheese and pâté for them, packed fruit and bottled water, and tried unsuccessfully to thrust crumpled euro notes, which she had squirrelled away in an empty jar, into their hands.

The taxi arrived. The Comtesse went to the gate to see off her 'exchange student' and to instruct the driver to deliver him safely at the departure terminal at Biarritz airport. She put the folded money directly into the driver's hands. 'He is just a boy, you look after him. I have paid you well.'

Sayid turned in the seat just as the taxi went round the corner. He waved at the Comtesse but his eyes looked up towards the window where Max stood. He was saying goodbye to his friend, not sure when he would see him again. Imagined fears of Max being hunted, of his best mate fighting for his life, stabbed at his conscience. Max's stubborn determination was scary at times. Whatever it was that drove him to take such huge risks was something Sayid didn't fully understand. But had he agreed to go to Morocco, his injury would have put Max's life in even greater danger.

Sayid would go home, he'd speak to Max's dad, explain everything – he'd know what to do.

Then he would wait for his friend to call.

'I've left Bobby's mobile in his room, Comtesse. I can't use it because the battery's flat. I'm sure he'll come back and I don't want him to feel he's let me down. Tell him there's no problem between us. I'd like us to still be friends,' Max said.

'I will tell him, and I will insist he finds you. He will phone me, he always does.'

'And my dad. You'll remember to phone my dad for me?' Max repeated it like an instruction. These were the final moments before he went on the run.

The Comtesse gave him a reassuring smile and her voice calmed his uncertainty. 'Of course, once you are well away from here.'

'My dad, he's . . . well, sometimes he doesn't understand things too well and he can't always take calls. If you have to leave a message with someone else, don't say too much, because then they might feel obliged to tell the cops in England.'

'I will be brief, but I will be explicit in my discretion. He will be told what is essential, but nothing more. You must not worry – only about yourself. Be careful. And remember what I said.'

Her eyes glanced at Sophie as she bent her head to brush his cheeks with her lips. She quickly whispered, 'About trust.'

Tishenko's plan would flush Max Gordon out of his hiding place, he was certain of that. The killer knew exactly where the monk had fallen to his death and that information had been passed to the authorities. Once Max Gordon was arrested, it would be the simplest of matters to have him snatched from police custody and brought to the unforgiving wasteland from where there was no escape.

Tishenko's assassin had failed to kill Zabala in his hut, then the second attempt on the mountain had been complicated by this boy. Fedir Tishenko should, by his own standards, have punished such a failure, but when he spoke to his ambassador of death, the killer was calm and confident, and expressed no regrets. The job had been done, and if this boy had been involved with Zabala before the killing, then that could not be laid at her door. Tishenko liked girls who killed. They were somehow more cold-blooded about the whole business. Like a glacier, as if their feminine emotions were buried beneath a mountain of cold intellect. He found that very attractive. But the greatest attraction of all was that no one ever suspected a girl could be an assassin.

In England a telephone rang, its soft but demanding tone echoing through the silent corridors of the specialized nursing home. Across the quadrangle, attached to one wing of the old estate, a huge brick and glass greenhouse brimming with natural fragrances from exotic countries created an ideal refuge for men who had spent their lives travelling the world, knew the jungle and needed the tactile comfort of stem and flower. Men who were now confined by ill-health to St Christopher's.

The telephone did not stop ringing. It waited for the orderly in charge of that section to answer. Ex-Royal Marine Marty Kiernan, all 1.83 metres of him, and 112 kilos, took a few paces across the beautifully crafted Victorian tiled floor and lifted the receiver. He listened, pressed a button on the phone's base, replaced the receiver and walked towards the mini-jungle that lay beneath the glass framework. His soft-soled shoes barely made a sound. Despite his size, he walked lightly. Old habits. Marty was a veteran of jungle and desert fighting. He had carried wounded men out of harm's way in different war zones, had knelt – as the trained medic he was – under fire, to save others' lives. And he had paid the price. In Afghanistan two bullets had torn into his big frame and rendered him helpless. It took six men to carry him to the medevac chopper – the wounds putting paid to his combat days. Marty suffered psychological as well as physical injuries, but he had been lucky and ended up in the only military hospital available in the UK. The people who cared for him gave him new hope, turning the black octopus of depression that gripped his mind into a positive, can-do attitude. Just the way he was before the bullets took his right arm.

You had to turn the emotionally draining negativity into action, he would quietly tell the injured men who were brought to St Christopher's. He didn't ask them any questions about why they could barely speak, why some of them just started crying for no reason at all, why others just gazed at a picture on the wall for hours on end. Sooner or later these damaged men would find a way out of the tunnel they were trapped in. And then they'd nod, or smile, and maybe even begin to talk. Until then Marty, and others like him who knew what damage combat can do to men, would care for them. No one else would.

One of his charges was unique. A long time ago this man had worked in Special Forces, became a well-known mountaineer, then used his education, his courage and skills to rove the world searching out potential, or inevitable, ecological disasters. Working for a privately funded organization had made him a lot of enemies, everyone from governments to powerful corporations, but Tom Gordon's actions had averted many environmental catastrophes before they happened, long before climate change became such a hot topic. Marty smiled. Hot topic. He liked that. He'd try that on as a joke, even though it was a lame one.

Marty and the other staff knew what had happened to Tom Gordon out in Africa, how a corrupt doctor had tortured him, screwing up his mind with toxic chemicals, trying to get vital information from him. Well, he hadn't, and Gordon's son, Max, had defied incredible odds and led the rescue of his father. Like father, like son, maybe.

It was humid in the vast greenhouse, and if some of the overhead vents hadn't been slightly open, it would have been hotter than the jungles of Borneo. He approached the man bent over the waist-high flower bed, digging around a brightly coloured plant. Marty stopped. It was never a good idea to approach men such as Tom Gordon from behind, particularly when they had something like a trowel in their hand. It could suddenly, and unexpectedly, become a deadly weapon for someone caught unawares and whose instincts were still frighteningly fast. He coughed. The man turned. A moment of doubt clouded Gordon's eyes. He knew this man. He saw him every day. What was his name? What was . . .?

He remembered. 'Marty. Hello.'

'Hi, Tom. Switchboard says there's a telephone call from France. I think it's Max.'

There were days Tom Gordon could not remember his son. He knew the boy phoned regularly, because Marty told him, but there were days when nothing made any sense.

'Max?'

'Yeah. Y'know . . .'

'Don't worry, Marty. Today's a good day.' Tom Gordon

smiled. He looked at the big man's face. 'He's in trouble, isn't he?'

'I am the Comtesse Alyana Isadora Villeneuve. Your son has asked me to phone, so that I can explain recent events here which might otherwise lead you to think that his actions have been dishonourable.'

Tom Gordon listened as attentively as he could. The woman sounded as though she never took a breath when she spoke, or that she only had enough breath to say something once, because then she inhaled again, rattling off another barrage of words lasting a couple of minutes. Max's dad had no chance of asking questions. Then, minutes later, after she had told him everything, she paused and her voice lowered slightly in a more measured tone.

'It has been an honour to talk to you,' the Comtesse said finally. 'And your son has qualities that are amazing, and which even he does not yet comprehend. I cannot think of any reason why my call would offer you any comfort; any parent would be anxious, I know, but I believe you should have faith, that your son will survive . . .'

Survive? Tom Gordon blinked. What was this woman talking about? But he had no time to interrogate her.

'. . . and that he will find a means of contacting you himself when the occasion arises. I offer you my heartfelt sympathy. Our children. Ah. Our children . . . what can one say? I urge you not to worry. He is a very capable and brave young man. Goodbye, Monsieur Gordon.'

Tom Gordon looked blankly at the receiver. Had he just imagined that conversation? It seemed unreal. He looked at

Marty, who waited patiently in case he needed to do anything for him.

'Everything OK, Tom?'

'A few days ago, did you tell me Max had been involved in an avalanche?'

'That's right. He phoned.' Tom Gordon had had one of his 'bad days' and couldn't take the call. Max knew how difficult it could be at times for his dad. 'You were busy,' Marty said, nudging Tom to remember.

His patient nodded.

'Max was OK. No harm done. He phoned to let you know that,' Marty said, and waited. Tom Gordon was collating the information from whoever had just phoned. 'Is there a problem?' Marty asked gently.

'Someone died in the avalanche and they think Max is involved. This woman, some countess, she said Max had asked her to phone. The French police are after him and he's looking for some kind of secret that the dead man gave him.'

Marty was never too surprised at some of the people who visited the patients at St Christopher's, or about some of the phone calls they received. 'So where is Max?' he asked.

Tom Gordon pushed compacted dirt off the trowel with his thumb, rubbed his fingers together to disperse the soil. He seemed deep in thought. Then he looked up and shook his head.

'I don't know,' he said.

Max and Sophie reached the main road. He wished he could just climb into the Mercedes he had taken from the Germans at the Château d'Abbadie, but it was parked a couple of kilometres away in a high-rise apartments' car park. Max hadn't wanted anyone tracing the stolen car to the Comtesse's château.

His plan now was to be as low-key as he could. An edgy certainty tugged at him. All his instincts said that going to Morocco was a huge step towards uncovering Zabala's secret. He would let Sophie lead the way. If she was his enemy he would soon know, as he was putting himself right on the line being with her. The sea fog comforted him, blurring shapes, then revealed a bus gliding almost silently out of the white mist.

When the bus pulled in he let Sophie board first. He kept his ski beanie low across his forehead and ducked his face when he followed her inside. She slotted the money into the small machine that curled out a ticket, and then he nudged her into a seat a couple of rows behind it, on the opposite side to the driver. He reasoned that anyone getting on a half-empty bus would automatically look towards the driver, then the ticket machine and then be drawn naturally towards the empty seats further back.

He sat upright, face turned, looking out of the window. Act natural, be natural. Two kids on a bus.

'I don't have enough money to get to Morocco,' he had told Sophie. She didn't think twice. She had a credit card and she would forward-book everything. All they had to do was get out of Biarritz, down to St Jean de Luz, forty minutes away near the Spanish border. Trains ran regularly to the Spanish town of Bilbao and from that old industrial town they could get a cheap flight into Morocco. The Spanish wouldn't be looking for him, not yet at least.

St Jean de Luz, a smart seaside town, still drew tourists even at this time of year but, compared to the bigger city of Biarritz, it felt like a crossroads between the Atlantic slamming against the sea wall and the Basque Pyrenees guarding its people and secrets. Sea mist still clawed across the coast road and railway line, and the damp night chill settled like dew on Max's jacket.

The railway station was almost deserted, the sea fog adding to his sense of vulnerability – an enemy could be on him before he saw them. He and Sophie had barely spoken a word since they left the Comtesse, and they now sat hunched on a station bench against the increasingly cold mist. Better to be in the open than caught inside. Small places meant an easier chance of being identified and the station café had a television on the wall. He didn't know how often French television had a news broadcast but he didn't want to be in there when it came on.

The train was late. Two dark-coated figures walked slowly towards them from the end of the platform. Each carried a sub-machine gun slung around his chest, hands resting deceptively casually on the butt. Their slow, steady pace showed their authority. They were gendarmes and they were walking towards Max and Sophie.

Stay or run?

There were half a dozen rail tracks to get across before the road. To the right the river's inlet meant an exposed footbridge.

The lazy grinding of the approaching train's wheels and the air-shuddering engine noise caused one of the gendarmes to turn. If Max was going to run, it had to be now. He looked at Sophie, whose eyes looked past his face, then quickly glanced back to his own. A barely perceptible shake of her head.

His mind raced. Were they on to him or was this a routine patrol? If they saw two teenagers on the platform it wouldn't be too unusual for the gendarmes to ask for proof of identity.

The damned train was taking too long to reach the platform.

One of the gendarmes shifted the weight of the sub-machine gun. For comfort? Or readying for action?

Sociopathic killer! Max's brain screamed at him. That's who they were looking for.

Cops – five metres away.

The train – twenty metres.

Sophie smiled.

Her hands cupped his face and her lips covered his. Her hand dropped and pulled his arm around her in a quick, easy motion, taking care of his dumbfounded surprise and his slow response.

He closed his eyes, caught between fear of the gendarmes, now standing almost next to them, and the warmth and safety of Sophie's embrace. Somewhere in the background, muted by his pounding heart and blood that stormed around his body like bad plumbing, the heavy metal wheels screeched and ground to a halt. Doors slammed open. A scratched and incomprehensible voice blared through the station's tannoy.

Max opened an eye.

The cops had moved on. One of them smiled – or was that a smirk? – to the other.

Without another look, or another word, Sophie was off

the bench and within four or five strides stepped into the train.

Max was right behind her.

It all seemed so calculated. Which is what it was, of course. Why was he thinking it was anything other than that? She had acted on impulse to save them. A perfect ruse. An ideal smokescreen.

Why hadn't he thought of it first?

He slammed the door behind him. She was already sitting, peering around, checking that they would have a clear view of anyone coming down the carriage. She looked at him but didn't smile. She pulled off her coat and beret. It was hot in the carriage.

Max looked out of the door window as the train pulled away. The gendarmes had sauntered to the café. There was no sense of urgency about the two men. It had been a routine patrol after all.

Max pulled up the window, caught his reflection and saw he was smiling. He checked his thoughts, then glanced at a stony-faced Sophie, who barely met his gaze. Reality check.

The train pulled away.

In the café Corentin wiped the condensation from the window and watched the carriages disappear. Thierry splashed two lumps of brown sugar in his coffee. Corentin's phone was at his ear.

They came like scurrying rats. Out of the darkness, a silent attack. One or two of them grunted in pain as the razor wire sliced flesh. They landed on the far side of the wall and the blackness swallowed them.

Only one light, high up, spilled out into the night, sea fog shrouding it – like a spectre.

Isolation meant danger could arrive in a leisurely way and the killers showed no sign of haste. They soon found the flimsy window catches and slipped into the silence of the old château.

The light from the Comtesse's bedroom sneaked into the lounge. The doors to the balcony were open and she sat, as she did every night when alone, letting the sea breeze and crashing surf caress her tired mind and the sadness in her heart. As much as she loved her children and Bobby, her only grandchild, it was her soldier-husband she longed for. How little people understood those who served their country. She sipped the rough red wine and inhaled the strong French tobacco. What no one knew was that she was dying. Too many cigarettes, not enough food, or just the hand of fate? She didn't know. She did not care. She was old. It was her time. And for some reason she had not seen it in the cards. It had been a life well lived. She had done her duty to her family, and even though she knew she lived in a half-world of fantasy, she had honoured the memory of the real *comtesse*.

The blanket clouds slid briefly away from the moon and bathed her in magical, veiled light, and that was when she realized the creatures had slipped into her sanctuary. The lack of panic surprised her. The four young men stayed back in the corners of the room; she could barely make out their features, but she could see their eyes. Dead. Soulless. Uncaring and unflinching. These boys would kill without a second thought. She stood slowly, turning her back to the sea and moon, hoping the light behind her would mask the fear that suddenly strangled her heart. But her voice was calm.

'Who are you and what are you doing in my home?' An imperious disdain filtered the words. She sounded just like the real *comtesse* used to. One of the boys took a step forward. There was no sign of any weapon but his face was frightening.

Spittle wet the edge of his lips, which seemed like a slash, pulled back against his pointed teeth. Was he smiling or was that how he always looked? she wondered. He took a step closer and the others moved behind him out of the shadows. A phalanx of fear.

'Where's the boy?'

'Boy? My grandson? I don't know. He's out. Who are you!?' she demanded.

Don't show them you're frightened. Don't yield to a threat. Stand your ground. Face the danger. That's what her husband would have done.

'Not him,' Sharkface said. 'Max Gordon. He phoned his father in England. From here. We know that.'

How could they know? Her mind pushed the thought away. Expressionless, she faced her inquisitor.

'I don't know any Max Gordon. You should leave now. My grandson and his friends will be home any moment. Trust me, you would not wish to see them angry! Get out!'

They took another pace towards her; she involuntarily stepped back, touching the edge of the big old sofa for support.

'We know about your surfing dropout. He won't be coming home.'

The flat, disinterested voice was like a slap across the face. What had they done to Bobby?

'Where is he!?' she demanded.

The jagged teeth smiled. 'Where's Max Gordon? He phoned his father from here. Or was that you? Where is he?'

She heard the click of the switchblade and saw the glint of moonlight on the knife one of the boys now held.

'You'll tell us, old woman. You'll tell us everything we need to know,' Sharkface sneered.

A small knot of warmth formed above her heart. It came, unsummoned, from somewhere deep within her and saturated her whole body. It was a longing for her husband. It was as if he held her, to protect her, an invisible shield between herself and the killers. Max Gordon would face these thugs, if he had not done so already, and he would have to fight for his life. Yes, they could hurt her and make her talk, she knew that. But she would not tell them what they wanted to know. She would not let these dogs loose after Max.

Her brave soldier husband, a hero of France, held her tightly. He embraced her, whispered his love for her, and gently, ever so gently, helped her take a step backwards on to the decayed balcony.

The moonlight filled her eyes; the crashing waves muffled the sound of splintering, shattered wood.

Her last breath was a sigh of joy.

She was dead before her body hit the ground.

16

Sayid made the taxi driver go past the entrance to the terminal and drive around the airport ring road. He wanted to see if there was any sign of the motorbike gang, even without their bikes, or any noticeable police presence.

He checked his passport and ticket and the piece of paper with the magic square of numbers they had found in d'Abbadie's château fell from his pocket. Sayid had shoved it in his jacket when they moved out of the library and into the observatory. What to do? If he was picked up he would be searched and this piece of paper might be a clue as to where Max was heading. Sayid studied the five-by-five box of numbers. Max might have the instincts of a wild animal for survival but Sayid had the ability to focus totally on anything mathematical.

He had used it effectively when cramming for exams. He supposed it was a bit like a musician being a sight-reader. The immediacy of what lay on the score, or in this case the page, allowed him to embed the relevant numbers in his memory. Up to a point, that is. *Heat-seeking missile, your brain is*, Max always said.

Sayid concentrated, locking out all sounds from the passing night, worked each line up and down, and saw the numbers take shape in his mind's eye, burning them into his memory. Then he wrote the other numbers that Max had dictated to him under the instep of his boot. Even Sayid's memory recall wasn't good enough to remember that sequence *and* the boxed numbers. Once he was satisfied the indelible ink had dried and there was no chance of misreading the numbers, he crumpled the piece of paper in his mouth and chewed it into a soggy mess and swallowed it.

That's what Max would have done.

It tasted horrible but at least part of the secret, whatever it was, was safe.

The taxi driver dropped Sayid off at the departure entrance. A car horn tooted. Like a Morse code signal. Calling him. Demanding he looked. He turned. A gush of relief making him forget his trepidation about the flight home. Bobby's van pulled up at the kerb.

Sayid limped towards the door that swung open.

'Bobby, where the heck have you been?'

Hands grabbed him, pulling him into the unlit van, and threw him roughly into the back. He cried out, but the van's engine was already revving as it pulled away. Someone had an arm around his throat, someone else bound his hands with gaffer tape, and then the tear of the sticky cloth as a strip was pulled across his mouth. Sharkface had split the hunting pack. Three of his thugs had staked out the airport while he had invaded the Comtesse's château.

There was a smell of neoprene and a tang of seaweed as they let Sayid fall against the black-clad body that lay trussed in the back of the van.

Eyes wide, he saw Bobby Morrell's lifeless form. Panic

nearly suffocated him. He had no idea if Bobby was alive or dead. He was unconscious, that was for sure. There was no warmth coming from his body, but that might have been because he still had on his wetsuit.

The van pulled off the autoroute, leaving behind the glare of the yellow motorway lights, which now snaked in the distance, beckoning like a welcoming shopping mall. But this place had a haunted misery to it. Sayid felt smothered by the claustrophobic darkness of the unlit industrial area.

The van stopped, the back doors' tortured hinges screeched open and, without any care for the well-being of their captive, the thugs pulled Sayid out by his ankles. His back thumped on to the ground, the pain knifed into him, his gasp smothered by the tape across his mouth. He twisted his head left and right, but the old buildings were in darkness. An abandoned site. Fear and desolation.

Bobby's body hit the ground next to him. Sayid heard a groan. Good! Bobby was still alive. Other men appeared; Sayid couldn't see their faces clearly, but then one of them bent down and he recognized him from the attack at the d'Abbadie château.

Their faces were ugly with violence. Someone kicked Bobby, another dragged Sayid to his feet. They were bigger and stronger than he realized. Now Bobby, too, was on his feet, shaking his head groggily. A fist in the back prodded Sayid towards the darkened interior of what appeared to be an abandoned warehouse. As he was frog-marched towards the doors, Sayid deliberately dragged his boot through a muddy puddle – he had to hide those numbers.

There were other vans parked in the background, sleek and

fat-tyred. Two older teenagers leaned against them, smoking; another was finishing off repairs to a rack of motorbikes that slid out on a ramp. Sayid realized those were the bikes Max had knocked over.

One of the men pulled back the other van's door, reaching for something. Peaches! She was unhurt, but sat guarded by another thug. She glanced up. She was probably terrified, Sayid realized. They must have caught her and Bobby down in Hendaye. He wanted to shout. Wanted to tell her not to worry. That it'd all be OK. But he couldn't and it wasn't going to be. The door slid closed on her.

A biker circled the fringes of light, dipping in and out of the gloomy shadows, filming everything with a small video camera held almost at arm's length. Sayid noticed there was an antenna on the roof of the van.

Another man stood in a pillar of light cast downwards by an overhead spotlight which threw an ominous shadow across his pinched features. He was leaning against a metal table, an old workbench, rusted but solid, which had an angle grinder resting on it.

This ragged-toothed man ripped the tape off Bobby's mouth, then Sayid's. Pushing his face next to Bobby's, he made the young American jerk back in fear, or maybe he had rotten breath with teeth like that, Sayid thought.

'Where's Max Gordon?' Sharkface said.

Bobby shook his head. 'I don't know.'

Sharkface nodded to a couple of the henchmen, who slammed their fists into Bobby. He was tough and fit, but Sayid could hear the sickening thuds and watched as the boy went down.

'Where is he?' Sharkface asked again.

Bobby gasped for breath. Shook his head. 'Don't know.'

'You tell us where Max Gordon is hiding and we won't hurt the old lady at the château.'

Bobby and Sayid couldn't hide their alarm. They knew about the Countess!

'Don't hurt her! She doesn't know anything!' Bobby yelled at Sharkface.

'Where is . . .?'

'I don't know! I left him at the place in Hendaye!'

Sharkface let his heartless eyes gaze at the boy and then nodded. 'Know what? I believe you.'

'Then you won't hurt her. Please!'

'She said you were due home. We told her otherwise,' Sharkface sneered.

'What!?'

'If you knew anything you'd have told us. To save her. Wouldn't you?'

'If you've hurt her I'll kill you,' Bobby shouted.

Sharkface grinned, which made him look as though he was going to tear apart a piece of meat. 'Too late, Bobby.'

Bobby yelled and threw himself at Sharkface, but the men holding him kicked his legs away and pinioned him to the floor.

There were tears in the American's eyes and his voice sounded as broken as his heart. 'You shouldn't have hurt her! She was an old lady . . . she was my gran!'

Sayid felt a wave of pity for Bobby. He knew what it meant for a loved one to die.

'I didn't touch her. She fell through a balcony,' Sharkface said dismissively.

He turned and looked at Sayid – who shuddered. A brief glimpse in his mind of the Comtesse falling through the derelict balcony flitted across the image of Sharkface staring at him.

'But *you* know where he's gone, don't you?' Sharkface said, wiping saliva from his leaking mouth.

Sayid shook his head vigorously. A spasm of vomit squeezed into his throat. He gagged, swallowed the acid taste and tried to think of what he could do. There was nothing. He was helpless. At their mercy.

The face came closer, like a shark coming out of the depth of the ocean towards a helpless diver. Closer, until the overhead light picked the button eyes out of the frightening face.

'How's the ankle?' Sharkface whispered in Sayid's ear.

'Listen, I don't know where he's gone. He does things his own way. I dunno. Honest. Just let us go. We won't say anything about any of this. We won't – I promise.'

As the words tumbled out of his mouth Sayid knew they were pathetic. Pathetic and desperate. There was no clear-headed thought for such a frightening moment. He didn't want to get hurt but neither did he want to betray Max. How long could he hold out?

Sharkface nodded at the bikers behind Sayid and they hoisted him on to the workbench, pinning him down. Sayid gasped for breath. He didn't want to cry, he didn't want to show these thugs how scared he was, but he could feel the tears sting his eyes. Heard the voice in his head shouting, *Please don't hurt me, please. . . don't*. But the words wouldn't come out of his mouth, not while he was gasping for each frightened breath. Strangely, for a moment, he felt more scared for his mother should anything happen to him. Sharkface looked down at him.

'That plaster cast must drive you crazy, yeah? Make your foot itch, does it?'

Sayid nodded.

'Why don't we take it off for you?' Sharkface said.

He grinned again. 'And I'm not talking about the cast.'

Sayid heard the terrifying screech of the angle grinder being started.

Money meant power and Fedir Tishenko had both. He moved those who worked for him around like a man playing a computer game, and this particular game was proving interesting. The boy, Max Gordon, had slipped away and the old woman had died without giving his men any information.

Tishenko stood before the wall of glass – four metres high and twenty long – that filled the huge rectangle cut into the rock face. The mountain lair was an incredible feat of engineering. Over the years tunnel-boring machines had scoured out vast caverns, bigger than road tunnels, large enough to house equipment fifty metres high, long enough to allow kilometres of cable to snake through the lower labyrinth. Here in his personal quarters he could gaze down from three thousand metres on to jagged valleys and the mighty glacier that edged lazily along the valley floor. Small aircraft would fly a couple of thousand metres below his eyrie, but no one could know Tishenko gazed down upon them like a mountain god.

Inside his mountain vertical fissures, scars from the ice age, had been reamed out and made into airtight shafts. Lifts dropped and rose, cushioned on air, a perfect vacuum – glass pods, steel supports and space-age technology – something that even the grandest, most innovative corporations around the world could not install. They were the fastest lifts in the world and, other than jumping from the small plateau of black, glistening rock outside his quarters, there was no quicker way to descend into his underworld of ice and stone.

Ascending in one of those lifts was the man Tishenko had summoned. Angelo Farentino was nervous, but he hid it well. He lived in his own fortress, a fortress of lies and deceit. Layers of misinformation surrounded him, protecting and hiding him from those who would love to have him arrested, tried and convicted for the massive betrayal he had inflicted on environmental groups around the world. But Tishenko knew where he lived.

Farentino had once been Tom Gordon's best friend. He was the man who published reports of ecological danger zones from scientists, adventurers and explorers such as Max's father. But over the years Farentino had played a game of deceit. He had turned his face and his bank account towards those who controlled vast sums of money and who wished to embark on massive projects that needed their environmental damage to be hidden.

The lift door opened and Farentino, casually but expensively dressed, stepped into the room. He had been summoned; not to have come to this grotesque man's lair would have proved bad for his health. He neither smiled nor greeted Tishenko. It was obedience not politeness that was required.

'Good timing, Angelo.'

Tishenko pressed a button on a console and a white surface the size of a small cinema screen appeared. It showed a recording, sent by Sayid's kidnappers. Max Gordon's friend had been snatched at the airport and the fear his men instilled in the boy gave them everything he needed.

Angelo Farentino felt his stomach lurch as if he had fallen down the lift shaft. Delicately, he dabbed the moisture from his upper lip with his handkerchief as he heard the angle grinder ripping the air above the screams of the boy held down on the workbench.

Screams of terror.

And the betrayal of Max Gordon.

Tucked up in the plane, Max allowed himself time to sleep. Who knew what awaited him in Morocco? It was important to snatch brief moments whenever he could. Even a twenty-minute catnap could invigorate him, and he knew soldiers slept at every opportunity, even if it was for only a few minutes.

Have to keep going. Take what rest you can when you can. Stay a player in a dangerous game. Why was he putting himself through this? Someone had died a horrible death and had trusted him to solve a mystery and find the killer – that's why. Giving up had never been an option. There were times he didn't want to go on, but something mingled with his blood as it pumped through his body. Intangible, undetectable by chemical analysis, invisible to any probing scans science could offer – it went beyond his DNA – it was who he was. Besides, Max hated analysing things. Start thinking too much about yourself and you end up tangled in a mental net that won't

225

let you go. Take it as it comes. Deal with whatever you have to; there'll be plenty of time to think about it later.

The journey became a series of dreams and jumbled thoughts. The turmoil in his mind tossed him around like the unrelenting power of the avalanche, and once or twice he gasped awake, gulping air. He slept fitfully for a couple of hours at a time, but at every unusual sound he awoke, heart banging, muscles tensed, ready to fight his way clear.

Sophie placed a hand on his arm and smiled. It wasn't just that she was calm, Max decided, but that she seemed emotionless – either that or extremely in control.

'We'll be safe, Max. No one knows we are here. Once we are in Marrakech we'll be only a few hours from home.'

'And your dad, how will he feel about you bringing a suspected murderer home?'

'He won't believe it any more than I do.'

Max looked into her eyes. The girl was still an unknown quantity to him and he could not help but feel that he was being lured towards a distant place where no one would know where he was. He really would be on his own. But isn't that exactly what he wanted? Wasn't that where the clues seemed to be taking him? He convinced himself that, like all the risks he took, this one was calculated. Trouble was, he also knew that maths wasn't his strongest subject.

He wished he had gone to the airport with Sayid. Being separated from his best friend made him feel even more edgy.

By the time daylight came he had overcome his need for sleep. Alertness was the key now, to make sure they had not been followed, that no ambushes awaited them.

The seats were uncomfortable, but that kept his mind focused. He had put himself into this dangerous situation. He could have gone home right after the avalanche. He need not have helped Sophie that night at Mont la Croix and earned Sharkface's enmity, or tried to save the wounded monk. But he had and he would face the consequences. Cause and effect. Max knew that whatever happened, whether he solved the puzzle or not, Sharkface would keep on hunting, like the predator he was.

He felt a deep-seated sensation inside him. Curled, like a fist.

It was not fear.

Max was ready to fight.

17

Noise and smells. Voices gabbling. Hands pecked at Max's clothes like hens at food. Colours dazzled; smoke and incense stung his eyes.

Marrakech, Morocco.

The souk, the market backstreets of the ancient city, teemed with people. Thousands of voices swelled in discordant symphony. Merchants vied for attention, fingers tugged at Max's sleeve, men jumped in front of him and tried to shove all kinds of goods in his face – silk and spices, jewellery, clothing, copper pots, beads and smouldering incense sticks.

'*Anji! Anji!* – Here! Here!' the shop owners and their touts shouted.

Pungent smells layered the confined alleys. Arguments broke out; men spat words at each other. Scooters and bikes, overladen donkeys and people – more peopie than Max had ever seen in such small alleys – jostled to get through the cramped passageways.

Sophie was ten paces ahead, sometimes hidden by the surging crowds, but she often turned back to look for him and, satisfied that he was still following, went back to pushing through the wall of bodies.

Max lost sight of her. Flies and sweat irritated his eyes, and the smells were beginning to overwhelm him. His concentration had wavered for a moment and the hungry sea of faces had swallowed her. He felt the urge to shout her name, but it would have been swept away in the noise of the alleys. Then someone grabbed his shoulder. Sophie. She stood in a darkened passage.

'This way,' she said, and turned into the cool gloom, where a scrawny kitten danced ahead of her.

Moments later she put her shoulder against a heavy wooden door and he followed her into an oasis of calm. An inner courtyard, blessed with diffused light, where mosaic tiles reflected differing hues of blue. A fountain gently splashed water across the centre of the stone yard.

And it was quiet. As if someone had closed a door to the cacophony of braying humanity.

Sophie unslung her backpack. 'We stay here for the night,' she told him, then called, 'Abdullah!'

'What is this place? Is it your home?' Max said.

'It's a riad, a traditional house,' she said.

'I know what a riad is,' he said.

She hesitated. 'Sorry, I didn't mean to patronize you.'

She walked away towards the entrance and called the man's name again. Max felt a twinge of remorse. He needn't have sounded so damned arrogant, but he wanted to score a point to give himself at least some sense of being in control of the situation.

He gazed around at the first-floor balcony that ran around the building with its delicate handcrafted ironwork, spiralled and shaped into an elaborate pattern. Across the courtyard where he now stood, an archway led to another enclosed area, where a swimming pool, edged with slabs of smooth stone, waited undisturbed for someone to leap and shatter its still water.

This was a small corner of paradise.

'It's a private hotel. Eight bedrooms, two suites and very expensive,' Sophie told him.

'You're gonna pay for this?' Max asked her, as he pulled off his boots and socks and let his feet cool on the stone floor. It felt great. He let the fountain's fine spray settle on his face like a cooling massage.

Before Sophie could answer, a man appeared. He was huge, with a barrel chest. His brown face bristled with stubble and his hair was cropped short to his scalp, like a shaved coconut. He wore traditional Berber dress, a djellaba cloak with broad sleeves and leather sandals. He grinned, spread his arms and embraced Sophie.

'Sophie! Good, good. It is my honour to have you in my home again,' the man said. 'My staff received your instructions and they have prepared two rooms, as you requested.'

Sophie had bought a phone at the airport and Max had seen her use it. So this was the call she'd made, he realized. Could she have phoned anyone else at the same time? He had to make a decision about her. Trust her or not?

'Max, this is Abdullah Boulkoumit. This is his place. Abdullah, this is Max Gordon. He's a friend of mine,' Sophie said, bringing the man towards Max.

Abdullah's gaze had not wavered from Max's face the moment he had turned away from Sophie. It was as if he searched out every event in the boy's life that had brought him to his home in the heart of the ancient city. For a moment Max felt awkward. He was barefooted, boots in hand, in the middle of a luxury hotel. He was grimy, unkempt, felt creased with all the travel, and realized one of his socks was floating away across the courtyard in the water from the fountain.

'You are welcome in my home, Master Gordon, and I see you are already familiar with our custom of removing one's shoes before entering. It honours me,' Abdullah said gently, delicately brushing aside his guest's embarrassment.

Abdullah shook his hand and then, as custom dictated, kissed the tips of his own fingers.

Two staff members waited inside the cool interior; one now eased Max's backpack from his hands and led the way down the corridor. Sophie walked with him.

'We'll go to my father's tomorrow. Abdullah will arrange transport. Freshen up and I'll see you in a couple of hours,' she said.

'I only take a few minutes to shower,' he told her as they stopped outside an iron-studded door which, once opened, revealed a luxurious room. He could get used to this, he decided.

'Well, I need longer. So, for once in your life, Max Gordon, slow down and be patient.'

She followed the other staff member and turned out of sight down another corridor.

Max stepped into the room. Beyond the huge double bed, steam rose from a sunken marble bath. Rose petals floated on the water's surface and a tangy smell of sandalwood filtered through the steam.

'Is that for me?' Max asked.

The man nodded.

'I'll pong like a dog parlour if I get in there,' Max said, not letting on that the sandalwood actually smelt quite good. And the bath was like a football club's locker-room plunge pool. Wasn't half bad at all, come to think of it. He might even practise deep-sea diving in there.

'Please,' the porter said as he gestured to the bathroom, and placed Max's backpack on a suitcase stand.

Max stepped forward. It was like something out of an *Arabian Nights* story. Beyond the bath, lattice screens offered privacy but also allowed him to see across the rooftops of the old city. Staggering snow-capped peaks rose up beyond the city skyline, tinged with the last rays of the setting sun. The Atlas Mountains. How far away? A few hours' drive? Somewhere beyond them was where Sophie's father lived, and that was where he felt sure Zabala's clue meant him to go.

The clues from the château, the link between her father and Zabala with the wild animals. There *had* to be a connection. Max knew nothing about Morocco. He remembered stories from when he was a kid. *Ali Baba and the Forty Thieves*, *Aladdin*, *A Thousand and One Nights*, but other than that he was in a part of the world that had sights and sounds – and smells – that were so exotic it felt as though they could sweep you along like an . . .

He stopped his thoughts right there, because the word that came to mind was 'avalanche'. And that thought sucked the warmth out of the room. The man was turning back the bed. Taking a bottle of chilled water from the mini-bar, he unscrewed it, poured half the water into a glass and settled it on a coaster – bead-sized stones delicately wired together by local craftsmen. He pointed to the lights, clapped his hands gently, and smiled as the lights came on.

That was cool. Max liked that big time.

The man, pleased to have amused his guest, bowed and left. Max checked the room. The bed was great: you could have a midnight feast on that with half a dozen of your mates. There was a CD player with a selection of music – international and local – as well as a bowl of fruit, a phone, computer connections, a mini-bar fridge stacked with fizzy drinks and fruit juices. Max reckoned he could survive a week in here.

He picked up the phone on the bedside table, got an outside line and dialled Sayid's mobile, but the standard recorded answer-phone message was all he heard. He left a brief message but stopped himself from telling his friend where he was. Sayid may have been picked up by the police. He hung up. Sayid should have been home by now and his phone back in use. But Max was realistic enough to know there was nothing he could do about it. He knew Sayid wouldn't tell the authorities anything more than he had to.

There was one more thing Max had to do before he could relax completely. He fished in his backpack and pulled out a small tube of superglue, one of the best repair kits for quick fixes. After fifteen minutes of concentrated work on his scuffed and torn trainers, using the blade from the mini-bar's corkscrew, he completed the task – managing the small miracle of not gluing his fingers together in the process.

Max let his clothes fall where he stood and slid in a CD. He popped a can, grabbed a mango and a packet of crisps and went through to the humongous bath. Rose petals or not, he'd have a long soak. He suddenly felt very tired.

He stepped over the broad edge of the bath, balanced everything he needed and slid into the velvet warmth of the deep water. He peeled back the skin of the mango and sank his teeth into the yellow flesh. It tasted of sunshine. And made a hell of a mess – juice everywhere – but he was in the perfect place to eat it. The packet of crisps followed, swigged down with the teeth-rotting cola. He didn't care. Someone in his mind was telling him he deserved to pig out for a while.

He clapped his hands.

The lights faded.

He clapped again.

The music got louder.

He clapped again.

Just for himself.

No matter how much money Fedir Tishenko possessed he could not control the Atlantic sea fog that blanketed the southern part of France and northern Spain, shutting down all air traffic.

Sharkface waited on a private jet at Biarritz. His destination was an abandoned military airfield south of Marrakech, where he would take control of the hunt for Max. But the plane sat on the runway, immobilized by nature's cloak. Others would now be needed for that job. Morocco was no further away than a phone call – Tishenko's promises scattered like gold coins into the dusty streets of the ancient city. Other killers would entrap Max.

Sharkface's vehicles, along with Bobby's van, drove slowly across France towards the Swiss border, hundreds of kilometres away. Sayid and Bobby still lay trussed up. Sayid's tears had dried and Bobby nodded at him, trying to offer some comfort, a gesture of understanding. Sayid had not cried because of the terror these killers had inflicted on him, though the shock at hearing of the Countess's death was like a body blow. No, he had wept because he had told them that Max was in Morocco. That gut-wrenching sickness of giving up your best friend embedded itself in his stomach like a blunt sword.

How much danger did that pose to Max? Sayid had very little information about his plans, but his friend had shared enough with him for his enemies now to have a clearer idea of what had been discovered.

Max had been given a crystal pendant by Zabala and had then found something in d'Abbadie's château, where the Germans and Sharkface's gang had attacked them. But Sayid didn't know anything else. Only that Max had gone to Morocco.

Sharkface had held the angle grinder across Sayid's plaster cast, lowering it slowly and deliberately, letting the white powder shower across Sayid. Just another couple of millimetres and . . .

Sayid had yelled at Sharkface. Screamed the information. Gave it out so willingly. Anything to stop the horror.

Now, as he lay in the van, he thought of how many times he had fantasized about being a hero. About how, like Max, he could save people, and that no matter how frightening the situation he would get through.

But so far the reality of his life had betrayed him.

Before Max's dad had saved his family in the Middle East, his own father had worked to help bring peace to the region. The terrorists came in the night and killed him. Sayid could still feel the air shattering from the gunfire, smell the cordite and hear his mother's screams. And his own. Moments later the darkness and smoke had been punctured with torchlight as British troops stormed their house. Gunfire flashed and echoed. More men died – the assassins. And then soldiers carried Sayid and his mother to a waiting helicopter. An Englishman, someone who spoke Arabic, comforted him and his mother. He was their friend. The man their father had called a brother. Sayid recognized him as the man who had shared food at their table. His name was Tom Gordon and he promised them he would care for them, in honour of Sayid's father – a brave and great man.

That is how Sayid had ended up at Dartmoor High with Tom Gordon's son. And now the avalanche, the fight at the château and his kidnapping all exposed Sayid's fear. He had betrayed not only his best friend but also his own father's memory.

The van jolted across a pothole. Sayid looked at the thugs up front. Yellow motorway lights flashed across the windscreen. He looked at Bobby, whose eyes were closed.

One thing Sayid had not given his torturers was the information on the piece of paper. He saw the numbers in his head. Reaching forward, he scraped the dried mud from under the instep of his boot. They were part of the mystery and they were important.

Sayid comforted himself. There was still something he could do to help Max. Solve the code. Get the information to Max. How? He didn't know. But somewhere deep inside he believed his friend would find him.

*

Abdullah put Max's passport in his personal safe and asked if he wanted to keep the pendant there as well. Max declined. He caught the look in Abdullah's eyes. A fleeting moment when he realized that Abdullah might know of its importance.

'A charm,' the riad owner said. 'It is a good luck thing for you, yes?'

'Yeah, that's about right.'

'If it is valuable, you should put it in my safe. You are going to the main square?' Abdullah asked, quite naturally.

'Yes. Djemaa el-Fna,' Max answered.

'The Square of the Dead,' Abdullah said matter-of-factly.

Was he trying to frighten him? Max waited a moment and held the man's gaze.

'I've heard it's pretty lively,' he said.

Abdullah nodded. 'But I am ashamed to say there are thieves in my city.'

Max thought about it for a moment and reached for the pendant as the man held out his hand. But Max simply took the slack in the leather thong, gave it a turn like knotting his school tie and tightened the cord until the loop sat closer to his throat.

'It's not valuable, just something a friend gave me,' he said nonchalantly. 'There.' He put a couple of fingers between the cord and his neck, a snug fit that didn't constrict his throat. 'No one can grab it now.'

'Not unless they cut your throat,' Abdullah said, unsmiling.

Djemaa el-Fna, the huge square in the centre of Marrakech, blazed with dozens of cooking fires. Coloured glass lanterns added to the fires' shadows; the shuffling crowds' movements fractured, as in a badly lit nightclub. Voices shouted. Food was cooked over the open flames. Traditionally dressed men with small, black-faced vervet monkeys on chains posed for tourists and let the tourists stand, more or less nervously, with the monkeys chattering on their arms.

A twinge of distress caught Max's heart. The small monkeys somersaulted, then sat cowering, staring at the higher species of primate that tossed a few coins into the upturned hat. A tug of the chain, a guttural command and the monkey would perform again. 'For the monkey! For the monkey!' the handler called, urging the bystanders to throw down more coins.

Max and Sophie edged deeper into the square. It was a close-up of faces, heads and shoulders as they angled and barged. Money changed hands, stained teeth grinned. Crumpled notes were pressed into grease-slicked fingers as locals and tourists alike bought the hot slices of lamb kebabs and roasted vegetables. This is where the locals came to eat, streaming out of the narrow alleyways. Smoke hung across the square like a blanket of cotton wool. Max's eyes stung, but they watched everything going on around him.

Groups of four or five men, playing flutes, tin whistles and cymbals, and beating drums with curved sticks, meandered through the throng. *Ganga* drums and *haejuj* bass lutes fought for dominance. Women sat having henna tattoos daubed delicately across their faces and arms. An old man, according to his small sign a doctor, surrounded by bottles of herbs, sat cross-legged, examining a woman's swollen hand.

Max and Sophie visited half a dozen food stalls and ate as much as they wanted. Max loved eating with his fingers – no table manners to be concerned about. Almost as good as being out on a camping weekend, except here all the food was cooked for you.

On the fringe of the square, cafés served mint tea and fruit juices.

'Everyone comes to eat here. Every night. It goes on really late,' Sophie said.

'Like a street party,' Max shouted. Conversation was always going to be a shouting match against this noise level.

'You look good,' she said. 'It suits you.'

Max tugged at the cotton djellaba he wore. There had been a moment of panic when he realized that the riad's staff had taken his clothes to be washed and left the djellaba in their place. Thankfully they had left his trainers and these were now peeping out from beneath the long flowing robe. It had felt a bit like wearing a dress at first, but within moments of slipping it over his head he saw the practicality of the loose-fitting cotton. It was cool to wear and made movement relatively easy.

Max eased his way through a knot of people, pulling Sophie behind him. She grasped his hand tightly, as if losing contact would set her adrift in the cross-currents of this human ocean. She watched as he cut a path through the people, allowing her thoughts to settle on the boy ahead of her. Max was a stranger here, threatened by unfamiliarity, escaping determined killers, but she felt the strength in his grip. Confident and protective. How little he knew of the inherent dangers here, where a life could be sold for the price of a meal.

Max was amazed how anyone got anywhere in these crowds. Stallholders had set up their wares. Piles of oranges, heaped in pyramids, were being cut and squeezed, dancing troupes joined the musicians, and fortune-tellers waved their hands, brushing aside people's misery.

He stopped next to a snake-charmer sitting on a faded tribal rug as he mesmerized a cobra. Rising up, its coiled body swayed languidly to the old man's flute-playing and the gentle teasing of his hand.

The snake's hood flared; its black eyes reflected the scattered fragments of light. It swayed and arched. It gazed into Max's soul. Held him with an illusion of calmness. The snake made a languid, hypnotic movement, a deceptive seduction that lowered a victim's defences.

Then the cobra struck. Its fangs bared, its hiss – like hatred.

The gathered strength of the unfurled body propelled it straight past the old man, directly towards Max and Sophie. Max jerked back, putting a protective arm in front of her, but the wrinkled old man, who looked half blind, simply swept his hand beneath the cobra's hood, twisted his wrist and let the snake curl about his arm. Then he raised the cobra's flicking tongue to his own lips and kissed the snake.

Murmurs of approval sighed from the crowd, a smattering of applause, coins tinkled into his upturned hat.

Max gave an embarrassed smile. Perhaps he'd been too quick to react. Could you be too quick when it came to a cobra strike? Sophie touched his shoulder. She knew how fast Max had moved – a brave and instinctive gesture. An attacking cobra was an old snake-charmer's trick. But Max wasn't to know that.

But those few seconds of reaction had sharpened his senses.

There was another danger. His instincts bristled, the warning insistent, demanding his attention. But what was the threat? From where? Max searched the immediate crowd. Something wasn't right. A man's eyes held his own for the briefest of moments and then flitted away. There were two men's faces he had seen earlier. He had been erratic in his choice of food stalls and entertainment, so it wasn't likely that he would spot the same faces twice.

He pointed over the heads of the crowds. 'Get to the edge,' he shouted.

She nodded. As fascinated as he was by the seething mass of people in the square, he realized he could be targeted more easily here than in the wilderness. In open space you can see your enemy; here they could be a breath away. But why feel that? Why would Sophie bring him here to entrap him when she could have arranged an attack at any time since they left Biarritz?

Paranoia. Fear. Get rid of it, he told himself – these feelings were just crowd fever. This place was like Wembley Stadium and twice as noisy.

The stifling mass now seemed impenetrable. Max pulled Sophie closer. He wanted her right there, at his shoulder, no more than a step away. A ripple of energy shuddered through the pressed bodies; hands reached out, clawing at him. Max felt the torsion on his skin as someone twisted his wrist. Sophie was at arm's length. Two men were between them, the back of their heads momentarily obscuring her face. Sophie's grip still held but he could feel it slipping. Images of Zabala falling from his grasp flashed across his mind. Sophie's face mouthed his name. Shouted it. One of the men turned. Same face as before. Dull eyes, uncaring, probably doped up on something. The man made a sudden grab at the pendant. Max blocked the move but the action forced him to lose his grip on Sophie.

Other hands scratched at his face. Screaming and chattering as they raked their fingers across his head. Someone had thrown a chained monkey on to his shoulder, its tiny nails scrabbling at his face and hair, and then Max felt it tug on the leather thong that held the pendant.

He swept his arm up, caught the monkey by its soft fur, but then yelped as it bit into his forearm. He threw the monkey away from him and lunged at its chain. He wanted the man at the end of it, but someone kicked his legs from beneath him and he went down hard on to the ground. Sandals and dirty feet, rubbish and bits of food swirled around his face. Max rolled, tumbled, struggled to get back on his feet. It was like another avalanche.

'Sophie!' he yelled, his elbows pushing against anyone trying to hold him.

Someone grunted; a man shouted in agony as Max's blow caught his cheekbone. He was being wrenched from side to side, unable to defend himself. Half a dozen smaller boys, ten- or eleven-year-olds who looked like street urchins, were attacking him now, but they too were hampered by the weight of the crowd.

A crushing fear – was Sharkface here? Max looked around desperately, but there was no sign of the ragged-mouthed teenager.

Bodies scattered and fell. Max saw Sophie throw a man twice her weight to the ground. This was close-quarter fighting. Her eyes darted across the swirling mass, seeking out his. But before she could speak another arm went around her neck. She twisted and was obscured from view as Max yelled, releasing his aggression. He hadn't noticed that a different energy now took control of the crowd. A surge went through it, like a shock wave. Voices were raised in protest, but then subsided. Max burrowed beneath the sea of legs, scrambling in Sophie's direction. The boys snatched at him, but he was scurrying fast, as in a body-jumbling fight for a rugby ball.

Five metres further on he pushed himself to the surface. People buffeted each other as a great battleship of a man bellied his way through the crowd. Abdullah. And behind him, like two escort destroyers in battle formation, came the two men from the riad. They made no sound, shouted no threats, just cleaved through the sweltering mass. Each of the two men carried lanterns, so Abdullah appeared to have two mighty wings of light behind him.

An angel of the night.

Max gawped for a moment.

'Abdullah!' Sophie cried, and the man's bulk turned, angling directly towards her.

Max was only metres away from her, but already Abdullah had struck out with a sturdy-looking stick and one of the attackers went down. Abdullah and his light-carriers walked right over him. That was probably worth a couple of broken ribs, Max thought. The urchins scattered as the second assailant foolishly tried to raise a hand against the unstoppable momentum. One light-carrier dipped the lantern over Abdullah's shoulder, the man shielded his eyes momentarily and Abdullah's fist struck him across the head like a mallet blow. Down he went.

Max reached Sophie at almost the same time as Abdullah. The big man didn't smile and spoke only to issue a command.

'We must go!' he said.

He turned, Sophie and Max fell in behind him, and the crowd opened like the Red Sea in front of Moses. They were safe for now.

But Max knew that the killers had found him.

18

Angelo Farentino had once known courage. He had worn it as lightly as one of his expensive suits. For countless years he had championed and supported those who roamed the world reporting dangerous practices that could wreak havoc with the environment.

And then one night he awoke – a frightened man. The darkness caressed his worst fears. He could no longer endure the intimidation and threats of the destroyers. The realization came that he could survive, be protected and become wealthy. All he had to do was betray those who trusted him implicitly.

Like a deep-seated disease, the seeds of deception had started months, perhaps even years earlier. It was, he realized some time later, caused by pain and jealousy. Of being denied something he could not have. A woman. His anger, like the claws of a beast, had torn something from his heart. And weakened him.

His courage had never truly returned, but his sense of survival was intact. Which is why he had argued with Tishenko. Less an argument, perhaps, more an impassioned plea. What Tishenko wanted could cost Farentino his life.

'You want me to go to England and speak to Tom Gordon?'

Tishenko had no lips, they had been scorched from him when the lightning struck him as a boy, but the gap that was his mouth widened into a grin. 'We know where he is. And we know his mind is as fragile as a kite in a storm.'

Farentino sipped the drink Tishenko had put into his hand. Drinking and listening allowed him to avert his eyes as often as possible. Tishenko's appearance had always given him a shudder of revulsion. For a man who cherished art and beauty as much as Farentino, the grotesque Tishenko was an affront.

Tishenko took his drink through a straw. 'You know his boy, Max. He has become involved in something quite extraordinary. He has slipped past my people, and he has discovered information that could cause me damage if anyone had the understanding and the knowledge to study it carefully,' Tishenko said quietly.

Farentino had once tried to have Tom Gordon killed and Max had been caught up in that assault as well. He knew the boy, all right. He knew how bloody-minded he could be.

'Why is Max Gordon involved?' Farentino asked.

'I am uncertain whether he stumbled upon the information I need by accident or his father has something to do with it.'

'Tom Gordon would never deliberately send his son into anything dangerous. That's ridiculous,' Farentino protested.

'There has been contact between father and son. If Tom Gordon knows anything about my plans he could cause me trouble. He could stop everything. My destiny will not be thwarted by a teenage boy and a man who has lost his mind.'

'And I am supposed to walk in on Tom Gordon and ask him if he is involved? He would kill me. On the spot. He would kill me!'

Tishenko watched the sun rise across the Alps. The ball of fire threw spears of light through the jagged peaks. The fiery orb gave life, but it would pale into insignificance if his plans succeeded.

He kept his gaze on ɯe sunrise, its warmth lighting the sky. 'Tom Gordon does not know who he is most of the time. He has only fragments of memory. But if he has instigated an investigation, using his son as an unofficial source of information, then he would be in command of his faculties – at least for these recent events. I don't care how you do it, Farentino. Go and speak to him. Convince him you are still his friend.' Tishenko turned and stared at the subdued Farentino. The disfigured face smiled. 'And then you can enjoy the act of betrayal yet again.'

After an hour's driving, while Max slept, Abdullah had pulled into the crease of a hillside, the darkness cloaking the Land Cruiser's bulk. He wanted to make sure they were not being followed. If word of their escape had somehow got out of the city there might also be ambushes in place. To learn patience was to survive. Besides, Sophie's friend was sick. Abdullah had stopped twice to allow Max to vomit. It was the monkey bite. Now he lay in a deep sleep, sweat dappling his face. But Abdullah didn't want to wait too long – the boy would need medical attention.

While Max slept, Sophie clambered into the back seat and used the vehicle's first-aid kit to clean and dress the bite on

Max's arm. As the desert's night chill penetrated the Land Cruiser, she pulled a rug across them both. Abdullah and his man would stay on guard.

Max felt marginally better when daylight came. He had barely moved all night. It seemed obvious that all his recent exertions had been responsible for accelerating the infection from the bite. The glands in his neck and under his arm were swollen, and his stomach muscles still hurt, but the giddiness had gone. His arm, though, was stiff and felt numb. Once he'd checked the dressing he realized it must have been Sophie who had cared for him. She lay curled across his lap, still sleeping. He gulped from the bottle of water Abdullah's man offered him. Dehydration from vomiting would have a knock-on effect and the day was going to be hot, so he needed liquid more than food right now.

Sophie moved slightly. Uncertain what to do about the sleeping girl, he decided to leave her undisturbed.

As the sun threw its light across the landscape the richness and beauty of the mountains and valleys surprised him. In the distance, to the west and south, a rugged, stone-flecked desert levelled out across the horizon – a shimmering warning that a harsher terrain was not far away. The Land Cruiser gripped the dirt track that led through the mountains and their snow-capped peaks that sucked in the orange warmth.

The 4x4 hit a deep rut, jolted and righted itself. Sophie was wide awake in an instant. She looked at Max, gazed through the windscreen, then licked the dryness from her lips. Max gave her the bottle of water. She drank thirstily and handed it back.

'Are you all right?' she asked Max.

He nodded. 'Thanks for doing my arm.'

She shrugged. 'It needs attention. My father will look at you. He knows about these things.'

'If it lives on the face of the earth it has probably bitten Laurent Fauvre,' Abdullah said.

They could see from his eyes in the rear-view mirror that he was smiling.

'And probably died from blood poisoning as a result,' Sophie said as she pulled her fingers through her hair.

'Sophie, go easy on your father. Show some respect, yes? He lives a hard life,' Abdullah said gently.

'And it takes a hard man to live it,' she said to no one in particular.

Abdullah shrugged. He knew about the friction between father and child. Max felt the tension. Sophie and her dad clearly had problems. What was he getting into?

'Is it much further?' he asked.

Sophie nodded towards the front of the vehicle. 'It's there.'

Max squinted through the dust-smeared windscreen. The low morning light gave a distorted reflection on the dirty glass. Across the distant, bare valley were what looked to be rows of hewn sandstone boulders, standing rigidly together like dominoes. They were almost indistinguishable from the mountains rising behind them, whose torn skirts of rock diffused the land's harshness with light and shadow.

Once Max focused more clearly he could see the tips of date palms and for a brief moment the glint of reflection as the low sun caught a slick of water tumbling down the mountainside.

'It looks like a town,' Max said.

'You're right. It's called Les Larmes des Anges,' Abdullah

said. 'It was once the toughest Berber stronghold in these mountains. Then, when we fought the French, they held it for years – I'm talking back between the world wars, 1920s. There was vicious fighting here. Neither side would think of surrender. It's the only walled town around here. During the final battle a rainstorm swept across the mountain between the sun and desert. The raindrops were lit by the sun's rays. Les Larmes des Anges – the Tears of the Angels. They blinded the defenders. The French garrison died where they stood. Now, when the wind comes down from the mountains, it is said you can hear the cries of the dying.'

The Land Cruiser left a wisp of dust behind it as Abdullah accelerated towards the ancient town. Sophie fell silent, gazing straight ahead at the crumbling walls and the place where her father waited.

Once they were closer the size of the walled town became more apparent. The walls had to be thirty, forty metres high. Two huge, iron-studded doors began to swing open as the Land Cruiser approached. Max wondered what was waiting for him as they drove beneath the entrance arch into the town the French had named the Angels' Tears.

There was in fact very little left of the town; it was mostly perimeter walls and a few other buildings that remained. The whole inside area was like a massive zoo. Huge, scooped-out troughs of earth, some filled with water, served as drinking holes for the animals. Others were natural enclosures for the assorted creatures. The walls were at least five metres thick and stretched for as far as he could see, until they buttressed the mountain's skeleton fingers that stretched down to touch the fortress town.

Towards one side of the wall Max could see cave-like openings, beneath which some craters dropped away. Twisting in his seat, he looked back as he caught a glimpse of deep orange and dark stripes. A tiger was climbing an old tree trunk conveniently laid against the face of the rock, allowing access to its lair. Fur and muscle glistened, rippling like oil on water as the huge cat, carrying a dead goat in its jaws, sprang the last couple of metres and disappeared into the darkness of its lair. But more awesome was the tiger that watched it. A big male reclined on a rock ledge, indifferent to the female's activities. The massive head turned its attention towards Max. Amber eyes, impassive but watchful, followed him.

'Did you see the tiger?' Max blurted out. 'It was huge. What is this place? It's like a safari park.'

Abdullah swung the Land Cruiser around the edge of another crater. Man-made obstacles, like an assault course, mixed with boulders and dead trees created a perfect haven for monkeys.

'That's the best way to describe it, Master Gordon,' Abdullah said, easing the big 4x4 towards a more open area where a gantry of iron platforms broke the skyline. 'Those big holes? They're bomb craters. They're perfect for a lot of the animals here. Don't forget, many of these are protected and endangered species. By good fortune, war and destruction gave these animals the chance to survive. The town was flattened, but they could not breach the walls. Sophie's father redirected the water from the mountains and created natural watering holes. The animals are as safe as they can be. Ah! There's Laurent.'

It was already getting hot in the shelter of the walls as Max stepped out of the Land Cruiser. They had stopped in front of the gantry, which Max could now see was scaffolding built as a trapeze platform straddling another crater. The steel bars reached up twenty-five metres or more and Max's eye was drawn to the figure swinging across space, gripping a trapeze bar.

Max shielded his eyes. He could see it was not a young man on the trapeze – his grey hair caught the sunlight; but despite the man's age Max could see his upper body was bulked with muscle stretching through the gymnast's cutaway vest. An Arab boy, dressed in white cotton shorts and T-shirt, stood on the opposite gantry – and swung another trapeze bar into the void. Max saw the man's biceps bulge with exertion as he hoisted himself into position, torsioned his body and let go in mid-air.

There was a moment, like a plane stalling, when he was motionless in the air. If he did not turn in time he would miss the approaching trapeze. He twisted, his hands slapping the approaching bar at just the right moment. With practised ease he swung across to the boy, who caught the trapeze. Laurent Fauvre sat on the support platform, dusted his hands with talcum powder, gripped a rope and slid down to the base of the tower.

Abdullah nudged Max, flicking his head towards the base of the trapeze, a scooped-out crater like the others, but this hole was full of jagged rocks.

'No safety net,' Abdullah whispered. 'He falls, he dies.'

Max followed Abdullah as he strode towards the scaffolding. Bad enough that Laurent Fauvre took his life into his hands every time he went up on to the trapeze, but now Max saw that he had lowered himself down the rope and placed himself into a wheelchair.

Fauvre dabbed his face and draped the towel around his neck. Abdullah bent down, kissed his friend's cheeks, shook his hand and held it for a moment in the warmth of friendship.

'Allah, the Merciful, keeps you safe, my friend,' Abdullah said.

'You've obviously put in a good word for me.' The Frenchman grinned.

Laurent Fauvre looked towards Sophie. Max hung back. Fauvre had already cast a glance in his direction and seemed to dismiss him immediately.

'Sophie,' Fauvre said, the love for his daughter obvious. The etched lines in his face, like worn leather, creased into a smile. She kissed him.

'Papa.'

She smiled, but Max could see it was not genuine. And Fauvre knew it. A shadow of sadness clouded his face for a moment, but left as quickly as it arrived. He nodded.

'Thank God you're safe,' he said gratefully. 'You cause me more worry than these animals I care for.'

'Don't start, Papa,' she said quietly.

Her father was going to say more but thought better of it. He looked at Max.

'And this is the boy who helped you?' He extended his hand to Max, who stepped forward and shook it. Fauvre's grip was firm, but there was no attempt to crush Max's hand in a macho show of strength.

'You are welcome.'

'Monsieur Fauvre, thank you. But I think I'm the one being helped now.'

Fauvre nodded, held Max's eyes a moment longer, then pressed the buttons on his wheelchair. 'We'll have breakfast once you're settled. Abdullah, let's talk. Sophie, show young Mister Gordon his room.'

The wheelchair purred away and for the first time Max noticed that wherever he looked an undulating track had been built around all of the animal pens. Laurent Fauvre could go anywhere he wished in his own walled town.

Max watched him leave. As Fauvre and Abdullah moved past an iron cage that enclosed a platform built above a cavernous gully, a male lion lunged at the bars. Teeth bared, its belly-growling roar caused monkeys to chatter in fear and Abdullah to jump back, hand on his heart. The surprise attack had no effect on Fauvre.

He shouted at the lion, 'Don't do that! You frightened Abdullah!' He reached through the bars, scratching the snarling jaw. The lion grunted and flopped down on his stomach, like a house cat content with the attention.

A car door slammed. Max turned. Sophie had grabbed their backpacks.

'Don't ever try that. That lion is a killer. All the big cats here are, except my father doesn't believe it. One day they'll take him. Come on, I'll show you your tent.'

Max took his backpack and followed her. Now he was going to sleep in a tent? Better hope Laurent Fauvre didn't put the cats out at night, like a moggy back in England.

He looked at the ancient fortifications. It would take a couple of hours to walk through this sanctuary. And anyone foolish enough to enter uninvited could end up as breakfast for at least a dozen wild animals. No point in having a 'Beware of the Dog' sign on the gate; 'Beware of the Cat' would be more appropriate.

Max would use the day to rest and then he would question Laurent Fauvre. For the first time in ages, he felt a sense of safety behind these vast walls. The fragmented clues were coming together in his head. He realized that the friendship and association between Zabala and Laurent Fauvre were vital to everything. When Max had laid the drawing of the triangle on the atlas, it was as if its longest side were showing him the way to this desolate place. And Zabala would not have brought the inheritor of his secret out into the middle of nowhere without a reason. It had to be *this* middle of nowhere. Max hoped that Laurent Fauvre was the reason.

Behind a ruined section of the town, where gardens had been established over the years in the Moorish tradition of creating tranquillity with the gentle sound of moving water, three or four tents stood under shady clumps of date palms. Max took it all in. This was an oasis. Not your average backpacker's tent, either. More like a Bedouin tent. Like a small circus tent, like a . . . well, it wasn't exactly luxury, but the layers of material, the pitched roof, the carpets on the floor, all made it look a bit Lawrence of Arabia-ish. All that was needed now was a camel and a . . .

The braying gasp of a camel stopped the thought there and then. He turned. Not ten metres away behind a thorn tree, a camel stuck its spit-slicked tongue out at him. He was about to return the compliment when Sophie pulled back the tent's flap.

'This is yours, Max.'

He stepped inside. The Berber tent was made of camel hair, goat's wool and canvas and, as in the others, hand-woven rugs, cotton pillows and cushions were scattered across the floor. The coolness was immediately apparent. Max dropped his backpack on the bed.

'It is basic, but I hope you will be comfortable. Your toilet and shower are through there. My father doesn't have many staff, they're here mostly to feed and care for the animals, so you will have to ask for your washing to be done.'

'This is luxury compared to the tents I usually sleep in,' he said. 'And I don't need any kit washing, thanks.'

'All right.' She was fairly close to him and reached out a hand to brush away the hair from his face. He instinctively pulled his head back. What was she doing?

She sighed. 'For heaven's sake, Max. Don't be childish.' And put the palm of her hand on his forehead. 'You're still running a temperature. I'll tell Papa.'

'Don't make a fuss. I'll be OK.'

He turned away, feeling the heat creeping up his neck and the increase in his heartbeat. He really was feeling sick, but what he felt now had nothing to do with running a temperature. He unpacked his change of clothing. Everything had been pressed and cleaned by the riad's staff. Wear one, wash one was Max's policy. Time to get back into shorts and shirt. Time for small talk.

'Do you have a tent as well?' He regretted saying it the moment the words slipped past his lips. It sounded as though he was inviting himself.

She raised an eyebrow, then smiled. 'I have a room in one

of the old houses. I need a greater sense of permanence than a tent.'

Now she was closer again. He tried to put a serious look of concentration on his face. These shorts definitely needed to be laid out on the bed a certain way. She touched his shoulder.

Smile bravely, Max. Look cool. Don't get flustered here. She's just a girl.

'What is that?' she asked, touching the pendant.

Like a feral cat enticed out of danger by a plate of food from a kindly person, he was still on his guard. And if the wildcat ate, it did so with one eye on the person feeding it, alert to anyone making a sudden move to trap it. One false step and the cat would bolt.

Max felt the bristle of danger tickle the back of his neck.

'It's something I picked up along the way. A friend gave it to me,' he said as casually as he could.

'But it's unusual,' she said, her eyes studying the pendant. She had tried to look at it when Max was asleep in the Land Cruiser but the way his body was lying meant the pendant itself was caught beneath his clothes and the fold of his shoulder.

'Oh, I don't think it's anything special,' Max bluffed.

'Can I see it?'

'Sure.' He fumbled with the cord, but sweat had tightened the leather thong. He couldn't undo it and he couldn't get it over his head. 'Well, maybe not.'

'That's OK. I was just being nosy.' She gave him a smile that could have charmed a monkey out of a tree. *But not this monkey*, Max thought to himself. 'See you outside when you're ready. Papa will look at your arm and then we'll eat,' she said.

The tent's flap dropped back, leaving Max alone. Flexing his arm, he felt the pain creep up into his shoulder. The nausea persisted, but he was sure he could shake it off. He had to. This place of safety suddenly felt like a cage.

'The wound must not be closed up. So, no stitches for you,' Fauvre said as he swabbed the monkey bite on Max's arm. The wound was looking bad, with vein-like tendrils creeping upwards beneath the skin.

Fauvre now wore a cool, loose-fitting white shirt and his withered legs were covered by white trousers. Max thought the clothes made him look a bit like a doctor, but that didn't offer much comfort.

'It hurts?' Fauvre asked as he eased the wound open.

'A little,' Max replied, wishing the probing fingers and stinging antiseptic would stop their pulling and squeezing.

'The infection is still there and you have some blood poisoning. It might be advanced. I cannot say, but that's what those red lines are going up your arm. When was the last time you had a tetanus shot?'

'Couple of years ago, I think.'

'Right. Tetanus and penicillin for you. Also I give you a multivitamin shot. Help boost your system. Those injections hurt more than the others; they feel like soup being injected. I hate them, but I give myself one once in a while.'

'Then I'd rather take a pill.'

They were in a small examination room, which Max reckoned Fauvre used for looking after animals. Fauvre turned the wheelchair and reached for a small fridge. Max noticed all the cupboards were at the same height, designed to allow the disabled man to live his life as easily as possible.

'Of course you would rather take a pill. That's the easy option and about as useful as sucking a sweet in these circumstances. Besides, handing out pills is not as much fun.' Fauvre smiled. 'For me, that is.'

He took the small glass bottles of medicine from the fridge and drew the liquid into the hypodermics. 'Animal bites and wounds can be hell,' he said as he unceremoniously jabbed the needles into Max's arm.

Max winced. He hated injections and this had been done with less finesse than a vet jabbing a cow.

Fauvre seemed to read his mind. 'No nice nurses here, only me. And I don't have much of a bedside manner.' He cleared the used bits and pieces away.

'That's all right. You weren't too bad. Thanks.'

Fauvre seemed amused. 'You lie very well, Max. It hurt like hell, the injections felt like snake bites and I have as much compassion as a charging bull elephant.'

'You save endangered species. You can't be that bad, Monsieur Fauvre.'

'That's not what my daughter thinks. And call me Laurent. You've earned it. Can you drive?' Fauvre asked.

'Yes,' Max replied.

'Then you are my chauffeur this morning, young man,' Fauvre said as he held one more hypodermic.

'What's that?' Max asked.

'You thought we were finished? No, no. This is the soup. And multivitamin shots go . . .'

259

He pointed at Max's backside. 'Drop your shorts and think of England.'

Max eased himself gently into the driver's seat of the golf buggy. The last jab felt as though Fauvre had used a screwdriver on him.

'We are feeding some of the animals. So, let us go,' Fauvre said, pointing out the direction.

Obviously, Max realized, the 'we' meant the staff were feeding the animals. Perhaps it was this autocratic manner of her father that Sophie disliked so much.

The golf buggy's canopy shielded Max from what was fast becoming a very hot day. Fauvre indicated the direction and Max pressed the accelerator down. Nice and easy, take your time, look around, get your bearings. Was there anything obvious that told him why Zabala had led him here? As his eyes scanned the jumbled ruins, he knew he was looking for more than just clues – if things go bad here, how to escape?

The old town looked as though it held plenty of caves, cut deep into the walls. Most of the big cats would be sleeping, but there were obviously many smaller creatures that had both shelter and plenty of room to roam once they ventured out and went down into one of the huge pits that had been torn from the ground. At the far edge of the town, unnoticed at first because of the backdrop of the mountain, was a vast aviary, almost obscured by the irregular shape of the netting. It dipped and stretched, pulled this way and that by jutting support poles. The birds could fly almost as if they were free.

That could be one way of escape. Climb that netting,

clamber on to the walls and down the other side. Max knew how to survive in the desert.

'You ask no questions,' Fauvre said.

'Just getting my bearings, I suppose.'

'Like one of my big cats looking for a way out of its pen.' Fauvre smiled. He needed to calm the boy; there were decisions to be made about Max Gordon. 'You are safe here. You saved my daughter's life. I am in your debt.'

'She's helped me as well. There's no debt as far as I'm concerned, sir. I mean, Laurent.'

Fauvre nodded. It was a good answer. Respectful. The kid had intelligence and knew when to apply it. He smiled. 'Most teenagers I have known either sulk and mumble like a constipated camel or ask endless inane questions that an encyclopedia couldn't answer. You do neither.'

Max did not like being patronized or have unwarranted praise put his way, but he was uncertain if that's what Fauvre was doing. It seemed to him that Sophie's dad had very little experience of teenagers, despite having one as his daughter.

Change the subject. Find out more.

'How long have you been here?' Max asked, keeping his eyes on the curving route towards wherever it was Fauvre wanted him to go.

'I started looking for a place fifteen, twenty years ago. I ran the Cirque de Paris. I knew back then what was happening to animals in the wild. Already I was sickened.'

'And you were the trapeze artist?' Max said.

'And ringmaster with my big cats. I trained them.' Fauvre's hesitation made Max glance at him. 'I love them,' Fauvre muttered.

Max guided the golf buggy along the curved pathways. A broken wall gave way to what looked like an old arena. Nothing as grand as a Roman amphitheatre, but the tumbled-down buildings around the space had created false tiers, like a small grandstand. Red, compacted dirt and sand made it look like a circus ring, except this space gave the appearance of an abandoned building site. Rusted steel girders lay at different angles, toppled against scaffolding; some lay smashed across old cars. Broken, low walls criss-crossed the space, while poles and ropes took a third of the area over on the western edge of the sand ring. It reminded Max of an army assault course set up for urban warfare. Fauvre indicated to Max to pull into the shade of a ruined building.

Abdullah sat in an overstuffed armchair, a canvas awning sheltering him from the heat as he sipped from a tall glass with sprigs of mint among the crushed ice. A cold box nestled at his side.

'*Bravo! Bravo! Ma petite princesse! Encore!*' Abdullah cried as he clapped his hands together.

Max raised a hand to shield his eyes. A puff of dust alerted him as the shadow that had been absorbed by the side of a wall sprang into life. It was Sophie. Like a marathon runner, she wore well-fitted shorts, tank top and cross-trainers. Dirt and sand caked her back with sweat – she'd obviously been training for some time. She kicked against an oil drum, leapt on to the back of an old donkey cart, flipped in the air and ran with aggressive determination at a rust-bucket of a car. Max heard her grunt with effort as she threw her body across the bonnet, seemed destined to smash into a pile of dangerous scaffolding, but instead twisted her body, caught the layers of pipework in two hands and, with a gymnast's skill, swung the weight of her body, using the momentum of her speed, to curl upwards and grasp one of the steel girders. She clambered like a monkey, using toes and fingers to grip the edge of the girder.

Ten metres up, the steel beam ended in space. Without hesitation she somersaulted into the air. Only then did Max realize a small hill of dirt was beneath her. After five metres she landed on her feet, opened her stride and raced to the bottom.

Finally, hands on knees, she bent over and sucked her recuperating lungs full of air. Sweat ran from her face, puckering the sand. Max hadn't taken his eyes from her. Her slight frame belied her skill and strength. Fauvre glanced at him.

'Young women today are so independent. Stay clear of them is my advice. They can be the cause of great pain.'

Was that a warning from the unsmiling Fauvre? Telling Max to stay clear of his daughter? Max brushed back the sweat from his face.

'You are all right?' Fauvre said.

Max nodded.

'Then drive. Over there.' An edge had crept into his voice.

Perhaps, Max thought, there was a darker side to this man's personality.

Max spun the wheel, wishing he had been honest and told Fauvre that he felt too ill to go on a sightseeing tour. But then he would have missed the incredible display Sophie had just given.

They drove towards an enclosure. Fauvre pointed at different caves and pits, the subject of his daughter replaced by his passion for the animals.

'It is mostly the big cats the collectors and hunters seek out. We rescue many of them and re-establish them around the world. I've had serval, ocelot, tiger, cheetah, jaguar, leopard ... and bears as well, they're a favourite for the scum who trap and trade them. I tell you something not many people know. A European monarch, only a couple of years ago, paid a fortune to a Russian peasant so he could shoot the village bear. The bear liked to drink beer. It would sit in the square and sleep, like an old man. And one day this king, this high and mighty person, arrived and shot it point blank. He needed a bear to add to his trophy collection.'

Fauvre closed his eyes for a moment, as if the pictures in his mind had hooks into his heart.

The image of the brown bear that attacked Max on the mountain leapt into his memory. The power and fury of the huge creature still awed him. More than that – it was an affinity – complete awareness of what that bear's existence was about. Smell is a powerful association for recall and he could almost taste the wet-fur odour at the back of his throat.

Fauvre sighed. 'The Chinese torture bears, did you know that? They keep them in bamboo cages, in a space they cannot even turn around in. Barbaric. They use their gall bladders for medicine. And we call ourselves the highest of the species,' he finally muttered.

Max glanced at the man's face. It was twisted in disgust.

'So I found this place. It took ten years of my life to get it like this.'

Max didn't know how intrusive he could be with his questions, but if he didn't start being pushy with this strong-willed man he wasn't going to get any closer to Zabala's secret.

'Have you always been in a wheelchair?'

That drew a sharp look from Fauvre. 'No. A tiger did this to me. My favourite tiger. He is called Aladfar.'

'That sounds Arabic,' Max said.

Fauvre nodded. 'It's the name of a star. It means claws. From Arabic astronomy. Do you know anything about astronomy?'

The question was like a hypodermic being pushed into his chest. A sharp pain that went straight to the root of the disease eating away at him – that determination to find the final pieces to Zabala's secret. And his killer.

So, Fauvre was playing games.

'I'm learning as I go along,' Max said noncommittally. 'How did the accident happen?'

Fauvre let Max sidestep his probing question. 'He is the perfect tiger. Three metres long, three hundred kilos. One day he decided to show me just who was in charge. He played with me as a cat plays with a mouse. He tumbled me and clawed my back. He broke my spine.'

'Was he shot?'

'Aladfar!? I would kill the man who laid a finger on him. He is magnificent – and now we understand each other.'

Max knew that Aladfar was the massive tiger he had seen when he first drove into the Angels' Tears. And it seemed the beast's pit was where Fauvre now guided him.

Where was the connection Max searched for? When did Fauvre first come into contact with Zabala?

'So was that when you brought your family here?' he asked.

'My animals are my family,' Fauvre said without emotion.

The blunt response silenced Max. Not much you can say to that. No wonder Sophie felt alienated.

Obeying Fauvre's hand signals, Max pulled up next to a walled crater. Two men stood by a handcart and were unloading a basket of old vegetables and fruit.

Fauvre spoke to them in Arabic and they stopped. 'Have a look,' he said to Max as he leaned across the low parapet.

The fever's nausea made Max's legs tremble. He needed shade and water, but he wasn't going to show Fauvre any sign of weakness if he could help it. He blinked away the sweat and carefully peered over. The crater's walls were almost sheer. It looked like the other animal pens. The sort of place Max could imagine bears living in captivity. Plenty of space, natural water, a shelter, good daylight and keepers to supply food. But for a moment he saw nothing except the wall at the other end of the crater, where iron bars divided this pit from the next.

The lower part of the wall had been replaced, or repaired, like the side of a cage and the bars ran for two or three metres. Max realized where he was. He'd come to the other side of the tiger's pit. On one side of the bars the massive, hungry-looking tiger prowled backwards and forwards. It wanted whatever was in this crater below Max.

Then he saw movement along the dark side of the wall directly below him, where the sun had not yet reached. Another two men stepped out and raised their hands – begging. They looked weak and unkempt. How long had they been trapped in this pit?

Max looked at Fauvre. The dispassionate expression scared him for a moment.

'Why are you doing this? Who are these men?'

'They came to steal. I have small animals worth a fortune. These creatures thought they could get away with it.'

'You're going to feed them to the tiger?' Max said incredulously.

'*They* think they are going to be fed to Aladfar. When I release them they will go back to whatever stone they crawled from under and tell others that you do not enter the Angels' Tears unless you are prepared to die.'

'That's sadistic,' Max said.

'It would be sadistic if I took pleasure in it. Which I do not. I am virtually alone here. I fight my enemies as I see fit, by any means at my disposal. And fear is the greatest weapon I have.'

Fauvre nodded to his staff, who tipped the basket of rotting fruit. The men below scrambled for the scraps. Clearly they had not eaten for some time.

Despite his feelings, Max knew Laurent Fauvre was a vital link in helping uncover Zabala's mystery. The information had to be dug out of this man, but he was afraid that it might prove more difficult than excavating one of these craters from the rock face. What Max needed was something explosive to tear Fauvre open.

'Did your wife die here?'

That got through, Max could see Fauvre's jaw clench. His mouth pulled down as if he'd bitten into a sour lime.

'Is that what my daughter told you – that my wife died?'

Now it was Max's turn to try and hide his shock. Fauvre was hitting back just as hard. Max nodded.

'My daughter lives in a fantasy world. Do not believe anything she tells you.'

Trust no one! Max's mind yelled at him.

'My wife went off with another man when my back was broken. I lay helpless and she ran off. It's the law of the jungle, Max. Nature always wins in the end.'

'And your son? Did he continue to run the circus?' Max was grasping for any thread of truth that might help him – anything that stopped the gnawing doubt about Sophie.

'My daughter has a deep-seated anger because I trusted a wild animal and barely escaped with my life. She blames me for everything – even her mother abandoning us. So she seeks danger and, along the way, someone she can love, like a brother, and who can protect her. Perhaps you are that person.'

Max winced.

'Then Adrien is dead?'

'Sophie went to Zabala because he had information about the animal smugglers – and something else that was important, I don't know what. I argued with her, but she was determined to go. She defied me at every turn.' Fauvre hesitated. 'Do you really want to know the truth?'

Max felt a sudden desperation. The truth? That always hurts.

'I do not have a son, Max. He is a figment of Sophie's imagination.'

Like a solid punch, the words shattered him. Everything was a lie. He felt as though he were going down. *Focus! Who are these crazy people? Don't give in!* He fought the nausea, wiped the sweat from his eyes and steadied himself against the wall. If Fauvre knew about his daughter's emotional instability, did he suspect anything worse of her? Could she have killed Zabala? Was she so determined to gain the secret information Max now held? Jumbled, erratic, nonsensical thoughts blustered through his mind like the desert sirocco wind, suffocating rational thought. *Must think straight. Have to shake off this fever.*

Fauvre had a mean streak in him, Max could see that. He cared little for others' feelings, even less for anyone who got in the way of his animals' welfare. Sympathy welled in him. Sophie needed help. There seemed to be no doubt she had emotional problems.

'Now,' Fauvre said quietly, 'why don't we stop playing games? My daughter is only a small part of this. Arab culture demands honour from a host towards his guest. Even an enemy under your roof is accorded the privilege of safety. But I am not Moroccan.'

Max wanted to run right then. But he could feel the strength seeping out of his body. *Tough it out!* Fauvre stared at him, his voice sombre and authoritative.

'I want to know why you are here. What it is you hope to gain. What you think is hidden here. You wear my friend's pendant. As far as I am concerned, there is enough evidence to convince me that you could have murdered Brother Zabala.'

Max's head spun. The fever gripped him.

Fauvre's men had turned and stood ready to do as he commanded. Aladfar roared and the vibration shuddered through the dry, hot air. A snarl exposed the curved canines

– those jaws would crush and those teeth would rip. Max glanced nervously down. It wouldn't take much to be thrown over the edge. The tiger would kill him in seconds.

Fauvre stared hard at Max. 'You have already absolved me of my debt. So why should I not avenge my friend and let nature take its course?'

19

In the Bible, Daniel went into the lions' den and calmed the beasts by his faith. Angelo Farentino had been told that story as a child, but every time his mother took him to the zoo he would look at those ferocious animals and know in his heart he would end up in their stomachs. He would have liked to think that she would die of grief because he had been eaten by lions, but, remembering his mother and the stick she beat him with, he knew it would be shame that killed her. Her son was eaten because he had insufficient faith!

Thankfully, Farentino had never had to put himself to the test and his mother was now an old crone who sat outside her house in the Italian village where she was born and still lived, shouting at stray dogs. She also moaned continually to the neighbours about how her son had abandoned her. They would commiserate. Children of today, what do you do with them? they would say, shaking their heads and occasionally spitting in the gutter to express their disapproval.

Farentino did not care. He had not been a child for more than thirty-odd years and he did not like his mother. Never had. Filial love was not an obligation he felt inclined to acknowledge. He had made a modest living as a successful publisher, he had spent his money on property and he had prospered. And he had his own faith – in himself and what he could achieve. He knew he had done some good. He had been a good man. Had been.

Helping the environmentalists over the years, he had glowed like an angel. He was righteous. A defender of the Earth's fragile balance. Scientists acknowledged the importance of his publishing house and those who cared about the world flocked to him to write about how this beautiful planet was being ripped apart by carnivorous men who had their eyes only on power, profit and sometimes madness.

And then he stopped being good.

He had taken the other side's money. Now he drove a Ferrari, had a villa on Lake Geneva, hideaway homes around the world and – most preciously – he had anonymity. False identities were bought and wealth was his joy. He had been safe. Until Fedir Tishenko summoned him. Now Angelo Farentino was stepping into the lion's den.

And Max Gordon's father was the lion.

The receptionist at St Christopher's made a phone call, then smiled and asked him to wait a few moments. He waited, nerves jangling. He calmed himself. Always find the positives, Farentino told himself. In less than fifteen or so minutes after seeing Tom Gordon he would get back in the car, return to Switzerland, report to the man who had threatened to expose him to his enemies and then slip away into anonymity again. Who cared what his visit might do to Tom Gordon's mind, or whether his son was targeted by Tishenko? The wonderful thing about being corrupt is that it takes away any sense of guilt. You are wicked and you know it. You have no morals and you don't care. You can cause grief and misery and turn a blind eye.

It was a lifestyle choice, Farentino decided.

'Mister Aldo, would you like to come this way?'

It took Farentino a second to respond to the false name he had given. A big man stood in the doorway; it was he who had spoken.

'I'm Marty Kiernan. I work on Mister Gordon's wing.' He extended his left hand.

Farentino hesitated, his right hand already reaching forward. He quickly corrected himself, but felt embarrassed by his social clumsiness. He should have noticed the man's disability, anticipated the gesture and reacted accordingly. He must be more rattled than he realized.

Marty's strides were twice those of most men and Farentino found himself awkwardly trying to keep up. Two strides to the big man's one. He felt like a child. Was there any way Tom Gordon could have seen through his request for an interview and his claim to be working for an Italian newspaper? Could he have known that Aldo was a false name and told this giant? Humiliation of an enemy is an old trick. Rattle your opponent's composure, put him on his back foot, take the advantage. This was a very bad idea, coming here. Angelo Farentino was not someone who should be placed under such duress. He craved a cigar. He could smell the delicate aroma of the Cuban Monte Cristo in the case tucked into his inside pocket. But regulations meant he could not smoke inside St Christopher's.

'How is Mister Gordon?' he asked Marty, anxious to stem his nervousness.

Marty opened a swing door and guided Farentino through into a corridor where white-painted, solid-wood doors with small brass name plates on them lined their route. The names gave no clue to the rank or status of the patients in each of those rooms.

'If you don't mind my saying so – I don't think it was a good idea you coming here,' Marty said quietly.

Farentino's heart sank. They knew! They KNEW! He looked for a fire exit. His step faltered, he wanted to run, was ready to surrender every last vestige of dignity. Farentino had always had a plan B. There was always a way of avoiding the net of authority – or the threat of personal revenge. Not this time. Tishenko had placed him squarely in harm's way. Thoughts flitted through his mind. The public humiliation of a trial, the stench of a British jail – the prison uniform! Where was it written that men incarcerated should have to wear such ill-fitting clothes?

With amazing calmness, Farentino looked into Marty's eyes. 'Why do you say that, Mister Kiernan?'

The big man had stopped outside one of the doors. The small brass plate had Tom Gordon's name inscribed on it. Marty's hand was on the doorknob.

'You'll see,' Marty said, and opened the door.

The lion's den.

Several hundred kilometres lay between Biarritz and Switzerland and Sharkface's gang took their time. They had driven Bobby's van at exactly or just below the speed limit. They didn't want to attract the attention of any bored traffic cops.

During the long night Sayid had lain in the back, still trussed up. Despite the cold nibbling at his fingers, he was grateful they had tied his hands in front of him. The passing glare of the yellow motorway lights was the only means by which he could see to scribble. He knew that as the tiring journey went on his mind might lose the numbers from the magic square that he had memorized. The violence and kidnapping had exhausted him and he would not be able to fight the tiredness that insisted he drift into a deep sleep. The only way he could attempt to solve the puzzle of what the numbers might mean was to write them down and play around with the sequence. If Max was correct and the boxed numbers held a secret message, there had to be something that would unlock the numbers' mystery and meaning. But every time Sayid tried to get in a position where he could begin writing out any sequences, one of the thugs always turned and checked what he was doing. How long could he stay awake? If he slept his mind might erase the numbers like a worn-out hard drive.

He had bunched his knees, turning his back towards the two thugs in the front of the van. Bobby was wedged more than he was and seemed to slip in and out of sleep. His injuries must have taken their toll, Sayid realized. One of Bobby's surfboards was strapped to the side of the van at floor level and Sayid had managed, over time, to edge himself closer. Now he could use his tied hands, his back to the driver, to write, in a tiny sequence, the numbers in his head. Sayid figured nobody would ever spot such a tiny scrawl, even in daylight, and besides there would be no interest in any of the kit Bobby had stashed in the van. Sayid concentrated. First line across of the magic square: 11, 24, 7, 20, 3; then down the left-hand side of the square: 11, 4, 17, 10, 23. Those were Sayid's memory triggers. Once they were in place he filled out the square.

This was his way of backing up his mental hard drive. He curled on to his arm. The numbers he'd written on his boot were there when he needed them, but for now he felt confident enough to sleep. He had to be as fresh as possible when he awoke.

Which he did after what felt like seconds, in reality an hour, when the van's engine spluttered. The driver cursed, glanced in his wing mirror and nursed the van along a few hundred more metres. Sayid could see the dull blink of the indicator light from the dashboard. The thug in the passenger seat pointed out something to the driver and Sayid felt a rumble as the tyres made contact with the verge. Less than a minute later the van slowed, then stopped. The two men got out. The side panel door slid open and one of the thugs clambered inside. Sayid looked away, not wanting to make eye contact with him. Sharkface's henchman kicked Bobby.

'Get up! What's wrong with this thing?'

Bobby's eyes opened; he seemed groggy. 'It's OK. I know how to fix it. It's a filter in the injector. Happens all the time.'

'Then get out!'

The man turned and stepped out of the van as Bobby, trussed up like Sayid, shuffled, got to his knees, braced his back against the van's side, pushing himself on to his feet. As he straightened upwards he whispered to Sayid. Bobby was alert, his grogginess a sham.

'Sayid, I'm gonna make a run for it if I get the chance. You OK with that?'

The thought hit Sayid like a thump on the head. To lose Bobby? To be alone? He realized that even though the American had barely moved for the last few hours the fact that they were together meant so much to him. A desperate loneliness surged through him. But he nodded. Of course. One of them had to make a break for it if they could.

'I'll get help, pal. I promise. And Peaches knows nothin', so they won't hurt her. I saw her in the other van.'

'I can help,' Sayid heard himself say, suddenly afraid of what he was about to suggest.

Bobby frowned.

'A diversion,' Sayid whispered.

'Hey! Get out now! C'mon!' the thug shouted. Some kind of Eastern European accent slowing his speech.

Bobby nodded at Sayid. 'Way to go, kid. But not too soon. Gimme time,' Bobby whispered as he jumped out of the van.

'I need a loo break,' Sayid called. 'It's been hours. Please.'

He heard his captors muttering and then the one who had clambered inside reached back in and snatched at Sayid, pulling him roughly towards the night air. He sat on the rim of the step, quickly orienting himself. They had pulled into a raised stopover area, like a picnic site – benches and tables and a small brick building which was the toilet block. At weekends this spot would have had long-distance travellers using it for a break, but now there was no one in sight except this killing crew. Their vans had pulled in behind Bobby's. He could see Sharkface sitting in front of one and he said something to someone behind him. The door slid open and a third man joined Bobby's van drivers.

Bobby had already popped the bonnet.

'I need my hands for this, unless you want diesel all over the place,' he said, offering his bound wrists to one of the men.

The man took out a knife and cut through the tape, then stepped back, watching Bobby as he dipped his head into the engine.

'And I need light in here. C'mon, guys, we're not all creatures of the night who can see in the dark.'

The man with the knife nodded to another, who found a torch in the cab and moved close to Bobby, shining it on to the engine. The other men stayed in the vans. Too many people milling around might draw attention; a broken-down van with a couple of people attending to it was less interesting.

One of the thugs hauled Sayid to his feet. His foot hurt and he hobbled. The man loosened his grip. 'I'm not carrying you, so hurry up.'

Sayid limped towards the toilet block, his eyes scanning the row of vans, the black strip of tarmac and the yellow glare of motorway lights. There wasn't much traffic, but there was a meridian barrier. Beyond that, across the other lanes, the land fell away into the darkness of trees and the countryside beyond. That's where Bobby would run, he was sure of it.

Sayid looked back to the vans. They had let Peaches out to stretch her legs. She wore jeans and a ski jacket, and hugged herself against the damp chill. Coldness or fear? Sayid stopped, leaned against a table to rest his leg, his guard a few paces away. Would Peaches run for it with Bobby when she saw him make his bid for freedom? Between the three of them maybe they could stop a car, or at least cause enough fuss to raise the alarm.

If only he could catch her eye. He would just nod. A simple nod and a smile, maybe. Just to let her know she mustn't be afraid.

Not as afraid as Sayid felt.

Fear. Flight or fight? Stand your ground and dig deeply into your own resources. Banish the panic. Pray – that was the best option. Farentino had discovered a new faith within the last few moments and he promised he would visit his mother, make a large donation to a charity and never again be so stupid as to do anything a man as crazy as Tishenko demanded.

The room was large and comfortably furnished, like an old country hotel. There was a single bed, an en-suite bathroom, a desk scattered with papers and notebooks, and through the French windows that led to a patio, Farentino could see the parkland gardens extending as far as the walled estate permitted.

Tom Gordon sat on a wooden patio chair. He was dressed as Farentino had often seen him – beige trousers, long-sleeved, heavy cotton shirt and boots. Even now the man did not seem to mind the chilled air. Farentino did not move, because Tom Gordon had not broken his gaze. His eyes held him. This was the moment of recognition when Gordon would be on him like an unleashed animal. He doubted that even the big man next to him would be quick enough to prevent the serious injury that seemed about to be inflicted.

Tom Gordon stood and took the few strides towards him.

He extended his hand. 'Mister Aldo, I hope you'll forgive me, but I can't remember your newspaper.'

Angelo Farentino immediately doubled the amount he would give to charity. Relief swept through him like a wildfire being chased by a hurricane. All doubt and fear incinerated.

Farentino sat close to Tom Gordon on the patio and looked into his eyes, searching for the most fleeting recognition. 'Do you not remember me, Tom?'

Tom Gordon waited a moment. The man looked familiar. Yes, he did know him. But from where and when? He shook his head. 'I'm sorry, Mister Aldo, my memory plays tricks on me.'

'That's all right. We used to work together.' Farentino felt a twinge of regret as he heard his own words. 'We were very close friends.'

He looked at the man he'd once considered as close as a brother, but who became someone he bitterly resented. All because a woman had come between them.

Tom Gordon nodded. 'I'm sure it'll come back to me. So, you wanted to ask me some questions for your newspaper. I'll do my best to help answer them for you.'

Farentino settled in his chair, relaxed, in control again. He would find out whatever he could and then report to Tishenko. Life was on an even keel again. He need not waste money on the charity after all, nor go and see his pinch-faced mother.

He smiled. 'Tom, would you mind if I smoked a cigar?'

20

The power of a tiger's roar stuns its victim, shocking it into immobility, allowing the biggest feline predator in the world vital seconds to attack. Max saw the snarl and felt the air tremble. He faltered, his legs gave way beneath him and he slumped against the low parapet as the fever leached his energy.

How could he defend himself? The men could kill him right now.

He was losing consciousness, the force of it drowning him in a flood of helplessness.

'*Ez ihure ere fida – eheke hari ere*,' he said, as quickly as reciting a mantra. A desperate means of reaching out to the old monk's friend.

Fauvre realized in that instant that Max had uttered words only Zabala could have willingly given him. Max fell to the ground. The men reached forward to help him in response to Fauvre's shouted commands.

Max tumbled into darkness. Tendrils of fear and pain snagged him, prickling like a thousand scorpion stings. His mind plummeted down a heat-enraged tunnel. The conflict in his body a battlefield.

'Careful!' Fauvre shouted at the men.

The boy was having some kind of fit; they couldn't hold him. The monkey bite must have been infected, the injections given too late. Max was thrashing around like a madman. But his eyes were wide open and his lips pulled back in a terrifying silent scream.

Sweat poured off him, his shirt clinging to his body as if he'd just dragged himself out of a river – a river of turmoil. From the shadows of his mind, Fauvre appeared, a giant of strength, not the old man in a wheelchair. He was reaching for Max. His voice did not match the image. 'Let me help you, boy. Let me help you!'

And like a child lost in a violent sea, Max knew he wanted to be helped. But not by the man who had threatened to take his life. He twisted and rolled, falling away from the outstretched hands.

'My God!' Fauvre cried.

Max tumbled over the low parapet. Slithering down the smooth-edged walls, his unconscious body flopped and rolled until it finally slumped on to the ground. That final impact penetrated his mind. He groaned.

Someone was shouting in the background. Where? He opened his eyes. The back of his head was resting against the sloping pit. Faces peered over, mouthing words in Arabic. He heard a few of them, understood none, except one – Aladfar!

Pushing through his grogginess Max managed to roll on to his knees, and tried to find the energy to push himself up. Half turning, he saw the slow, deliberate tread of the tiger, its paws the size of dinner plates, its head slung low,

282

its unwavering gaze locked on its prey as it stalked forward.

Fauvre looked on in horror. The tiger would strike any second. The boy would be torn apart and he would be responsible. The boy had been sent by Zabala – that was now obvious – but his only chance for survival was if the male tiger responded to Fauvre's commands.

'Aladfar! Back! *Ecoutez-vous!* Listen to me! *Ecoutez!*'

What happened next was uncertain. Fauvre believed the animal stopped, gazed up into his face and lay down submissively, keeping its eyes on Max. The Berber keepers later told Abdullah another story. They were looking down into the unlit shadows of the pit and could see the boy. He had rolled clear, was half obscured by a jagged tongue of rock face, but stood up. His hands opened like claws at waist height, the sunlight changed, the shadows moved. The one man swore Max's body curved like an animal, his teeth bared and his body became bigger – on the grave of his beloved mother, he swore to Abdullah that he had witnessed *djinn*, an earth-bound spirit that can assume animal form. The other argued it was a shadow that loomed up near the boy when the sun caught the old rooftops and that is when Aladfar lay down. The size of the shadow and the fact the boy took a step towards him made the big cat cautious. No one, not even Fauvre, had ever challenged Aladfar in a direct confrontation.

The tiger saw only the boy, bigger than a goat, but an easy kill. The smell of fear from the two other men held captive behind those bars had alerted his senses. And he was hungry. When the boy-creature fell he could have pounced, but a voice carried on the air. It was the old man, but Aladfar, cat-like, would always choose when to defer to man's commands. He lifted his head not because of the old man's demanding voice but because another scent filled his nostrils. Animal. A beast he had known in some previous time when he had the freedom of the mountains and jungles. Aladfar feared nothing except the violence of man, and even then he would attack if forced to. But this defenceless creature evoked energies that were beyond understanding; a time remembered from the forests and mountains; a primeval force which spoke only to Aladfar's sixth sense.

He would wait, as his instincts told him. So he lay down.

Fauvre wasted no time. He drove his wheelchair down the ramp, opened the iron gate and went into the enclosure. He spoke softly to his tiger, soothed its passion until he was close enough to reach out and stroke its head. Aladfar knew the gentle touch and the smell of the old man. He stood up. Fauvre, sitting in his wheelchair, barely came to the tiger's shoulder.

The privilege of being so close, so intimate, with the true king of the jungle always affected Fauvre. 'I know you are the greatest beast in the world, my Aladfar, but we must not let this boy die,' he whispered, stroking the great cat's ruff, nurturing the animal's instincts.

Fauvre had left his fear in the circus ring all those years ago, when Aladfar punished him for his human arrogance. Now he felt only a deep love for the huge animal. Gently, ever so gently, he turned the big cat away, guiding him to the passageway that led to a locked cage.

Settled by the gentle vibrations of the old man's voice and

the uncertainty of the boy who had not yet moved, Aladfar allowed the man he had once mauled to close the gate on him. The tiger lay down and purred.

Fauvre turned back to Max, gesturing his keepers to enter what was now a safe pit and help the boy. By the time they got there Fauvre had moved closer. Max still stood, his eyes still open, a look of stone-set determination on his face, as if he drew energy from some deep recess of his brain.

Once again Fauvre spoke softly, as if to a wild animal. 'Max, it is all right now. You will not be harmed. I promise you. Can you hear me, boy?'

Fauvre heard the two men approach cautiously behind him and raised a hand to stop them. No one should approach a wild animal in fear of its life. For in that moment Fauvre, sensing the same energy Aladfar had, believed that is what he was witnessing.

Max blinked, looked at Fauvre, nodded and sat, slumping back into unconsciousness. At last the men could approach and lifted him out of the enclosure. Abdullah and Sophie had heard the shouts of alarm and reached Aladfar's pit as the men brought him clear. Abdullah took him in his arms and carried him to his tent. Sophie, running ahead, gathered the medicines her father had instructed her to fetch. She returned to find her father checking Max's pulse and Abdullah bathing the boy's face. They had laid him in the near darkness, where the air was cooled by the layers of the tent.

'It's more than the infection. Something else is going on inside of him. If the fever breaks in the next few hours he'll live,' Fauvre said.

'We need a doctor,' Sophie said.

Fauvre opened the medical bag Sophie had brought him. 'By the time he gets here his presence will not be required. For one reason or another,' he said, preparing another injection. 'He will have recovered or he will be dead.'

'We should try!' Sophie said impatiently.

Abdullah touched her shoulder. 'Sophie, there is a dust storm coming. No doctor would risk it.'

The injection administered, Fauvre nodded, satisfied he had done all he could do for now. 'Keep him cool, bathe his face, try and get him to drink as much water as he can. Can you do that?' he said to Sophie.

She knew her father was giving her responsibility for Max's nursing. She nodded. Fauvre turned away, beckoning Abdullah to join him. Sophie squeezed out the wet cloth and mopped the sweat from Max's forehead. She put her face close to his, trying to imagine what was happening inside this boy, whose lips trembled and who groaned quietly as the fever took him. Her fingers touched the knotted cord around his neck and felt the dull stone trapped in the pendant's grip. It was only after her father and Abdullah had left that she noticed they had tied his wrists to the bed frame.

Over the next few hours, as Sophie sat with Max, Fauvre nursed his own thoughts. Months ago Zabala had entrusted a package to him, to be opened only when another was delivered. Or when – as Zabala believed to be inevitable – he was killed. Fauvre had followed his friend's instructions, but the drawings in the thick brown envelope showed nothing more than an astrologer's prediction twenty-odd years ago – the very thing that had caused Zabala's downfall. Old business that had cursed a man's life. Why the hell hadn't Zabala forgotten all this nonsense? It had been such a waste of his abilities.

Fauvre sipped a cognac, his old friend on his mind. The ridicule Zabala had faced all those years ago had sent him on another of life's journeys, a passage of time dedicated to two things: helping Fauvre relocate some of the endangered animals and uncovering the Truth. That word, that deceptive, irritating word, which held so many meanings to different people, was always written by Zabala with a capital T. Exposing the Truth was the monk's ultimate aim, because it would vindicate his theories and – as he had always insisted – stop a massive disaster from striking Europe. Madness. An incomprehensible event dreamed up by a discredited scientist.

When Zabala had sent word those few weeks ago that he had information about the animal smugglers, the 'Truth', this secret, was never disclosed.

Fauvre could not go to the Pyrenees himself, but Zabala had insisted that this information was crucial, it had to be put together with those documents Fauvre already held. The monk had planned to bring it to Fauvre himself, but he was convinced he was being watched. Zabala feared for his life. Only months ago a friend had betrayed him. The killers were closing in.

Fauvre wanted that secret. He wanted to grasp the madness that had driven his friend for so many years. And now Max Gordon had appeared – the messenger delivering the package? Which was what? What had Zabala told him? Somehow the boy had been given enough information to reach the very place Zabala had intended – here. The old monk had given him the ultimate warning in a language so few could speak. There was no doubt, Max Gordon held the key to the Truth.

The weight of the sickness drifted away from Max's body; his youthful strength had fought and won, but the healing sleep kept him locked deep in darkness. More time was needed before his body would be capable of following commands from his mind.

Sophie had left the tent when his fever broke; now she returned, slipping quietly between the wind-flapping folds of the tent. Checking his temperature, she laid a hand on his cool forehead. Her father could return at any moment to see his patient, and with the leading edge of the dust storm splattering sand against the walls, it would be sooner rather than later. It was time to do what she must.

She gazed at Max for a second longer, a look of both regret and tenderness. 'It's almost over,' she whispered.

With almost surgical skill she laid a razor-sharp knife next to the slowly pulsing jugular vein that carried his life's vital blood supply.

She kissed his forehead.

The blade cut.

Sayid knew Bobby would make his break for freedom at any moment. The American had taken his time stripping out the diesel van's faulty injector and their captors had relaxed their guard. Earlier, one of the older men who Sayid had seen fixing the damaged bikes at the industrial estate nodded as he checked Bobby's progress. The kid knew what he was doing, so why should *he* do the job? he had asked Sharkface. The broken-toothed killer turned to Peaches, said something to her, and she climbed into the back of the van. Then he got back into the passenger seat. Sayid didn't want to look too long at the killer in case those dead eyes read his thoughts.

The others had found somewhere to sit. One of them had clambered back into Bobby's van. Sayid had begged to be allowed to sit out at the picnic table bench, wanting the cold night air rather than the confined box of the van – besides, he was hardly going to escape, was he?

Sayid couldn't concentrate on the numbers in his head, his heart beat too quickly – anticipating the moment Bobby might make his break. Sayid had worked out that if he stumbled and fell down the grassy incline from where he now sat, that might distract a couple of the thugs. One might even run towards him, away from Bobby, though he hoped it wouldn't earn him a beating.

Watch Bobby.

Wait for a glance. A nod. Anything.

Peaches stepped out of Sharkface's van again. She had a mobile phone. Why? Sharkface must have given her instructions to phone someone. Who? It had to be Sophie. That was it. Sharkface had told her to phone Sophie, pretending everything was all right, and if Sophie answered they might find out where she was in Morocco – and where Sophie was, so was Max. No. That didn't add up. Sophie had told him that she had dumped her mobile after those men in Biarritz had followed her. He watched Peaches. Now she thumbed a text message. For all Sayid knew, she had convinced Sharkface that she had wealthy parents who would pay a ransom for her. Or maybe Bobby's family. Whatever the reason, it made no difference now. Bobby was bent over the engine, his right hand reaching for a spanner. It fell from the van's bodywork. Bobby's head was still looking down into the engine when Sayid heard him mutter.

'Damn. Get that for me, would you?'

Without thinking, the thug who held the torch did the most natural thing in the world and bent down. And that's when Sayid cried out and threw himself down the slope – the second before Bobby lashed out and kicked the thug flying.

As Sayid rolled and tumbled, kaleidoscope images blurred his vision.

Bobby ran, the kicked boy staggered, van doors yanked open and Sharkface screamed commands, spittle flying from his mouth. He pointed at Bobby's dark form as it ran beneath the lights' yellow glare, and then at Sayid, who was now almost at the end of his fall. One man ran towards him; others burst away from the vans, scattering like a net cast outwards from a fisherman's hands to snare the escaping prey.

Peaches ran towards Sayid.

'Don't! Leave me! Run!' Sayid screamed.

But it was too late. The man got to him first, yanked him to his feet and slapped him hard across the back of his head. The impact sent Sayid spinning. Flashes of light and dark scattered across his eyes. The blow momentarily deafened him. He saw Peaches shout at the man and then she ran for the road.

Go for it, Peaches!

Cotton-wool silence in his ears suddenly popped clear as the thugs screamed instructions to each other. The last glimpse he had of Bobby was of the wetsuited figure limping from his previous injuries, but running as hard as he could for the possible safety of the treeline across the far carriageway.

Then a sickening sound came out of the night. Car tyres locked in a terrifying skid. Tortured rubber compound tore from the treads. Shouts mingled, headlights skewered the yellow glare – a car spun out of control, its driver attempting to avoid Sharkface's men on the road.

Moments later a stomach-churning thump.

A body was hit.

Metal screamed. Glass smashed.

Silence.

Sayid watched as some of the gang ran to the damaged car. Sharkface ignored the slumped driver behind the wheel and ran back twenty metres. Peaches leaned into the wreck as two of Sharkface's men helped ease the driver to his feet. The man was alive, groggy on his feet; then he collapsed.

Sayid's eyes picked out Sharkface and the others. They bent over a body on the grassy verge. A black-clad body.

And then they turned away.

'Bobby!' Sayid screamed into the night.

Sullen faces turned towards him. Sharkface and his men ran back towards the vans. Sayid was thrown into the surfer's van. The door slammed closed. A jumble of voices outside. A minute's worth of spanners being used. The bonnet slammed. The engine started – the thugs were back in charge.

The van rumbled across the verge, rolling Sayid against the walls. Fear coiled around him – a snake squeezing the life from his lungs.

Max. Help me. Please.

Think, Sayid! Think! Another part of his brain shouted back, ridiculing his silent cries for help.

What was it? What didn't fit? What had he seen?

The car's lights – whipping out of control.

The gut-churning impact.

The crash – slow motion.

Bobby lying dead or injured. Sharkface shouting to the others. Everyone running back to the vans. The gang running back to the vans . . . the gang running . . . the gang and Peaches running back to the van.

And that's when Sayid knew what was so terribly wrong.

21

The sandstorm's ferocity was not as violent at this time of year, so it did not scour the soul of anyone caught unaware. The dust swirled, bending heads, covering eyes, a shield behind which enemies could hide. And Max Gordon's enemies were close.

Dark-eyed, blue-skinned men who lived in the wilderness, whose ancestors fought vicious and brutal battles and who still lived by these skills, crept closer to the town's walls. There were still places a 4x4 could not go as easily as a horse and as the sand buffeted the town's walls, half a dozen of these desert warriors threw covers across their horses' eyes and muzzles. Their own turbans, several metres of blue gauze wound across their faces, not only kept the sand from penetrating their mouth and nostrils but also, according to their beliefs, kept evil spirits from entering their body.

Their grappling hooks snared the walls. While two men held the horses' reins, four of the blue-skinned warriors began to climb.

Fauvre's concern lay not only with the fever-stricken boy but also with Aladfar, who had been forgotten in the turmoil and was still caged. As he turned his wheelchair on to the ramp that would take him down to the tiger's pit, he saw the dust clouds take the edge off the stars as the first wave of sand spilled over the town walls.

Out of the blurred night, ropes dropped down; the wind caught the intruders' billowing robes. Fauvre knew these assassins would have struggled to scale the height of the walls and their intense determination meant they were here to kill.

The big cat was already on its feet as Fauvre hurriedly unlocked Aladfar's pen. He took the length of chain hanging on a hook and whispered a soothing murmur to the tiger. Clipping the snap-hook to Aladfar's collar, he turned the wheelchair and urged the beast on.

The tiger's sharpened senses picked up on his old master's urgency. It was as Fauvre hoped – the loping tiger could easily pull him along faster than he could move under his own power.

'On, Aladfar, on. You can save us all. *Très bien, mon ami.* Well done. That's it, faster.'

The distant figures separated, quartering the town – searching. Fauvre saw they were armed, some with rifles, others with AK47s. They stopped, knelt down in the sand and pulled something that looked like a short pole which had been secured to each man's back. A moment later small flames licked the end of these sticks – tar-soaked rags, which then burned fiercely. Fauvre knew why no ordinary torch beams cut through the night; these flames would offer some protection against Fauvre's wild animals.

By now Fauvre and Aladfar had reached the wall of the building where he had treated Max. His fingers scrambled for the wall switch's cover, but Aladfar's strength tipped him from his wheelchair. The tiger was pulling him away from the alarm button.

He let the chain's leather handle go, saw Aladfar lope into the night and crawled towards the wall. Arms outstretched, he managed to reach the windowsill, his back and arm muscles powering his lower body upwards, and in a desperate lunge reached for the switch.

The side of his fist hit the knurled red button and a slow moaning wail began to fill the night air. Within seconds the old air-raid alarm siren howled at full volume.

Max sat bolt upright. Released from the deepest of sleeps, he felt as if he'd been given an intravenous drip from a bottomless well of nature's energy.

Canvas flapped, a gritty scuttering of dirt rasped across the roof and somewhere in the night a tiger roared. He instinctively raised his hands to his throat. The pendant was missing. Max saw the frayed rope on his wrists – he had been tied but someone had cut him free and sliced through the pendant's cord.

As the siren wailed Max was already out of the tent. A veil of sand swept away from the starlit sky, the swirling dust shifting as quickly as it had arrived. Fire singed the darkness – he counted three, no, four men with burning torches. Men with blue turbans wrapped around their faces. An orange blur, the perfect camouflage, streaked across the shadows. Aladfar! Was that why the siren's cacophony deafened him, because the tiger was loose? No! Those Arabs were armed. This was an attack.

Max ran hard across the compound towards Fauvre's quarters. The intruders searched buildings quickly and thoroughly, one of them headed for the tents. Straight towards Max. The man's strength was apparent and Max would be hard-pressed to fight on the warrior's terms. He sidestepped, ran across the edge of a parapet, the pack of Ethiopian wolves swirling below in the pit's shadows like piranhas in a dark river. The man followed him, matching his sure-footedness pace for pace. He tossed the flaming torch into the wolves' enclosure, scaring them into a frenzy, perhaps hoping to unnerve the boy a few metres ahead of him, who now kicked dust, leapt on to a two-metre-high concrete drainage pipe, ran to its end and jumped on to a steel girder that lay across old rusted cars. Hard physical demands of desert living made the chase easy. He would take the boy in another half-dozen strides. Sweat moistened the palm of his hand, making the sword's handle slippery. He could unsling the assault rifle and shatter him with a burst of gunfire, but any warrior of the desert would rather kill by the sword. He tightened his grip.

Max heard the powerful man pounding across the dirt behind him. He had deliberately slowed, as if faltering, wanting the man's thundering energy to help defeat him. The warrior couldn't help but let out a cry of victory as he lunged right behind Max, the sword making a lethal whisper through the air. Max spun, leapt for one of the rusting girders, felt the coarse metal under his grip and swung his body to one side. The man's downward slash tipped him off balance and, as he fell forward, the sword smashed into the old car. As steel met steel, the warrior's blade snapped. His shoulder took the brunt of the impact as he fell and for a moment he lay stunned.

Max wasted no time. Using the girder as a back brace, he kicked a nearby oil drum on to the man. He heard a grunt, saw the man slump, but then get quickly to his knees.

And all Max could see were his eyes, wild with hatred and anger. The slap of flesh against metal was audible as the warrior pulled the AK47 into his hands. Max dived, full length, away from the man into the dirt on the other side of the wrecked car as a roar of gunfire shattered through the sound of the siren. Clanging ricochets screeched as bullets slammed into the steel beam where Max had been seconds earlier.

As Max hit the ground, he took the impact on the palms of his hands, curled his body, tucked in his neck and rolled into the dirt, twisting and squirming as fast as he could towards another wrecked car that stood on blocks. He caught a glimpse of the warrior holding the gun above his head and firing wildly over the top of the car that momentarily stopped him from chasing Max. But then he saw the man clamber across the bonnet.

Max was boxed in. With no other option, he dived head first into the car, knowing the man would spray it with gunfire. Mind blurred, ears ringing from the gunfire and siren, he felt himself fall into the carcass. There was no escape now.

A chattering thunder shattered metal, punching holes into the old car, the bullets' mushrooming impact scattering lethal shards as the bodywork punctured. The man kept on coming, kept on firing, a stalking assault to murder the boy.

The metallic screams stopped when he ceased firing and stood, weapon still at the ready, gazing through the gunfire's smoke that clung to him. He peered forward, looking for the bloody remains of his victim. But the wreck was empty. There was nothing inside. No floor pan, no steering wheel, just a hulk.

He didn't hear the scuff of dirt behind him, but he felt the sudden agony as a scaffolding pole was slammed against his back, and then, as he fell to his knees, the realization flashed into his mind that the boy had rolled clear beneath the wreck and got behind him. Max hit him again – a baseball-bat swing that clipped the man's turban and floored him. At last the man went down and stayed down.

He ran back towards the buildings. Fauvre lay in the dirt, pushing with all his strength to right the overturned wheelchair. Max had never felt fitter or stronger. Righting the battery-powered wheelchair, he grabbed the man under his arms and dragged him into the seat.

'Aladfar is loose!' Fauvre gasped.

'I saw him. But these men . . .'

'Tuareg!'

Max had heard of them. Horsemen warriors, old enemies of the French colonial powers and the Foreign Legion, they had a fearsome reputation. Known as the Blue People – their skin stained by the indigo dye used to colour their *ghandouras*, traditional robes worn over white kaftans – their faces and heads swirled by black or blue turbans. The blue dye soaks into the skin, giving them protection against the desert heat, locking in the body's moisture. And gave the warriors a wild-eyed ferocity that could chill the bravest of men.

'Behind you!' Fauvre yelled.

One of the Tuareg had run around the edge of the building,

the flaming torch alerting Fauvre before the man stepped into view. There was no time to think. Max reacted immediately as the warrior attacked without warning. The building held straw and hay bales; Max grabbed the nearest weapon he could find – a pitchfork. The warrior slashed the flaming torch across him with one hand while reaching for the AK47 slung on his back. Within seconds his free hand had brought it to bear. Max had escaped one assault rifle attack, but there was no protection where he stood now. And Fauvre was helpless.

No time to be squeamish – Max lunged, aiming for the man's arm. The attacker jigged to the left, but one of the pitchfork's tines jammed itself into the end of the gun's barrel. He couldn't shoot now, not without it blowing up in his hands. Max twisted and pushed, felt the gun yank free, but now the pitchfork was useless. The man grunted in disbelief and rage and reached for the curved knife sheathed on his waist, slashing left and right. Max gave ground, desperately trying to stay away from the cold metal that burned blood-red from the reflection of the flaming torch.

Max stumbled and fell – at least that's how it looked to his attacker. Max knew it was difficult to assault a victim who is rolling round on the ground. Denied a slashing attack, the man would have to commit himself to reaching down, to try and stab Max. Which he did. Max swung his right arm in a powerful curving arc and let loose the rock he had snatched up. The blow stunned his attacker, throwing him back on his heels. Losing balance, he thudded into the ground. The burning torch arced away, the knife dropped into the dirt. As Max sprang to his feet, Fauvre had already manoeuvred the wheelchair and caught the groggy man from behind, his muscled arms encircling his throat, choking the air from his lungs. The warrior slumped.

'I'll tie him, Max. You must get away. You must hide. I saw another three men. They have come for you!'

Fauvre was already binding the man's arm, using the length of turban, but no sooner had he warned Max than a whoosh of flames sucked air into the storeroom and spewed out a fireball of burning straw. The attacker's torch had caught the tinder-dry bales.

Max got between Fauvre and the fire, pushing him to safety as another tongue of flame licked out into the night. They beat burning embers from their hair and clothes. Soot streaked Max's face – he looked like a commando on a night raid.

'I can't hide, Laurent. We can beat them! They won't be expecting a fight. Abdullah and his man are here somewhere. We outnumber them.'

Fauvre looked past his shoulder and shouted – a guttural mixture of French and Arabic. Max spun round. Aladfar snarled, his body crouched in fear by the roaring grain store. The mayhem of the night's terrifying sounds of gunfire and the scent that only men give off when they hunt had confused the big cat and he had run back to the only man ever to have commanded him.

Fauvre's extended hand and his words held Aladfar's gaze. Like a domesticated dog, the tiger slunk to the shelter of the stone wall.

'Where's Sophie? Have they taken her?' Max shouted above the roar of the fire.

'I don't know. She could have outrun them.' A father's anguish caught hold. 'Find her, Max!'

Max moved, but not before Fauvre's iron grip caught his arm. Once again the man spoke rapidly to Aladfar. Urged him, caressed him with a language that soothed the animal's fear.

Gunshots and screams, yells of confusion and threats, echoed across the Tears of Angels. Hunting dogs yapped, big cats roared and monkeys screamed as the ear-bashing siren still threw its noise across the desert. Aladfar was on his feet, eyes searching the night, jaws open, panting with excitement. Fauvre reached down and picked up the chain.

'Take him and find my daughter,' he said to Max, pushing the leather grip into his hand.

Max grasped it, as if it were the most natural thing in the world to have a three-hundred-kilogram tiger on the end of a chain in the middle of a night attack by ferocious Tuareg.

The store was an inferno; sparks leapt upwards to join the stars. They coughed from the acrid air. Before Max could answer, Fauvre turned his wheelchair, leaned down and grabbed the warrior's knife.

'I'll get help!' Then he was gone.

Five metres of lightweight chain joined them. Max ran and the chain tightened as Aladfar kept pace with a boy who ran like an animal – a loping gait, nowhere near full stretch, but ready to respond to unexpected danger.

In the flitting shadows Max saw Abdullah fighting one of the Tuareg. The big man grappled with the attacker, grabbed his clothing, lifted and half turned him, then slammed him into the ground – a powerful wrestler's throw that knocked the man unconscious.

Three down – one to go.

He was wrong. The sounds of fighting had reached the remaining two horsemen on the other side of the wall and, as any warrior wants nothing more than to join the conflict, one of them scaled the wall into the compound.

Max and Aladfar ran across a stone causeway, a small bridge that separated different animal pens. A nightmare figure ran screaming at them from the darkness – a shrouded warrior hurling himself forward, a curved sword in one hand, a flaming torch in the other.

Abdullah heard the man's battle cry, turned in alarm and saw the determined attack on Max. His bellowed warning was swallowed by the siren. He had seen another warrior drop down from the wall and cut in from Max's flank, running silently, sword held above his head, ready to slash down and kill.

Max heard a heart-stopping roar. Aladfar attacked, leaping metres towards the first charging warrior. The force of the tiger's lunge pulled Max off balance just as the second man came at him from his blind side.

Thrown on to the ground, Max was twisted around by the tiger's power as he gripped the chain. The sword, a shimmering blur, swung with enough force to sever an arm or leg, smashed into the stony ground. A moment of slow motion saw Aladfar trying to smother and rip the first attacker, but the man had miraculously rolled clear, his clothes shredded, blood running from Aladfar's claws. With a fearful scream he threw himself across the nearest parapet to escape the final killing bite. Max knew the attacker had been lucky more than once. He'd escaped Aladfar and dropped down into the safety of the monkey pit. These images flashed through Max's mind, just as the chain went slack. Aladfar had turned.

302

Another roar.

A bellowing snarl that summoned up every iota of fighting energy.

Fear struck the attacker's eyes. He had time to slash backwards and kill the boy – it was a practised skill – but instead he felt the veil drop from his face, knew that his belief could kill him, because evil would strike into his heart through his exposed mouth and nose. That roar had come from this boy, from this changeling shadow that loomed up before him like a massive creature. Was it the raging fire that distorted everything?

Aladfar scuffed and jigged, wanting to strike for the kill, but the man was being beaten by this other creature that held the chain that bound him. Finally, it was no punch but a sweep of Max's arm that felled the man, and which threw him to the mercy of Aladfar.

The tiger sprang.

Max made a noise, a sound he didn't understand. He had sucked in the night's inferno and turned it into something that resonated with authority and command.

The sixth sense Aladfar had experienced earlier with this boy returned. He backed off, felt the chain tighten – another bond that held him to this creature of the wild.

Max's mouth was as dry as sand. He looked up, taking in the scene around him. He was on his knees, pressing into the unconscious warrior's back, while his hands bound the attacker with the cord that held the man's clothing.

The siren slowed, reluctantly giving way to silence. Max saw Abdullah in the distance, the big man lumbering towards him, dirt and blood streaking his once-spotless djellaba.

Fauvre called out to him as he emerged from the smoke and Abdullah pushed the battery-driven wheelchair towards Max.

'Her room is locked from the outside. She's not here,' Fauvre said.

Animals still chattered and roared, but the stillness gripped Max. He was coming back into the moment, released from the frenetic, adrenalin-saturated fight.

Max lifted his head and stared into the amber eyes of the massive cat, which sat less than two metres away – watching. Slowly, deliberately, it blinked its eyes. A cat's expression of contentment – that all is well.

It was over.

Max, Fauvre and Abdullah, and the other men, felt the aftermath of the fight. Muscles cramped and ached, cuts and scratches irritated. Hot, sweet tea helped ease them into the new day as dawn lit the night sky, the moon giving way to her brother the sun. Minor wounds were treated and the animals calmed, fed and watered, as their routine demanded. Max had washed quickly in a water trough; he needed to talk to Fauvre and look at Sophie's room for any clue as to how involved she might have been in this attack. But first he needed other information – once Fauvre got off the phone.

The police could not reach the town until later that day. The dust storm had blown between it and the city, they were undermanned and it was not the first time the crazy Frenchman had had intruders into his animal sanctuary. They would get there when they could. In the meantime, keep the prisoners under lock and key.

None would speak of why they attacked, but it was obvious to Abdullah, after those others' efforts in Marrakech, that they had been paid to find Max.

And now Sophie was missing.

Not kidnapped, but gone off into the night. Gates for a loading ramp at the far end of the town, once used for bringing in trucks carrying the animals, had been opened – and closed again – and that's where Sophie had driven Abdullah's Land Cruiser. Fauvre had cursed, furious at his daughter's behaviour. The mood swing from being desperately concerned about her during the attack to this condemnation made Max realize just how fickle grown-ups could be. What he didn't tell Fauvre was that she had taken Zabala's pendant. He needed more information first. Fauvre phoned half a dozen people. Contacts at the airports, the banks, anyone who might know where she had run to. He cancelled the credit cards he'd given her and closed her bank account. She would soon turn for home.

Max needed to interrupt Fauvre's anger. 'I've brought this trouble on you, Laurent. I'm sorry for that, but this is connected to Zabala and now to Sophie. What did he send you?'

Fauvre took him down a ramp into what were once the town's dungeons. Fetid air caged the memory of lost souls and dull light bulbs gave a murky glow to what was little more than a tunnel dug from the soft sandstone.

'I always knew that if Zabala was not a crazy man, then what he had sent might be of importance. No one would come down here to search for it,' Fauvre said as he unlocked and pulled open a walk-in safe's door.

The bulky documents, mostly handwritten, were almost

illegible to Max's eye. But when they returned to the brighter light of Fauvre's office and spread the sheets out, it was obvious that the documents were in precise, chronological order – from his earliest investigations, suspicions and theories. They still made little sense, but the photograph and drawings did. And so did Fauvre's explanation.

'I have known Zabala and this man –' he pointed to the photograph that Max had seen before: the gaunt man who stood with Zabala in front of the Château d'Antoine d'Abbadie – 'for nearly thirty years. The man with Zabala was one of his few friends. He betrayed Zabala, who was going to go public with his information. He was determined the world would listen to him this time, but this so-called friend tried to steal the information from him. I don't know what happened to him. He just disappeared.'

Fauvre turned more pages. 'Zabala knew his friend had betrayed him to someone powerful, but did not know who.'

He opened a folded letter and passed it to Max. The scratchy writing was almost frantic in its untidiness. 'He was convinced they would send someone far more lethal after his secret. And before he could get the information to me, the killer struck.'

He shuffled through the documents and laid out the same drawings that Max had found at d'Abbadie's château. The circle, the angles drawn within and the numbers.

'That's a birth chart,' Max said.

'Yes, correct. Do you see this French name on the chart, right here?' Fauvre said.

Max squinted at Zabala's tiny writing. 'Beetle something . . . beetlejuice?'

Fauvre smiled. 'Betelgeuse. It is an enormous red star. Massive. Five hundred times bigger than our sun. History suggests it represents a catalyst for a terrifying event.'

He saw the look of uncertainty – or was it disbelief? – on Max's face.

'It's true, Max. Astronomers believe that in the next thousand years this supergiant will explode and destroy everything, but astrologers have recorded its influence over the centuries. It was there on 9/11, the tsunami in Indonesia, even as far back as the Great Fire of London. If Betelgeuse is in a certain position in the heavens, it always indicates catastrophe.'

Max felt overwhelmed. Star charts, predictions and heavenly conjunctions of planets. It might be more ooby-gooby stuff. Waffle. Messages and influences from the stars weren't something he could see as solid, no-nonsense facts. One thing was certain, though. Enough people believed in this stuff to have Zabala murdered and send attackers after Max. Those were facts. That was something he could believe in.

'And someone has killed him to retrieve the information, and has sent people after you because you now hold his secret.'

'Maybe this is what they're looking for. I have a birth chart exactly the same,' Max said, pulling out the drawing he'd found at d'Abbadie's château.

Max put the two pieces of paper side by side. The sketches seemed identical and made by the same hand. Although he knew nothing about astrology, he realized that with a bit of practice he'd get the hang of it. Maps, sea charts, star maps, they all had a logical system to them.

Max traced the symbols he didn't understand.

'There's a difference,' he said. 'On Zabala's original drawing I've got there's an extra triangle drawn inside the circle of the birth chart. On yours – it's missing. They're not the same.'

'So that's why he sent me this chart. You must have something else, something that shows the difference between these two predictions. The first was incorrect, but the second . . .'

Fauvre glared at Max. He realized Zabala's pendant was missing.

'Where is the stone? Did you lose it during the attack?'

'No, Sophie took it. That's why she ran. And I need to see her room.'

The stone-walled room was once part of a cluster of single-storey houses. Ruins each side blocked any means of entry other than the one door. Like other teenagers, Sophie Fauvre kept her room locked. It was her sanctuary. One of Fauvre's men brought bolt cutters and squeezed the blades over the padlock's thick shackle.

Two of the walls inside were plastered with an ochre-coloured clay screed. Small windows, covered by muslin curtains, allowed a faint light to penetrate the darkness. Max tried the light switch; nothing happened. In the cool, shadowy room he could see a single bed covered with a brightly embroidered cloth. Books filled shelves on one wall, and music CDs another. Candles, trapped in their own spilled wax, were dotted around the room, many of them barely puddles of colour from being burned so low. A faint scent clung to the airless room. Max realized it was Sophie's fragrance.

A makeshift desk was used mostly as a dressing table, its top cluttered with make-up, a glass pot full of hairgrips, an assortment of combs and brushes, while a mixture of dust and body powder showed where essential oil bottles – lavender, marjoram, thyme – had left sticky ring marks.

Fauvre had edged his wheelchair into the room. He gazed as mesmerized as Max at the unfolding world of his daughter. Photographs, posters, the girl's drawings and sketches – slashes of colour on squares of canvas, muted pages of charcoal-anger scribbled by a furious hand – a world of pain and despair.

Max looked at family pictures from when Sophie was obviously a child. The strongly muscled Fauvre before his accident, the beautiful, dark-haired woman without a face. Every picture showing parents and child, right up to what were obviously recent years, had the mother's face burned out or scratched away.

But Max's attention was fixed on the wall above Sophie's bed. Clustered together were pictures taken far from Morocco's sun-baked harshness. They were of startling white landscapes, prickly green fir trees dusted with snow and brightly dressed skiers in competition. But this was no downhill racing; these skiers stretched their limbs across differing terrain. Some of them knelt in a firing position, a rifle to their shoulder, others stood and aimed at targets, while in the same picture skiers pushed away into the background.

'This is a cross-country skiing competition,' Max muttered to himself.

'That's right,' Fauvre said. 'A biathlon. Last year in Norway. Sophie was a junior competitor in the fifteen-kilometre ski and shoot. She didn't get placed. She had the stamina but her target shooting was not good.'

Max looked closer. A figure had been captured in one of the photographic sequences. Flurried snow indicated the skier had had to stop and shoot at a target. It was a standing pose, rifle to shoulder. Max's stomach fluttered. It was almost a mirror image of when the killer shot Zabala.

His eyes followed the sequence of pictures of the shooter's progress downhill to the marksman range, until finally the same competitor, cheek nestled against the target rifle's stock, was in close-up.

This skier's Lycra race suit was the same scattered white on black design as the murderer's, but the face was clearly in focus.

Max's breath was trapped in his chest; his heart tried to hammer it free.

He knew the clear-eyed girl with her finger on the trigger.

The killer whose name he couldn't pronounce – Potÿncza Józsa.

Peaches.

22

That's what was so wrong.

Peaches had run back to the van with Sharkface's men. Sayid gulped. Something invisible gripped his throat and stabbed him in the heart with an icicle. The look she gave him didn't need words.

The vans burned rubber, found the nearest exit from the motorway, took it easy along country roads for the next fifty kilometres and slipped back on to the silky-smooth blacktopped autoroute.

Sayid's mind was in turmoil. Bobby was probably dead, another man injured and Bobby's girlfriend was part of this whole terrifying mess. Desperately alone, he began to shake with fear. The shock was going to shut him down and he couldn't help but let out a gulping sob.

'Shut up, you snivelling brat!' one of the bikers yelled from the front seat.

The tone in the boy's voice had an unusual effect on Sayid. In that brief moment of temper, he realized they were rattled. Things hadn't gone to plan, had they? No, they hadn't. These evil, violent people had been as shaken by events as had Sayid, but for a different reason – the fear of being caught in an unexpected situation far from home. There was still time for other things to go wrong. For someone to stumble on them.

He brought his scattered thoughts back under control. The magic square numbers burned even more brightly in his mind: perhaps they held essential information that might stop these killers.

Sayid concentrated – the heat-seeking missile was back on target.

Max had to fight the obvious: Sophie was in league with Peaches, involved in killing Zabala and a member of Sharkface's gang. Bobby Morrell hadn't abandoned him and Sayid at Hendaye, he had been betrayed, maybe even killed by Peaches. These thugs worked for someone so powerful his reach could stretch across the world to get what he wanted by any means possible. Zabala's cry, *Trust no one – they will kill you*, had even more resonance now. Had the whole thing been a charade? Sharkface's gang attacking Sophie, Max riding like an idiot to the rescue, drawn in and seduced by her vulnerability, only to be used as a means to an end – to find Zabala's secret?

Obvious? So it seemed, and he wished it wasn't. Distrust eats away at you like a terrible disease.

'Why did she take it?' Fauvre demanded once they were back in his office, his hands sifting through the old monk's papers. 'She must have known its importance. There can be no denying that! Damn her! She's selling it for money, isn't she? She's found a buyer for something invaluable. Selling a man's life!'

The distraught man's anger was at a destructive level.

Whatever Sophie had done, Max convinced himself she was not a killer. She could have cut his throat when she took the stone. That gave him some hope, a glimmer of understanding.

Max needed this man on his side, because he had to get out of the Tears of the Angels and back to Europe.

'She's caught up in something that she doesn't understand,' Max said. He had pulled Peaches' photograph from the wall in Sophie's room. 'Do you know this girl?'

Fauvre shook his head. 'She is someone Sophie knows?'

'She's the girl who killed Zabala,' Max said quietly.

The man's shock was genuine. The flush of anger drained from his face. His shoulders slumped and he suddenly looked old and beaten. He held the photograph in a trembling hand. 'What has my girl done? Why is she with these people? May God forgive me for not loving her enough.'

He poured a drink and gulped it down like medicine, wincing at the whisky's sharpness. He sat shaking his head. After a moment Max saw a resolve creep back into his body. His broken spine straightened, his voice became more convincing.

'She is in danger. I must help her.'

'Then you need to help me,' Max told him. 'Do you see that pattern on the girl's race suit? I've seen it a couple of times and each time violence has been attached to it. Look at the other competitors. Some of them have sponsorship logos. Do you think that design could mean anything? If it did and Sophie has gone to this girl, it might help us find where she is.'

Fauvre nodded. Now there was something he could do,

something positive. He banged on the window. Abdullah was outside, making sure enough water was being poured on the burning embers of the feed store so no sparks got caught on the wind and started another blaze.

The riad owner came inside; rivulets of sweat scarred his soot- and dirt-caked face. Fauvre handed the photograph to the big man.

'Abdullah, take this to the computer room, scan it in and see if that design means anything.'

Abdullah nodded, asked no questions and turned away towards the next building.

'We have a good scanning system here. We use it to compare animals' faces with those photographed in the wild. It's a recognition package. Abdullah can do these things much quicker than I can.'

'I have a friend who's the same,' Max said grimly, thinking of Sayid, who was who-knew-where.

'And that is all we can do? Hope to find an obscure link?'

Max knew he had to play his final card. 'No, we can do more than that. We can see what your friend Zabala hid on the pendant's stone.'

Max reached for the short-bladed knife that served as a letter opener. Sitting quickly, he pulled off one of his trainers, dug the knife into the heel and gouged out the cushioning gel.

He held the stone between his fingers.

'Sooner or later someone would have snatched that pendant. I replaced Zabala's stone when I was in Abdullah's riad.'

'Then Sophie?'

'Has a piece of cut stone from a drinks mat. She has nothing,' Max said.

Angelo Farentino had enjoyed the first half of his cigar. Max Gordon's father really had no idea at all who he was, and the hulking bodyguard-cum-nurse was out of earshot, so none of this conversation would be remembered by anyone. Except Farentino. But what Tom Gordon had told him dried the moisture in his mouth. The cigar had gone out and the cloying, stale tobacco coated his tongue with a bitterness that had more to do with the bile of fear than the life-threatening habit of smoking.

Tom Gordon had made a casual remark, a meandering explanation of how he and other explorer-scientists had gone to Switzerland many years ago. Farentino immediately became more attentive. Gordon's memory was like a jigsaw puzzle and not all the pieces fitted, but the scraps and recollections began to form a complete picture for Farentino.

Environmental groups had investigated the huge nuclear particle accelerator establishment in Switzerland and had been invited to see for themselves the safety measures in place. Farentino remembered those days, could almost recall the article someone had written, and that he had published, about the melting glaciers in the Alps and the danger of causing any electromagnetic energy that could contribute towards climate change in that area. Quietly, so as not to cause alarm, safeguards were initiated for the underground research work – like a firewall on a computer. A barrier. But no one knew if it was sufficient should a major catastrophe strike the area.

The lying, deceitful Angelo Farentino had now inadvertently

been given information which Fedir Tishenko must be told. Even Tishenko could not have predicted the destruction that he would bring if he went ahead with his plans to harness nature's energy. Could he?

If Farentino went to the authorities they would arrest him, whether they believed him or not about this long-forgotten theory. Nor could he hide. If this information was correct, everything Farentino owned, every scrap of wealth would be destroyed. Stock markets would tumble, banks would close, property would become worthless. Meltdown. Massive destruction.

If he tried to run, to shift money around the world, to go and live in Brazil or on a rock in the middle of the Pacific Ocean, Fedir Tishenko had the resources to find and kill him. If he did not run, everything was finished anyway. It was a no-win situation. It wasn't that vast numbers of people would die or the environment would be irreversibly contaminated that bothered him – his wealth was going to be destroyed. That's why he had betrayed everyone in the first place. Vast wealth. This was so unfair. Why did he have to learn about this? Why hadn't fate put someone else in the hot seat?

Ângelo Farentino was no hero, but he had to use every charming, persuasive skill he possessed to convince Tishenko that what he was planning could create hell on Earth.

The vans stopped to refuel, but Sharkface kept Bobby's van out of sight on the slip road to the garage and restaurant complex. They filled containers with diesel and refuelled it in the darkness of the trees.

Sayid turned his body around and braced his back against

316

the panelled sides, making sure his plaster cast hid the scribbling on the bottom of Bobby's surfboard. The door slid back – Sayid flinched. Peaches climbed in. She looked at him and he averted his eyes. *Don't make eye contact with anything dangerous*, Max had once told him.

The girl gave him something that looked like soggy cheese in a flaccid roll filled with bits of stir-fried vegetables. It tasted like a sweaty sock full of garden cuttings but he was starving and he was desperate for the cup of hot chocolate she held.

Outside he could hear Sharkface telling the others what route they would take. Snatches of place names, including the city of Geneva – he couldn't catch the rest; his chewing was making too much noise in his ears. He gobbled the food, scared that the cold-faced Peaches might take it away from him. She sat on her haunches, watching him. Her eyes studied every bit of the inside of the van, searching for anything that might allow Sayid to make an escape, or cause problems on the road.

Sayid made sure his foot did not move away from the surfboard. Dare he risk provoking her by asking questions?

Be nice. Be grateful. 'Thanks, Peaches. I needed that.'

She nodded and gave him the hot chocolate.

Ask her. Be careful! 'I don't understand why you're with these creeps,' Sayid said quietly. 'I mean, Bobby was such a nice bloke.'

She snatched the hot drink away from his bound hands, splashes scalding him. She threw the contents out on to the ground. 'You're not here to ask questions, Sayid. You can't talk and drink at the same time – so you've just made your choice.'

'I don't know anything about what's going on!' he said

angrily, desperately wishing he could have had the warmth from the drink.

'We figured that, but you're more use to us alive than dead for a while longer. You don't think your friend would abandon you, do you?'

Max! They were using Sayid as a trap! How? They didn't know where Max was exactly unless ... Sayid's thoughts slammed into a brick wall. What was the common denominator? Sophie. That's who Peaches had sent a text to. Peaches and Sophie were working together!

Peaches smiled, climbed out and slammed the door closed. The tomb-like van held the darkness, its chill enfolding the helpless boy like a spider spinning its web of death. Sayid had to find the answer contained in these numbers. And somehow get that information to Max.

Because once they had Max, Sayid was of no use to them.

They would kill him.

Fauvre wiped the sweat from his eyes, wheeling himself backwards and forwards, gathering pieces of equipment. He shifted a crude, old-fashioned microscope into position. Once cutting edge, now years out of date compared to modern technology, it still had a use in a shoestring operation such as his.

Fauvre held out his hand for Zabala's crystal. Max felt a possessive surge grip him. He had been entrusted with it by the dying man, fought for his life to protect its secret and was now handing it over to the father of the girl who had betrayed him.

After a moment's hesitation he dropped it into the

outstretched hand. Fauvre rolled it between his fingertips, caressing it as if it were a priceless diamond. And it *was* priceless if its secret could be understood.

Fauvre felt the boy's hesitation. 'All right. Let's see what my friend was killed for.'

The air in the room was heavy with sweat; the breeze helped cool it a little, but the acrid stench of burnt straw still caught their throats. Fauvre wiped his eyes with his sleeve and lowered his face to the lens. The darkened room was lit only by the diffused glow from a light box. Max could barely breathe with the tension. If Fauvre understood what was on that crystal it would be tantamount to opening the vault of a secret tomb.

Fauvre's rasping breath was the only sound as he concentrated. His head jerked back, eyes glancing at Max – a glimmer of alarm. After what seemed a long time, he pushed himself back from the table.

'Give me the birth charts,' Fauvre said.

He spun his chair around and clamped the two pieces of paper on to a whiteboard – the original chart Max had found in the château and the latest that Zabala had sent to Fauvre. He quickly made a bigger drawing of them so they could both see exactly what they were talking about.

Max watched the black marker slide across the whiteboard, like the killer gliding across the snowfield. The felt tip squeaked as Fauvre sketched the same-shaped triangle that was etched on the crystal, placing a letter at each corner – E, S, Q.

'Several years ago three new distant bodies in our solar system were discovered,' Fauvre said as he wrote them out, Eris, Sedna and Quaoar, pronouncing each one as he did, like a teacher back at school: 'Eeris, Sedna and Kway-o-are.'

He touched each point of the triangle. 'E, S and Q. Zabala could not have known of their existence all those years ago. Back then the planets told him a major disaster was going to happen, but there was something missing – these planets and their conjunction.'

'Their alignment? That's special, is it?' Max asked.

'Exactly!' Fauvre said. 'These are the triggers and they are now in the correct place in the zodiac.'

Max wasn't getting it. He just couldn't pull all the information together. This whole astrology bit was making his brain fuzzy. But he concentrated as if his life depended on it – which it might. He knew the moon affected the Earth's crops and tides, so perhaps these planets could also exert subtle forces. Max's fingers hovered across the diagrams, touching the unlocked secret which as yet didn't make complete sense.

'Zabala had all the vital pieces for his prediction,' Max said. 'He wanted you to have the pendant. Because he had sent you the new chart he made.'

Fauvre spoke carefully. 'I am convinced Zabala's prediction of a natural disaster is correct and it will be brought on by a man-made force. Those three missing heavenly bodies now lend an enormous weight of conviction to it happening.'

Max could only go so far with crazy ideas, but this was getting to him now. It was all too airy-fairy.

'I can't deal with this stuff. There's no logic. There's no reasoning behind it. All of this because of a lousy triangle!' he blurted out. His dad had always taught him to be practical; to see the reality behind the façade of non-scientific claims.

'You're wrong, Max! This information would have died with Zabala had you not taken responsibility and seen this thing through.' Fauvre spoke slowly and precisely, letting the boy's frustration settle. 'Max, this is not the idiocy of reading a horoscope in a daily newspaper. This is a scientist – my friend Zabala – discovering a powerful universal force.'

'I want something more definite to go on,' Max replied.

'This is precise. It is definite,' Fauvre replied. He drew the new triangle into the diagram Zabala had sent him. 'This gives us the planetary alignments at the exact hour, day and year that this catastrophe will occur: 11.34 on the 8th of March.'

'Two days' time,' Max said.

Fauvre held up the numbers he'd scribbled on a pad, taken from the crystal:

7 24 8 – 10 4 9 12 25 – 7 11 9 17

'But this is one part of Zabala's secret I cannot understand. What do you think these numbers mean? I do not believe they have any bearing on the astrological horoscopes. There is no relationship between them and the drawings.'

'It's a code of some description,' Max said, and as he did so, his stomach plummeted. Sayid! His face intruded into Max's thoughts. There was nothing he could do about his friend. Not right now.

Fauvre saw the look of anguish on his face. 'There is something you haven't told me?'

Max nodded. 'There was a sheet of paper with a square of numbers, twenty-five numbers. It made no sense except they all added up to sixty-five no matter which way you added them.'

'Then that square holds a message. Zabala was passing on

vital information, perhaps even telling us how the catastrophe might be averted.'

Max racked his brains. There was no way he could remember the magic square numbers. 'To encrypt anything you need a word or a phrase. The people writing the code and those deciphering it have to know it. It's like a combination for a vault.' Max was sunk even if he had the magic square. He did not have the keywords.

'We only found the numbers in the square and those on the crystal,' he said. 'We never found the keywords to help us decipher it.'

'But don't you see, Max, somewhere Zabala *has* given you those keywords to unlock his message. You've seen them, or been given them, or been told them. Where is the piece of paper?' Fauvre insisted.

'My mate's got it.'

'And where is he?'

'He should be home, but I haven't been able to get hold of him. Maybe the cops have him back in England. It doesn't matter right now.'

Max moved to a wall map. 'The triangle brought me here from Biarritz. The other two sides join up . . .' Max's finger traced a line. 'Here.'

'Geneva,' Fauvre said, alarmed.

Fear twisted Max's stomach. 'The particle accelerator at CERN.'

'You know about it?' Fauvre said.

Europe's organization for nuclear research. Max was supposed to have gone on a school trip there a couple of years ago but was in a cross-country competition instead. Sayid had gone and said it was stunning. A hundred metres underground a huge circle of accelerator tubes, eight and a half kilometres across, twenty-seven kilometres in circumference. It was the size of London Underground's Circle Line. Massive. Biggest, most complex piece of machinery in history!

Sayid tended to get excited about science.

This was every physicist's dream. The big-bang theory. They were going to accelerate beams of protons at very nearly the speed of light. The beams would smash particles together, creating an unbelievable burst of energy. 'Bang! Bang! Bang! BANG!' Sayid had shouted, stamping his feet like a madman, nearly falling over himself with exhilaration. In fact he rabbited on for days about it. Drove Max crazy. Now Max wished he'd listened more attentively.

Fauvre tapped the map. 'Those scientists are attempting to find out how this universe came about. They want to determine when the known forces of nature were born – one trillionth of a second after the moment of creation,' Fauvre told him. 'It makes sense. Zabala once spent months in those mountains.'

Max's gaze stayed locked on Lake Geneva, trapped between the mountain ranges. Suppose, just suppose, every single thing he had discovered was true? A disaster striking that area would cause death and destruction on a vast scale.

'The particle accelerator. The Big-Bang Boys. Sophie must be taking the pendant to someone there,' Max said. 'But when she delivers it and they discover it's worthless . . .'

He didn't say anything more. Fauvre's stricken face reflected his own. Sophie would die.

Zabala had given them the date and time of the catastrophe,

and now Max knew where it was supposed to happen: the French–Swiss border at 11.34 a.m. on 8 March.

Their stunned silence was broken by Abdullah barging into the room, gesturing with Peaches' photo. 'That pattern on her ski suit, it can be many things.' And then he smiled. 'But two things for sure it is!' He put a couple of printouts on the desk. 'This is a photograph of chain lightning. See, it is like a piece of coral in the night sky. And this –' he shifted the other sheet into view – 'this is the corporate logo of Perun Industries.'

'Lightning,' Max said, realization stabbing him. 'Brings light . . . *Lux Ferre* . . .'

'What? Zabala used those words in one of his letters . . .' Fauvre said, scrabbling among Zabala's documents. 'Here!' He held up a crumpled sheet of torn paper. '*Lux Ferre*. This is what he feared! He says so. It made no sense to me.'

'They were clues,' Max said. 'What sort of company is it?'

'Oil and gas. The exploration and commercial rights were sold years ago, but the man who owned Perun kept the name. There are no shareholders. It is a private company worth billions. It would appear the man became a recluse. His name is Fedir Tishenko, a Ukrainian. And he lives somewhere in Switzerland.'

Max knew he had found his enemy.

And Fauvre was correct – Zabala *had* given him the keyword. He'd shouted it moments before he died.

Lucifer.

Sayid. Where are you?

L-U-C-I-F-E-R

The key.

23

Fedir Tishenko massaged aloe vera cream into his scaly skin. Climbers used moisturizer because altitude and wind would parch their faces, but for Tishenko it had been a daily ritual since the lightning god had struck him. Small pieces of dead skin would peel away under his fingertips and his hairless body was like that of a reptile.

Was it the cruel hand of nature that created monsters or were they born? He did not care. Society had rejected most of those who worked for him. Either through gratitude or through fear, they did his bidding. Loyalty was bought one way or another. The core group of scientists, though, were his fellow outcasts. Some had a physical disability; others had experienced uncaring, almost cruel treatment because of their mental state. Each one driven into his own hell of desperate loneliness, all had wanted a better, fairer life, and they had found their champion in Fedir Tishenko. Only he among them had the driving ambition and desire for immortality, and the money to achieve it. He had offered them the chance to strike back at an uncaring world. Tishenko would harness the awesome power of the universe in a shattering moment of light and fire, the intensity of which had not been seen since the creation.

This quiet madness had embraced him years earlier, embedding itself deeper into his psyche until it became quite normal. Tishenko was going to create a new life form, so it was only to be expected that many others would have to die in order for his ambition to be achieved. He was no raving lunatic twisted with hatred, planning to commit wanton acts of genocide – he was chosen.

As far as anyone else outside his group of scientists was concerned, Fedir Tishenko was investing everything he owned to research and create an alternative energy source, much needed by a wounded world. So Angelo Farentino, in all his ignorance, standing in the room and telling him of the enormous disaster that might befall vast tracts of Europe if he went ahead with his project, had no bearing on his plan.

'So the connection between Max Gordon and Zabala is purely coincidental?' Tishenko asked as he peeled another layer of skin from his cheekbone.

'Yes!' Did this madman not understand his real discovery – the disaster about to befall them at Tishenko's own hand? This fool was going to kill them all.

Tishenko nodded. Neither the boy's father nor his scientific friends at the environment agencies were involved. Good. The boy's presence was a fluke – but he had information that Tishenko needed. Fate had put Max Gordon in the path of a cosmic train and he would die. Yet he had proved impossible to stop so far. He had survived an avalanche, escaped Tishenko's hunters, avoided capture by the police and another attack at d'Abbadie's château. He had fled with Zabala's secret and survived the backstreets of Marrakech. Of the attack on the animal sanctuary there had been no word. Failure, once again, had to be the outcome of that operation. Perhaps Max Gordon was charmed, protected by a supernatural force.

It did not matter – only he was the Chosen One.

'When I was a teenager,' Tishenko said, as he poured a tall glass of mountain water, 'I was travelling through Kraminsk, a small town that has two bridges over its river. I and the men, my *vucari*, travelled across the second bridge, which was virtually deserted. Then, Angelo, I heard cries and screams. A small child had fallen in the river from the bridge upstream. It was cold, violent water, so the girl was helpless, a rag doll at the mercy of the current. I am not afraid of anything, so I jumped in and saved the child.'

Farentino stayed silent. Tishenko seemed desperate that he should understand.

'I pull the child out. She is alive. I get back to the bridge and the people cheer in their happiness and excitement at this heroic act. I wanted no credit. I asked for no applause. I desired only to save an innocent child. But then I get closer to the crowd, they see me and how I look. Smiles turn to revulsion, then hatred and fear. The hero had become a monster. It is a cruel world, Angelo, do you not agree?'

Farentino nodded. Tishenko's question did not expect an answer.

'So I threw the child from the bridge back into those terrifying waters and she died.'

'What?' Farentino whispered.

'Prejudice killed that child. Not me.'

'You haven't heard what I've been telling you! This isn't about one child dying, this is about a massive rupture in the Earth's surface that will kill thousands. It will kill us.'

Tishenko pressed his remote handset and the screen flared with a three-dimensional view of the mountain ranges surrounding them. Criss-cross lines divided the picture and three distinct grid patterns ran out from his base, like torn edges of paper, through glaciers, towns, Lake Geneva and the heart of Europe.

The slash that was Tishenko's mouth widened into a travesty of a smile.

'Not thousands, it will kill hundreds of thousands. And in twenty-four hours the devastation will begin and a new world will be created.'

A wave of nausea surged from Farentino's stomach. No one could stop this madman.

Tishenko nodded to someone behind Farentino. Before he could turn, two of Tishenko's security men grabbed him so tightly the pain shot through his arms into his shoulders.

'You will not be a part of our new creation, Angelo. You have nothing to contribute. Your gene pool is as empty as my glass,' Tishenko said, turning his glass upside down.

'Someone will know what you're doing! There's someone out there who will find out!' Farentino screamed, moments before the strong-arm men threw him down a flight of stairs. The Italian landed hard, his face battered by the impact, his ribs seared by pain. He did not hear Tishenko's final words to him.

'It will make no difference. No one can touch us now. It has almost begun.'

Abdullah's man pumped diesel from a bowser into an old pick-up. Fauvre had got Abdullah to use his contacts and arrange a flight out of Morocco and into Switzerland for Max. French airports might have him posted on their wanted list.

Abdullah's Land Cruiser had been found abandoned near the coast. Sophie had caught the hydrofoil ferry to mainland Spain and from there a fast train through Europe. She had a twelve-hour start, but Max could get there before her. And do what? Fauvre had pushed an envelope stuffed with cash into his hands.

'You tell her if it's money she wants, then she can have it. Tell her the pendant is worthless. Tell her everything. Yes?'

Max nodded. He didn't think Sophie's problem was only about money, but maybe it would buy her off and convince her to stay away from Peaches and the company she kept.

'I'm not responsible for what she does,' Max said. 'She's the one who's caught up in this whole thing. I've got to try and find a way of stopping this Tishenko bloke.'

'There are people at CERN I can talk to. I will try and convince them that they should stop all experiments and research for at least forty-eight hours. In this day and age, if I warn them of a possible terrorist attack they would close down the whole of Switzerland. Max, I do not want my daughter to spend the rest of her life in prison. If she is caught by the authorities I will not be able to save her.'

'And what about me?' Max said.

'You can't stop any of this. You cannot. Accept it. Give the money to Sophie and then turn yourself in to the authorities. I will speak on your behalf. Then, perhaps, they will believe you and conduct a thorough search of the area. Leave it to the professionals, Max. There is no time left.'

*

Max was packed and changed. He was going from the desert to the snow. Once he got off that plane he'd be back into winter. He was ready.

Now all he had to do was say goodbye.

Max stood in front of Aladfar. The caged tiger lay asleep next to the bars. His tufted ear twitched, his tail thumped on the ground. A dream or a memory? Max wondered.

Aladfar woke up and lazily turned his gaze on Max, who stood, unmoving, close to the bars. Why did the boy's eyes look into his own? The tiger edged away cautiously. Human beings were unpredictable, but he recognized this one, knew of the strange sensory vibration that passed between them. The boy showed no fear. The tiger remembered the previous night. It had been good to be free again. But he had let this boy command him. Those instincts confused him.

Aladfar lunged, teeth bared, his mighty head ringed with a striped ruff that flared in attack. A snarling roar to challenge the boy who gripped the bars with both hands, who stood his ground. Aladfar's head dropped, his amber eyes watching.

The boy reached through the bars, first one arm and then the other. He whispered low sounds, soothing, his eyes slowly blinking. The tiger heard a word he understood: 'Aladfar, Aladfar.'

The huge cat padded closer, sniffed the hands that opened before him and allowed the boy's fingers to close on the thickness of his neck.

'Aladfar, you are magnificent. The most beautiful creature I have ever seen,' Max said gently – the awesome moment nearly overwhelmed him. He could smell the tiger's heat, feel the deep layer of fur covering the thick muscle below it. 'I'll come back and see you again one day. I will never forget you. Ever.'

It was hot. Aladfar panted. The tiger sniffed and licked the boy's hand as it stroked his face.

Max walked away. Fauvre and Abdullah waited for him at the pick-up. He shook Fauvre's hand – no more need be said between them – and climbed into the stiflingly hot cab.

As the pick-up turned, Max looked back towards the tiger.

Aladfar was standing, full square, his body casting a giant shadow. His eyes followed Max, watching the boy take his freedom. And then Aladfar gave a roar that echoed around the walls of the Angels' Tears.

A tremor of fear fluttered through Sayid. The old van was struggling. The last thing he wanted now was for it to be abandoned. The numbers on the surfboard had been scribbled and crossed out a dozen times as he tried to find the phrase or keyword needed to decipher the magic square's numbers.

The one thing the journey had given him so far was time – time enough to remember Max's spy game. Once you had the keyword it was easy. Lay the letters out in the same box as the numbers, don't repeat any letter, use the numbers Max found on the crystal to translate and it was done.

Easy.

If only he had the keyword letters to lay out! He had tried every word associated with his dilemma: Sharkface, Château, Biarritz, Atlantic, Surfing, Ethiopia, Zabala, endangered species, Morocco – that made him think of Max, wishing his friend was right there in the van with him. No, not that. He wanted

Max and himself to be free, to be back home. But the more he thought about that, the more his courage seeped away.

The van stopped. The driver lowered the window. Peaches and Sharkface appeared. They both looked past the men in front to Sayid. He turned his face away, pretending to sleep.

'Carry on,' Sharkface said in his spittle-lipped way. 'Peaches stays, the vans follow. We wait here with the bikes. The girl's coming. Take the kid up there.'

A gust of cold air blew snowflakes into the van. The window went back up, Sharkface thumped a signal to go on the van and the engine started again.

The girl? That meant Sophie. Was she bringing Max with her? How could Sayid warn him he was walking into a trap? He couldn't. Not yet. But perhaps when he got 'up there' – which was where? A building? A mountain? Wherever it was, Sayid realized, that might be the only place he could reach a phone. This was way beyond Max being wanted for murder; he needed the police to find him before murder was committed.

This was like playing tag with the devil. He hooks you and you're it.

Dead.

And that was the answer he'd been searching for. Take your mind off the problem, give it something else to think about and, like smoke under a door, the devil whispers in your ear.

Lucifer.

Another two hours. Low gear, winding uphill. The squeak of rubber against windscreen as the blades struggled against the snowstorm. The men smoked and cursed, and Sayid felt sick from the cigarette fumes and lack of air. Thankfully, the windscreen began to mist up and the men were forced to open the windows slightly. The fresh air cleared Sayid's head. He had the magic square rewritten. Max's story of the code breakers was clear in his mind now. He had to lay out each letter of the keyword alongside each number of the square, but he must not use any of the keyword's letters more than once.

Once those letters had been used, you then had to carry on with the alphabet. So once the word 'Lucifer' had been written next to the numbers, he had to continue with S, T, U, V and so on. Trouble was there were twenty-six letters in the alphabet and he had a square of twenty-five numbers. That meant two of the letters had to share and, if Max's story was correct, the Second World War code makers used I and J.

Sayid carefully wrote out the key word, L-U-C-I-F-E-R, beneath the numbers.

11	24	7	20	3
L	U	C	I/J	F

4	12	25	8	16
E	R	S	T	U

No, the U was wrong. Can't repeat a letter if it's been used. He crossed it out and started the line again.

4	12	25	8	16
E	R	S	T	V

17	5	13	21	9
W	X	Y	Z	A

10	18	1	14	22
B	D	G	H	K

23	6	19	2	15
M	N	O	P	Q

The driver changed down a gear. The engine lurched. One of the men swore and hit the dashboard. 'Come on! We're almost there! Heap of junk!'

The men pushed open the doors and stepped into the swirling snow. Their muted voices still carried, but it sounded as though they had had enough. Sayid heard the other vans pull up: tyres scrunched; doors opened and slammed. The shiver that ran through him had nothing to do with the high mountain air. He knew that if the van had finally given up, then they would put him in one of Sharkface's vans – and he'd be separated from the magic square.

Sayid squirmed towards the cab, reaching for one of the bottles of water the men had shoved between the seats. There was no time now. He had to take the risk. He could still hear their voices, but because Bobby's van had no windows in the back he couldn't see where they were. More voices, a couple of them raised. Someone moaned. 'I'm not towing it! We'll never get up the pass. Leave it!'

Sayid spilled the water across his boot and rubbed the accumulated mud and caked slush away. The numbers Max had given him from the crystal revealed themselves. When Sayid took each of those numbers, found it on the magic square, he would then see the corresponding letter. He was a dozen letters away from discovering Zabala's secret message. The pendant's first number was 7 – Sayid saw that that was the letter C on the square; the next, 24, was the letter U . . .

Sayid's eyes darted across the magic square. The voices were getting closer – he wrote quickly. If they ever searched him when they got to wherever they were going, he had to make sure they would not find the deciphered code. And if he was going to find a way of telling Max the secret . . . Concentrate! Number, letter, number . . .

He had to do something! If they ever found this van they had to know he was still alive. Sayid tugged the *misbaha* from his pocket and hooked it over the tail fin of a surfboard.

One of the men wrenched the back door open. The glaring snow meant he couldn't see clearly in the gloom of the van. Sayid slipped the pen into his sleeve.

'Get out, kid!' the man shouted. 'Come on, hurry it up.'

As one of the men leaned in to drag him out, Sayid lashed out with his plaster cast as if struggling to comply with their brutal commands. He kicked the surfboard from its bracket and it fell flat on to the floor of the van. Whatever happened next, at least none of these men would see his scribbling on the board's surface.

They made no concessions for the slow-moving boy. One of them pushed him and he stumbled, but within half a dozen strides of being hauled and kicked across the snow he was flung into the back of one of the vans. It smelt of oil and grease. Motorbikes. The grooved channels on the floor reminded Sayid that each van carried three bikes and they and their riders were back in Geneva. Waiting for Sophie.

The doors slammed closed.

Sayid wrote down the last two letters.

The message. It made no sense.

Max had left the Tears of the Angels in an old pick-up driven by Abdullah. Now the dusty road reached beyond the horizon.

The old pick-up didn't have the luxury of Abdullah's Land Cruiser and the rutted road shook Max's spine. For a long time Abdullah remained silent, but then he turned and spoke to Max.

'Those men who attacked us, they were Tuareg.'

'Yes, Laurent told me,' Max answered.

'You know about them?'

Max shook his head. 'Not much. Desert warriors.'

Abdullah nodded. 'It is the men who wear the veil. They believe evil spirits can enter their bodies through their nose and mouth. The women do not wear the veil. Tuareg women are different from other Arab women. They can fight. They are taught from when they are young to wrestle. They are strong. Strong women. Not many men can like this thing – only Tuareg. The women are special and they are permitted to choose the men. You understand me? They choose. The men, they accept what the women choose.'

Abdullah stopped talking for a moment and waited, as if expecting Max to grasp the reason why he was telling him all of this.

'I see,' Max said, because he didn't have a clue why Abdullah was giving him lessons in tribal culture.

Abdullah shrugged. He would have to explain further.

'Sophie's mother was Tuareg.'

Now Abdullah had Max's attention. The image of Sophie wrestling the man to the ground in Marrakech began to make some sense.

Another shrug from the big man. Now did the boy understand?

'The attack last night was about Sophie's mother?' Max asked uncertainly.

'No! Nothing to do with it! You are not listening to me.'

Max sighed. He thought he'd been most attentive. 'Sorry, Abdullah, what exactly are you trying to tell me?'

The pick-up hit a bone-jarring rut. Abdullah crashed the gears, found an easier route and steered them clear.

'She is Tuareg. She found herself a man who was not crippled.'

'That's cruel,' Max said, feeling the uncaring act of desertion.

'It was her choice! No matter. Laurent is a Frenchman. His pride as well as his back was broken. And Sophie, no, she could not accept it either. Laurent tried to hold the girl with what love he has left, but she is different as well. His daughter has Tuareg blood. Yes?'

'I suppose she has, yes.'

'And now you understand?'

'Er . . . no, not really.' Max gave a helpless smile. It was beyond him.

Abdullah shook his head. This boy knew nothing. 'Sophie will fight for you. She has chosen you.'

Laurent Fauvre thought of his daughter as he had watched Max and Abdullah leave. Secrets were being exposed, frightening power might soon be unleashed. Did he believe in any of Zabala's predictions? He was uncertain. But his daughter was a part of this madness. And Max Gordon? How much did he care about him?

He knew the telephone number he dialled by heart. The man answered.

'*Oui?*'

'Where are you?' Fauvre said.

'Marseilles.'

'Get to Geneva. My daughter will be there in a few hours, at the train station. Max Gordon is flying in.'

'We'll leave now,' said Corentin.

24

The vans pulled into a vast underground area. It had an industrial chill. In the depth of the tunnels that led off from this massive cave torn out from the mountainside, Sayid could see machinery, lots of it – big earth-moving equipment, tunnel-boring machines, excavators; this was the workman's entrance.

The men pushed and pulled him towards a set of lift doors. An armed, uniformed guard without insignia watched them approach. He nodded to Sayid's captors and pressed a button. Doors hissed open and Sayid was pushed into a crystal lift. It felt as though he was inside a diamond: purposefully cut edges illuminated with soft-glo halogen lamps splashed colours about, like refracted light. They ascended rapidly. Light flickered, catching the bare rock face visible through the etched crystal, every scar on the rock's surface throwing back the colours. It was like watching the swirling night sky when an electromagnetic storm throws cosmic dust across the heavens.

There was sufficient distraction for Sayid to stop being scared for a few moments. The lift slowed, its power source purring gently, bringing it to a halt. Only when the doors opened did he realize just how high up he was inside the mountain.

His captors pushed him out. In front of him was a massive window. Clouds drifted below. He must be thousands of metres high. The temperature was cool; the smooth, polished rock floor gleamed with reflection. Modern. Efficient. Cold-hearted.

'I hope you are impressed,' a voice said, from across the far end of the room.

The man moved closer and Sayid squinted against the mountain-top light, trying to make out the man's features as he got closer. When he did, he shuddered.

'And scared, I see. Good. You should be,' Fedir Tishenko said.

Abdullah's words bothered Max during the flight to Geneva. Just what did he mean? Sophie had chosen him? And would fight for him? But she had stolen the pendant. That was theft and betrayal. Who was she selling out to? No. It didn't make sense. One thing did, though – the clock was ticking and it seemed to be moving faster than usual. Twenty-four hours and Zabala's prediction was going to smash this area like a hammer on a walnut. Max gazed down at the banana-shaped Lake Geneva as the plane banked for landing. The city huddled along the western shoreline, nudging the border with France. Max looked across the runway. Barely a couple of kilometres from the airport, modern shed-like structures huddled together on the open plain. That was CERN. How or why they were involved in Zabala's disaster Max did not know, but he could see that if anything catastrophic went wrong there, Geneva would be wiped off the face of the map.

Beyond the lake and city, piranha-toothed mountain peaks raised themselves skywards, snapping at him like a morsel being tossed into their jaws. Welcome to the land of cuckoo clocks, chocolate and violent death.

Corentin watched the passengers move through Geneva international airport's arrival hall. Max Gordon would be heading for the airport's train station, which would take him to the centre of town, six minutes away. He didn't want to miss the boy. Trains ran every fifteen minutes, but if Max Gordon spotted him he would run – and that could ruin everything. There were other kids milling around, a damned school trip. He flipped open his mobile. Thierry was looking out for Sophie at the Gare de Cornavin – the main train station in town.

'She there yet?'

'Train's running early. Another five minutes.'

'Damn. It's too close, Thierry. He's gonna miss her. Stay with her. I'll take the kid here.'

Corentin broke cover. He had to flush Max into the open. Make him run. Scare him into panic. That's when Corentin would get him, when the boy's head gave him wrong directions and few choices. Out the doors, into the streets – vulnerable. Traffic, and the chance that the kid didn't know Geneva, would give Corentin the edge.

Max mingled with the school trip. The Italian youngsters chatted and shouted, excited about going to Lake Geneva; the cacophony of voices mangled any chance of the teachers' instructions being followed. Nonetheless, their practised herding abilities shepherded the children towards the main exit doors.

Max allowed the surge to carry him along, his eyes looking beyond them, flitting along the scattered people in the terminal. He checked a wall clock. Still time. Sophie's trans-European train wasn't due for another half-hour. As the school tour swarmed, shoal-like, Max stepped out from among the confining bodies. He quickly made his way towards the escalators at the end of the terminal that would take him down to the platforms. If he could reach Sophie he'd get straight on a city train to the nuclear research centre and warn them. Had Fauvre got through? Had he convinced them of anything? Or was Max going to arrive and be met with blank incomprehension – or the police?

As he passed one of the automated ticket machines he saw the dark shape of a big man in a leather jacket. And his eyes bored right into Max. It was the same hard man from Mont la Croix who had tracked him to the hospital at Pau. How had he found him? Here! In Geneva? It didn't matter, Max was already sprinting for the escalators, but he could see that the big man moved just as fast – he was fit and strong. The escalator's grooved tongue swallowed Max downwards, but not quickly enough. Max got his backside on to the rubber handrail and slid down faster than he could run.

A train clattered away. The platform was empty except for a couple of bewildered tourists. Max sprinted towards the end of the concourse; he'd jump down and run if he had to, right between the tracks. He didn't have to look behind him to know that the man chasing him was close. Max was younger and fitter, he would outrun him. He would make the older man suck air until his lungs couldn't take it any longer. But that wasn't happening. If anything, the man was gaining on him.

Max was running out of platform. The tunnels would be dangerous, but there was no choice. He had to jump on to the tracks. In the split second of his decision he saw a service door to his left. The no-entry sign was for the rest of the world, not Max Gordon. Throwing his weight against the push bars, he tumbled into the corridor. Halfway up the service corridor's walls red, blue and green stripes ran like London's Underground route map. If only it were, he'd know exactly which direction to take. The doors slammed open behind him.

'Max Gordon! Stop!'

Max ran on, momentarily bewildered as to why the hard man called him by name. He ran deeper into the corridor, bounced his shoulder against the end wall as he turned left, almost ricocheted off the opposite continuing wall, and saw another door, painted red, another sign – it indicated 'High Voltage Danger'. It was a T-junction. Blue line left, green line right.

He ran left, saw the flight of stairs, knew he'd made the right decision and leapt up the first four steps.

Double doors, one-way exit. Fresh air blasted his face. It was a stunning day. The cold air gave him a spurt of energy and the brightly lit sky was a glorious cosmic arc lamp that beamed down, adding power to his legs.

Running hard along the side of the building, he saw the area was enclosed by security fencing – access was through a manned barrier four hundred metres away. If he didn't get out of this enclosed space, the man chasing him seemed intent on only one thing.

Max reached the fence. Coiled razor wire meant he could not go over the top. He turned, pushing his back into the mesh, using it as a springboard to push himself away again. The bulk of his pursuer loomed a metre away. How had he caught him so quickly! He anticipated Max's dummy jig to the right, an arm caught Max around the neck, and suddenly he was smothered. But the man didn't squeeze the life out of him, he held him, letting Max squirm and fight and yank at the encircling arm. Max kicked hard against the man's shins. He never flinched. Max was held like a wild animal in a net and the more he fought the quicker he weakened.

He was not going to die! Not without a fight. He slumped, let his weight fall, knowing it would take the man by surprise as the wriggling mass suddenly became limp. Then he would roll free.

It didn't work.

The man went down on one knee, supporting Max's weight, and twisted his arm, so that Max was turned away from him. His knee pressed into the small of Max's back as he held him with a grip that felt like iron.

Face down, arm behind his back, cheek pressed into the tarmac. This was the end. Max knew it. This gorilla was going to snap his neck. *Dad! Help me!* Max was blacking out, the air forced from his lungs. Yet still he tried to kick and squirm. A useless attempt to stave off the inevitable. The sunlight blinded him, blood pounded in his ears. He saw peaks and snow, remembered Aladfar's warmth, smelt the mountain bear's musty fur as the eagle's scream echoed through his memory. But no strength came to him. No animal power surged through his body.

Max had become an endangered species.

*

344

Sayid shivered. The men searched him, ripped apart his backpack, shredding it for any evidence the boy might have about Zabala's clues. They found nothing. They let him get dressed, but Sayid's trembling was due not only to cold and fear; his body needed food and drink. His throbbing foot hurt, the pain robbing his nervous system of what little stamina he had left. If he could only sleep for a few hours he would be fine. His mind would be alert again and he would think of a way of getting the message to Max. They were waiting for Max and he couldn't do anything to warn him.

Tishenko knew Sayid had little value other than to entrap Max. His killer had sent word to the Moroccan girl. She would bring Max Gordon to Geneva because no one would let their friend die. Not that it mattered. In a few hours they would all die anyway.

'Get him a wheelchair,' Tishenko said to one of the men.

He sat opposite Sayid, his scaly fingers lifting Sayid's chin so he could not avoid Tishenko's eyes. 'You are tired, boy.'

Sayid nodded. He did not want to begin any kind of conversation with this man.

'And you are in pain from your broken foot. I understand pain. It can suck the life out of you, take you to a point where you no longer care whether you live or die. Are you at that point?'

'No, no. I don't want to die.'

'Of course you do not. There is nothing for you to be afraid of. I will not cause you any pain, I promise you. But you would like some hot food and to sleep?'

Again, Sayid nodded. The whisper-like voice almost hypnotic.

Tishenko turned to the men. 'Bring him,' he said, as he stepped towards the lift's doors.

They plummeted silently to below ground level. This was a different area from any that Sayid had seen before. The glistening machinery, pristine in its technologically sophisticated environment, hummed with subdued power. A fan-like structure towered above him; it had to be at least sixty metres high, taller than a cathedral. Sayid felt the size of an ant as Tishenko walked across the vast floor. Immense cables encased in copper-coloured bindings, conduits thicker than a bus, snaked away from the machine's rim and disappeared back into the rock face. Tishenko watched Sayid's amazement.

'You like science?'

Sayid could only nod. The complexity of what he was looking at was beyond his comprehension.

'Twelve years, thirty-seven billion dollars, fourteen interlocking tunnels with a twenty-one-kilometre particle accelerator circuit, one hundred and fifty metres below ground – and the best brains money could buy. Each scientist completed his area of speciality and then left. Only I and a chosen few understand the importance of what we shall achieve here.'

'Which is what?' Sayid said, hoping the man's ego would allow him to give away vital information.

'An energy source the likes of which no one has dared contemplate. That capacitor you are looking at weighs nineteen thousand tonnes. It will store energy for a micro-second, then blast it to the heart of the mountain, where . . .'

Sayid watched the man's barely moving features, the skin destroyed so long ago it was like a mask. But the eyes sparkled

346

from a mind's-eye vision of something beyond imagination. Tishenko had stopped short, allowed his secret to remain buried, and looked again at Sayid.

'I don't want to bore you with the details. You need your sleep.'

Sayid felt tears of fear well up again. There was something final in those last few words.

They went deeper into the tunnels, the colder air creating plumes of breath, sapping the last of his strength. Even the men shivered, but Tishenko showed no signs of discomfort. Sayid could stay awake no longer. His head dropped on to his chest. He snapped it up again. He must be hallucinating. Blurred figures behind a wall of ice moved away, the colours from their clothing seeping into nothingness. He was in a chamber like the inside of an ice cube. Moist air flowed around him and froze. Forcing his mind to beat the exhaustion, he opened his eyes. They hurt. Frost stung them. He tried to lift his arm and wipe away the frozen tears, but something held him. He was pressing against an invisible wall. His body was restrained. What little warmth remained in it retreated under the onslaught of the freezing air.

Starlight glistened, the sky so black it was impenetrable. Shooting stars flickered across his eyes; surging waves of deep blue, purple and whiter than white light stole his consciousness. A small whisper took perverse pleasure in telling him that his core body heat should not fall below 37 degrees centigrade, that when it reached 35 degrees hypothermia set in; below 33 death was likely.

Sayid's mind teased him with numbers that meant death. He was already much colder than that.

347

He held one last breath in his lungs.

His final thought before the swirling stars turned to dark matter and nothingness was how to get the decoded message to Max.

Max sat strapped into the front seat of the black Audi. The big man had scared the life out of him less than ten minutes ago, but now he was more relieved than he could imagine. The hard man's name was Corentin and ever since Sophie Fauvre had run away from her father to seek out Zabala he and his partner, Thierry, had been paid to shadow her. To make sure she didn't get into trouble. They didn't know at the start how Max was involved but when they lost her at Oloron, they traced him to the hospital. Find Max Gordon, find Sophie Fauvre; but Max had given them the slip. They thought they'd succeeded in scaring Sophie home when they finally caught up with her at Biarritz and let her see them. They followed her to the old château, kept track of the two of them down to the station and watched them get on the train. Corentin's job was done. Fauvre was a dear friend – from the old days when Corentin lived in Paris. He had phoned again, when Sophie ran from Morocco to Geneva, and asked him to protect both her and Max.

The ex-Legionnaire kept the car in low gear as he cut and thrust through the traffic, his mobile phone attached to the dashboard. Thierry's voice gave a non-stop commentary.

'I can see her. She's heading across the bridge for the park.'

'Don't let her see you. She'll spook and we'll lose her,' Corentin replied as he floored the accelerator and powered past slower-moving traffic.

'Shut up and do your own job,' Thierry sparred back. 'How close?'

Max could hear he was running.

Corentin ducked his head and checked their position, his eyes flitting between rear-view and wing mirrors, searching for any gap in the traffic where he could take advantage.

'Two minutes.'

'There's another girl. She's seen another girl, walking towards her now. She's slowed. Something wrong here . . .'

'Damn!' Corentin swore as a city trolley bus blocked his way. He thrust a street map at Max with one hand, swung the steering wheel with the other. 'Can you read a map? Get us to Parc La Grange!' Corentin didn't wait for an answer. 'We're on Rue du Roveray.'

Max's eyes scoured the street map, but his mind raced faster than the engine revs. Who was the girl Sophie was meeting?

Max's finger traced their intended route as the big car swung through the traffic. 'Rue de Montchoisy, left!' Max instructed.

'No! Gridlocked! Next! C'mon, kid, c'mon!'

The pressure was on him, but Max stayed focused. He was the navigator now and the big man had to follow his instructions. 'First left Rue de Nant, it's one way – in our favour.'

Corentin was driving fast and expertly, ducking and weaving. Horns blew. A near miss. Brake. Heel, toe, clutch, change down, high revs, engine screaming. Redline the rev counter.

'I see it!' he told Max.

Thierry's voice: 'Can't get any closer, Corentin. Come on! How close?' Demanding. Urgent.

'One minute . . .' Another surge of power.

'I have to take her now. They're arguing. She's got a necklace or something. Trouble! Bikers!'

'Give them the pendant!' Max shouted. 'It's worthless!' But he knew his cry of alarm meant nothing. 'Turn left, fifty metres, then right!' he ordered Corentin.

'Dammit, kid! More warning!' Tyres burned rubber as Corentin heaved the big car across the intersection. 'I see the park!' he yelled at the phone. 'Three hundred metres! Two . . . one-fifty! Thierry, where are you?'

Thierry's laboured breathing heaved down the phone. 'Picnic site . . .' Interference scrambled the line, then the last words picked up again: '. . . fighting . . . Get here!'

Max gripped the dashboard.

Corentin's face was dark and threatening, eyes locked on to the park entrance. He shuddered the car to a halt and was out of the door before Max could release his seat belt.

Max ran. Sedate rose gardens and sculpted ponds lay further to the left, then the park merged into trees and open grassland. He could see the rolling fight two hundred metres ahead. Thierry was already throwing one of the bikers to the ground, the machine's wheels spinning dirt and grass, roaring as the throttle jammed. The kid had no chance against Corentin's partner – he was unconscious before he hit the ground.

Bikers swirled like attacking wasps. Corentin, fifty metres ahead, was already grabbing one of the outriders, literally kicking the bike from under him. Max knew what those iron fists were already doing to the rider.

He saw Sophie run after the girl whose back was to him. She spun around, faced Sophie and grappled with her.

Peaches!

Max almost stopped running in shock. Two other bikers headed for the girls. No sign of Sharkface. Where was he? He had to be here. Had to be.

'Peaches!' Max yelled.

His ploy worked. The girl lost concentration for a split second, looked across towards him, and fell hard to the ground as Sophie stepped in and body-slammed her down.

The two bikers would have reached Max but for Corentin and Thierry, who were playing their own game of block-tackling. The hardened ex-soldiers had known war and conflict, had endured physical and mental punishment few could imagine, so those two bikers were going to get stopped. And hurt.

Max was just thirty metres away now. He knew that Peaches was not only a strong athlete but also a killer, and she wasn't going to let Sophie win an easy victory. She scissor-chopped with her legs. Sophie went down, rolled, grabbed the edge of the nearby park bench, pushed her legs like pistons, balanced, twisted her body as if she were on a pommel horse in a gymnasium, and was back on her feet.

Max could see that Peaches had the pendant wrapped around her fist. That didn't matter any more. Saving Sophie did.

It was then that Peaches spun like a karate expert. Generating enormous power, she gripped something else in her fist: a cosh – black, short, heavy and deadly. Sophie recovered her balance but not from her confusion. The two men who had been after her in the Pyrenees were now in the park with Max. What was going on? How did Max find her?

'Look out, Sophie!' Max shouted.

His warning saved her. She lurched back. Another grapple and she would have Peaches at a disadvantage. But it was her own body that defeated her. Sudden pain made her think she'd been shot. Searing agony flashed through her leg, her knee no longer able to bear the weight of her body. She could not know it, but like many young athletes her body was overstrained; she had made too many demands on it. Doctors would tell her later it was her anterior cruciate ligament that had broken. As her leg gave way, she fell badly, going down on one side, her head hitting the concrete base of the park bench.

Max saw her slump. She was unconscious.

'Corentin!'

The warning cry was no sooner out of Max's mouth than he saw the hard man react. Max sprinted after Peaches. She had all the answers.

Corentin was almost at Sophie. 'Look after her!' Max yelled, then ran as fast as he could towards the escaping girl.

There was no further threat from bikers, who were all down. Max sucked in air, pumped his arms and drove his legs. He was gaining.

Sharkface loved his crew. They were the only family he had ever known. And he was well aware that Tishenko could hurt one of them if he didn't succeed – that was a hold the withered-faced man kept on him. But now Tishenko's killer, the pretty one, the one who looked so glamorous, who had no physical blemish – she was taking the glory. She had replaced Sharkface, a common thug, in Tishenko's favours.

Once she delivered the pendant she could have whatever she wanted from the madman.

Sharkface waited, silent and unmoving, in the cab of a 4x4 in the trees. From his vantage point he saw the men in leather jackets fight his boys, saw them getting hurt, and watched as Max Gordon ran into the fray. Tishenko had told him that only the Fauvre girl and Max would arrive. But these two men were professionals. Their presence was a mystery.

Peaches had won her fight and she ran towards him. Sharkface's instructions were to get Peaches, the pendant and Max Gordon back to the mountains. But the situation had changed. Max and Sophie were outnumbered, but these two men had turned the tables. Priorities shifted. Sharkface could not take on the English boy. Not that he couldn't beat him, he thought, but it was he and Peaches who were now outnumbered. It was the pendant Tishenko prized more than anything. Deliver that and Sharkface could have whatever he wanted.

He knew the Hungarian girl was a cold-hearted killer and he also knew that if their roles were reversed she would grab the opportunity that now presented itself.

The engine was idling. She was running straight up the hill towards his vantage point. He was far enough back in the trees not to be seen. She ran hard, but Max was less than thirty metres behind. He was going to catch her. Sharkface dabbed the headlights. This way! She sprinted, made up some lost ground and crested the hill.

Sharkface floored the accelerator and two tonnes of 4x4 traction leapt forward from the trees. Potÿncza Józsa, the smiling Peaches, the chic expert skier, adored by young men and a ruthless killer, took the impact full on. The last thing she saw before life went out of her eyes was a smiling ragged-toothed mouth.

Sharkface slammed on the brakes and skidded five metres – straight at Max, who threw himself to one side. He tumbled and rolled down the incline. By the time he was on his feet, Sharkface had retrieved the pendant, leapt back in the car and roared away, the wheels tearing grass.

Max raced through the trees and caught a final glimpse of the 4x4 as it slowed, dipped out of view and then moments later joined the main road, heading east. East! Why east? It was the wrong way! If there was going to be a problem at CERN, the nuclear research centre lay to the west! Then the 4x4 disappeared from view.

Moments later Max's trembling hand touched Peaches' neck. She looked as though she was sleeping, curled on her side. But there was no pulse. Conflicting feelings confused him. Was he afraid of touching the girl he had once thought of as a friend who was now dead – or fearful of resting his hand on a killer?

Corentin checked Sophie's injuries. She was slipping in and out of consciousness. Thierry tied up the bikers, leaving them face down, wrists bound to ankles.

'Police will be here any second,' Corentin said. 'We're taking her through to the hospital.'

Max nodded. 'How badly hurt is she?'

'I don't know. A crack on her head and something wrong with her leg. There's blood, look, in her ear. I think it's a fractured skull. We have to be careful with her.' Corentin turned away, whistled Thierry to join him.

Max pushed back the hair from her face. 'Sophie, what's going on? I don't get it.'

Her eyes opened, blinked a few times, and stayed open, as if she was just waking from sleep. 'Max?' She smiled. 'Thought I was dreaming. Knew it was you. I'm sorry.'

'Why did you steal the pendant? You should have told me everything.'

She was weak but she could hear him. Her voice faltered. 'You were sick. You did not trust me.'

Her words hurt, but it was the truth.

The Audi rolled across the grass towards them. Sophie tried to reach something in her jacket pocket. 'Max, he's in the mountains. My phone, get my phone. She told me, Peaches told me. That's where they have him . . . in the Citadel.'

Max pulled out her phone. She nodded. She was losing consciousness again.

'Sophie, hang on. Your dad sent these men to help us. We're OK now.'

She shook her head. 'Sayid . . .' she whispered. A brief smile and she reached up her hand to touch his face. 'I tried . . . Sorry, Max.' And then her eyes closed.

Max held her, not wanting her to die.

Corentin eased her away from Max, checked her pulse. 'It's OK, kid. She's alive. We'll get her to Emergency.'

Corentin and Thierry lifted her gently on to the back seat of the Audi.

'Get in,' Thierry told him.

He wanted to. But he shook his head. 'I can't. I have to go on and try to stop this thing. Whatever it is. Look after her, Corentin. If you hadn't been here they'd have killed her. Thanks.'

Max pulled his backpack from the car.

Corentin was behind the wheel and Thierry cradled the unconscious Sophie on the back seat. They had done their job. Max Gordon was not their problem, but Corentin admired the boy.

'And you? What thing? Where are you going?'

It was suddenly all too big a problem. As if someone had told him to climb a sheer wall of ice dragging a Land Rover behind him. 'Somewhere called the Citadel. I'll find it.'

'Other end of the lake,' Thierry told him. 'Mountain ranges. You can't go there, kid, it's lethal. Weather's coming in. You don't have the gear. Come with us.'

Max looked at Corentin. They both knew he wouldn't.

The stubble-faced man pushed a folded map through the window. 'Take this. You'll need it.'

Max nodded his thanks, then said, 'Corentin, if you know anyone in the French security services, cops, anyone, talk to them. Any contacts you might have.'

'And tell them what?'

'Check back with Laurent Fauvre. He'll explain.' He snatched the folded drawings and notes from his backpack and shoved them at Corentin. 'There's a triangle. It pointed to CERN, the nuclear research centre. Here! Geneva! I was wrong. I got it wrong. The line crossed those mountains, same direction, different location. You tell them there's going to be something huge, in these mountains. It's critical. Tell them!' Max pulled the pack on to his shoulders and was already running as Corentin eased the Audi away.

Sirens announced the police were on the way. Pitched battles in a public park in genteel Geneva were not a common occurrence and the place would soon be swarming with cops.

Max looked at Sophie's mobile phone. Why was she trying to reach it? She wanted him to have it. Why? He pressed the buttons, found the text messages and his heart almost thudded to a halt.

```
Man who takes the animals has Adrien. Bring
monk's pendant and Max to Parc La Grange,
Geneva 7. Sayid is with me. I can help.
    Your friend, Peaches.
```

Sophie had realized her friend was a liar and had betrayed them all. There was no Adrien. He did not exist. Peaches could not have known that.

But they had captured Sayid.

Today was the 7th. Zabala predicted catastrophe for the morning of the 8th. Max had been wrong about Sophie. She had tried to save Sayid. Abdullah's words now made sense. She had fought for Max. Now it was up to him to fight for Sayid. He had to get to the mountains to save his friend.

And stop the madness.

25

Panic spiked him. Clawing anxiety was taking hold. He had to get on the lakeside road or back to the train station. Either way it would eat precious time. Slow down and think about it. Taking the road south of Geneva would cross the border into France before he could curve north towards the end of the lake and the mountain kingdom that held Sayid. That route posed the risk of being spotted by the police. And he couldn't chance being held in custody. Go on the north road around the lake, staying in Switzerland, and he'd sit in traffic. The couple of hours' journey might take twice as long as that. The lake was seventy-odd kilometres long, and then there was the trek into the mountains – how much time did he have?

Max looked at the rows of fancy yachts and motor cruisers moored at their pontoons in the marina opposite the park. Moving quickly down them, his eyes sought out a boat, any boat, he could take. Steal was the word, he reminded himself. He was going to have to break in and get it started. Then he heard the soft spluttering of powerful engines. A boat snuggled stern in to the pontoon, where a woman was about to tie the boat's lines. White leather seats contrasted with the midnight-blue hull, which shone like glass. A man had walked to the bow of the speedboat to check that fenders protected the shiny hull. The woman was a few metres away on the quay, trying to slip the rope around a cleat, when Max stepped unseen aboard. The engine idled in neutral. Gripping the walnut steering wheel, he braced his legs and shoved the throttle's four levers forward. Angry-sounding triple diesel engines, frustrated at having their power curtailed, churned water, the stern drives eager to thrust the scalpel-sharp hull through the calm surface. The man tumbled overboard; the woman screamed, but her voice was already muted by the roaring engines. Like Aladfar! The wind pushed across the raked windscreen. The boat surged to thirty knots and the speedo showed it could reach fifty.

The power scared him. He'd handled speedboats before with his dad, but this was like going from a bicycle to a Formula 1 racing car. He curved away from the shoreline. Visibility was good, but darkening clouds approached the mountains. Bad weather was going to be his companion in the hours ahead. The police would come after him, but this was what Max wanted. To lead them to the Citadel. This boat was worth a million, so stealing it should get someone's attention. Max would hopefully have the law at his back when he got there. It was time to let the beast go – he pushed the throttle levers forward and the boat nearly leapt out of the water. Max laughed away his fears as the surge gave him flight and he raced the wind.

Relief and disappointment mingled as he realized, forty minutes later, that no one was in pursuit – perhaps bureaucracy was to blame, as the border between France and Switzerland cut the lake horizontally. Odds were no one could decide who should be chasing him and by the time he calmed the throbbing engines and eased the sleek craft into the empty beach, he knew he was still on his own. Against the soaring mountains he felt isolated and vulnerable. But energies other than fear drove him on. Like the engines' shuddering power, Max felt a gathering storm of anger. Sayid. Was he injured? Was he still alive? They must have taken him at the airport in Biarritz. All this time and Max had had no idea his friend had been captured. The dull ache he felt at the base of his heart was guilt. He should have taken better care of him. Well, he'd make up for that now.

Snow whipped across the peaks, drifting into ravines and crevasses, but no flakes fell from the darkening sky. Max had jogged for several kilometres, making greater demands on his legs as the narrow track grew ever steeper. A sign stopped him. It was in English, French and German – to make certain there was no misunderstanding. He levelled his breathing. *No Entry. Road closed 1 kilometre ahead. Scientific Research Area: Wild Animal Resettlement. Beware Wolves.*

Better than any warning about guard or attack dogs – wolves would stop everyone in their tracks. Max took the map out and balanced his compass, finding the direction of the Citadel's peaks. He was on course. The contours were steep; the mountain ranges soared to thousands of metres in the near-distance. How was he going to get up there? Snow would be a problem; the cold too. That sign warned people off. It was definitely where Max had to go. As he started jogging again he pushed a nagging thought to the back of his mind: how many wolves were running loose in these mountains? And there were no farms anywhere, no natural prey, so what did they hunt and eat?

As he turned a curve in the road he saw the first barrier. A wire mesh gate several hundred metres along the track. This was an ordinary gate, four metres high, supporting a fence that merged into the rock walls. Another sign repeated the previous warning. Max climbed over. In the distance he could see a snow-swept vehicle. Bobby's van!

There was no need for caution. Max could see it was abandoned. No footprints were visible and the van's sides were corrugated with drifting snow. He yanked open the driver's door. Stale smells escaped – old packets of food and cigarette butts. He climbed inside. It was a dark, cold box and it had imprisoned his friend. As the breeze entered the van something swayed, a trinket hooked over the skeg of a surfboard – Sayid's *misbaha*! He'd been here! Max clambered into the back, held it tightly in his fist. If only he could bring his friend back simply by wishing for it. But he knew it was going to take a lot more than a wish – it was going to take a tough, unrelenting search.

There was nothing else that he could see which might help him learn any more about his friend. There was no sign of blood, thank heavens. A couple of surfboards, sleeping bags, a mattress. Just as he remembered it, except now it held the frightening sense of harm. Max rummaged in the van. A couple of packets of crisps and a half-empty bottle of water. He shoved them into his pack and pushed the rear doors open.

A few metres further along the track, the second obstacle

was more challenging – galvanized gates and fencing that ran hundreds of metres up each side of the mountain until it embedded itself into rock face. Razor wire was rolled out several metres beyond that and ten metres further on was a secondary electrified fence. He could see that the road went on into the mountains, but even if he got over the gate he would have to cross this no man's land. At each vehicle-crossing point rows of dull red lights illuminated side barriers – like a high-street shop's security gate to stop shoplifters.

The wind gusted; the cold metal van creaked. The clock was ticking. There was no time to scale these mountains to try and get past the barriers. Max climbed up the van's rear ladder and yanked the restraining straps on Bobby's covered surfboards.

The one that lay flat in the back of the van, where Sayid had worked out the message from the magic square, stayed as Sayid had intended – unnoticed by anyone, including Max.

It took twenty minutes of back-breaking effort to climb the eighty-odd metres to a narrow plateau. Once there he cast aside the windsurfer's cover, readied the board, pulled on his goggles, shoved his feet into the supports and heaved up the sail. It crackled with energy. The wind funnelled through crevasses and curves, snatched at the board's wing and hurtled him forward. He nudged the sail, pulled the wishbone control bar to him and shredded the face of the snow wave. He needed speed, direction and a jump-off point to clear those inhospitable fences. This was Bobby's own windsurfer. The champion had the fastest and the best, and Max didn't know if he could handle it. Built for speed, the short board skimmed across the snowfield. Max tugged on the wishbone and the twelve-square-metre racing sail responded, the rigid aerofoil holding him on course. The wind gusted and he trimmed the sail again; it pulled at his shoulder sockets, while the cold air stung his cheeks. The power-hungry speedboat he had stolen could reach fifty knots, but these windsurfers came close to matching that when they raced across flat water. This was flying! He was really moving now. But it was no joy-ride. He was speeding towards the lip of the rock's curved snow face. When he hit that he would be plucked into the air, thrown like a sycamore seed into the wind, spiralling away – how helplessly he didn't know. The angle of his take-off dictated he would gain a lot of height quickly and then somersault. He was suddenly back in Mont la Croix and his snowboarding failure. He had to get a mighty lift here; control the topsy-turvy spin or he was finished. This was more than losing face – this was about losing your life. The razor wire could savage him and leave him bleeding to death or, if he hit the electric fence, he was toast.

The board hissed across the snow. The wind chased him, white flurries tumbling ahead of the board's snout. Max saw the void, the wind's swirling confusion, the point of no return. Wham! The wind socked him, nearly wrenching the wishbone from his hands.

Silence. The board left the ground. A whoosh of air. The blurred, transparent sail creaked with pressure as it cartwheeled through space. Giddying images of the wire and electric fence swirled below him. Could he clear them? Did he have the distance? He seemed to be in the air for ever. The board righted itself; he shifted his weight instinctively, helping the board find its balance. He thumped into the ground, nearly lost control, exactly the same as he did at the snowboarding competition, but this time he let the seat of his pants drag down in the snow and used the sail's wishbone to keep the board steady. He had cleared everything by barely a few metres.

Max yelled a triumphant cry. That was better than any competition prize.

Steadying the board, he picked up the wind again, flattened the sail, easing out the wind's power, and headed for where the road took him. With a quick glance behind him, he saw Tishenko's defences. He'd beaten them. It gave him an added boost of strength. Nothing could stop him now. He was getting closer to the mountain and the man who held his friend. And closer to impending disaster.

Tishenko descended inside his mountain. Here the black rock walls, scarred from the blades of the tunnel-boring machines – as wounded as the man himself – corrugated the dull light and held the cold in ice sheets, a metre or more thick. Machinery and piping lay snug against the rock face: this was where the engineers and construction workers left all their equipment. The hoist lift was far removed from the super-smooth lifts that usually whisked him to his high lair. The open platform was used for bringing equipment down into this cavernous chamber.

Running water ran between the back of the cages and the wall, a sluice carrying melting ice that had tumbled into underground caverns and, as water will, sought out the line of least resistance. It had served Tishenko well, for this was where he had kept captured animals over the years – before he honoured them with the hunt.

Steel cages, several metres square, were bolted to wall and floor along each side of the hoist's open shafts. Like a fortress prison, the freezing-cold air corroded the bars, but they were secure enough to hold the strongest beasts. Most were empty, though the floors still had straw and animal droppings on them. Tishenko walked along the cages, the strong animal smell drawing him closer to one in particular. The additional chill of the cold water soothed the heat that seemed to always lie beneath the layer of his burnt skin. This was the last beast held captive. There had been no need to build the big square cages at this end of the cavern. Only the front wall, from where Tishenko's men could toss dead fish and blubber-rich seal to the great creature, was rigid with bars. The remaining walls were translucent sheets of ice.

The near-freezing water from the sluice spilled into a pool before continuing on its journey. Ideal for one of the most fearsome creatures from the far north. The polar bear's head broke the surface of the water and gazed at him. With a flurry of water the giant dragged itself clear and raised itself up to its full height.

Tishenko measured him with his eyes. He was magnificent. Over three metres high, weighing six hundred kilograms. Massive strength and unrivalled hunting skills. Frightening. Take the DNA of a wild hunting beast and merge it with human intelligence. What creature might be born from such a genetic union?

Climate change meant the bears were losing the ice earlier each year in the frozen wastelands of the Arctic. Their food resources were becoming scarcer and their aggression towards humans more pronounced. Tishenko had paid a small fortune to have him captured and brought here. He was the biggest, most aggressive male they could find. His DNA had been taken; now he would be the last animal Tishenko would hunt down before ... The thought of tomorrow stopped him. Tomorrow would be the most awesome of days.

His phone rang.

Sharkface had returned.

Max climbed around what appeared to be a massive entrance at the base of the mountain and, as he clambered hundreds of metres up the side of the mountain, he saw Sharkface's 4×4 pass beneath him and disappear from view. He told himself he'd made the correct decision by stealing the boat. Sharkface must have been held up by traffic.

Max scanned the uninviting rocks. There were several fissures in the almost sheer face of the north wall. This coldest and darkest side, encrusted with snow and ice, offered no easy climb, but Max spotted a cleft that would allow him to edge towards one of the chimney-like funnels. Of all the ridges and crevasses only one did not have snow or ice on its rim. Warm air was coming up from somewhere. It had to be an opening. That was Max's way in. *Don't go where your mind hasn't been first.* Max studied the route, visualized where to climb, identifying footholds and fist-jams.

It took almost an hour to free-climb across the treacherous face of the mountain. As he edged higher he saw the distant sun devoured by jaw-like peaks. To the north a rumble of thunder heralded the beginning of a storm. It was at least eighty or ninety kilometres away, but Max knew that if it advanced rapidly this was the last place he wanted to be. A crevasse on a mountainside was a favourite place for lightning strikes.

Max squeezed down into the chimney, his headlamp casting its light a few metres beneath his feet. The sharp rock split about ten metres below. Bracing his back and legs, he edged downwards. The lamp couldn't penetrate the darkness, but he knew his decision had been correct. From the void to the left, too narrow to clamber through, was the unmistakable smell of animals – like a zoo – pungent and rich. There were no sounds, but it was this rising air that had warmed the chimney. The tunnel below his feet on the right was wider and he might be able to squeeze down, but he could see the dull reflection of ice. An ice crevasse is impossible to descend without the right equipment. What was the choice? Climb back out? No. He'd get down the ice chute somehow.

Max wedged his legs against a sliver of rock, unslung his backpack and searched for a small plastic container, no bigger than a matchbox, that was tucked in a Velcro pocket. Sharp edges of rock caught his knees, sweat ran into his eyes, and if he slipped from this tenuous foothold he would plunge into the narrow pipe of rock and shatter his legs. Shock, pain and loss of blood would mean he'd be dead in less than an hour. The claustrophobic chimney started to get to him. He hated small spaces at the best of times, but imagination can make matters worse. No! The rock walls were not moving closer! He steadied himself, taking comfort from the headlamp's glow.

His fear back under control, Max scrunched down again

and lifted one foot clear of the slippery rock. His off-road trainers had good grip but not enough for that ice chute – however, they did have four small sockets in each sole to screw spikes into for additional grip. He blew on his fingertips. He dared not drop any of those slender spikes. After a couple of minutes he completed the task. Now he had some grip for the ice wall. Max pulled off his headlamp, eased it over his left foot, tightened the strap, so the lamp angled downwards but was clear of the spikes, and took his first tentative step into the unknown.

Having convinced himself that the mountain had caves or excavated chambers inside, it seemed logical to believe that the wild animals were on one side and there was a separate chamber on the other. Logic doesn't always work like that, but he had no choice. Besides, it made him feel better to believe it.

Legs straining, back pressing as hard as possible against the wall, his backpack allowing at least some traction, he lowered himself into the dangerous ice. As his left foot found purchase on the wall the light shone downwards. Max could see what lay beneath him. A curve in the chimney was coming up. He prayed that it didn't turn into a sheer drop, because if so he had no chance.

The angle steepened. There was a faint blue tinge of light creeping up the shaft that was not from the lamp strapped to his foot. Tendons and muscles stretched as he tried to slow his downward slide. The spikes were ripped from the soles of his trainers; he was going to hit *something* soon. But what? He pulled his knees together, bent his legs slightly, got his arms up around his head, elbows tucked in, and took a deep breath. He plummeted down.

An eerie blue glow flashed across his vision as the chute spat him out. Where the mouth of the chimney ended, a frozen undulating wave of ice curved down from the rock face into a huge hall. He was ten metres up from the floor, but the rolling curve caught him like a theme park ride, breaking his fall.

Max skittered across the gleaming black stone floor and thumped into a wall of ice. Somewhere in the background rushing water broke the silence. He got to his feet. The dull glow was emanating from very soft lights, but the blue tinge came from the ice that surrounded him. It was like being inside a glacier. But as soon as his eyes adjusted he felt a sudden panic rise in his chest. It was below freezing, his breath plumed, but it was not the sudden shock of cold that made him fearful. Dozens of eyes stared at him.

Eyes of the dead.

26

Tishenko had listened to Sharkface's description of the attack in the Parc La Grange.

The death of his girl killer caused no feelings of regret. Survival depended on an individual's skills and determination. Luck was a fickle companion.

Sharkface told him of the assault and how the tough-looking men had arrived with Max Gordon and had run over Peaches. It had not been possible to capture the English boy, but Sharkface did have what Tishenko prized most – the pendant. All Sharkface had ever wanted was to be accepted by Tishenko as a *vucari* – a wolf man, one of the chosen few.

Tishenko instructed the boy to get food; he would reward him later. He brought the stone closer. It yielded nothing to his gaze. It seemed so ordinary. His people would examine it under microscopes so powerful they could look into the eyes of microbes!

At last. The secret Zabala had hidden within the stone – the information he had died to protect. Fate had now cast the pendant into Tishenko's hands at such a vital moment. The monk had spent more than twenty years tracking the stars, seeking out the Truth – that explosive moment when heavenly powers flung down a shattering fireball of creation. Zabala *knew*! And had tried to warn an unsuspecting world. But the scientists had ignored him. Ridiculed him. Tishenko had not. Zabala's friend had betrayed him; told Tishenko that at last the mystic monk had found the proof of the catastrophe that had eluded him for so long. A fragment of knowledge that Tishenko yearned for. A final nudge from the gods that would confirm everything he planned tomorrow, when the lightning would be controlled. Tishenko had the power. His mother *must* have known when she named him. Fedir – a gift from God.

The storm was approaching. The grumbling sky reverberated with mounting anger. Tomorrow it was expected to be at its most violent. That he had secured the monk's pendant only hours before he was to leave the Citadel and take himself into the desolation enforced his belief that the great mystery of the universe guided him.

Not only would he challenge the storm, he would embrace his destiny. Out of the devastation and fire he would create life. *Lux Ferre* – the bringer of light.

Max crouched like an animal ready to run, his mind racing to take in what he saw. He was in an ice cave. Specks of frost clung to the walls and roof, so everything shimmered as if some magic spell was being cast. But the creatures' eyes that stared back at him were unmoving. No light, no glimmer, just the vacant stare of death.

It was a natural history museum of frozen animals, teeth bared, in natural poses. A muscled silver-back mountain gorilla glared, a black rhino stood full square, proud, curved horn majestic. A leopard lunged upwards at a very rare Tibetan antelope, startled but, like the others, frozen. Two lions fought, the huge male, his mane dusted with frost, poised over the female, which was twisted in a snarling defensive position. Max could almost sense the African dust rising from their scuffling paws. Orang-utan, lynx, all stood as if caught by flash photography. A leatherback turtle, bigger than any Max had seen before, was suspended in an ice block, as if swimming through the ocean. There were animals Max had seen only in photographs, such as a rare snow leopard, its softly mottled coat blending into the snow bank that had been created around it.

He moved slowly among the creatures in a freeze-frame time warp, in silent wonderment at being so close to the great beasts of the world. Then he realized that this was a very specific collection. They were mostly predators. From the big cats to wolves, hunting dogs to jackals.

The jackal. Its dark shape subdued as it stood on a black boulder. Realistic and magnificent. It gazed down at him with wise eyes, touching his memory of a jackal's guidance when he was in Africa.

A Bengal tiger, not as big as Aladfar but huge nonetheless, crouched, eyes glaring, claws gripping the ground, its breathless snarl and silent roar mute witness to a magnificent creature that once roamed free of man's interference. This private museum belonged to the man who smuggled animals, many of them endangered. A bear, about the same size as Max, stood on its hind legs, its front paws held up defensively, as if uncertain what the human being who killed him was about to do. The look of surprise on its face was accentuated by the black circles around its eyes. This was the small South American bear Sophie had mentioned to him when they first met. And this is how the poor creature had ended up.

The cold air carpeted the floor with a thin crust of ice, so that Max's footfalls crunched. This was too spooky. And he wasn't on a sightseeing tour. He moved quickly to the other end of the hall, forcing himself not to look over his shoulder – in case the dead came back to life. They all looked ravenously hungry.

A double stainless-steel door barred his exit. There was no sign of a handle, a switch or code box. Nothing. It had to be a remotely operated door. Further along the wall a hole gave a brief glimpse of a spurting torrent of water. It was no larger than the ice tunnel he had just slid down and the water gushed white with the tremendous power of a waterfall before disappearing into the blackness below. The volume of water told Max it came from somewhere higher in the mountain – run-off from melting snow.

He stuck his face closer to the pounding water, pushing his shoulders into the hollow wall. Wasp stings of spray pricked his face; the roaring water deafened him, but there was a different sound in the background. It was barely distinguishable, but it was of water splashing, falling into other water. This was some kind of sluice, a natural underground stream. He'd seen something similar when potholing on a school trip. How far down was it before the water tumbled into deeper water? Was it a lake? A pond? Whatever it was, it was below the level of this ice cave.

It might be the lower-level chamber beneath the air-vent

chimney that was too small to crawl down. The water chute was the only way out.

This was extremely dangerous. In fact extreme didn't quite cover it. But it was a risk he had to take. He opened his backpack, pulled out a plastic bin liner and began stripping. As each layer came off, the freezing air snared itself around him, barbed-wire sharp. He knew he couldn't hang around too long or it would freeze him into submission. With all his clothing stuffed into the plastic bag in his backpack, except his boxer shorts and trainers – whose tough soles might help deflect any sharp-edged rocks on the way down the waterfall – he was already relishing the thought of dry clothing at the end of this nightmare plunge. He was shivering violently. You had to know what freezing-cold water would do to you in order to survive it. Cold water strips away body heat twenty-five times faster than cold air. The moment Max got into that sluice his blood pressure would rise and he would start hyperventilating – and that was dangerous. The sudden shock would stop him from holding his breath. Even the strongest swimmers have drowned in cold water. Knowing what to expect would help him survive, but not knowing how long he might be in the water was the frightening part. After three minutes his body temperature would drop, hypothermia would set in, his muscles and limbs would be unable to keep him going.

Experts called it Sudden Cold Water Death.

Max pulled his backpack on across his chest – this would stop it snagging and also give him a buoyancy aid. He clambered on to the rock sill, tried to stop his teeth chattering and took a deep breath, mentally locking it into his lungs. He needed that air as long as possible.

He pushed into the tongue of water and immediately gasped, losing vital oxygen. Water spilled across his head, his neck felt as though someone had pinioned him with icicles and his throat constricted with the cold. *Control it! CONTROL IT!* his mind shouted at him. He suppressed an urgent desire to yell as he felt the water-smooth rocks disappear from below him. He plunged from darkness to dim, glowing light in the space of twenty seconds. His stinging eyes saw the drop – only three or four metres – before he splashed into a pool of water.

It felt as though broken glass pulsed through his veins. The cold was shutting him down – rapidly. He couldn't function, his arms were useless, his mind unable to grasp the deep sleep that threatened to suffocate him. Images danced across his vision. Snow and ice packed the edges of the pool below, and the remains of something dark and bloody stained the smudged snow. This was the end. He had gambled and lost and now the dark ice would take him. A deep instinct for survival, a small glimmer in his brain, told him there was time for one more gulp of air. And then he went down into the water.

The impact, the resistance of the water and then a floating sensation. Downwards. *Out of your depth. Too far down.* The cold left him. That meant he was either unaware of the terrible effect the temperature was having on his body and he was slipping into deep unconsciousness, or he had warmth and protection, like a young polar bear.

The pool's water was marginally warmer, not by much, and its salty content stung his eyes. At first it seemed as though daylight streamed down into the depths, but then his achingly cold mind told him that it couldn't be. These were artificial lights allowing something to see beneath the water. What something?

A white monster smashed into the water. A mature polar bear, its huge paws, thirty centimetres across, scooped away water. *This* was the something.

Fear-generated strength gushed through Max. An unusual feeling of clumsiness encumbered his body. He was dog-paddling, pulling water beneath his body, back legs kicking awkwardly, bubbles streaming from his nostrils as he peered through the gloom. White turbulence from the surging water came into view as it coursed through the pool and escaped onwards over a lip of rock.

He dared a look behind him. The polar bear was striking up from the deep pool, broad paws swatting away water in an almost lazy fashion, as if in slow motion. It was an illusion. The bear was so strong it made his power seem effortless. The fury and violence if he caught the intruder in his territory would be terrifying.

The watercourse was the escape route. Max didn't know how he had stayed under the surface for so long, or how his body had coped with the heart-stopping cold, but he went as fast as he could, broke the surface, reached up on to the packed ice on top of the rock ledge, and tried to haul himself out of the water. The backpack strapped to his chest made it impossible. The horror of having his legs dangling in the water with the predator less than a couple of metres below spurred the strength back into his limbs. Twisting his body, he levered himself ashore using an elbow and the biceps of one arm.

On all fours he clambered across the rock, through the

bloody remains of the seal, heading for the sluice that funnelled the water away. To his left an ice wall blocked his escape – but the slushing sound of water behind him told him the bear had hauled itself clear and was within lunging distance. Max dived into the sluice and sensed rather than felt the power of the polar bear as he heard it bellow, its paw slashing through the air, missing Max but connecting with the ice wall. It sounded like someone scraping their fingernails down a blackboard.

He had missed savage injury and certain death by seconds, but if he stayed in this fast-moving watercourse he would be swept away into the plunging water that disappeared at the end of the rock cave, forty metres away. He flung out his arm, caught hold of something cold and hard. Steel. The edge of a steel cage.

There was no more strength in him. To hold fast against that flow and haul himself over the rim of the channel into the cage was beyond him. Better to die now. Just let go and die. It was so easy.

Sayid's face looked up at him from the back of the taxi taking him to the airport at Biarritz. That was the last time he had seen his friend. It was like being punched in the stomach – his friend needed him. That's why Max was here! Right now he didn't care about a crazy man causing devastation. He wanted to save his friend. But first he had to survive.

Max tightened his grip. He wouldn't give up, but the effort needed was still too much – and then nature took a hand. The water twisted him; he floundered, kept his grip on the steel bar, but he was now belly down, facing the surging water. He couldn't breathe.

It happened so quickly that the thoughts were barely formed when the force of the water slammed against his backpack, still strapped on his chest, and threw him upwards with the force of the current. It gave him an instant to twist and fall on to the straw floor of the cage whose steel bars he had clung to.

He lay still, the prickly straw making no impression on his frozen body. A blue tinge covered his skin, like the beginning of a bruise. But he was alive. The white noise of the sloshing water seemed like a lullaby. No longer a threat, it offered a soothing comfort to his battered body. The other sound he did not understand – a persistent, desperate scratching.

The alarm bell that rang loud and clear was in his head. He needed warmth and food. His body was desperate for sugar and carbohydrates. The deep straw stank of stale animal smells but he would have happily burrowed deeply and slept. Instead he forced his painful, trembling limbs to stand and undo his backpack. Everything was still dry. He plunged his arms down into the bag, fingers searching for the energy and chocolate bar he knew he had tucked away. He tore off the wrapper with his teeth and shoved the contents into his mouth. Fruit, nuts and chocolate clogged his teeth. He sucked and chewed, still shivering but gloriously happy to feel the energy seep into his stomach. He pulled out the dry clothes, but he needed to get his circulation going first, to rub warmth into his skin. There was a pile of sacks tacked against the far wall beyond the cage doors. He pushed. The cage was bolted. Max reached through the bars. The bolt was jammed; the damp air had set it fast. He tried to wriggle the bolt's handle but it barely moved. If he tried to hammer it with the heel of his hand he'd cause damage to himself. Removing one of the sodden trainers, he slipped his hand inside and used it as a buffer for his fist.

Then he realized what the scraping sound was.

The polar bear was on its hind legs, standing full height on the other side of the ice wall – there were no cage bars between Max and the bear's enclosure. It was scraping furiously to reach him. And those giant claws were rapidly destroying the half-metre-thick wall.

Max still lacked strength but the urgency drove him to hit the stubborn bolt as hard as he could. The impact ran through his wrist into his forearm and shoulder, but that was the strongest way to deliver a blow.

The ice wall gave way. A hole crumbled open, big enough for the bear to get his paw and shoulder through. He grunted and snorted and seemed to relish the effort of reaching his meal. Max did his own grunting as he thumped away at the rusting bolt.

He could smell the bear now. Its breath plumed rapidly, its head forced further through the hole. It retreated for a few seconds, scraping more ice, then, clambering like a giant teddy bear, its back claws found more purchase to force its body through.

Max felt the bolt give. He yelled as loud as he could, forcing the energy into the strike, and hit it again. It was enough. Pushing his shoulder against the cage door, he fell clear. The bear burst through the ice wall like a stuntman jumping through a fake window in a movie. Ice particles shattered, the bear stumbled, then was on all fours and came at Max.

Max shouted at the bear. 'Not today! NOT TODAY!'

And laughed crazily as the bear pressed itself against the iron-fronted gate that Max had just managed to close. He slumped barely a couple of metres from the frustrated, growling bear, repeating this mantra the only thing his mind seemed capable of doing. 'Not today. No, not today. No thanks, not today. I'm not on the menu today.'

Fear finally released its grip on him, but the cold did not. He was worn down beyond anything he had ever experienced. He shuddered and felt a wave of relief. Tears stung his eyes. He had been so frightened, so scared. There was no shame in being human. A vulnerable human being. *Dad. Oh, Dad, I was so bloody terrified.* He couldn't stop his body racking from huge sobs. The terror needed an escape route and found its release through tears.

Max took a couple of deep breaths. He was all right now. He blew the snot and spit away. He sighed. He was OK. He was OK! What a sight he must look. Exhausted, sitting on the cold floor, his boxer shorts halfway down his backside, one shoe on, one shoe off, hair matted with bits of smelly straw, his skin goose-bump blue and a monster of a polar bear still fancying him for dinner.

His ears still hurt from the cold-water ride; the sounds of the gushing sluice and the bear's short, sharp grunts and growls were muted. Better that way. A bit of peace and quiet was exactly what he needed right now.

Max grabbed one of the empty sacks and rubbed the coarse hessian all over his body. He had to get warm, get his core body heat back up. At last he felt the blood prickle his skin – it hurt, pins and needles – but then came the satisfying comfort and warmth as his circulation returned. In between getting dressed he shoved every bit of food he could find into his mouth. The stale crisps and bottled water from the abandoned van followed. Now he felt alive. His trainers were still wet but the dry socks and clothes made him feel 100 per cent better – which, given his condition, wasn't as great as it sounded.

Max looked around him. This huge hall was more utilitarian, like a massive holding area. Empty steel cages, maybe twenty or more, lined the wall where the polar bear still paced. Lifeless machinery, wooden pallets and a fork-lift, sacks filled with salt. So that's why some of his cuts and bruises were stinging. They must use salt in the polar bear's pool. And there was the way out! A mechanical hoist rose up between the empty cages, its platform open, big enough to roll a fork-lift on to, and obviously used for bringing anything heavy down below, like the machinery and all those sacks.

Then he heard a sound from one of the cages just beyond the hoist. It was slight, barely audible above the rushing sound of water which plunged out of view into the depths further down. It was a voice. Someone was weakly crying for help.

'Sayid?' Max called as he ran past a couple of empty cages until he came to where the whimpering emanated from.

The cage was locked and straw covered the floor. A body lay curled next to the bars, his face badly bruised and covered in stubble and dirt. His eyes sought out Max's, his hands raised, pleading for help.

'Max,' the hoarse voice whispered.

Max stood at the bars, the shock rendering him helpless for a moment. The man lying in tattered clothing encrusted with dried blood was Angelo Farentino.

Tishenko had never needed to attack anyone physically. There were always others to do his bidding. Within the caverns and hallways of the Citadel mountain he had a core group of armed guards. They were mostly from his home area and they sought refuge in Tishenko's power. Like their fathers before them, these killers were part of the *vucari* – the tribe of men who invoked fear, not only through simple people's superstition but also because of the clan's taste for violence. For the privilege of being part of a group that was virtually a small private army, they did as they were told without question. And one of them had just slammed the butt of a sub-machine gun into Sharkface's stomach.

Sharkface thudded across the floor. Bewildered and in pain, he lay crumpled against a wall. He had served Tishenko loyally for years, ever since the burnt man had picked him and his gang up from the streets in East Berlin nearly eight years ago. Kids into killers. Sharkface had earned his cold-hearted reputation, but now tougher, meaner men were going to hurt him.

'The pendant is worthless! A stone, a common stone! Zabala did not die because of a trinket!' Tishenko hissed.

'That's what I took off the girl. That was all she had,' Sharkface said, his mind desperately racing, trying to figure out how it had all gone so horribly wrong. He was only seconds away from death – but then Max Gordon inadvertently saved his life. One of Tishenko's scientists came into the room.

'Someone was in the ice cave. Thermal imaging shows he came through a ventilation shaft,' the man said.

Tishenko touched a button on a control panel, the screen flared into life and the red glow of a body came into view. The blurred shape moved slowly, the hot areas of the body glowing – head, eyes and stomach. Set against the ice cave's frozen blue atmosphere, the liquid red ghost was an unmistakable intruder.

'And now?' Tishenko asked the scientist as the red blip merged and disappeared into the surroundings.

'He went into the water.'

It was unbelievable that anyone would choose to do that and Tishenko had no clear thought for a moment. Then it made sense.

'He's in the cages.'

The statement was a command. Armed men ran from the room. There were no thermographic detectors down there, there was no need. It was only the preservation of his private collection that needed a constant freezing temperature.

One of the armed guards remained standing over Sharkface, the sub-machine gun levelled for a quick, killing burst.

'Don't kill him,' Tishenko ordered. 'Not yet.'

Max stepped back in shock. It couldn't be the man he and his father had once entrusted with their lives.

'Max, please help me. There's not much time,' Farentino muttered. 'I know you must hate me. But Tishenko is going to –'

'Shut up!' Max said harshly. His mind jumbling a dozen questions to ask and knowing there was insufficient time to ask them. Stay concentrated! Think of what you're doing here! 'Where's Sayid? Where's my friend?'

Farentino shook his head, as if trying to clear his mind. 'Who? I don't know him.'

'He's fourteen. My mate. He's injured. They brought him here.'

'How would I know? Max, never mind him. There's going to be a terrible disaster.'

Max turned away. Farentino thrust his arms through the cage, desperately begging.

'Max, Max, my boy. I understand, I do, I understand. Listen to me, please . . . listen . . . I saw your father!'

Max spun on his heel, reached through the metal bars and grabbed the pathetic man by his shirt front, pulling his face close. Farentino winced in pain.

'Liar! My dad would've clobbered you. He'd have *killed* you!' he shouted, throwing the man back into the stinking straw.

Max trembled with rage. This was insane. Whatever Farentino had got himself into was his own problem. Max had to find Sayid.

'The man who's doing all this, he sent me to him. He thought you were working for your father, ever since you were in the Pyrenees. I *had* to go and see him. To make sure you weren't working for him.'

Max was rooted to the spot. Fists clenched, legs trembling with adrenalin, wanting to punish the wretched Farentino. But he was in a pitiful state, beyond contempt, and Max knew he couldn't inflict violence on him. If he did, what would that make Max? A thug? A mindless attacker overtaken by revenge? The conflict in his mind fought him for seconds, which felt like minutes. He *did* want to punish Farentino. Maybe Max's instincts were that basic. He shook his head.

'You're not worth it, Angelo. You can stay here till you rot.'

Farentino had to break through Max's anger. He whispered hurriedly, as if confiding a great secret, forcing Max to listen, demanding he concentrate, in case he missed any vital information. 'Your father, years ago, before you were born, he knew about this area, he was part of a team – listen to me, Max, listen to me, you have to, because your father told me. He *told* me.'

Max hesitated, surprised. 'Told you what?' he said, seeing Farentino's shoulders slump with relief, having hooked Max's attention.

Farentino's words tumbled, hissing like the fast-flowing sluice. 'Telluric currents, natural electromagnetic waves, grids of energy that lie below the Earth's surface. Like hairline fractures in the Earth's crust.'

Max understood. His dad had explained it once when their compasses went haywire. These electromagnetic currents could be measured at different points in the world. Companies used the data from the energy flows for prospecting, to identify electrical changes in the Earth and locate petroleum reservoirs, fault zones – anything from geothermal water supplies to underground volcanoes. The intensity of these currents influenced weather patterns, created atmospheric electricity and huge thunderstorms. The Americans even harnessed them back in the nineteenth century for their telegraph system.

So what?

'I don't care, Angelo. This is too big. I can't save this place, or you. But I can save my mate.'

Max turned away again. Somewhere in this mountain

385

kingdom Sayid Khalif was being held and every ounce of Max's energy was going to be spent in saving him.

Farentino shouted after him, 'This madman's going to create a blast that'll destroy Geneva! It'll crack the lake! It will destroy the nuclear research centre! Max! Stop! The shock wave and water will cut a swathe from here to Paris! This mountain and half the Alps won't be here in a few hours!'

Farentino was right. There were only a few hours left. Max knew that. Time had slipped away from him. He was leaving everything too late. He didn't even know where Sayid was, never mind how to get him out.

As far as he was concerned, Angelo Farentino was on his own. Max felt a ripple of uncertainty at his own cold-bloodedness. He was leaving the man to die.

The hoist's platform hummed into life. Someone on one of the upper levels had pressed the call button. Max ran for the slow-rising platform. He was within a metre of grabbing the platform's substructure. He would ride up undetected.

And then Farentino's desperate shout pierced him like a spear.

'Your mother! I know how she died. How she *really* died!'

27

Farentino's words captured Max. He'd left his escape too late. The platform eased down and four men came into view, each levelling a machine pistol. There was nowhere to run, but Angelo had stunned him and momentarily taken the fight out of him. His mother. He knew she had died in the Central American rainforest during a research trip when he was eleven. Maybe Farentino was playing games; saying anything to get Max's help and escape.

Tishenko's guards kept a firm grip on him as the hoist climbed upwards. Max stayed alert, searching for anything that might come to his aid when he escaped, because escape he would – he needed to be certain Angelo Farentino wasn't lying.

Max figured the hoist was a crude lift mechanism used only for these lower levels. Tunnels hewn from the rock face went off in different directions on each floor they passed. Generators, power plants and general storage would be down here.

The hoist stopped and the men pushed him off the platform, across a more cared-for area and into a sleek, modern lift. Moments later Fedir Tishenko turned to face him when the express lift's doors opened. Max's stomach lurched. A stocky man with skin like a lizard looked at him. Half his face was covered in hair as dense as fur. It was fur, Max realized, trimmed close to the puckered skin. Max kept his reaction under control.

An armed guard stood over Sharkface. Max hadn't seen the sky in hours, but now he looked through the massive window cut in the rock face. This must be three thousand metres high. A blue velvet sky shimmered with stars. You could almost reach out and take a handful, but what held Max's attention was the cloud base a thousand or more metres below. The black carpet would cut out the night if he were on the ground, but from up here it swirled, in a conflicting tide, and small lightning flashes ricocheted through the dense cover.

Tishenko saw Max's fascination. 'That is a damp firework display compared to the apocalyptic event that will take place in only a few hours. My name is Fedir Tishenko. Where is Zabala's stone?' He tossed the useless pendant at Max.

So, Max realized, Sharkface had landed himself in it.

'Where is my friend?' Max said, daring to bluff confidently.

'He is dead.'

No way. Max wasn't going to accept Sayid was dead until he saw his body. This monster was trying to scare him. Max didn't show his emotions. 'That's a pity. He had the stone.'

'Oh, brave try, young Mister Gordon. You have dogged my ambitions for some time now. We searched the boy, he had nothing. You, however, are the kind of threat I could make no allowances for in my plans. You have it. You must. Why else are you here, other than to make a futile attempt at stopping me.'

'I'm here for my friend.'

'But you did not know he was here until a few hours ago. Who told you?'

'No one,' Max lied. He looked at Sharkface. 'I saw your thug here kill Peaches.'

'Why am I not surprised to hear that? Ruthless ambition can do strange things to a person. And then?'

'I followed him here.'

'Liar! No one followed me! I swear it!' Sharkface yelled, desperate for his life.

Max smiled. 'You're rubbish, mate. I could have followed you with my eyes closed in the middle of the night. You led me right here. I found Bobby Morrell's van, and my friend left a clue there for me.'

Max was looking around, taking in as much as he could. There were big screens dotted around the room. Satellite pictures from space. Gathering storms across the Atlantic. Cold-weather, low-pressure fronts projected across Europe and a swirling, snake-like coil of clouds twisting towards the Alps. That was the expected monster of a storm. Hours away.

Max tightened his stomach muscles and faced the disfigured man. 'Your people have been so careless it's downright sloppy. If you think you're going to rule the world or whatever insane scheme you've got planned, you should hire better staff.'

There was a stunned silence. And then Fedir Tishenko did something he could not remember ever doing before – he laughed.

'All right, you have courage. And you did not cringe when

389

you saw my face. I like that. I am going to show you something.'
He curled his finger, beckoning Max to him.

Max stepped further into the room, which angled away. A CGI map of Europe filled the wall. It was easy for Max to see exactly where he was. Red veins criss-crossed the map.

'You know what this is? What those lines are?' Tishenko said.

Max didn't but it wasn't difficult to guess. 'Telluric currents.'

'Very good,' Tishenko acknowledged. 'Watch.'

Tishenko pressed a button – an electronic clock appeared in one corner and the hours and minutes spun fast-forward. The projected path of the storm centred over Lake Geneva, and at the Citadel mountain a huge graphic flash appeared – a rod of golden light shafted into the three-dimensional mountain, a shock wave of energy rippled downwards and out along the veins. Surrounding mountains crumpled, the lake burst like a water-filled balloon and every red line on the map glowed. It was as if the sun had exploded below ground. A black swathe of destruction collapsed a path across Europe.

It was, Max realized, the complete and utter devastation of a huge area. That was a shock he could not disguise.

'Now I see you understand. Zabala knew of the geophysical danger here. Switzerland is fragile and his original prediction almost came true twenty-odd years ago. But they reinforced the tunnels at the nuclear research centre – then they thought they were safe. And Zabala was ridiculed. I offered them billions of dollars to include my regeneration proposal, but the governments involved did not dare accept my challenge.'

'So all of this is about revenge and death on a big scale?' Max said.

'No. This is about revenge and life on a gargantuan scale. Do you understand metamorphosis? The changing of man into beast?'

Max could only nod, his own dark world of shapeshifting still a mystery to him.

Tishenko pointed a remote control at the far wall. It was merely a screen. Shuttered steel slid to one side. He gestured with pride and stepped on to a narrow gangway. Max had never before seen anything like the huge shimmering light that lay a hundred metres or more below them. It was a spiked crystal. It must have measured twenty metres across and thirty high. Its jagged arms were like miniature missiles pointing outwards at every angle.

'Geothermal water in the mountain created this. I discovered it when I first started tunnelling. Within the crystal is life.'

Max looked down. Copper-coloured conduits, each ten metres thick, locked the crystal into steel girders twice its size, securing it to the rock face. Behind that, hundreds of metres beyond the vast cathedral-sized tunnel, was what appeared to be a gigantic fan. It was so enormous that it filled the height of the room. Max thought it looked like a huge generator whose blades would feed power into, and light up, the crystal.

'Many years ago the Japanese perfected a technique of storing DNA in a crystal, using liquid nitrogen. They froze every cell into deep hibernation. And then the experiment was stopped. They were afraid of what life form they might create. But I am not.'

Tishenko stepped closer. Max curled his toes in his trainers, imagining he was gripping the floor to stop himself from backing away.

'Regeneration. I found people like me, scorned and rejected by our so-called civilized society. I found the emotionally wounded, and those who struggled to keep the demons in their minds at bay, and those whose bodies were malformed, whose twisted limbs caused fear in others but whose minds were scalpel sharp. I offered these people everything. I bought their intelligence, I secured their loyalty and I offered them a new life in the future. Just as I have decided to offer you a new life,' Tishenko said quietly, in awe of his own power.

Before Max could say anything, two of the armed men grabbed him and sat him in a chair. A white-coated man, whom Max hadn't noticed before, stepped forward. He carried a small kidney-shaped dish and a hypodermic. Max struggled, heaved and pushed, but one man held his head in a vice-like grip and two others held his arms and legs down in the chair. The needle slipped into the vein in the crook of Max's arm and the white-coated man drew a phial of blood. A small sticking plaster was carefully placed over the puncture wound.

Tishenko nodded and the men stepped away. Max kicked the chair across the room, wanting to back into a corner to defend himself.

'Death is only a bridge between two worlds. Look what I offer you,' Tishenko said.

He slid back a frosted-glass door. Inside was a cabinet with a couple of dozen phials of amber liquid.

'Your blood will be mixed with that of one of the animals

whose DNA we have stored – and then placed deep inside that crystal. The scientists at CERN believe their particle accelerator can find that moment, that fraction of a second after this world was created. At dawn tomorrow my lightning charge will blast through my own particle accelerator and its design is more powerful. *I* will re-create creation. Not a microsecond afterwards, but the exact moment. And life will, years from now, grow from that crystal. Charged with power, it will evolve man and beast. Intelligence and strength that will determine a new world species. Symbiogenesis: it is the creation of a new form of life through the merging of different species.' Tishenko smiled. 'I have built the new Noah's Ark.'

'I've seen supermarket trolleys with a wheel missing that are more stable than you,' Max said, unable to hide his disbelief. 'You're certifiable.'

Tishenko's insanity was all the more frightening because of the power he wielded and the resources at his command. It would make no difference if a warning had reached CERN. It lay in the path of the underground surge. Once Tishenko triggered that power, it would rupture and tear apart the nuclear research facility and everything that lay beyond it.

Tishenko looked with pity at the boy who had backed into a corner, crouching, as if ready to fight for his life.

'You will die, Max, before I unleash the storm. You will be dead by then. I promise you.'

Sayid had to be found. And Angelo Farentino had given him another reason to survive – to discover the truth about his mother's death.

Max knew he had no chance unless there was more time. Never give up.

'You've got the wrong time for your big-bang theory,' he said.

'And why do you say that?' Tishenko asked carefully.

'Because I have seen Zabala's stone and the alignment of the planets – that's what you're looking for, isn't it? Well, that's all supposed to happen at twenty-six minutes to twelve tomorrow morning.'

'And you think I am going to believe you?'

'You have to. I have the stone.'

Max knew he had to hand over that last vital piece of Zabala's prediction, because without the extra few hours' grace he had no time to make a plan.

Tishenko shuddered. An involuntary ripple of expectation. At last; the exact moment for his ambitions to be realized.

He held out his crinkled hand.

From where Corentin and Thierry sat, the distant mountains looked more formidable than they had ever seen. The lightning flashes were fairly constant now and the thunder reverberated across the valleys. The peaks were lost from sight as the advancing storm funnelled into a dead end of mountains. Sophie had begged them at the hospital to help Max. If they didn't there'd be destruction on a massive scale. And Max was trying to save his friend. Corentin and Thierry would do that for each other, wouldn't they?

Corentin had phoned an old friend, a former Legionnaire who now worked in the French DGSE, the Direction Générale de la Sécurité Extérieure, their secret service. Corentin's urgency ripped through the usual formalities. Governments were frightened now. Pieces of the puzzle were beginning to fit more neatly. Intelligence communities and the French police were liaising, scientists were forced to look at a possible disaster scenario, and while no one could actually agree and put a plan together, Corentin and Thierry had made their own.

A flurry of sleet danced around the car. Corentin opened the boot and hauled out two huge hold-alls. Each man pulled out the equipment he needed: ropes, climbing gear, two Heckler & Koch machine pistols with laser sights, extra clips of ammunition, grenades, flares, two-way radios, bullet-proof vests and night-vision goggles. They slung the equipment around them like beasts of burden. Thierry led the way. They couldn't destroy the obstacles in their path – that would warn Tishenko's people – so, like Max, they had to find another way in. Corentin's contact had told him about the *vucari*. Private armies were one thing, but blokes who thought they were so special they called themselves wolf men needed a lesson in reality. Reputations were one thing – doing the business another. It would take time, but Corentin and Thierry would climb round, find a way inside the mountain and engage the enemy. That had a nice ring to it.

That felt good.

Max had cut the stone out of his trainer's heel and within minutes it was confirmed that this was indeed the vital, final part of Zabala's secret.

'And those numbers etched into the crystal?' Tishenko had demanded.

Max could only shake his head. 'I've no idea. Part of some code. But I don't know what.'

The truth of Max's ignorance convinced Tishenko. Numbers meant nothing now – the time was what mattered.

He gestured to his men and Sharkface was pulled to his feet. 'I shall give one of you the opportunity to die quickly – the other will be torn apart by wolves.'

A gaping hole led out on to a snowfield. Churning clouds muscled each other aside as they rolled across crevasses and peaks. The cold air bit into Max's face, but it wasn't the chill wind that made him shudder.

Max and Sharkface stood on a steel grid. A pack of about twenty wolves yelped and snarled five metres below their feet. These animals had been deliberately starved.

'You two seem destined to fight each other,' Tishenko said.

He gestured to his men, who grabbed Max and Sharkface. They attached a stainless-steel clamp to Max's left wrist and another to Sharkface's right. Two metres of chain joined them. Max had been chained to Aladfar, but this boy was a far more dangerous beast.

'You have ten minutes to run before my wolves and I give chase. Two kilometres away, on the edge of this escarpment, you will find two ice axes. If you live that long, I expect one of you to kill the other, and then I, or my wolves, will kill the survivor.' Tishenko checked his watch. 'I suggest you start running.'

Max leapt forward, Sharkface half a second behind him.

They ran through hardened snow covered by a few centimetres of powder. The two boys were dependent on each other at least until they found those ice axes – after that Max didn't even want to think about.

The confused sky crackled and rumbled, but the lightning stayed locked in the clouds. Despite the darkness there was enough light to see the sweeping valley and the mountain's jagged claws of bare rock reaching down into the ghostly white. Max took a handful of the swaying chain, tightening it, making it easier to run. After a moment Sharkface did the same. Max glanced at him. Spittle flecked away from the boy's jagged mouth. Was Sharkface fit and strong enough to keep this pace going for a couple of kilometres?

It was almost as though Sharkface had heard Max's thoughts.

'I'll kill you, Max. I'm not ending up as wolf bait. You'd better keep up.'

'You worry about yourself!' Max said, breathing hard, the sweat already clammy under his clothes.

'He'll come out of the sky. It's how he hunts. We have to keep watch,' Sharkface grunted.

Max looked over his shoulder. The cloud obscured just about everything except the lower thousand metres or so of the Citadel. A dull light flickered from the cave-like hole they had left, but a couple of hundred metres higher a broad tongue of shiny dark rock stuck out, from where another light glowed within the mountain. Max saw a giant bat flutter, drop momentarily, then rise and level out. It was a black-winged paraglider.

Max stumbled and fell. Sharkface went down with him. The snow felt like sandpaper as he piled in. Sharkface was on his feet in an instant, grabbing Max by the front of his jacket, shaking him angrily as he hauled him to his feet.

'Get up, you fool! Every second counts!'

Max shoved his opponent's arm away. 'Keep your hands to yourself!'

They glared at each other, tightened the chain again and ran on – desperation powering them forwards. A lone wolf cry called the pack to the hunt – then others took up the call, their voices changing as they answered. They were loose.

The sickening realization that the wolves could soon be on them gave added strength to their legs, but now Max also knew that Sharkface was strong. He had lifted Max out of the snow with little effort. How could he beat such a strong opponent?

Their laboured breathing was steady; their footfalls crunched the snow almost in unison, their fast pace matching each other. Tears from the cold air blurred the distant ground, yet Max's instincts were operating at maximum. Blood pounded in his ears, but he was attuned to any shift in the wind, any unseen rocky outcrop illuminated by the lightning breaking free of the clouds.

He heard the flutter of wind against fabric and dared another glance over his shoulder. Max barely believed what he saw. The winged hunter was less than fifty metres behind and above them. Tishenko wore a wolf-skin mask. A lightning flash threw a harsh glow across him and glinted off the arrow shaft that he now held full back into his shoulder.

Max dug his heels in, yanked the chain with both hands and twisted Sharkface down into the snow. The boy grunted, surprised and shocked, a savage look on his face ready to curse Max.

The arrow thudded into the ground with a terrifying *thwack* at exactly the place Sharkface would have been in another two strides. Max knew every hunter aimed ahead of a moving target and his instinct had saved Sharkface's life.

Sharkface knew it too. He nodded. Both boys were back on their feet, running full tilt – zigzagging, making themselves a difficult target. Tishenko would need to steady the paraglider, get himself into position before loosing another shaft. But the longer the boys weaved and dodged, the more ground they had to cover. And the closer the silently hunting wolves would get.

Max concentrated on their running pattern, but he could hear the ruffle of air entering the wing's vents each time Tishenko changed course. The paraglider fluttered dully in the night air, the canopy resisting the wind. Tishenko was giving away his location. They were on a level stretch of snow and lightning shattered the low clouds, showing them the broken landscape about half a kilometre away. Pockmarked globules of snow and ice, cracks and jagged shapes – the edge of the glacier – dangerous, unstable ground. Two hundred metres to the right of that a marker flag fluttered. The ice axes had to be there.

The mountain raked down, obscuring the valley to the left, where there was a lot of lightning activity. It danced and shuddered in a confined area, and Max could see the tops of what looked to be two towers which attracted the creased lightning. But there was no time to consider what they might be, as Tishenko had altered course dramatically, curving the paraglider, finding a position to steady himself for the next attack.

There was no flash of lightning this time and Max strained

to hear anything that might alert him to the arrival of the next arrow. There was no warning. It came out of the darkness, a rushing, lethal whisper that lanced downwards across his face. A couple of centimetres less and it would have pierced Max through the neck and into his chest.

Sharkface's terror was as vividly evident as Max's. The arrow had embedded itself between them. All very well that Max had nearly died, but had he gone down, the fast-approaching wolves would have had Sharkface at their mercy. To hell with Max Gordon getting killed by Tishenko; he didn't want to be torn apart chained to bloodied dead bait.

The ice axes were fifty metres away. If Tishenko got another shot off, it was likely to be third time lucky. For him.

Max and Sharkface saw the ice axes at the same time. Their curved, serrated picks wedged into compacted snow, the adze – the flat rear blade – protruded, catching slivers of light from the diffused lightning in the clouds. The axes were the same length, each long enough to stand from ankle to thigh with a pointed end at the base of the rubber grip. Max and Sharkface yanked them free.

The wolves were eighty metres away, splitting into smaller packs. These highly intelligent and courageous hunters would not be frightened by two teenage boys carrying ice axes.

'Go left!' Max yelled, tugging the chain so that they veered sharply towards the rising ground.

Tishenko needed a headwind to keep his momentum going. There were no thermals to catch; this was a cold night in turbulent conditions. No sane man would be up there in the sky now, but Tishenko must have extremely good equipment to manage it, perhaps even specially designed military gear.

Whatever it was, Max thought he knew how to stop him.

The thunderstorm buffeted the far mountains, but the wind was fairly constant in this valley – that's how Tishenko could fly so accurately – but where the ridge's gnarled rock formations obscured the distance, the air would be turbulent, and this wind shear was something all pilots dreaded. A rolling vortex of wind can create high-speed surges. Even Tishenko could not control his paraglider in those conditions.

It was the uneven ground and crevasses that slowed the wolves, and as Max and Sharkface leapt in unison across one of the narrower gaps Max felt the wind shift. Snow powder gusted and swirled.

'Keep going! Jump the gaps!' Max shouted, seeing that a pack of several wolves had found its way across the face of the slope and was coming at them from a different direction.

Where was the winged hunter?

'Check out Tishenko!' Max yelled as he took in as much of the ground as he could.

Sharkface looked back. Max tightened the chain, keeping it as taut as possible, controlling their run, while the other boy took his eyes off the way forward.

Tishenko watched the two boys – saw the ragged teeth in their usual snarl as the boy looked up towards him. Max Gordon was cleverer than he had thought. He had obviously sensed the place of danger for the paraglider. With the growling clouds several hundred metres above his head and the funnelled wind across that rock face, Tishenko could not control the big wing in any effective manner. Turbulent air like that would collapse the paraglider now buffeting above his head. And then he would be the one lying injured on the glacier, waiting for the wolves. This was only sport, he told himself. More serious considerations needed his attention. Tishenko would return to the mountain and prepare himself to harness this threatening storm and bring the greatest power in the heavens down to earth.

Max Gordon had survived this far. He felt a grudging admiration for the teenager. But the wolves would finish the job and he doubted Max could beat the stronger Sharkface.

Tishenko did not care who died first. In a few hours it would all be over anyway. He trimmed the wing and turned away from the doomed boys.

'He's gone!' Sharkface said.

They were still running, but now they were being cut off by two different packs of wolves and, with the storm's dancing shadows, the light played tricks on their eyes. Max was uncertain whether the shapes he saw across the icefield were wolves or not.

'Hold it!' he said.

Desperation could finish them off if they didn't think their way out of the encircling wolf packs. There was a low whimpering, as if the predators were communicating with each other. Max loved wolves and had always admired them; he knew they seldom attacked humans, but this was the cold reality of being face to face with a starving pack kept by a madman who had found ways of controlling them.

Max tried to identify the alpha male and female. These wolves don't always lead the pack, quite often leaving that to mature subordinate animals, but the alpha pair would control and direct the wolves' behaviour. The attack would come – but which wolf would be the one to trigger it?

What neither boy had seen was that the ground they were on was like a spit of land. They were boxed in on three sides by wolves. Beyond them was another crevasse. Max tugged at the chain, edging them closer to the void.

It was some three metres wide, which was about the size of the battered old sofa in the common room at Dartmoor High. It was nothing. But with this gaping drop into blackness it was as wide as the Grand Canyon. And the ground was icy underfoot. They would have to jump that space together. If either lost his footing . . .

'We have to jump this and we have to get it right.'

'Too far!' Sharkface said, eyeing the gap.

'You think there's a choice? We need a run at it,' Max said, turning to face the wolves, which had crept closer.

Max and Sharkface needed several metres to gather momentum and the wolves were twenty metres away and closing. How many could they kill if they were rushed? Max doubted they would manage even one or two. Wolves pull their prey down; they go for the throat and no sooner are their victims on the ground than they start to eat. And these wolves were hungry.

There was a sudden snarling fury. One of the subordinate males had made a run for them and a big male had lunged, bitten and barged the impertinent youngster. Its yelps and body language showed immediate submission. There he was, Max realized – the alpha male. Its ears were up, its tail held high and its eyes gazed fearlessly at the two boys.

The pack merged into a semicircle, knowing it had run its prey to ground. Now it was only a matter of who went in for the kill first. Max locked eyes with the big wolf, raised his ice axe like a trophy and howled as loudly as he could. He'd made his profile bigger and his presence known in no uncertain terms. The wolves faltered. Even Sharkface felt his blood chill at the sound of Max's howl.

'Now!' Max said.

They turned and sprinted for the crevasse. The wolves surged forward. Max's foot hit the rim first, Sharkface, heavier and slightly slower, right behind him. Max bicycled his legs, like doing a long-jump on sports day. As his feet hit the far side, he threw himself down and slammed the ice axe into the ground. No sooner had he secured a firm grip than the chain yanked his arm backwards. He twisted, crying out in pain as his shoulder wrenched. Sharkface screamed. He hadn't made the gap and had only managed to snag his ice axe on the edge.

'Help me! Help me! Hurry!'

Max dug his heels against a lump of ice, twisted his body and pulled his left arm towards his chest, taking the strain of most of Sharkface's weight. The wolves snuffled and growled on the far edge, desperate to reach their prey, but they were helpless as they faced the gap.

Sharkface could be seen just below the rim, his chained right hand clawing at the snow, the other through the axe's wrist loop. Max shifted the strain of holding him to his legs, feeling the muscles in his thighs tighten. He held Sharkface, but now he was facing the wolves. He could smell their breath and it seemed as though their snarling jaws could still reach him.

Were it not for the back-breaking strain he'd have taunted them, laughing in their faces, but if he didn't get Sharkface off that rim the ice could give way and there'd never be the sound of laughter again.

Max found firmer footing and brought his own ice axe free of the ground. Sharkface had managed to drag himself a little higher, but Max could see the sweat running off his face. This was ridiculous. He was trying to save the life of a boy who, the moment he was rescued, would try and kill him. Why didn't he just slam the ice axe down on to the chain and sever it? He raised his arm and a shiver of lightning caught the blade.

Sharkface wasn't going to get a free ride.

'Where's my friend? What did Tishenko do with him?'

'Go to hell!' Sharkface grimaced.

'After you!' Max yelled, and dipped his shoulder as if to strike.

'No! Wait! All right! The tunnel above the cages. He's got him there. I swear it!'

Max realized he must have been close to Sayid when Angelo Farentino had spoken those barbed words about his mum.

'All right. You listen to me. I don't know if these wolves are hungry enough to risk that jump, but if we keep our heads and we work together, we can get back to the mountain and stop Tishenko. You understand? You don't owe him any favours.'

Sharkface nodded. How much longer could Max bear his weight?

Max pushed his ice axe down towards Sharkface, who grabbed it with his chained hand. Now they had an even purchase and Max backed away, muscles straining as he pulled the floundering boy from the brink. Sharkface was clear.

The exertion took its toll. Both slumped to the ice. The wolves ran backwards and forwards, trying to find a way of reaching them, but the big male stood still amid the scurrying. Max was on all fours and gazed past Sharkface to the wolf. A silent understanding, which Max could not have explained, bridged the void. The alpha male turned and loped away. Momentarily confused, the wolves seemed uncertain what to do, but then they too followed him. After fifty metres the pack's leader turned his head, looked back at Max, raised his head and howled. The other wolves took up the cry. For a second it reminded Max of the siren at Les Larmes des Anges.

A warning.

Sharkface attacked.

28

The axe scythed across the space between them. Max couldn't bring his own axe to bear and block it. He flicked the chain instead and the slack caught Sharkface's pick's serrated point, yanked and the blade dug into the ice a hand's width from his thigh. It was a vicious attempt to disable him. He rolled, heaved on the chain, pulled Sharkface to him, shouldered his chest and, as he spun and the chain tightened, brought up his own axe.

They slammed blows on each other. Max managed to get both hands on the length of his axe and block a vicious downward strike. He twisted Sharkface's axe away but couldn't follow through because of the chain. Sharkface was fast, his recovery instant. He swung left and right, bearing down on Max like a gladiator. The axes thudded and screeched as blade hit blade. Parry, thrust, lunge, strike, kick and shoulder-slam.

This was a fight to the death.

Both boys sucked in air, yelling to give their arms strength. A furious battle that could last no more than a few minutes – so intense was the assault. It was hand-to-hand combat in its most brutal form.

They scuffed backwards and forwards into the icefield. Small crevasses making them turn on a heel, change position quickly, strike and block, a ballet of death. Max stepped inside a curving blow aimed at his back, grabbed Sharkface's axe shaft, pulled as hard as he could and slammed the bigger boy's chin with the top of his head. Something crunched and Sharkface spat blood.

As Sharkface fell, he pulled Max down with him. The chain determined neither could escape. Sharkface bucked and rolled, throwing Max clear. Max felt his feet slip into space. Another crevasse. He slid quickly. Now it was Sharkface who had to bear the weight. The edge crumbled. Max jolted downwards. He gasped. He couldn't swing his axe and get a grip. It was only the chain holding him. His hand clung to a freezing-cold rock on the rim. Sharkface did not even hesitate. Max saw the look in his eyes as they locked on to Max's wrist. If he chopped off Max's hand he would save himself and kill Max. The axe was a blur. It swooped down like an executioner's blade. Max twisted his arm. The blade struck the rock, severing the chain, and Max slid down the ice wall into darkness.

The last thing he saw was his attacker peering over the edge. His bloodied mouth, like a shark's having savaged its prey, and above him rolling black clouds torn by lightning.

It was a vision of hell and the devil's dark angel.

Jonah and the whale. Crazy thoughts. An all-encompassing darkness swallowed him, its cold breath as dank as the deepest grave. After a few metres the ice wall curved into the crevasse, became a slide and scooped Max along. He reversed the ice axe, held the pick close to his armpit, leaned back and heard the grating tear as the blade dug in like an anchor. It was a terrifying, hurtling ride. He might drop into a void a thousand metres deep or rocks could be lying in wait to mangle him. He pushed his heels together. He was slowing. He was sure of it. The huge black ice slide was flattening out.

Now he was horizontal, his body still skidding, but barely moving. He thumped into a wall of ice, grunted with fright and surprise, tucked his knees up and rolled. He lay still for a moment, then gingerly reached out to feel the ground around him. There was no drop. Perhaps he was at the bottom of the small crevasse, or on a ledge. He felt confident enough to stand, pushing his back against the cold wall. Lightning crackled somewhere overhead and, although he couldn't see the sky, light bounced down. He saw he was in a labyrinth. Dirty-looking ice, contamination from dust and rock, twisted this way and that, as if some great force had ripped it carelessly apart. He was on the bottom, grateful that the drop had been only about fifty metres. His hand touched the ice wall, like someone feeling their way in the dark. He stood still, waiting for his eyes to grow accustomed to the dark. There was an almost negligible tremor under his palm. But it *was* there. A vibration.

He closed his eyes, letting his mind settle into the black hole that surrounded him. Every creak of slow-moving ice, every faint flicker across his eyelids from the ricocheting light, centred his thoughts. He liked the dark and trusted his instincts to guide him through it. Other senses came into play. He heard a slow, regular drip of water somewhere ahead and to the left. Probably ice meeting warm air; possibly an overhang that was melting slowly. The machine hum was far away and the cavernous, twisting walls distorted its source, but there was something else. A smell.

Wolves and bears can smell their prey kilometres away. No human could match this, but now Max's senses went beyond such limitations. The faint odour told him the animals were a couple of kilometres away. The musky smell of a bear and the tang of wolves reached into his mind and gave him direction. These were animals he already knew. The wolf pack and the polar bear. What was it that allowed their smells to reach him? Some kind of underground cave system perhaps. Right now it didn't matter. His senses told him that those animals were back where they belonged, at the mountain, and that there was a way out from down here.

Max moved forward, one foot just nudging in front of the other, and then, when the reflected light filtered down from the sky into the underground world, he moved more quickly.

It took over two hours to edge further along the passageway until he was in such complete darkness that even the lightning could not penetrate. This was rock face now, not ice. He could hear a deep hum and the vibration was much stronger. He listened, then let his hand follow the wall. It curved; he hugged it, edging along, and then he saw a thread of light. He followed it, more bravely now, confident he was not going to fall. Above him, cut in the side of what must be the mountain's lower slopes, was a tunnel. It was easily three metres high and the same wide. Max clambered up, using the dim glow from the tunnel's soft lights to find his way. The air moved down the passageway; it was this that had allowed the barely detectable smells to reach him.

What appeared to be a pipeline ran through the tunnel. Max might be disoriented, but he felt certain that the towers he'd glimpsed lay to his right and the mountain to his left. This was no pipeline carrying fuel; it was the high-energy conduit Tishenko was going to blast his energy source along to smash into whatever contraptions he had installed inside the mountain.

Max heard a soft whine. He saw a steel rail above his head. Someone had to inspect this tunnel – and this was how they did it. Out of the tunnel's gloom a slow-moving metal chair crept forward. It was double-ended so an observer could use either end, depending on the direction of travel. Max clambered on top of the pipe and, as the ski lift-type chair approached, climbed on board. A toggle stick, like a small gear lever, was set on the side arm. Max pressed it forward and the chair's speed increased. This tunnel was bound to end at some kind of docking platform in the mountain. He leaned back; this was just like being a driver on the London Underground.

A hard hat was placed strategically in a holder – clearly a necessity for the operator. Max ignored it – he'd live dangerously for once.

A control room looked on to the docking area and Max saw a white-coated figure sitting inside. As the chair emerged from the tunnel he eased himself, unseen, alongside the humming pipeline.

Max knew there must be at least two vertical shafts that carried the lifts inside the mountain and the various levels were both above and below him. Clambering across the small platform, he hunched and ran for a door marked with a zigzag sign indicating descending stairs, ever watchful of the person in the control room. The white-coated man looked up from what he was doing. Max froze. It is movement that catches the eye. The man looked right at him – and turned away. Max couldn't believe it, but then realized that the platform was darker than the control room and that, combined with the window's reflection, would stop anyone from seeing past the glass. But Max was shocked to see the time on the clock above the man's head: 9.57 a.m. It was as though the storm had swept away the hours. Max had less time than he thought before Tishenko blew the mountain apart at 11.34.

The stairs were like a fire escape: reinforced steel bolted to the rock wall. Above him the tentacles of hundreds of cables snaked into the rock ceiling seventy-odd metres above his head. This was like being in a gigantic inspection pit beneath a futuristic time machine. The crystal Tishenko had shown him must be up above somewhere. He ran down further – another hundred steps. It was darker, quieter. He could see the hoist at the end of the passage. Two industrial-sized pipes of different thickness were bolted along the rock wall. He touched them. One was warmer than the other, which was ice cold, but without any condensation furring its sides. Both had gauges showing an unchanging pressure.

What was down this end where the darkness led to a single blue glow? If Sayid was on this level, as Sharkface had said, where could he be other than towards the far end of the passage? Max was torn. The hoist would take him down to Farentino and the information about his mother. Who first? He ran down the passage.

'Sayid? Can you hear me? Sayid? Where are you, mate?'

There was no echo to his voice. The walls were closer here, muffling his words. Max listened. No response. He ran on. The air suddenly became freezing cold. He had stepped into the blue glow. He shuddered. It was an ice grotto. Max walked on, gripping the axe in his hand more tightly. Something was wrong here. It felt as though the ice was going to close around him, blocking the way out.

That was when he saw Sayid.

And knew his best friend was dead.

Tishenko had given his final orders. The Citadel was guarded by twenty of his most faithful gunmen and a skeleton staff of scientists monitoring the equipment. Those who stayed awaited, with an almost fanatical zeal, the moment when the surge of power would create life. For many it was the culmination of years of devotion to creating a scientific miracle in an environment far removed from a sneering world. Fedir Tishenko *was* the chosen one for them.

Tishenko stood alone inside the caged control room at the top of one of the two purpose-built forty-metre-high towers that Max had glimpsed three kilometres from the mountain. Lightning danced and clawed at the structures, but he was perfectly safe. The latticed steelwork crackled with high-voltage energy, but inside the cage lightning could not touch him. It was the only place where the electrical field was zero.

Lightning coursed down through superconducting coils entwined about the towers. Each coil was made up of nine thousand filaments, each one-tenth the thickness of a human hair. Supercharged energy slammed its power into the underground acceleration chamber cut three kilometres into the base of the mountain. The energy charges built up a huge source of millions and millions of volts, jamming particles together like nose-to-tail traffic on a packed motorway. When the massive power of cosmic high-energy particles seethed through the storm, delivering a lightning strike into his waiting hands, he would slam it into the particle accelerator like a high-speed pantechnicon ploughing into a traffic jam.

The big bang.

Sayid was suspended in a block of ice, as if he were floating in a deep sea. His eyes were closed, his lips slightly parted, as if he had fallen asleep. A look of anguish creased his face. Perhaps there was a moment before he slipped into unconsciousness when he tried to push away those constricting walls of ice.

This chamber must be where Tishenko froze the animals. Cryogenic gas for deep-freezing was used to keep powerful heat conductors for the particle accelerator at manageable levels. Sayid had been slowly frozen to death.

Max pressed his face against the ice. He'd failed to save his friend. It was all his fault. He could trace back every inch of their journey and chastised himself for allowing Sayid to tag along.

A surge of violent, uncontrollable anger erupted. Max hacked the axe again and again into the ice. He stopped himself. It was a useless waste of energy. Sayid was embedded too deeply. Max swore at his own childish tantrum. Anger had blinded him to his friend's intelligence and courage. Sayid had believed in him right until the end. Sayid's hands pressed against the ice and Max saw the unmistakable message written on his left palm. It was slightly blurred because of the ice, but it could be seen by its thick black lettering – an indelible ink pen:

cut bears claw

'Cut bears claw'? Max said it over and over in his head. He knew that Sayid had cracked the code, that the piece of paper with the magic square decoded the numbers on the crystal. Sayid had both. And in those last minutes before he died he had believed that Max would find him.

'Well done, mate. You're a bloody genius. And I'm not leaving you in there. I'm gonna get you home to your mum. I promise,' Max muttered.

Bear's claw? Where? How? Polar bear? Frozen bear? It defied understanding, but if this was Zabala's coded message, then it was vital. Max clambered up behind the ice cage that held Sayid, his hand seeking out the fat warm pipe. He turned off the valve; the pressure gauge dropped. Balancing his feet against lower pipe work and his back against the rock face, he swung the ice axe as hard as he could.

Water spurted from the gash, power-washing over the ice. Max had ruptured the pipe carrying geothermal water from deep below the ground. Its heat dissipated on the ice, steam filling the room.

Max heard echoes of gunfire and small rapid explosions. The lights went out. For a few seconds it was pitch black and then a dull glow tried to lessen the darkness as an emergency generator kicked into life.

There was an attack going on inside the mountain. Max

watched the ice melt away slowly, but it would still take time to release Sayid's body. Something rumbled above his head. It sounded like automatic doors being closed and then the final thump as they locked. Soft, deceptive gunfire carried down the hoist shaft. That meant the fight had moved further away. If demolitions were being used and created any major malfunctioning of Tishenko's equipment everything could blow up inside the mountain anyway – without Tishenko's lightning surge.

This place could end up as a tomb for both Sayid *and* Max.

Max was dripping wet; the steam soaked through his clothing. Sayid's body had not moved as the hot water continued to gush over the ice block. The water flooded the passageway, spilling down the hoist shaft. Max heard someone crying for help. Farentino.

The hoist still worked and, as it slowed its descent into the caged area, Max jumped clear. Farentino was at the front of his cage shouting, his arms jammed through the bars. Fumes and smoke from damaged machinery were beginning to fill the cavern.

'Max! Thank God! Get me out of here! Hurry. There's shooting. Someone is attacking.'

Max looked around the area carved from the rock face. There was still a tunnel-boring machine, maybe he could cut through the wall of rock. No, that'd take too long. Max felt as though the whole mountain was on top of his head. Any serious flooding or damage and it would shatter. The tunnels and caves cut into it over the last twenty years would have weakened the inherent structure.

'My mother!' Max demanded.

'I'll tell you everything, but we have to get away, Max. You see that, don't you? There is no time.'

Max grabbed Farentino's wrist and tore free the Rolex.

'What are you doing?'

Max snapped the expensive watch on to his own arm. It was 10.46. Just under one hour to get Sayid's body out of the mountain and stop Tishenko.

'In five seconds I'm smashing the bolt free from that polar bear's cage. You won't be going anywhere, Farentino, you scum. I want to know how my mother died.'

'All right, all right. She was in the jungle. Something went horribly wrong.'

'What went wrong?' Max yelled.

'I don't know. Please, Max, get me out.'

'Tell me! What happened?'

Farentino's tone changed. The defeated man's face looked defiant in its anger. 'You want to know the ugly truth? All right! Your father abandoned her. She was sick, she was dying and he ran!'

'Liar!'

Farentino sensed he had the upper hand. He had an emotional hold over Max that no one had ever had before. 'She died alone, Max, because your father saved himself!'

'My father wouldn't do that! Not my dad!'

'He did it and he can't live with the shame! Why do you think he stuck you away in that boarding school? Why do you see so little of him? WHY? Because he knows he killed your mother!'

His words struck Max like an assassin's knife ripping into his chest.

417

'Why should I believe you? You've betrayed everyone who ever trusted you!'

Farentino lowered his voice, tender memories softening his anger.

'Because I loved her. I loved your mother with all my heart. But she would not leave your father for me.'

Max didn't move. He couldn't. Farentino gently touched his arm and spoke quietly. 'Get me out, Max, and I will tell you everything. Please. I promise.'

Max had to break through the crippling numbness that gripped him. Gunfire rattled on one of the levels above. It was close. The smell of gunsmoke and cordite clung to the air, stinging eyes and throat. It snapped Max back. He felt cold, but it wasn't the temperature. It was his heart.

He turned to the machinery against the wall, pulled a heavy-linked iron drag chain from one of them and passed it through the cage's bars. Then he jammed a metal rod through the end of the chain to hold it fast.

Feeding out the links, he heaved its weight to the hoist. The hand-held control switch dangled in the air. Max pressed the 'up' button and the platform rose. He stopped it when it reached head height, then snagged the chain beneath the hoist's structure. He pressed the 'up' button again and the platform rose slowly, taking the chain's strain.

'Stand back!' he shouted to Farentino as metal screeched and strained. The chain wrenched the cage apart. He lowered the hoist to head height again. Farentino staggered from his cage, but Max wasn't interested in helping him. He saw no reason why a trapped polar bear should die down here. He ran to the cage where he had escaped the angry bear, pushed

418

back the bolt and saw the bear rise up from its icy pool.

'Come on! Picnic time! Plenty of bad people to eat out here!'

The sound of his voice had an immediate effect and the bear began to climb through the ice wall's hole between the two cages.

Farentino had already clambered on to the hoist's platform. Max jumped, with the bear fifteen metres behind him. He grabbed the control buttons and lifted them up to the next level.

'I need help with my friend,' Max said to Farentino, dragging him off the platform and into the flowing water.

Gunfire, loud now. Explosions. Grenades. Men crying in pain.

Farentino cringed in fear and offered no resistance as Max bullied him along the passage. Max had sent the platform down to where the bear could clamber up; the rock face should give it enough grip to climb out. He had done all he could. *Cut bears claw.* It meant nothing! He grabbed Farentino's arm and pulled him into the darkened tunnel.

It looked as though Sayid lay sprawled backwards across an ice bench. Everything had melted except for one block at the bottom. The hot water still gushed but had cooled.

Max cupped Sayid's face in his hands – there was no neck pulse. He slipped his hand under Sayid's jacket and shirt; his chest was ice cold and there was no heartbeat.

'He's dead,' Farentino said matter-of-factly. 'We should get out.'

Max gripped Farentino's arm. Saw the pain register on the man's face.

'The entrance is too narrow. I can't carry him on my own. Take his legs.'

An explosion somewhere nearby – the fighting was almost upon them. Farentino grabbed Sayid's legs as Max took most of his friend's weight. They shuffled past the hoist and into the open area.

Max laid Sayid's body down gently.

Two alien-looking creatures dressed in black, with rubber faces, bulging eyes and carrying machine pistols, ran out of the cavern's gloom. Pencil-thin laser beams from their gun-sights cut through the near-darkness and settled on Farentino's chest.

'Don't shoot!' Farentino cried.

Corentin and Thierry pulled the night-vision goggles from their faces.

'Max!' Corentin said. 'Is this the boy?'

'Corentin! How the . . .?'

'It was Sophie,' Thierry said, as he knelt next to Corentin, who was already checking Sayid. Thierry slipped a backpack from his shoulders. 'There's a small army of French and Swiss support troops outside. They're too late as usual. We did the business in here.'

'Wolf men! Puppies more like,' Corentin said.

Corentin cut Sayid's clothes with a wicked-looking combat knife. Thierry took a battlefield medical kit from his backpack. Both men worked silently, no longer determined professional soldiers but field-trained medics. Thierry prepared a hypodermic.

'Epinephrine,' he said to Max's worried look.

'Save him, Corentin,' Max pleaded.

Corentin placed small spoon-sized paddles from a mobile cardiac resuscitation unit on each side of Sayid's ribcage. Thierry plunged the needle into Sayid's heart. There was still no pulse.

'Clear,' Corentin said.

He triggered the unit and Sayid's body jolted.

'Come on, Sayid! Come on!' Max begged.

'The boy is dead. You waste your time,' Farentino said.

Corentin's look could rip out your stomach. 'This boy's ice cold. He's not dead until he's warm and dead.'

Corentin and Thierry tried the procedure three more times, then Corentin looked at Max and shook his head.

'There's a casevac chopper outside. We'll take you boys out of here now. C'mon, this place is secure. And there's a hell of a storm waiting to explode out there. Choppers won't fly much longer.'

Max gazed down at the lifeless body of his best friend. Where were the tears and the throat-closing sobs? Why didn't he feel anything except this animal-like desire to pursue his prey?

'Kid, you're exhausted. Let's go,' Thierry said, as Corentin lifted Sayid into his arms.

Max looked at the watch: 10.59.

'I can't. Tishenko's going to blow this place sky high in less than forty minutes. He's in a tower a couple of kilometres down the valley. There's an underground rail system –'

Thierry interrupted him. 'Listen, boy, that tunnel was booby-trapped. It's caved in. The pipe's still there but there's no way out. Best maybe we forget the crazy man, eh?'

'No one's going down that valley, Max. It is too much to ask. The lightning is everywhere,' Corentin said quietly.

Max shook his head. 'Get him to hospital, please, Corentin.'

Sayid's limp arm flopped. Max tucked it back and stroked his friend's face. Now he felt tears in his eyes. But there was a shadow part of Max Gordon that pulled him away. He turned his back and ran as fast as he could for Tishenko's private lift.

He pressed the button. It wasn't an express lift any longer, but there must have been an emergency capacitor that held an energy store specifically for it, because seconds later he stepped into the room where Tishenko had bragged of his plans for immortality. The wall panels were open, the crystal hummed and glowed – power was still surging into it. That meant that underground pipeline Max had travelled along was the vein of energy – the particle accelerator that would reach the speed of light in . . . He checked Farentino's watch – 11.15. Nineteen minutes to go.

Cut bears claw.

Sixty metres of living accommodation ran along the rock face. Two huge doors waited at the end. Max hauled one open and was blown off his feet as the storm surged in. This was Tishenko's viewing platform, which was now battered by cloud and rain. Max rolled clear as the storm forced its way in and vandalized Tishenko's quarters. Then he saw the wolf mask draped on a bronze head sculpture of Tishenko. Max snatched it from the cold metal. Its fur soft, its cutout eyes creepy. The hunter's mask. Max slipped it over his face. It felt as though he was inside the wild animal's skin. A mirror reflected the creature that stared back at him. A shudder. Muscle rippled. His heart raced. A deep-seated urge to attack swept through him. Then he remembered – there was another platform, from where Tishenko had launched the paraglider. And that was Max's only chance.

The lift dropped rapidly.

11.20.

Lightning struck the side of the mountain, shattering huge flakes of rock. It clawed, just like Tishenko's logo. Max stepped into a cave purposely made and big enough to house a small aircraft. But instead of any aircraft it housed at least a dozen paragliders hanging from the ceiling. It was a drying room for the canopies. They hovered like vampire bats, shivering in the draughts that forced their way through the doors from the storm outside.

The clouds swirled four hundred metres above his head. Violent lightning tongued through darkness, ghostly images exposing the inside of cloud formations. Max needed a headwind. He pulled open the access doors. It was like being inside a tornado. At this height the air was calmer, the wind pushing against him. But it was the perfect vantage point. Max could see exactly where the two towers stood, an incredible display of lightning crackling between them. Tishenko was drawing nature to him and turning it into dark power.

11.22.

Cut bears claw.

Strapped tightly into the harness, Max threw the fabric he held bundled in his arms into the storm. Like a dog with a rat, the wind snarled and snatched it, tossing him into the air. Max plunged into a surreal world. Snow and ice below, turbulent black clouds above. Lightning cut across the valley, showing him exactly where to go. He tugged on the paraglider's risers, spilling air from the canopy. The web of lines connecting him to the wing above his head sizzled with tension. A compass and air-speed indicator were stitched into the harness. Max knew where he was going, no need for the compass, but he was buffeting along at nearly sixty kilometres per hour.

The air bit his skin; pellets of hail stung his hands. He fought the gale to stay on course for the towers. As each lightning flash crashed across the landscape Max saw movement below. Wolves. They shadowed him, perhaps believing it was their master beneath the black wing. And if he fell? They would soon realize that the figure wearing the mask was not Fedir Tishenko. It didn't matter. He felt as if he was running ahead of the pack. Leading them.

Max saw he was too high; he would overshoot the towers in less than a kilometre. He pulled down on the risers, collapsing air out of the canopy. The drop was dramatic. Too much. He corrected, shifted his weight, threw a hand up to protect himself as lightning slashed across the veiled rain. This was the wildest ride of his life.

The two towers were in a compound. They looked like watch-towers in a prisoner-of-war camp, but they were only two hundred metres apart. And there were no huts other than a brick-built structure, half underground, which looked like a generating room. It squatted at the perimeter fence. A raised hump of ground went from the base of each tower into this building.

Max was tossed across the sky. A gust had swept around the side of the mountain. This was the wind shear he knew Tishenko had avoided. Now it forced Max to fight for his life. He pulled this way and that, cascaded down the side of the far reaches of the mountain, turned into a confused wind and spilled even more air. He was going down. Fast. And aiming straight for the compound.

Fire strangled the towers. But then Max realized that what he saw were cables carrying the lightning strikes down into the ground, along those humps in the ground and into the building.

A figure stood in the wire-mesh control box at the top of one tower. Lightning laced itself around the cage, trying to reach him, like a frustrated monster. But as long as Tishenko stayed in the zero field he was safe. One finger outside that safety zone and he would die like an insect flying into a bug-zapper trap. He manipulated the two control levers that guided the ten-metre parabola – like a big satellite television dish. It caught lightning and threw it into the pre-set dish on the other tower. Sometimes the lightning divided itself and struck both parabolas at the same time, creating an even more powerful electrical charge.

Tishenko neither saw nor heard Max's approach, but he turned and gazed into the night, his sixth sense as strong as ever. A black-winged creature with the face of a wolf swept out of the sky. Max Gordon had survived and still attacked. So, the boy wore the mask of a wolf man? Then he must be prepared to die as one.

Max knew he was coming in too fast. If he tried to turn now he'd be dragged into that cheese grater of a fence. He let go of everything, covered his head with his arms and tucked his legs back into the paraglider's seat. *When all else fails – panic!* a voice shouted scornfully in his head.

By releasing the tension on the control lines, the canopy

fluffed with air, rose two metres and then stalled. Max dropped less than the height of his dorm table at Dartmoor High.

Unbuckling the harness, he ran into the devil's furnace. Lightning exploded, tortured wind screamed through the tower's wire-mesh cage, and in the far distance a rolling ball of fire tumbled down the valley's sky, parting the clouds like a meteor scars the night sky.

Over the storm's deafening smash he heard a man scream. Tishenko. Cursing Max Gordon.

11.30.

The inner core of the second tower was a lift. He pressed the button. No doors – an open platform sped him upwards. Max was inside what felt like the biggest exploding firework in the world. A flash blinded him. Blank, melting blobs swam in front of his eyes. Tishenko had swept the dish down and thrown a bolt of lightning at Max's tower. And again. The power slammed the cage where Max now stood. Two game-like control levers sat on a console panel. Whatever Tishenko had pre-set was immediately unlocked by Max pressing the 'manual control' button. Max heard the hum of power as he tweaked the handles. The dish on his tower responded immediately. There was no time lag between command and response.

As Max swung the dish into the sky he saw the fireball ever closer. Beyond this valley Lake Geneva sat trapped between two mountain ranges. An anvil blow along this telluric line would shatter the valley's floor, like tapping an egg against the rim of a frying pan.

11.32.

Two minutes left!

Tishenko struck Max's tower again with another bolt of lightning. It shook and for a moment Max felt that it would shudder itself into a crumpled heap. His dish caught a bolt of lightning and threw it against Tishenko's tower. If it was a game Tishenko wanted, Max was up for it. He knew how to play Sayid's computer games.

The natural phenomenon tearing across the sky now looked like a fiery meteor crashing to earth, but it was the spear tip of a mighty lightning strike. It could not have been foretold by anyone. But catastrophe was about to strike and a scientist-monk had predicted this very disaster. The chain-mail fist of fire was going to pulverize the inside of a mountain in less than ...

11.33.

Cut bears claw.

Tishenko had killed Sayid! Max's anger burned as brightly as the storm, his concentration blocking out the shattering noise. Tishenko and Max traded blows. Lightning bolts clashed like medieval swords in personal combat across the two-hundred-metre battlefield between the towers.

Tishenko slashed Max's tower again, an enormous strike that lit the whole area. Max reeled. Tishenko saw the boy stumble, the impact slamming him to the cage floor.

The flash of light held the valley in its glare. Max stared at the looming black monster of a mountain. It rose up into the heavens, forcing aside the clouds, its peak like a bear's head, its jagged ridges grasping the valley floor – claw-like.

Cut bears claw.

Max's mind did not reason, his thoughts did not question.

The cosmic lightning struck.

Max twisted the controls. The fiery bolt seared from the dish and severed the bony ridge of mountain that looked, in that instant, like a bear's claws.

Every moment of Fedir Tishenko's existence encapsulated itself in a microsecond. He was the fire god who would destroy and create life. Touched by the power from the sky when a child, he could not be harmed again. So he was baffled at the searing pain that shafted through his chest and thrust him against the cage's mesh wall. The eye of the storm recognized its long-lost son, reached out with a cruel stiletto lightning strike and took him home.

Time moved in slow motion for Max. His tower was collapsing; the mountainside exploded and Sharkface stood in the fire-lit snow, next to a motocross bike, his arm still extended, having loosed the arrow from Tishenko's hunting bow. The shaft had pierced Tishenko's chest and then thrust its steel tip through the cage wall, offering itself, and its victim, to the lightning.

Max's tower collapsed slowly, crumpling as wearily as an armour-clad knight beaten into submission. He clung to the control box, heard tearing metal as the structure flattened the perimeter fence and then the tower's death rattle: its steel groaning in final surrender.

The earth trembled, wind snared the clouds and within one hour the crystal-clear night settled a frost across the land and Max's crumpled body.

Then the wolves came.

*

Silence can be bought; events can be explained with half-truths and scientific explanations. There were more than a dozen deaths from the battle inside the mountain that Corentin and Thierry fought alone. Official reports stated that seven of these men were members of a climbing team caught on the notorious north face of the Citadel. Inexperienced climbers, they were caught by the minor earthquake that shook the region that night, and five rescue workers died trying to bring them off the mountain. It was a tragedy.

There was considerable damage to one of the lower-lying villages but, thankfully, no fatalities. An undisclosed number of scientists monitoring seismic activity in the Citadel research centre had been rescued, which explained the presence of Swiss and French forces in the area that night – a wonderful example of cross-border cooperation, a government spokesperson said. The truth was that Tishenko's scientists were held in undisclosed secure centres where their psychiatric health would be examined over a number of years.

Climate change and a phenomenal weather pattern were blamed for everything.

'Wake up, boy,' Corentin said roughly.

He shook Max, brushing frost and snow from his body, slapping him gently – as gently as anyone like Corentin could manage – until Max awoke.

'OK, I'm OK ... Corentin ... what happened?' Max said.

The big man hauled him to his feet.

'The cavalry came, late as usual, but they'll take all the glory,' Thierry said. 'They always do.'

Max remembered Tishenko's death. 'Where's Sharkface?'

'Who?' Corentin asked.

'There was a boy here. He killed Tishenko.'

'Give the kid a medal,' Thierry said. 'There was no one here except you and the wolves.'

'A pack of wolves?' Max asked.

'That's right. A polar bear was on the loose. He was very interested in having you for breakfast,' Corentin told him.

'I don't understand,' Max said.

'The wolves, they were in a circle around you, one big wolf . . .'

'One big bad wolf,' Thierry laughed, interrupting his partner as they helped Max to the Audi.

'He would not let anyone near you – and the pack, well, it was not something I have seen before, but they kept that polar bear away from you.'

'You didn't kill the wolves?' Max asked, suddenly alarmed.

'A few shots in the air. The alpha male, he stood his ground to the end, but Corentin here talked to him like his poodle at home, and he left you alone.'

'I don't have a poodle, or any kind of dog. Don't be stupid,' Corentin sighed as he opened the Audi's front door and eased Max into the passenger seat.

Max had never been so thankful for a ride home. He felt as though he'd been run over by a steamroller.

'I sit in the front,' Thierry moaned quietly to Corentin, who walked around to the driver's side.

Max saw Corentin grin. 'I get sick in the back,' Max said.

'Me too. Get out,' Thierry ordered.

'Leave him. I don't want him puking in the car,' Corentin said. 'He's already had a rough enough ride.'

He passed a bottle of water to Max, who guzzled it.

'And me getting sick?' Thierry said.

'Hold it in,' Corentin told him as he fired up the engine.

Thierry squeezed into the back seat. 'I'll have to have the window open.'

'Fine.' Corentin wheeled the car away from the devastation, the studded tyres crimping the snow.

'And don't go fast on the corners,' Thierry warned him.

'Shut up.'

Max never heard the ongoing sparring between the two mercenaries. He fell into a deep sleep and woke up sixteen hours later in a Swiss private clinic.

The beauty of Switzerland is not only its magnificent countryside but also its secrecy laws. Everything was hushed up. Anyone connected with Max's ordeal was taken into safety, nursed, cared for and debriefed by government agencies and scientists.

Scientists explained that the slab of mountainside Max had exploded crashed down into the fissures and crevasses beneath the valley floor and stopped whatever shock wave there was from cleaving Lake Geneva, devastating the CERN research facility and destroying the environment and countless lives. How had he known to do that? they wanted to know.

'Zabala. He did it,' Max told them.

'The discredited scientist?' they scoffed.

There was no proof Max could offer. The pendant stone

431

had disintegrated with Tishenko. Perhaps it was enough that Max knew the truth. What Max did know was that it was good to be alive and breathe this high mountain air without fear lurking behind every rock.

Sharkface had escaped that night. There was no sign of Tishenko's wolf mask that Max had worn. The killer must have thought Max dead and taken it before the wolves arrived. Who knows? Maybe it was enough for the outcast boy to have killed Tishenko and taken the mantle of the *vucari*.

'What happened to the huge crystal in the mountain?' Max asked Corentin.

The rough-looking man shrugged. What did he know? He was just an ex-Legionnaire being paid to save a couple of kids. Not that Max needed their help.

It was a great compliment from the fighting man, but Max knew his DNA had been mixed with a predator's and stored in that crystal. Where was it? The doctors and scientists he had questioned denied any knowledge of it.

It was a closed matter. None of it had ever happened – officially. It didn't matter; that was what governments did. Max just felt lucky everything had worked out the way it had. Did he believe in luck? Or was that just superstition? He didn't care – luck was essential.

Three other figures lay on wooden loungers in the late-winter sun, their injured legs propped up. Sophie Fauvre had had the best orthopaedic surgeon in Switzerland work on her damaged knee. She had beamed when Max arrived, but she saw his weariness. Battle fatigue, Corentin told her. Max had been through something huge. Probably something he wouldn't be able to talk about for a long time. Give the kid some space.

He'll need it. Sophie understood. She would go back to her own father and help with the endangered species and she hoped Max would return home and find a way of talking to his dad.

She had hugged Max. 'Hey?'

'Yeah. It's cool,' he had said, smiling.

Bobby Morrell had been brought to the clinic from a French hospital. He was still a little quiet. His broken arm, leg and ribs would heal in time, but the pain he felt over his grandmother's death would take much longer.

But as far as Max was concerned luck had been the most generous to Sayid. He was prodded and tested for a week. Not since a Japanese man had recovered from being frozen on a mountain top some years earlier had anyone survived such intense cold. The doctors agreed – Sayid had fallen into a hypothermic state similar to hibernation. His brain and organ functions were locked away as if in a cyberspace retrieval system, and were protected without being damaged. He'd made a complete recovery.

They all sat wrapped in blankets, gazing out across the clinic's gardens, towards the snow-capped mountains. They sipped hot chocolate brought by a nurse Bobby Morrell really fancied.

'I don't know how you found me,' Sayid said to Max, knowing Max would tell him the whole story one day.

'I heard you snoring,' Max replied.

They laughed, but Max soon fell silent, letting them talk and shout each other down as they excitedly told how each had survived their own experience.

Farentino had disappeared in the confusion of the rescue

operation by the Swiss and French forces, but his words were as sharp and hurtful as when they were first spoken. What had really happened to Max's mother? Did his dad know about Farentino's love for her? An uncertain future faced Max. He had to find the truth behind his mother's death.

And whether his father had lied to him.

Max heard the distant, echoing roar of a bear, and the answering howl of a big wolf. It made him shiver. It was as if they called out to him.

'Did you hear that?' he asked the others.

'Hear what?' they said.

Max shook his head and gazed back into the mountains.

'Nothing.' Max smiled. 'It must be my imagination.'

Author's Notes

Mont la Croix and Montagne Noire are places I created for this story, but if any of you are budding (or even experienced) skiers or snowboarders you should make sure you understand the safety guidelines for going into the mountains. Our climate change means there's an increased risk of avalanches, so if you are going off-piste take a transceiver with you – probably the only way a rescue team can reach you in time if an avalanche strikes.

The Château d'Antoine d'Abbadie exists pretty much as I have described it, though the elderly French caretaker is a character of fiction and nothing like the charming French lady who helped me there. I will have pictures of the château on my blog.

Biarritz is a great European surfing destination and although the Comtesse is a fictional character her château can be seen just about where I described it. It's a private property, so I can't be more specific than that.

CERN, the European Organization for Nuclear Research, did have a tunnel collapse in 1986 and Switzerland is considered by its government to be at risk from earthquakes. The country lies on the edge of the Eurasian tectonic plate and the area of Valais – where Tishenko was based – is considered to be particularly at risk. Experts fear tidal waves could be triggered by landslides falling into the country's lakes and reservoirs.

Telluric currents have been known since ancient times and geobiologists, among others, now use telluric and magnetotelluric currents for exploration below the Earth's surface.

I discovered quite a lot about lightning during my research. A Russian scientist, Alex Gurevich of the Lebedev Physical Institute, proposed the theory that lightning strikes are triggered by cosmic rays which ionize atoms, producing an avalanche of relativistic electrons directed through the clouds.

In 1901 Nikola Tesla constructed his famous Tesla coil, which generates electrical charges – high-energy 'lightning' strikes. Lightning is a phenomenon about which little is still known, but lightning towers, based on the Tesla coil, have already been built. Continuous discharges of lightning can be 'thrown' between the two towers. Experiments along these lines – to harness lightning – go back as far as 1932, when two scientists stretched a cable across two peaks in the Alps. Sparks of several hundred feet were created and the scientists planned to install a tube for the acceleration of particles, but the death of one of them caused the project to be abandoned.

Crystals, of course, do carry energy and information, and scientists at Stanford University have succeeded in putting a three-dimensional image (of the Mona Lisa) into a quartz crystal and then retrieving it. There are also some theorists who maintain that life began in crystalline form, then genetics took over and developed life into cellular form.

One of the most interesting challenges in writing *Ice Claw* was to try and find planetary movements that were synchronous with events on Earth. I wrote *Ice Claw* in 2007, setting it in winter 2007/2008. The book would be published in summer 2008, so I needed to predict a potential disaster for about March 2008.

My dilemma was how to explain that Zabala, a scientist and astronomer, who also understood astrology, could have been so wrong in his predictions of a disaster twenty years earlier. I was looking for a feasible situation in which planetary alignments would reflect potentially catastrophic events on Earth at a given location.

Over the months I worked with an accomplished astrologer, David Matthews, and he realized that three planets, Eris, Sedna and Quaoar, had recently been discovered and these had astrological properties – or energies – that could reflect events here on Earth. My old astrologer monk, Zabala, could not have known about them and so was missing vital information when he made his original prediction. Then my astrological expert discovered these were the same stars and planets that lined up in exactly the same place in March 2008 as they did in March 1988.

Some stars and planets connect with events on Earth. Not necessarily causing these events, but reflecting them. The universe is a complete unity, so it might be considered that 'as in the heavens so it is upon the Earth'.

So now I had a chart that showed me the same degrees of planetary conjunction in 1988 as in 2008. Human-created powers being unleashed are represented by the planet Uranus – lightning and energy – and so, unexpectedly, this planet was also (as were others) in the right place in the sky to fit very neatly into my story. Pluto and Capricorn represent great transformation at this exact time. The relevant research fell neatly into place.

And what about the wild animals in *Ice Claw*? Not only is our climate change destroying species and placing others at risk, but there is a terrible trade in endangered animals. I've only touched on it in this story, but illegal trapping, shipping and killing are widespread. For more information on this, there are books in libraries and interesting facts on websites. Here are some you might want to look at:*

wwf.org.uk

kidsplanet.org

newscientist.com/channel/life/endangered-species/

* These links are to third-party Internet websites, which are controlled and maintained by others. These links are included solely for the convenience of readers and do not constitute any endorsement by Penguin Books Limited ('Penguin') of the sites linked or referred to, nor does Penguin have any control over or responsibility for the content of any such sites.

Acknowledgements

There is not a great deal known about the Basque people, their culture and language – and so I am extremely grateful to Louise Letoux for translating the text I wanted to use into Basque. David Matthews, astrologer, spent many patient hours with me as I tried to create a feasible catastrophe. Elizabeth and Victoria Chiazzari advised on some technical points for whitewater kayaking. Oliver Wren kindly read, and commented on, my snowboarding sequences, and Dr Grenville Major has, as always, advised me on medical matters. Any errors in the text, deliberate or otherwise, from these experts' help are mine alone.

Once again, thanks to Keith Chiazzari and James McFarlane for their invaluable input. Isobel Dixon, my agent, manages to calm the storms before they escalate into hurricanes. A safe harbour for a sometimes stricken vessel.

I am fortunate to have a great team at Puffin Books and their ongoing enthusiasm for Max Gordon and Danger Zone is a constant encouragement. Tom Sanderson plays nicely with his colour box and creates wonderful covers. Carl Rolfe, Andy Taylor and Brigid Nelson do a special job of flag-waving. My editor, Lindsey Heaven, lavishes her skills on the story, while Wendy Tse and her copy-editing team pick up all my mistakes.

Thanks to Emily, Sophie and the hugely energetic Jodie Mullish, who has always made 'going on the road' so easy. May she enjoy her own adventure in the Amazon and find her true compass bearing beyond the horizon.

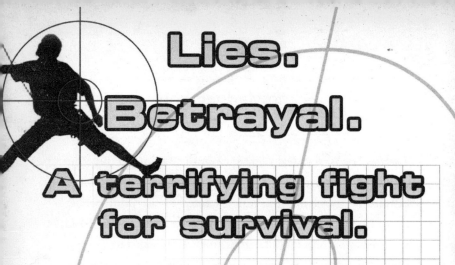

Lies.
Betrayal.
A terrifying fight for survival.

Desperate to uncover the secret of his mother's death, Max Gordon is chased into the night by a ruthless mercenary.

The clues take him from the desolate hills of Dartmoor to the endangered rainforest of Central America – where the devastation hides a sinister and fearful secret. Drug smugglers, deadly caimans, man-eating snakes and flesh-stripping piranhas await Max at every turn.

In a heroic battle against a lethal enemy, Max joins forces with a lost tribe of children. But faced with the terror of an ancient sacrificial ritual, has Max's quest for the truth led to an answer for which he'll pay the ultimate price?

Join **MAX** in the next *adrenalin-pumping* **Danger Zone** adventure coming in **2009**

thedangerzone.co.uk